ANCIENT ECHOES

Also by Joanne Pence

ANCIENT ECHOES

ANCIENT SHADOWS

ANCIENT ILLUSIONS

DANCE WITH A GUNFIGHTER

THE DRAGON'S LADY

SEEMS LIKE OLD TIMES

THE GHOST OF SQUIRE HOUSE

DANGEROUS JOURNEY

The Rebecca Mayfield Mysteries

SIX O'CLOCK SILENCE

FIVE O'CLOCK TWIST

FOUR O'CLOCK SIZZLE

THREE O'CLOCK SÉANCE

TWO O'CLOCK HEIST

ONE O'CLOCK HUSTLE

THE THIRTEENTH SANTA (Novella)

The Angie & Friends Food & Spirits Mysteries

MURDER BY DEVIL'S FOOD

COOK'S BIG DAY

ADD A PINCH OF MURDER

COOKING SPIRITS

COOK'S CURIOUS CHRISTMAS (A Fantasy EXTRA)

ANCIENT ECHOES

JOANNE PENCE

QUAIL HILL PUBLISHING

Quail Hill Publishing

PO Box 64

Eagle, ID 83616

Visit our website at www.quailhillpublishing.net

First Quail Hill Publishing Printing Book: April 2013 Second Quail Hill Publishing Print Book: August 2018

First Quail Hill E-book: May 2013

ISBN: 978-1-949566-09-3

ANCIENT ECHOES

PART ONE

The Travelers

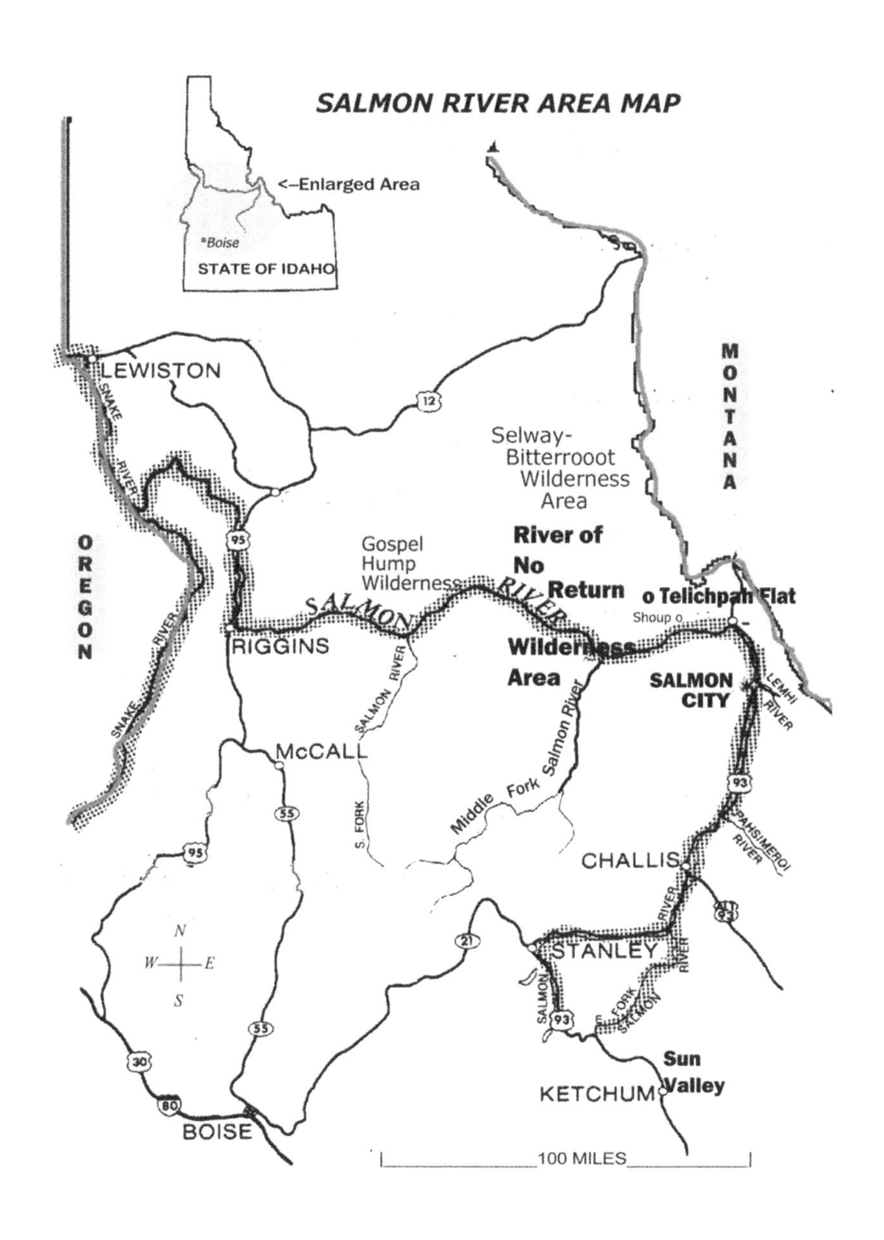
SALMON RIVER AREA MAP
<--Enlarged Area
Boise
STATE OF IDAHO
LEWISTON
SNAKE RIVER
12
MONTANA
Selway-
Bitterrooot
Wilderness
Area
OREGON
95
Gospel
Hump
Wilderness
River of
No
Return
Wilderness
Area
SALMON RIVER
o Telichpah Flat
Shoup o
RIGGINS
SALMON RIVER
SALMON
CITY
LEMHI
RIVER
SNAKE RIVER
McCALL
Middle Fork Salmon River
S. FORK
55
93
PAHSIMEROI
RIVER
95
CHALLIS
RIVER
93
N
W
E
S
21
STANLEY
RIVER
SALMON
93
E. FORK
SALMON
55
30
Sun
Valley
KETCHUM
80
BOISE
100 MILES

ONE

Mongolia

Michael Rempart flung back the thick, musty brown quilt, rekindled the metal stove's dying dung fire, and dressed in heavy woolens and an insulated jacket before stepping out of the small *ger*.

The bitter winds of western Mongolia's Bayan Ölgiy region slapped at his face and dried his eyes until they ached. Normally, the sky above this cold, barren plain was bleak and pale and gray at the edges, as if viewed through an ice cube. This sky was a murky mustard color that made him uneasy. He'd seen this before on the Gobi Desert as a prelude to a sandstorm.

His archeological dig team should have been busily moving about the camp. But the camp was empty. The two aged Soviet-built GAZ trucks used to transport men, equipment and supplies to the dig site were also gone.

Last evening, everyone had retired for the night in high spirits. After weeks of anticipation, skepticism, and hope, the dig had reached a depth from which they would learn if they had discovered an ancient tomb filled with riches, or if all their work had been a colossal waste of time and money.

Today would tell the story. But why was no one here?

A treeless, dreary expanse of low grass and scrub edging the snow-capped Altai Mountains surrounded the camp. From China, the jagged peaks arched through Kazakhstan to Mongolia and then to Siberia. The air was thin in these high mountains, the land empty of humans except for wandering bands of nomads...and Michael's dig team.

A tall, angular man, Michael Rempart was one of the world's top archeologists. His face, burnished and browned by the bright sun and cruel wind, had a high forehead, sharp cheekbones, and long, straight nose, while hair the color of soot fell haphazardly to his shoulders. Only the slightest crinkling of skin beneath deep-set brown eyes and edging a firm mouth hinted at his forty years of age.

Michael's assistant, Li Jianjun, had insisted on locating the dig site a full two miles from the camp. If Michael had placed the camp any closer to the site, he wouldn't have found anyone willing to work for him. Even here, despite his best efforts, the workers had remained fearful and jumpy.

It was because of the *kurgans*—long, shallow mounds of black and gray stones that jutted eerily over the barren landscape to mark graves. *Kurgans* were death-filled reminders of the ancient cultures that once wandered over Central Asia and southern Siberia from the eighth century B.C. to the thirteenth century A.D. Remnants of those cultures and their traditions were believed by many to still exist. To this day, numerous stories were told of the dead who walked among them.

Near them, darkness hovered, and the earth seemed abnormally still. Near them, every nerve in Michael's body grew taut and tense.

The place they needed to dig sat between three such *kurgans*.

Michael ran toward the *gers* that housed his team. The nomadic tents were commonly known as yurts in the West, but that was a Russian word and never used by the fiercely independent Mongolians.

He swung open the three-foot high door.

No one was inside, but on the ground stood a rounded object covered by a white cloth. White candles circled it. White signified death in many East Asian cultures, much as black did in the West.

Michael snatched off the cloth.

A human skull smiled up at him. It had browned with age, and its few teeth were yellowed and worn. He studied it a moment, then lifted it.

The skull had been placed atop a square of material with a picture of two demons. One had a bright green body, huge belly and monkey's head. The other, a red dragon-like beast, had a human face in a snake's head with four golden fangs. Both demons glared with furious, black, bulging eyes.

Michael squatted low and fingered the material. The silk looked and felt quite old. The art work was Tibetan, a land whose culture and religion had influenced the Mongolian people from their earliest days.

The demons seemed to dance before his eyes, mocking him.

He hurried back outside and searched the bleak, treeless emptiness, hundreds of miles from civilization, for any sign of what had happened to his companions.

He was completely alone except for the *kurgans* in the distance.

TWO

JERUSALEM

"Charlotte! It is good to see you again, my friend." Mustafa Al-Dajani kissed Charlotte Reed on both cheeks. She stood a whole head taller than he and bent forward with a stiff and awkward smile as he gripped her shoulders for the warm greeting. Thirteen years had passed since she last saw him.

They stood at the entrance to a two-story gray office building near Hebrew University's Mt. Scopus campus. Years ago, Charlotte had studied there.

Only a handful of Arab scholars such as Al-Dajani taught at the University. A leading scholar of Egyptian history, culture, and language from the Middle Kingdom through the Ptolemaic period, roughly 2000 B.C. to 30 B.C., he served as an external lecturer for the Institute of Archeology. And he was one of the world's few experts on early alchemical texts.

"It's good to see you, as well, Dr. Al-Dajani," she said. He had gone quite gray, and his stomach, a gentle paunch thirteen years ago, was rotund. He seemed prosperous and happy.

She knew that when he looked at her, he no longer saw the willowy, enthusiastic twenty-four-year-old student she had been, but someone more angular, sinewy. Harder. Her once flowing blond hair was short and straight now, usually worn tucked behind the ears. She wore no make-up. Large blue eyes, analytical and cold, dominated her face.

"You look better than ever," he said.

"So do you." Her head inclined as her reserve slipped ever so slightly. "And we're both terrible liars."

He chuckled as he led her into the building, past the security guard at the entrance, and down the hall to his office. The university secured the building due to the stature of its scholars and the value of the artifacts they studied.

When the two first met, Charlotte Reed had been a doctoral candidate in Al-Dajani's field of expertise. But one day, after having lived and studied in Jerusalem for over a year, her life abruptly changed.

Her husband, Dennis Levine, had been seated in a small café when it was blown up by terrorists. He was killed instantly. She gave up her studies and returned to Washington D.C. where she found a quiet desk job as a Customs agent dealing with forgeries and smuggling of Near and Middle Eastern art and antiquities, an almost forgotten area ever since ICE, U.S. Immigration and Customs Enforcement, had become part of Homeland Security.

Then, one week ago, she received a baffling call from Al-Dajani.

"I have just learned of something that greatly interested your husband before he died," Al-Dajani had said. "It's complicated, impossible to explain over the phone. But if you have time to come to Jerusalem, you may find it of interest."

Despite the calmness of his words, he sounded excited, even desperate, to share his discovery.

But then he added, "I hesitated to contact you after so many years, Charlotte, to bring up the past this way. And also, if you have moved on from those terrible days, if your life is full now, I will understand if you choose to stay away."

In truth, her life wasn't full. Pleasant, at best. Boring, in truth. She liked her home, her job; she had friends, even occasional lovers. Yet, at times, her surroundings felt oddly temporary, as if she missed something vital, crucial.

Al-Dajani gave her a reason to return to the place where her life had swerved so violently awry.

Hearing his voice, talking to him once more, made her realize that the past couldn't be laid to rest by simply ignoring it.

But traveling here, being here now, was even more difficult, emotionally, than she had expected it to be.

An ancient quote played through her mind: that the world was like a human eye—the white was the ocean, the iris was the earth, and the pupil was Jerusalem. The center of all things. The center of her life.

As the sights, sounds and smells of the city flooded over her, a bit of her heart, what little she had left of it, broke all over again.

Al-Dajani's office changed little from the way she remembered it: one small window, dark wooden shelves overflowing with books and folders, and a desk piled high with papers. He offered her tea heavily spiced with cinnamon and cardamom. While the tea brewed, he prattled on with animation and obvious love about his wife and three daughters. She offered few words about her job. He didn't bring up her private life, and neither did she. Finally, impatient and abrupt, she said, "Your call intrigued me."

"Yes. We must talk about it," he murmured.

She braced herself. "I would say so."

He flinched at the coldness of her tone. "At first, I found it merely amusing," he began, "that an American professor who specialized in the Western expansion—cowboys and Indians (your 'Indians,' as you call them) —should come to me about ancient Egyptian alchemical texts. I wondered if he planned to become an alchemist himself."

Al-Dajani's grin mixed mockery and humor at the American, but his words surprised her.

She probably knew more than most people about alchemy and alchemists. Many Americans formed their opinions from children's books and movies in which alchemists were depicted as sorcerers or wizards with pointy hats and long white beards, spending their lives in dark, dank castle laboratories trying to change common metals into gold.

Al-Dajani's gaze caught hers as his expression changed to fear. "Soon after the professor left, strange incidents began to occur. I felt watched. Someone broke into my office. I couldn't help but feel more was behind this than appeared on the surface. The American had been referred to me by Pierre Bonnetieu in Paris. I believe you have met him."

Her world shifted as the past rushed at her once more. Bonnetieu was curator of the Cluny Museum in Paris. She shut out the onslaught of memories of being with Dennis in Paris, of how it felt to be young and in love in that magical place. "Yes," she murmured. "I've met him."

Al-Dajani continued. "The American professor, Dr. Lionel Rempart, had been at the Cluny asking to see medieval writings about alchemy. When Bonnetieu couldn't answer, he referred the professor to me."

"What did this professor want you to do? Create some gold for him? Professors don't make a lot of money, you know."

Al-Dajani's round face crinkled into a smile. He lifted his hands, palms up. "Who knows? But at least that would make sense!" Then he turned serious. "This professor acted nervous, impatient, and arrogant. I explained that everyone had made up stories about alchemy from day one. But Rempart's only interests were in the author of the Emerald Tablet, and in a Kabbalist scholar named Abraham who, some believed, wrote down the information from those tablets. Do you remember your studies regarding any of that, Charlotte?"

Charlotte felt like a student again, a wayward student who'd forgotten to do her homework. She smiled. "All I remember is that about 1900 B.C., a scholar known only as Hermes Trismegistus produced the earliest writings on alchemy, the Emerald Tablet. Hermes believed all life, human, vegetable and mineral stemmed from one single source. A few centuries after his death the Emerald Tablet was lost, but many adepts claimed their own writings included information from those original texts. The most well-known of these adepts, Geber or Jabir, is mostly remembered because his name became the root of the English word 'gibberish,' which tells what people thought of him."

Al-Dajani chuckled mischievously. The mystical East baffling the materialistic West remained a constant source of amusement to him. He took a loud slurp of his tea. "Dr. Rempart seemed to think an ancient book of alchemy had been brought to the western part of your country many years ago, during the time of some early explorers...Lewis and Clark, I believe their names were. As I answered his questions, his excitement grew. His last words to me were '*Maranatha*, it exists.' Then he left."

"What exists?" Charlotte asked.

"The same book that your husband wanted to know about," Al-Dajani said.

"My husband?"

He looked surprised. "You don't know?" At her blank look he shifted, nervous and chagrined. "I'm so sorry, Charlotte. I thought you knew. It's what your husband was investigating when he was killed, the reason for his trips to Paris, and his meetings with me. *Maranatha* was the last word I ever heard him say."

Her mind whirled with confusion. She had introduced Dennis to Al-Dajani, but she had no idea they had ever met beyond that.

"You're telling me Dennis questioned you about alchemy?" Her voice rang with doubt. Dennis used to laugh that deep, throaty laugh of his about the Egyptian mysticism classes she took from Al-Dajani. She could almost hear him now. No, she couldn't imagine Dennis investigating such a thing. Not her Dennis. Al-Dajani had to be mistaken.

"I'm so sorry, Charlotte, if I'd known you were unaware I wouldn't have asked you here at this time. It will take a while to explain. Come this evening so we will have time to talk and we won't be disturbed by confused undergraduates." Al-Dajani patted her hand. "What I've found is incredible. An ancient secret. One that extends from this area to China and then to the New World—your world. A secret some men have died to learn, and others have died to keep."

"I don't understand," she said.

He nodded sadly. "I'm glad you decided to come and hear what I have found. If the tables were reversed, if it were my wife who had died and you had learned something about what she had been pursuing..."

She stared at him, scarcely able to believe what she heard.

He glanced at his wristwatch. "I must be off. Shall we meet here at six o'clock?"

"Fine."

He quickly signed a pass to get her admitted through security after hours, then walked her to the door, and took her hand. "Don't be late!"

"I won't," she said, still somewhat dazed by all he had stated and implied.

"*Insh'Allah,*" he called. God willing.

THREE

Idaho

High gray granite walls cast a gloomy shadow over a narrowing trail as six anthropology students, a professor, a teaching assistant, and their guide trudged through the bitterbrush and beargrass that covered the canyon floor of central Idaho's River of No Return Wilderness Area. Jagged mountains, deep canyons, white-water rapids, glaciers, and high mountain lakes filled its scantly charted two and a half million acres.

Little to no human intrusion had been made in the area, ever. Cascading mountains soared to ear-popping heights and then plummeted to cavernous streams and snaking creeks. Even game was scarce.

"There's a reason the Indians avoided this area," visiting anthropology professor Lionel Rempart said to the students. Rempart had arrived at Boise State University two weeks earlier to spend the school year doing research. A tenured professor at George Washington University in Washington D.C., and one of the country's leading Lewis and Clark scholars, BSU treated his visit as if it were the Second Coming. That he was brother to the dashing, world-famous archeologist, Michael Rempart, who dated Hollywood stars and was a darling of magazines and TV specials, heightened the buzz surrounding him.

The students stopped talking and complaining about the trek and listened.

"Their stories of it being a 'bad' place weren't pure superstition," Rempart said. "One tribe did live out here, an offshoot band of the

Tukudeka. Most Tukudeka were found farther south, around the Middle Fork of the Salmon River. The exception was that one small group. And then, they disappeared. *Poof!* Just like that.

"Legends began not only about a band that disappeared, but of wealth. Of gold." At the skeptical look of the students, he added, "If we can find their stronghold, the discovery could be unimaginably important."

"It sounds like a fantasy," Melisse Willis said. The graduate teaching assistant was one of three women on the trip. Six feet tall, with short, head-hugging pale blond hair, and sculpted muscles, she looked like a Nordic body builder. She grew up near Montana's Flathead Lake, and knew survival techniques in isolated, mountainous terrain. Nevertheless, important people had to pull strings to get her on the field trip.

Melisse softened her tone for the good of her career. "To find something like that in this enormous wilderness, we need more than the five days we've scheduled."

Rempart gave a small, mysterious smile. "I've discovered more about its location than anyone else ever has. And we can always come back."

Melisse hid her skepticism and said nothing.

A chartered bus had carried the university group the three-hundred plus miles from Boise to a place called Telichpah Flat. No more than a few buildings alongside a dirt road, its population reached ten in summer and dropped to zero in winter. There, they met their guide, Nick Hoffman.

From Telichpah Flat, they planned to hike two days in, spend five days at the site, and then two days back out.

Nick Hoffman had excellent credentials as a guide and his references checked out, but the photo he used must have been thirty years old. The six students squeezed into the bed of his old Chevy step-side pickup while Hoffman, Rempart, and Melisse Willis sat in the cab. Hoffman drove out the narrow Salmon River Road, and then onto fire roads heading west. Once the roads ended, they left the truck and hiked inland as far as they were able before they made camp for the night.

Rempart and the guide disagreed with each other almost from the outset, and their disagreements quickly grew. At camp the night before, the students became restless and uneasy, nerves twitched, and in the morning, each complained that when sleep finally came, strange, disturbing dreams filled it.

Now, Rempart stopped and pulled out a map. Hoffman folded his arms and waited.

Watching Rempart and Hoffman, Devlin Farrell knew which one he'd listen to. A second-string wide-receiver on BSU's football team, Devlin found himself on the disabled list when he broke his pinky. He knew, even before that, he'd never have a football career. He exulted in being outdoors and having aced several anthropology classes gave him the edge to be selected for the field trip. The trip offered a chance to decide if this should be his chosen field.

Devlin eyed Rempart, a pasty, soft-muscled man in his fifties, with thinning blond hair, glasses, and surprisingly delicate features. His khaki slacks, white polo shirt, navy blue wind blazer, and Merrell hiking shoes were more appropriate for a stroll through a vacation health spa than exploring a forest. Devlin heard he had been divorced three times, had no children, and enjoyed the company of coeds. That any coed would look twice at the tallow-faced professor told Devlin he would never understand women.

Nick Hoffman, however, looked and sounded every bit as craggy as the surroundings, as if he'd spent his entire sixty-plus years scouting this wilderness. Wiry and hard-muscled, with a long Buffalo Bill mustache, he wore a battered, wide-brimmed cowboy hat, the type commonly seen throughout Idaho with the exception of Boise. A true Idahoan never wore one too new, too high, or with a brim too wimpy.

Rempart and the guide's argument raged on, growing more virulent and bitter by the minute. The trail had been closed due to a landslide, and the surrounding mountains were steep. Nick Hoffman insisted the route the professor wanted to take was too difficult for the students. They were young, yes, but a week at a ski resort was about as grueling as their lives got. Hoffman didn't waste his breath on Rempart's own pitiful physical condition.

Rempart pointed out that taking one of the approved U.S. Forest Service trails around the landslide would add at least a day's walk in each direction, leaving little time at the site. His voice grew high and impatient. "I only brought you here because the University required a guide. I didn't expect you to interfere!"

"It's too dangerous to leave the trails." Hoffman's wide-legged stance projected no nonsense. "Why do you think that soil slid? The land is steep, and the silt is loose. It's like trying to stand on talcum powder. Step on it, and you get no footing. The question is, why are you so damned determined to get to that particular part of the Wilderness Area? The land out there is all the same."

"How can you know if you haven't been there?" Rempart snapped.

Hoffman attempted to keep his voice calm and reasonable. "Because those who went said so. If you want evidence of Tukudeka activity, you need to head south, like I told you."

"Nonsense. I want to see this spot." Rempart jabbed the map with his forefinger. "And I'm the one in charge here!"

"That's fucking pigheaded!" Hoffman shouted. His words stunned Rempart. The much vaunted instructor couldn't believe he'd been spoken to that way. Hoffman continued. "With the trail gone, we can't safely get there from here in the time you have. Period. Besides that, your map isn't complete. A half mile over is a gorge. It fills up in winter and spring. This time of year it's dry, but too damn steep even for mountain goats. It's not shown on your fancy geo-what-the-hell map, but it's sure as hell there. And once you're off the trails, there's no way to easily get help if someone is injured. I won't lead you and a bunch of kids into danger!"

The students backed up as the disagreement spiraled out of control.

"We're not going around the landslide." Rempart folded the map and tucked it in his jacket's breast pocket. "This field trip is no longer your concern. From here, we'll find our own way."

"This isn't a park." Hoffman's voice sounded low, threatening. "It's an empty, perilous land. Your cell phones won't work, it's too big to patrol, and the wild life can be deadly. I'm the one in charge of your safety."

"Not anymore," Rempart said. "You're fired."

No one moved.

Finally, Hoffman spoke, trying to sound reasonable despite the rush of color to his face, the vein that throbbed on his forehead. "All right." He took a deep breath. "I shouldn't have spoken that way. You're the boss and I apologize, but we need to stay on a trail. We'll have time to reach an area a bit south and west of the spot you wanted to go, but it'll be fine, I'm sure. It's all the same out in that wilderness, believe me."

Rempart drew himself up to full patrician haughtiness, then turned his back on Hoffman to his preferred route. Over his shoulder he called out, "You know nothing about what's fine for anthropologists. Pack up and go."

"I'm not leaving these young people, Rempart!" Hoffman faced Melisse. "You've got sense. Do something!"

Devlin saw the struggle on the powerfully built teaching assistant's face, but Rempart held her future in his hands. Melisse didn't dare confront him. "I'm sure," Melisse said, "Professor Rempart would never do anything that might endanger himself. Or anyone else."

Hoffman took his case to the students. "You don't want to do this."

Devlin's gaze met those of tag-along Brian Cutter, his best friend who tried to do whatever Devlin did and never quite succeeded.

Baby-faced, stocky Ted Bellows jutted out his chin as he waited for Devlin and Brian's decision. He tried to look macho and burly, but with thick carrot-colored curls and a red-tinged pug nose, he only looked porcine. His mother sat on the university's board of trustees and had insisted that her son take part in the activities of the famous Dr. Lionel Rempart.

Vince Norton's eyes showed fright as he peered through black-framed glasses at his fellow students. A wispy man with a boy's body, glasses and shaggy brown hair that never saw a comb, Vince's claim to fame—and reason for being on this trip—was his ability as a computer nerd. He oversaw care of the equipment, including a satellite computer connection back to the University.

Devlin faced the two remaining students, Rachel Gooding, the Anthropology Department's best student, and Brandi Vinsome, the child of aging hippies who built their organic farm into a multi-million dollar business. Brandi's round face was red from exertion, and her overly generous hips and pendulous breasts had been squeezed into too tight jeans and a skimpy red Nautica hoodie. No one understood how in the world she had been chosen for this trip.

The girls, too, looked to Devlin for a decision. Alarms jangled in his head. To stay here without a guide and to be led by someone who knew nothing of the area was foolhardy in the extreme and potentially deadly.

His inner self urged retreat as his senses sharpened to every sound, every smell. Somewhere, a branch snapped like a gunshot, and nearby, an owl hooted. Many Indians considered owls a portent of death.

But it didn't take him long to realize, just as Melisse had, that Lionel Rempart controlled his future. He stepped closer to Rempart. As he did, his shadow, Brian, joined him, as did the porcine Ted, and scrawny, quivering Vince.

A moment later, Rachel followed, as did Brandi, who looked more scared of going off alone with someone as scruffy as Hoffman than of staying.

Hoffman's world-weary gaze slowly moved from one to the other. "Heaven help you," he muttered, then spat, gathered his belongings, and without another word, walked away.

FOUR

Mongolia

Back in his *ger,* Michael desperately tried to reach someone on his telecommunications equipment but heard only static.

The loud engine of an old GAZ truck sounded in the distance. He ran out of the *ger* and watched as it approached.

His assistant, Li Jianjun, jumped out of the truck first. Born in Beijing, he was now a Canadian citizen. Of medium height, with a slim build, his appearance and demeanor were more like that of a college student than a man of 35 years. When he was eight, his family moved from Beijing to Hong Kong, and from there to Vancouver, Canada. He worked at Microsoft in Seattle, bored out of his mind, when he met Michael Rempart. Michael needed someone with Jianjun's technical abilities, and Jianjun needed someone who would use and appreciate the full capability of his programming skills and computer hacking know-how. They worked together the past seven years.

Right after him, the two field experts, Batbaatar and Ravil Acemgul, exited the vehicle.

"The men, they've run away," Jianjun said to Michael. "We tried to find them, but couldn't. They were too scared. Long gone. They stole a truck."

"I saw the skulls and demon pictures." Michael folded his arms. "Who did it?"

"We don't know," Jianjun answered. "None of us saw or heard

anything. When we woke up, we saw that someone had managed to come inside while we slept. Creeped me out!"

"The men can't be blamed." Acemgul felt deeply embarrassed. He was responsible for the workers. Middle-aged, he was of Kazakh descent as were many people in the western part of Mongolia. With skin burned dark by the sun, he had broad cheekbones and a high, straight nose. His bearing held all the strength and athletic ability of a master horseman, common among Kazakhs. "They are superstitious, uneducated."

"People in the mountains did it. People who watch the *kurgans*. They protect everything here. They want us to leave," Batbaatar said. An ethnic Mongolian, he stood five-foot five, with a broad and stocky body and a round, flat face. Mongolians used only a single name, and "baatar" was a common ending. It meant "hero." A recent graduate of the Polytechnic Institute in Ulaanbaatar, the country's capital and only modern city, he operated the equipment, made radio contact with the world beyond Banyan Ölgiy, and handled all things meteorological.

Michael found that hard to believe. "We've been here for weeks mapping, imaging, and now digging. Why didn't we hear from them earlier? This is crazy."

Batbaatar continued, "These mountains, this land, are filled with much that makes no sense to you who are not Mongolian. But that does not make it less deadly." He held his head high as if he enjoyed talking about his strange countrymen. "But what they did doesn't matter because nature will stop us. A sand storm is heading this way. A huge one. It will hit around noon. We need to take strong cover by that time."

Despite the strangely colored sky, Michael could see for miles in every direction. The storm wasn't near them yet. "A sandstorm could set us back a week or more."

"The sky is still clear," Acemgul said. "I say, let's see how far we can get before it hits."

"None of you are listening to me!" Batbaatar's red-tinged, wind-burned face frowned deeply. "This storm is a monster. Even here at camp I don't know how safe we will be."

Michael made the decision. "That's all the more reason for us to hurry." He got into the truck. Reluctantly, the others followed, and soon they reached the dig site.

The dig involved going straight down over a relatively small area. To prevent the earthen walls from collapsing as they dug, Michael's dig team employed step-trenching, creating a series of large, wide steps heading downward as the hole deepened.

As the dig neared the underground cavity, Michael bored a three-inch hole through the soil and inserted a long tube with a periscope head and a light. It revealed an open area containing a large rectangular object as well as two smaller objects.

He had found something, but what it was could only be learned by physically entering the chamber.

Michael expected to have plenty of time to breach the underground cavity, but they no sooner reached the site when Batbaatar incredulously announced that the storm had grown and picked up speed. Jianjun had rigged up an Iridium satellite connection to Batbaatar's laptop so he could continuously monitor tracking from NESDIS, the National Environmental Satellite Data and Information Service polar orbiting satellites. The storm spanned a full three miles across and would reach them by eleven o'clock rather than noon.

Michael climbed down into the pit with a pick and shovel, determined to find out more about his discovery. Acemgul and Jianjun helped.

Michael and his team had dug within three feet of the tomb when Batbaatar called out, a desperate edge to his voice. "The storm is moving even faster. It's still growing. In one hour, the first wave will hit. We've got to finish up here and leave."

Michael refused.

The three furiously yet methodically swung the pick in the dry, rocky ground. Twenty minutes later, the moment Michael had dreamed of since first entering Mongolia happened. He broke through an opening.

Flashlight in hand, he lay on his belly and looked down into a secured chamber about eight feet below. He shined his flashlight onto wooden boxes, one of them large and ornate enough to be a coffin.

The group high-fived congratulations all around.

They worked rapidly to shore up the opening so it wouldn't collapse while making it large enough for a man to descend into the chamber.

Batbaatar used an electronic meter to check for carbon monoxide, methane, mold, bacteria, and other contaminants. Given the all-clear, Michael and Acemgul donned hard hats with battery-powered Petzl caver's headlamps, and carried tools, rope, and a digital camera. They lowered an extension ladder into the hole along with ropes to hoist up finds. Jianjun and Batbaatar remained at ground level watching not only weather instruments but also those that gave warning of any sudden shifting of the earth.

Michael descended first. He inhaled stale air with a sharp, rancid undercurrent. He breathed through his mouth, trying to keep the fetid smell from his nostrils, yet feeling as if it were pressing against his face, cutting off his air. Sweat broke out on his forehead as it always did when he went deep underground, loosening terrifying memories of his first significant dig. He had been only twenty-six years old, in Kenya. A cave-in had buried him. When rescued, he appeared dead, his breathing and heartbeat nearly imperceptible. Not until several minutes passed did he regain consciousness.

With those memories, as always, the idea struck that perhaps this time would be his last.

Michael flipped on the light on his hardhat as Acemgul climbed down after him.

The chamber measured ten feet long by eight feet wide. The rapid flashes from Acemgul's camera created a bizarre, almost strobe-light effect. In the center stood a coffin. The ornately carved wood was dry and rotting. Two small lidded crates lay beside it. A wave of exultation filled Michael. They'd done it. The stories and legends were true.

They'd found the tomb and treasures of Lord Hsieh, governor of the wild, uncontrollable northwestern provinces during the ancient Han dynasty.

FIVE

Jerusalem

Charlotte Reed lit a cigarette as soon as she stepped out of Al-Dajani's office. A little calmer now, she headed for the Old City with its ancient arches and stone alleyways. In the Muslim Quarter narrow, crowded streets wended through the souk where shops and outside vendors carried fresh produce, crafts, tasteful art objects, and cheap trinkets. Arab music blared, and the strong scent of shawarma, cumin, and cardamom enveloped the area.

A lopsided wheelbarrow tilted toward her and she jumped aside to avoid being struck. As she turned, she noticed a figure dart behind a hanging rug as if trying to avoid being seen.

She hurried on as old terrors came to mind. The crowd grew ever larger, closing in on her, jostling, pushing. She gripped her shoulder bag tight against her side. As an ICE agent trained to go up against art smugglers and thieves, she always carried a 9 mm Glock 19. It was her constant and most trusted companion even though she had only fired it once on the job to shatter a padlock.

Charcoal smoke filled the air and brought tears to her eyes. Tamarind stung her nostrils. Arab women wearing hijabs, Orthodox Jews in black and white, and Christians wearing everything from jeans and Birkenstocks to cassocks and habits gave her strange looks.

The sense of being watched strengthened.

At the Wailing Wall she warily took in her surroundings and the people nearby. Behind her, she heard a muffled din of devotions; to the left, the piercing call of the muezzin from a minaret; and to the right, the peal of sonorous church bells. No one paid any attention to her, she told herself. And why should they? She was a tourist, nothing more.

She chided herself for baseless nervousness and found an outdoor café for *kanafeh* and tea. She took a seat against the wall facing the street, shook out a Benson and Hedges menthol and lit it as she carefully watched the passersby.

Soon, she left the Old City and went up to the Mount of Olives with its magnificent views of Jerusalem. She sat stiffly on a bench near the Chapel of the Ascension and from that high lookout finally allowed herself to do what she had both longed for and feared ever since returning to the Holy Land.

She became lost in the past.

Another saying about the area came to her, this one attributed to the Hasidic spiritual leader, Rebbe Nachman: *Wherever I go, I am going to Jerusalem.*

In a sense, ever since fleeing the city after her husband's horrible death, no matter how much she fought against it, she knew that one day she would need to face the past.

Memories washed over her. Some felt wonderful while others held more pain than anyone should have to bear. She had spent years telling herself she had moved beyond it, but in reality she simply had refused to deal with what had happened here thirteen years earlier. Now, she steeled herself to face it. To remember.

She attended George Washington University in Washington D.C. as a first-year graduate student of Middle Eastern art and history when Dennis Levine entered her life.

Ten years older than her, with short, tightly waved dark brown hair and glasses, his remarkable intelligence rather than his looks caught her attention. His brilliance in her field of studies made her feel like a complete amateur, grasping at straws and trying to learn through books what Dennis already knew, lived, and breathed to the marrow of his being.

Their casual coffee dates quickly became serious. Two months after they met, he asked her to marry him and go with him to Jerusalem where he worked with the State Department. He needed to return immediately. Without a moment's hesitation, she agreed. That was when he added that he was, in fact, a CIA officer.

They explored the city together, spending endless hours walking everywhere, learning to love the modern city as well as the ancient one.

She rose from the bench and turned toward Mt. Scopus for her upcoming meeting. She didn't mind the long walk; she wanted to feel the pulse of the city beneath her feet once more. As she walked, the sights before her faded, and in their place were ghosts of the past.

Once in Jerusalem, she had applied for transfer to the graduate program at the Hebrew University. Dennis's position had a lot to do, she believed, with the ease with which she'd been accepted. Nonetheless, her classes on the history, art, language, and culture from Egypt to Sumer captivated her.

Dennis seemed to think she'd be interested in joining him in the CIA someday, and that her knowledge of the Middle East would be useful to the agency. He taught her to use handguns and rifles, and insisted she carry a small handgun whenever she went out alone. She never did. As a student, she had firmly believed handguns should be banned and the nations of the world disarmed. The irony of her now being an armed agent with ICE wasn't lost on her. Back when Dennis was alive, she had feigned interest in the CIA because he adored his job and she wanted to make him happy. In truth, such a career held no appeal for her. She hoped to become a professor and naively wished to use her knowledge and admiration of this land to help soothe, in some small way, the international tensions surrounding it. But all her dreams had turned to nothing.

And now, she found herself in Jerusalem again, alone and trying to learn what she could about her husband's death. Ancient secrets. A bizarre American professor named Lionel Rempart. Alchemy. She found it hard to believe any of them could possibly be connected to her practical, both feet firmly on the ground husband.

Before she knew it she had reached Al-Dajani's office building. She tapped on the glass door to get the attention of the guard and then plastered the pass Al-Dajani had given her against it. The young guard read it and with a smile and nod, hit the buzzer to let her enter.

The door no sooner opened when, from behind, she heard running footsteps coming closer.

SIX

Mongolia

Michael could scarcely believe he had found Lord Hsieh's tomb. The exploration had been beset with trouble from the outset.

Even the way it started was strange.

Michael and his older brother, Lionel, weren't at all close, which wasn't surprising given their family and upbringing. That was why Michael found it curious when, over a year earlier, Lionel had contacted him for help.

Lionel told him a strange story. Many years earlier, a Chinese foreign exchange student found materials indicating that a medieval French book on alchemy had been brought to the northwestern United States and ended up in what is now Idaho. After returning home to China, the exchange student had apparently become a geneticist, but Lionel could find nothing more about him.

Since Michael was in Beijing attending a symposium on archeological discoveries from the Shang dynasty, Lionel had asked him to contact the scientist for more information. The idea that a Chinese scientist might know anything about an ancient alchemy book in the U.S. sounded far-fetched, but Michael asked Jianjun to attempt to find the man.

Jianjun succeeded, in a sense.

Dr. Chou An-ming was dead, but others in his family were living in Beijing.

"I appreciate your agreeing to talk with me," Michael said with a slight bow as he met Dr. Chou's daughter, who introduced herself only as Mrs.

Yang. She was a plain woman, her clothes as boxy as her build. Michael and Jianjun met her at her small apartment.

Michael felt awkward about being there, about having to ask personal questions, and wondered why he had agreed to Lionel's request. "I understand your father studied in the United States."

"He was quite proud of his time there," the daughter said. "He studied at George Washington University in Washington D.C. He was a good man who died much too young."

"I'm sorry."

Mrs. Yang nodded. "He went to New York City for a symposium put on by a big American company, Phaylor-Laine Pharmaceuticals. And also he planned to meet with his best friend in college, a Danish scientist. Meeting the Dane, I've heard, truly excited him. Unfortunately, as he crossed a street, a truck hit him. He died instantly. It was fifteen years ago."

"He died in the United States?" Michael asked, surprised.

"Yes. In New York City, near the United Nations building. He never got to meet his Danish friend."

After words of condolence, Michael got to the point of his visit. "Did your father ever speak about alchemy, or about an ancient text on alchemy being in the U.S.?"

At the word "alchemy," the daughter turned to Jianjun, who had remained quietly seated up to that point, for a translation. She looked quite bemused when she got it.

"My father's work involved genetic engineering. He did botanical and genetic analysis of early Chinese herbal medicine, concentrating on herbs used in far-flung regions. It certainly had nothing to do with anything as silly as alchemy."

"Yes, I can imagine," Michael said with a smile. "But did he ever mention alchemy at all?"

She thought for a moment. "Now that you mention it, he told me one story, both interesting and sad. I think that's why I remember it. It obviously moved him deeply."

She sat stiff and upright as she relayed the story. "During the Han dynasty, from 206 BC to 220 AD—the period in which the Chinese empire expanded into Central Asia—its major problem soon became control of the newly conquered population. A wealthy man, Lord Hsieh Ch'en-yu, was named governor of the northern outskirts of what is now the Xinjiang province. His wife refused to accompany him to such a barbaric region. One day, as he rode through a village, he saw a beautiful young woman. He demanded she become his concubine. She had no choice—if she refused, she and her family would have been killed.

"He forced the concubine to accompany him to the desolate outpost. She was very much afraid, and for protection brought with her many ancient herbs and potions to perform her magical arts, namely alchemy. She had been taught how to use them by her grandmother."

She paused to see if this was the sort of story Michael sought. As an archeologist, anything going back two thousand years fascinated him. He nodded.

She continued. "In Central Asia, Lord Hsieh soon discovered that he could not hold back the freedom-loving nomads. Swords drawn, they swarmed over the Chinese. The new governor was among the first killed. As the Han Chinese soldiers continued to fight, the concubine urged them to flee into the mountains of what is now Mongolia, to a more desolate area where they might live. She took Lord Hsieh's body with her. There, her retainers built an underground tomb for Lord Hsieh. Stories traveled back to the eastern capital of the magnificent woman who led her people, trying to find a safe haven for them. The young woman's bravery so humbled and impressed the soldiers that—although a lowly concubine from a poor family—they honored her with the title 'Lady.' But soon after her people completed the tomb, nomadic tribes found them and attacked once more. Lady Hsieh knew there was no hope.

"She told the soldiers they were free to leave, to escape back to their homes if possible. She also set free all Lord Hsieh's slaves and retainers, and then, in the dead of night, she disappeared. Everyone knew she desperately wanted to live, and many believed she used her magical arts to that end. To this day, however, no one knows what happened to her or to her husband's gold and possessions."

For reasons he did not understand, Michael could feel the young woman's terror at facing death far from everything she held dear.

"Over the centuries, the tale of Lady Hsieh slipped into the mists of time except in Bayan Ölgiy where she escaped. In Bayan Ölgiy it is believed that whoever finds Lord Hsieh's tomb will possess untold riches." Mrs. Yang folded her hands, her story ended.

Michael soon thanked Mrs. Yang for her time and left.

He reported on Dr. Chou's death to his brother. But the story of Lady Hsieh haunted him. One of his earliest lessons as an archeologist was to learn to listen to local legends. Before long he decided to search for Lord Hsieh's tomb.

Michael first sent Jianjun to the western Bayan Ölgiy area to see if anyone there could confirm the history behind the tale. The story was corroborated, and the areas where the tomb might have been located were narrowed to a manageable degree.

Many difficulties, political as well as geographic, hampered his plans. Mongolia wasn't quite as paranoid about strangers as China, but almost. And, although Mongolia was an independent country, China maintained a high degree of influence over its government.

For a reason he could not express, the dig soon became an obsession. Michael never considered giving it up. While Jianjun located men and heavy equipment, he dealt with the government. Officials told him "No" for months, then out of the blue, like a drain unplugged, everything opened up. It seemed nothing short of miraculous.

He wasted no time making a site surface survey. This being Mongolia, he had to mount the sensitive resistivity meters and ground penetrating radar equipment on a cart pulled by yaks. Fortunately, it worked. Echoes from radio pulses reflected back changes in soil and sediment, and the depth of those changes. Scans revealed the location of a cavity some twenty-three feet below the surface with a diameter of ten feet or so.

The size fit that of a tomb.

In China, archeologists already had excavated more than forty Han dynasty tombs, all made of brick or stone and placed deep in the earth for preservation. This was the first, as far as Michael knew, found outside of China.

And now, he had entered the tomb.

Michael started with the small crates and quickly opened them. Inside he found pottery and jewelry of jade, gold and semi-precious stones. The quality and value, however, were minimal. They weren't anything to give rise to the reputation the tomb had for riches. It didn't worry Michael, however. The most valuable treasure was usually buried with the body.

Michael and Acemgul turned to the coffin. With surprisingly little effort, they lifted off the lid.

Inside, a skeleton stared up at them. The flesh was gone, its garments worn away to nothing but a gray gauzy film. The rest of the coffin was empty.

Michael was stunned.

"So it comes to this," he murmured, his disappointment palpable.

"Air clear. Ground stable. Storm is six miles across and will be here in less than thirty minutes!" Batbaatar called down.

Just then, dirt fell from the ceiling. A cloud of dust burned Michael's eyes and nostrils. "Watch it up there," he yelled, needing to keep Batbaatar and Jianjun away before they caused the whole roof to collapse, smothering him and Acemgul along with the worthless corpse they'd found.

Michael perused the tomb with dismay. "I don't get it. Why set up such an elaborate site to bury the old governor and a few items with little value?"

Acemgul turned toward the ladder when a loud *crack!* filled the chamber. The floor opened up beneath him, and he dropped.

Michael dove toward him. He landed on his stomach and grabbed Acemgul's arms as the assistant tried to hold on to something, anything, to prevent himself from falling into the unknown.

The floor under Michael's chest began to sag. His body slipped forward. "Batbaatar! Get down here! Help us," he yelled.

Acemgul held onto him, his eyes wide with fear as he squirmed, his legs flailing to find support for his feet. "There's nothing under me," he said, his voice tight, quavering. "I don't know how far down..."

"I know," Michael said. "Move your hands. Grip my arms."

Heavy footsteps sounded on the ladder. "Not too close," Michael warned as Batbaatar reached the floor.

Batbaatar knelt on the ground, and looped thick arms and hands around Michael's waist, pulling him back. The muscles along Michael's arms and shoulders felt ready to tear from Acemgul's weight. Acemgul wasn't very tall, but he was solid and muscular. The strain on Michael's arms became unbearable.

The small Mongolian shifted forward, stretched, grabbed Acemgul's jacket, and used it as a winch to pull the Kazakh from the hole as if he weighed no more than a child.

Jianjun carefully descended half-way down the ladder in case his help was needed.

Michael and Acemgul sat on what they hoped was a solid floor and waited for the tremors to cease in their quivering muscles. A heavy, musky, almost sweet smell in the air. It wafted up from below.

"Flowers," Michael murmured as he struggled to stand. "It smells like flowers." He repressed a visceral reaction to the strong floral scent in the enclosed space. It brought back terrible memories of his mother's death. He was only ten-years old, but he would never forget the overwhelming smell of the flowers that surrounded her casket, or how it had nauseated him.

"Peonies," Jianjun murmured as he checked the air meter. It gave no indication of a problem gas. "Much loved in China."

A sudden loud whistling of the wind through the main burial chamber paused any further conversation.

"The storm is like a mountain filling the entire western sky," Batbaatar said. "Truly, we must go."

"The demons tried to swallow me up." Acemgul stood, his back, shoulders and neck aching. "The sandstorm is a curse cast upon us for desecrating the grave."

Such superstitions outraged Michael. "Go, if you feel that way!"

Acemgul's eyes were hard, his expression rigid. "I gave my word to help you. I will stay until you say otherwise."

Michael nodded, sorry for his harsh tone. He moved toward the new hole in the floor and shined his flashlight into it. "Another chamber, a little smaller. The ground is eight or nine feet down. It explains why the radar reads indicated a deeper tomb than the one we found. I'm going to check it out."

"The storm is visible." Batbaatar sounded firm yet resigned. "It will be here in a matter of minutes."

"Wait. I'll get you another ladder," Jianjun told Michael as he headed up to ground level. "If you insist on going down there, I won't stop you. But I'm not going down! No way. One ladder, coming up!"

"I'll go with you, Michael," Acemgul said defiantly, his dark eyes boring into Batbaatar as if challenging the Mongol to dare to argue against their boss' wishes.

It was reckless, Michael knew, given the storm, and that there were only four of them. But then, his whole life had been reckless.

He and Acemgul chipped away at the decayed wooden floor until they reached a solid section. When Jianjun brought down the light aluminum extension ladder, they rested it there. Michael felt a surge of excitement, the kind he had felt in the past before making an important discovery.

"Wait here," he said to the others. "I'll take a quick look."

He descended the ladder to a second chamber. The floor seemed to have solid ground beneath it. But the scene puzzled him.

The space was empty except for a large, rectangular wooden box.

Before he knew it, Acemgul and Jianjun joined him.

"You?" Michael said, bemused, to Jianjun.

The strong light of the Petzl headlamp showed Jianjun's pale face. The worry in Jianjun's eyes bothered Michael. His assistant loved to talk and complain, but he rarely showed any sign of fear. Usually, he took command of a given situation with the technical knowledge and equipment to handle just about anything that came up. And anything he didn't know, he knew someone who did. Michael might be his boss, but Jianjun tended to mother hen him, and more than once his cautious worry saved Michael's life. At the same time, on a few other occasions, Michael's selfless courage returned the favor.

"Don't ask, Michael. Just don't ask. Let's get this show on the road so we can all get out of here."

Some kind of resin sealed the lid. They pried it off with knives.

Saffron-colored silk, faded and dry, covered the inside. Michael attempted to lift it, but it turned to dust in his hands.

Underneath he found a second large chest surrounded by lacquered bowls and porcelain figurines of tigers and bears. Old, but crude and not remarkable by any means.

In the early Han period, wealthy Chinese often used a two-layered coffin system with an inner and outer receptacle. The inner container would be painted and lacquered with scenes of heaven including spirits and strange animals.

Michael realized this might be a coffin after all, but larger than those found in prior excavations.

Batbaatar lowered himself half way down the ladder. "You must come now," he shouted excitedly. "Sand is already falling into the first chamber. It will be all we can do to get back to the *gers*."

"Two more minutes," Michael said, as he and Acemgul studied the second box. Made of teak, floral designs were carved into it. They decided against attempting to lift it out and instead pried off the lid. Inside, they found yet a third chest, also teak, about five feet long and two-and-a-half feet wide.

"Is this a joke?" Michael muttered.

Batbaatar climbed down the rest of the way, stepping lightly to test the floor as he moved closer. "What's keeping you here?"

"This might be like one of those Russian nesting dolls." Michael waved his hand dismissively at the find. "One chest inside the other until you get to the last one which doesn't open or is empty."

The wind whistled ominously.

"Empty? You're risking your life, and ours, for an empty crate?" Batbaatar gazed longingly back at the ladder, but didn't go toward it.

"We don't know for sure that it's empty," Jianjun said, defending his boss and friend. "That's why we've got to see what's here while we have the chance. The storm will bury all this. If it's as worthless as the first coffin, we can let it stay buried and go home."

"Someone or something doesn't want us here," Acemgul murmured. His eyes lifted to the ceiling, to the opening that could lead them out of this tomb.

Michael peered closer. "There's a design on the chest."

The design had faded over the years, but they could make out two overlapping triangles with two veed lines and a circle in the center. It wasn't carved, but appeared to have been painted in red dye:

"What does it mean?" Jianjun asked.

"It's not a symbol I recognize," Michael replied. Batbaatar and Acemgul were similarly mystified.

Michael attempted to force open the third chest the way he had the earlier two. It didn't work. Some kind of wax or substance that hardened to a granite-like consistency hermetically sealed it.

The howl of the wind grew loud and commanding.

He gave the okay to Acemgul to help him chip away at it with a hammer and chisel. Normally, he'd never treat any find that way, but this one seemed worthless.

Outside, the wind kicked up a loud ruckus. Opening the last chest was taking too long. Batbaatar and Jianjun grew more nervous. Acemgul prepared to take a crowbar to it when Michael raised a hand to stop him. "I've got it."

The surprisingly heavy lid required the four of them to lift it off.

They gasped in astonishment at the silk banner inside as bright and soft as the day it was created. Silk paintings often served as burial objects during the Han period.

Against a vermilion background, the scene depicted heaven at the top protected by a dragon, with the sun and a crow on the right, and the moon with a toad and rabbit on the left. Below it, a beautiful woman leaned on a walking stick while three female attendants helped her on her journey upward. Below them, the underworld swirled in darker hues of blue and purple.

On one side near the end of the box lay a piece of paper with a map. They all bent low to study it.

"I am familiar with this," Batbaatar said with awe on his face. "Our Buddhism comes from Tibet. This type of map gives the dead a means to find their way in the *bardo*." He gazed with superiority at Acemgul and explained. "As described in *The Book of the Dead*, the *bardo* is the transition period in the afterlife."

His words confirmed that the chest was a coffin. Acemgul stepped back as he realized what it must contain.

A chill crept along Michael's spine as he proceeded to peel back the silk, piece by piece. It remained as sheer, fine and soft as if freshly spun.

Ten layers down, a shape began to appear. It became more pronounced as he removed more layers of the silk cloth. Hair and style of dress began to show through the silk. "It's a woman," he whispered. "Lady Hsieh. It has to be her. So, she died after all, and her servants hid her body so her corpse wouldn't be desecrated before they fled."

The sudden pulsating shriek of the wind all but stole his words.

He took hold of the last layer and slowly lowered it. First, he saw her hair, as black, shiny and thick as it had been in life, arranged in a high, fashionable style with coils held with combs of gold and rubies.

Next, he saw her face.

She was beautiful with flawless skin, the color of pale ivory, her cheeks lightly rouged as were her lips. A small stone, a deep but brilliant blood red color, lay against those lips, as if she were kissing it.

She wore a dress of pure white silk, delicately embroidered in shades of blue. It skimmed her body showing a slim, youthful figure.

A jade medallion with a gold design in its center of the same interlocking triangles seen on the coffin, had been placed on her chest. His gaze rose again to her face. To see her so perfectly preserved startled him. He couldn't take his eyes off her.

"It's impossible," Jianjun said. "No way. No way at all." He had been standing close to the body, but now he eased back.

A sharp metallic *clang!* made them all jump. The storm, now gathered to an ear-splitting force, had slammed the aluminum ladder from the wall it leaned against onto the opposite side. The noise resounded in the narrow chamber.

Michael ignored the storm. "What process did they use?" he whispered, as much to himself as to Jianjun. "A modern taxidermist can't keep a body so lifelike. No culture has been known to mummify a body so perfectly or so completely." He turned to Acemgul and Batbaatar. "How can this be, here in the Mongolian desert?"

Just then, the first grains of sand whipped down upon them.

Her face looked bloodless, yet the skin appeared as fresh and natural as if she simply slept. A stray lock of hair touched her cheek—a stubborn lock as if with a will all its own.

Batbaatar ran to the ladder and began to climb up. "We've got to get out! We'll be buried alive!"

Michael stared at the woman. He knew better, but couldn't help himself, and reached out to brush back the lock of hair, his fingers delicately traveling along her face.

Where he touched, the skin felt soft. Warm. His breathing quickened. He lightly pressed down, and when he lifted his fingertips, her skin reformed with the elasticity of living flesh.

Jianjun saw, and Michael heard his sharp intake of breath.

How could she have been preserved this way?

And what...

He bent low and studied the strange red stone over her lips. He had never seen or heard of a stone that particular color in nature and wondered if it wasn't an alloy of some sort.

More sand fell. The storm had arrived in full, violent fury.

"We can wait no longer," Acemgul cried. He began to follow Batbaatar out of the pit. "This will be your own tomb if you don't hurry!"

Ignoring the sand and chaos behind him, Michael glanced at Jianjun who read his mind. "No!" Jianjun whispered, but then the scientist took over. His shoulders slumped, his demeanor embarrassed that he showed himself to have been frightened, and he said, "Yes. Yes, of course. You must."

As the air of the chamber grew thick with sand and dust, Michael tried to keep his hands steady and used only his forefinger and thumb to grip the red stone. He slowly lifted it from the body's mouth.

Then, unable to believe what he saw, he stood mute and frozen in place.

The woman's eyes opened, and she looked straight at him.

SEVEN

JERUSALEM

At the sound of footsteps running toward her, Charlotte's uneasiness from earlier in the day combined with her ICE and terrorism training kicked in. She lunged inside Al-Dajani's building to seek a secure position.

Behind her, the guard shouted. Then, a sickening pop, the sound of a silencer on an automatic handgun.

Down the hall she found a narrow side corridor and spun into it. Heart pounding, she slid her hand into her shoulder bag and gripped her Glock.

"What's going on?" Al-Dajani flung open the door of his office at the end of the main hall.

A stranger with frizzy, close cut black hair, an olive complexion, and wearing tan slacks and a black sweater stepped into view. He stared at Al-Dajani. The .357 magnum in his hand looked like a cannon.

With no word, no hint of danger, no warning, he lifted it and fired.

"No!" Charlotte shouted. She pulled the trigger three times in rapid succession, her unsilenced handgun loud and reverberating in the hallway. The stranger fell.

She ran to Al-Dajani. He lay on the floor, the top of his head a gaping black hole of hair, blood, and white matter.

Bile rose in her throat. Unbelieving, her gaze darted over the office where she'd sat with both joy and curiosity that very morning. Blood had splattered over the walls, furniture and floor. Then she turned to the gunman. She'd never shot a man before. Had never killed. Her head swam.

Something about him...had she seen him earlier? Near the Wailing Wall? She wasn't sure. But what if she had been followed that day? There was no "if," she realized. How else could the gunman have been so close behind her when the guard unlocked the door?

If she had acted faster, shot to kill sooner, would her friend still be alive? Had she hesitated? The thought crushed her. If she could have saved Al-Dajani...

A police siren sounded in the distance.

With sudden clarity, she realized she had to get away. Three men lay dead. To become involved with the Israeli police investigating a triple homicide verged on madness.

The siren grew louder, closer.

On top of Al-Dajani's desk she saw a stack of papers about alchemy.

His words flooded her...alchemy, the American professor, Dennis...and she found herself snatching up the papers, clutching them tight against her chest as if they might contain some answers. As she turned to run from the office, she remembered having heard a slight jingle of keys as Al-Dajani walked. His jacket lay draped over the back of the desk chair, a surprisingly normal and homey touch considering all that had just happened. He had always parked his car in a small lot in the back—a perk for those with offices in this building. She reached in one pocket then the other before she found his keys.

At the door to the office, she checked to be sure there wasn't a second gunman in the hall.

She ran to a stairway down to the parking area and paused, clutching the cold steel of the railing, as she listened for footsteps on the staircase. All remained silent. She plunged down.

"What I've found is incredible," Al-Dajani had said.

He had complained about being followed, his office broken into, and feeling he'd been followed. Foolish paranoia, he'd called it. But it wasn't paranoia.

The only thing that connected her and Al-Dajani was the reason he had called her—the subject he claimed Dennis had investigated before his death. Did that cause Al-Dajani to die?

A thought, unbidden and terrifying, hit her. If someone killed Al-Dajani now because of Dennis' investigations thirteen years earlier, could Dennis' death have been—

No! She couldn't think that. His death had happened because he'd been in the wrong place...because of bad luck.

Or had it?

Al-Dajani had said she might want to know the truth.

He was right. She did.

As she exited to the parking area, she pushed the remote, and saw the welcoming flash of the headlights on an older Mercedes.

She got in. As she started the car, a tall, muscular man, with short blond hair, a thick jaw, ran towards her from the back of a neighboring building. He aimed his gun directly at her.

EIGHT

Mongolia

The *karaburan* or "black hurricane" swept over the desert at one-hundred-twenty miles per hour, burying everything in its path with layers of sand. This one was larger than most, a true Sahara-like sand storm caused when individual particles of sand vibrated and flew upward, and then slammed back to earth. As they repeatedly struck the ground, they loosened other particles that did the same thing, causing the storm to grow and revolve, much as an ocean wave churned and swelled as it raced over the water.

Jianjun pulled Michael out of the tomb and forced him to hurry. Above them, the sky had turned a sickly brown. In the distance a wall of dust, sand, and dirt rolled toward the site. It looked as if the entire desert had been lifted up and formed a thick ochre cloud that would smother everything in its wake.

"There's no more you can do now," Jianjun shouted as the wind grew louder. "You covered the coffin. It survived two thousand years; it can survive a few more days. We'll dig it up again when the storm passes." He hooked one arm with Michael's, and with the other grabbed Batbaatar's shirt as the Mongolian led them to the jeep, with Acemgul pushing from behind.

"Get in quickly," Batbaatar begged. He'd seen sand hit so hard it tore the skin off a man, and he wasn't about to get stuck in it, or to let that happen to his boss. Despite himself, he liked the difficult, solitary American, but the man had a death wish.

They jumped onto the jeep. Michael pulled his jacket off and covered his head and face with it. The winds advanced, swirling as if in some wild, syncopated rhythm. Depending on how the sands hit, the entire excavation could be wiped out in an instant, burying Lady Hsieh deep underground once more.

Batbaatar drove as fast as he dared across the desert. The first waves of sand punished the jeep, tossing it about as it struggled forward. Batbaatar used every ounce of strength to control the wheel. Yet, Michael's thoughts remained at the tomb.

Once inside the *ger*, although the storm shook its ribbed walls, its round construction helped withstand the area's brutal winds. Two sturdy wooden vertical posts supported the entire structure while wooden latticework framed the circular walls. Slim poles slanted upward from the walls to form a circle at the center of the roof providing a means to vent the stove. The walls were swathed in layers of thick, natural-colored wool with a top layer of off-white canvas. Overlapping rugs of hides from yak and horses along with richly patterned wool carpets covered the floor and portions of the walls.

Acemgul handed Michael a glass of *airag,* a sour brew of fermented mare's milk, and made him drink it straight down. Batbaatar gave each man a bowl of hot tea laced with salt and yak milk in the Mongolian style. Michael didn't realize his fingertips were nearly frozen from the temperature drop in the sunless sky until he touched the hot bowl.

To forget the sound of the storm, Batbaatar took out his stringed *huqin* and began to sing traditional melancholy songs of brave deeds of warriors past. Soon, the wind's howls grew too loud for even that simple pleasure. The temperature plummeted further, and they all burrowed beneath rugs and quilts to stop shivering.

Michael leaned back against a pile of pillows, holding another glass of *airag*. Candles cast shifting patterns on the *ger's* walls, suffusing it with a subdued and gentle mood within the raging storm. Michael looked over at Batbaatar and Acemgul, and even Jianjun, now convivially joking and drinking in this land of no power lines, no fences, not even a road sign.

He felt alone. Again. He shut his eyes, hoping for the relief of sleep.

The winds grew louder, thundering around him.

She opened her eyes and looked straight at me.

Gently, Jianjun lowered the lids, and they had stayed shut.

Her skin had been warm and soft. Jianjun saw that, too. Or had he?

He repeated to himself she was dead, she had to be, and yet...

He tried to convince himself he only wanted to find out how Lady

Hsieh's body could have remained without putrefaction or decomposition for over two thousand years. He knew of a few instances of that happening, but none for that length of time. In the west, Catholics believed the body of Saint Bernadette of Lourdes remained preserved after death as in life. In Japan, the tooth of the Buddhist monk, Nichiren Daishonen, honored by the Soka Gakkai cult, was said to have a piece of the monk's gum on it, and that the gum was living flesh.

At the other extreme, the Soviets had tried to preserve Lenin's body in a glass enclosure, but it rotted away and they had to rebuild him in wax—a sort of Communist homage to Madame Tussaud's famous museum.

Michael had never heard of an instance of a body of someone who wasn't a saint or a holy man surviving unblemished. But he had no interest in saints or sinners, no interest in the spiritual or ethereal. Cold, rational science interested him. Or so he tried to persuade himself.

Somehow, he would find a way to sneak Lady Hsieh out of Mongolia. Bribes or whatever it took, he would do. He would succeed. He must.

She wasn't just a mummified corpse to him, but much more.

And he had to find out why.

The winds grew louder, thundering around him.

Michael left the *ger* hours later, drunk and miserable, while the others slept. The brunt of the storm had passed, but the night was cold and dark. He wanted the solitude of his own *ger*.

He paused, needing to think, but the world swayed under his feet and he stumbled forward.

He angled toward his *ger*.

It was gone. Smashed by sand. Blown away.

His mind couldn't function. What had he been thinking? He should go back inside. Back to sleep. But not to dream. He hated his dreams.

It must have been the rush of air entering her mouth when he removed the red stone that caused her eyes to open that way. No other rational explanation existed. No rational...

He raked his hands through his hair. Only here, in this quiet loneliness, could he admit what he saw, what had both frightened yet electrified him. When her eyes were open, they were alive. Not the flat, unseeing eyes of the dead, but focused. Warm. They saw him, and somehow formed an unbidden, unimagined connection. They seemed to understand his innermost, darkest, most frightening thoughts.

The connection felt deeper, stronger, than anything he had known before; perhaps because it had been so startlingly unexpected. And real. He would swear that to his dying day.

Why was he out here? Suddenly, he didn't know if he was awake or asleep, or if this was one of those dreams so vibrant that when you woke, you could scarcely believe it wasn't real.

He sensed her again. Lady Hsieh. She called to him. Even as he argued with himself about the impossibility of what he heard, something drew him toward the *kurgans,* away from the camp, out into the open. He couldn't fight it. He turned toward the dig. To Lady Hsieh. He needed to see her again, to answer her call.

He rose as straight as he could, shoulders broad and squared, and forced his steps toward the dig.

The air remained thick and murky, the stars and moonlight dim. All road marks had been covered by a heavy layer of sand and dust that sucked and grabbed his boots.

Yet, he knew he headed in the right direction. She drew him to her, led him there. A dream, but not a dream. He pressed forward.

Another burst of wind and sand hit, and he pulled his scarf low to cover his face. Head bowed, he stumbled, blinded, and then slid down a steep embankment into nothingness.

NINE

Paris

Charlotte hailed a taxi to take her from Charles de Gaulle airport into the city.

The night before, in Jerusalem, as the wail of sirens filled the streets, a gunman had been ready to shoot her as she drove Al-Dajani's Mercedes. At the same moment, a police car sped by. The gunman faded into the darkness.

At the Tel Aviv-Jaffa airport, she purchased an El Al ticket to Paris. When living in Israel, she had always carried her passport, papers, and credit cards with her and had reverted to that system without thought. The few clothes, books, and toiletries back in her hotel room weren't worth going after.

She went through the special internal security division, showing her U.S. Homeland Security credentials and weapon. She scarcely breathed until the plane left Israeli air space. She feared security cameras had captured her leaving the parking lot in a victim's car. She had no idea how long it might take before the Israeli police identified her.

On the plane, she looked through the papers she had picked up from Al-Dajani's desk. Most of them were photocopies of ancient Egyptian Demotic script. She remembered a few of the consonant glyphs, but would need her books and dictionaries to make any sense of the writing. The only thing clear to her was a symbol drawn on a sheet all by itself:

Given Al-Dajani's area of study, the symbol very likely had an alchemical connection. In alchemy large outer circles represented boundaries of energy fields, and the four elements that made up all matter were represented by triangles.

But she had no idea what the complete symbol represented, particularly with its center having two vee shapes and a solid circle above them.

The taxi brought her to the Latin Quarter. She got out at the Rue Saint Jacques, two blocks south of the Seine, and began walking. The Musée National du Moyen Age Thermes de Cluny with its flamboyant Gothic turreted walls and dormers with seashell motifs was located nearby, on the Place Paul-Painlevé.

She slowed to make a thorough scan of the area, then hurried to the Cluny. The medieval mansion housing the museum had been built originally for Benedictine abbots in the fifteenth century. In 1515 it became the residence of Mary Tudor, daughter of Henry VII and Elizabeth of York, and widow of Louis XII. The newly formed French republic confiscated in 1793 and turned it into a museum in the mid-nineteenth century.

She entered an open cobblestone courtyard with gargoyles peering down from beneath a stone parapet. At the museum entrance, she gave her name, and asked to see the curator, Pierre Bonnetieu, saying she needed to see him about a mutual friend, Mustafa Al-Dajani.

After a short wait, a pointy-faced woman led her up the stairs to the administrative section, past the rotunda which housed the six Lady and the Unicorn tapestries, the museum's most famous collection.

Bonnetieu's office was paneled in dark wood covered with paintings. Shelves held fine pottery and figurines as well as leather bound first editions. The curator sat behind a massive inlaid mahogany desk. He wore an expensive but overly snug suit, as if refusing to admit his weight. His brightly florid face with sagging jowls spilled over a too-tight collar.

As he rose to greet her, he studied her face. "Miss Reed? You look familiar. I'm sorry, I can't quite place ..."

Although her heart pounded, her stance remained stiff, devoid of expression. "Many years ago I met you through my husband, Dennis Levine."

His eyebrows rose with recognition. She watched his expression shift as the full impact of the memory hit. "Dennis ... oh, my. Yes, I do remember. I'm so sorry for your loss. He was a good man. A brilliant scholar."

"Yes, thank you," she murmured, then hurried on. "The reason I'm here may have something to do with what he had been investigating when he died." She said no more, wanting to gauge his reaction to those words.

He showed no surprise. "Please sit." He gestured toward the leather chair facing his desk. "May I offer you something to drink? A liqueur? Tea, perhaps?"

"No, thank you," she said curtly, then added, "Mustafa Al-Dajani is dead." The words were a sharp crack in the air.

His face drained of color.

She quietly relayed the details of her visit with Al-Dajani, and how he'd mentioned the possibility of danger. "He said that after speaking with you about the visit of Lionel Rempart, an American professor of anthropology, he began to piece together information, and that caused him to think about what Dennis investigated. Perhaps it had to do with alchemy. Do you know what he referred to?" she asked.

The Frenchman grew agitated as he thought about her words. "*Non. Impossible.* The American, he wanted to know about an old alchemical text. Nothing special; nothing dangerous. That is all. I showed him the information I had, and when he asked what the symbolism meant, I referred him to Mustafa who is the greatest scholar of alchemy in the world ... or, so he was." He placed his hand against his mouth and whispered, "*Mon Dieu. Mon ami.*"

She waited while he composed himself. "Please, you must tell me what you know," she said, her gaze hard.

He took a deep breath, his hands atop the desk, clasping and unclasping them. "Texts on alchemy are always written in symbolic, poetic language, impossible to understand. Mustafa and I learned that one book, and only one, existed which made everything understandable. We wanted it; we dreamed of finding it."

Bonnetieu crossed to a wooden cabinet and poured two glasses of Courvoisier. He handed one to Charlotte.

"The book we looked for had once been owned by an alchemist who lived here in Paris in the fourteenth century. It was called *The Book of Abraham the Jew*. It is the text Professor Rempart asked about."

She put down the drink. Her hand shook. "Did Dennis talk to you about that book as well?"

"He did." He drained his glass. "I think it will be best if I show you, just as I did him. The book, you see, vanished centuries ago, if it ever truly existed. Most people think it did not. They say it is merely apocryphal, and legends of its existence are simply that, mere legends."

Their footsteps echoed loudly as Bonnetieu led Charlotte through dark, stone-covered medieval corridors filled with exhibits from the Middle Ages.

Bonnetieu unlocked the room with the Nicolas Flamel display. The space had a musty smell, the stone walls dank and cold. He switched on the lights. Several didn't come on at all, leaving the room heavily shadowed.

"No one paid any attention to this collection for years," he said. "Periodically, there's a flurry of interest in Flamel, then it all dies down again. The last time was because of *Harry Potter and the Philosopher's Stone,* or the *Sorcerer's Stone* as you renamed it in the States. The book mentioned Nicolas Flamel, and people were shocked to learn there actually once lived such a man. But, few are interested now, so we rarely bother to open up this display."

The Flamel materials, tracings of engravings, stone sculptures, and a manuscript allegedly written by Nicolas Flamel himself, fit in a single glass case. Beside it were translations in a number of modern languages.

Bonnetieu waited patiently as Charlotte read.

Born around 1330, Flamel had been a bookseller and had a stall next to Saint Jacques la Boucherie in Paris. Copyists and illuminators did their work at his house in the Rue de Marivaux. He married a slightly older widow named Perenelle. They had no children.

Flamel's quiet, happy life changed when a stranger in need of money came to him with a unique book to sell. He wrote:

... there fell into my hands for the sum of two florins, a guilded Book, very old and large. It was not of Paper, nor or Parchment, as other Books be, but was only made of delicate rinds (as it seemed unto me) of tender young trees. The cover of it was of brass, well bound, all engraven with letters, or strange figures; and for my part I think they might well be Greek Characters, or some such like ancient language ....

Upon the first of the leaves, was written in great Capital Letters of Gold the words: Abraham the Jew, Prince, Priest, Levite, Astrologer, and Philosopher, to the Nation of the Jews, by the Wrath of God dispersed among the Gauls, sendeth Health.

Flamel concluded his description by writing:

After this it was filled with great execrations and curses (with this word Maranatha, which was often repeated there) against every person that should cast his eyes upon it, if he were not Sacrificer or Scribe.

Charlotte stopped reading. A chill came over her. "*Maranatha*....Mustafa said both Dennis and the professor, Lionel Rempart, used that word. Do you know what it means?"

"Ah, an interesting question," Bonnetieu replied. "Saint Paul used it in the first Epistle to the Corinthians and currently it is interpreted to mean 'The Lord comes' or 'The Lord is coming.' However, he used it right after the word 'anathema,' a curse for damnation or excommunication. And since ancient Greek has no punctuation, in the past many kept the two words joined in their mind. As a result, *anathema maranatha* was believed to be the most extreme sort of curse, as in 'The Lord is coming to execute vengeance.' The word has now mostly lost its negative connotation, but in Flamel's time, it was a strong, horrible curse. I believe the book contained the warning if anyone not permitted to read it did so, they would be forever damned."

Charlotte heard a quiver in his voice as if he believed such nonsense.

TEN

IDAHO

Lionel Rempart hadn't said a word to the students after the guide left them. Instead he marched off in the direction he alone had determined. The others trailed behind, silent and fretful. Soon, they reached the powdery silt Nick Hoffman had warned against. They made an effort to climb it, but kept sliding back down. Even crawling on hands and knees, they would reach a point where the loose soil and steep ground could no longer hold their weight.

Rempart, his pale skin red and perspiring from the effort and the sun, studied the topographical map once more, and every so often took out a second map. That one appeared to be hand-drawn, but he didn't allow anyone else to inspect it. The more he referred to the two maps, the more nervous the students became. He led them through a stand of quaking aspen and pine, and then down a treacherous naked slope to a jagged canyon with talus and jumbled boulders.

By the time they reached the bottom, they were too exhausted and nervous to go on. The students spoke among themselves as they made camp. They had expected to hike two days before reaching the anthropological site, but now they wondered how far out of their way they had gone.

The next morning the group started early. Hours later, past a grove of willows, they found a creek with crystal clear water flowing over rocks and white sand. Two men, rough and hard-looking, stood by a couple of beached orange rafts.

"Hey, there! What brings all you out here?" Everything about the man who spoke was big, from the filthy, misshapen cowboy hat, to his beefy shoulders, enormous belly, and thick legs. He wore a stained flannel shirt, heavy boots, and dirt-crusted shapeless jeans. His companion was as skinny as the first man fat. Similar small eyes and bulbous vein-covered noses were surrounded by thick beards and hats pulled low. Each man held a can of beer.

Rempart answered the big stranger's question. "We're trying to get around a landslide on the Sheep Hill Trail and then to head northwest. But the topography keeps forcing us south." He held up his folded map as he spoke, as if to blame it for their troubles.

"Where you goin'?" The barrel-chested fellow asked as he and his skinny friend ambled toward the students.

Rempart clearly warred with himself before answering the question. He had kept an important fact from the guide and Melisse when they asked why he insisted on following his map. It was a secret, something he didn't trust others to know about until he had succeeded in his quest. But since the map didn't match what he saw on the ground, divulging the secret might mean the difference between finding the site and not finding it. He decided. "I'm trying to find a couple of pillars, tall and upright. I don't know much about them. They're probably made of wood. Have you ever seen anything like that out here?"

The river rats glanced at each other. "Why? What's so special about them? Are they valuable?" the skinny one asked.

"Not of value to anyone but archeologists and anthropologists," Rempart stated. "We're the latter. Any Tukudeka tribe artifacts around those pillars may be invaluable to the scholars of the area."

The thin guy looked at the barrel-chested one. "Sounds like a lotta bull crap to me, Kyle."

Big Kyle bellowed with laughter. "Yeah, me too, Buck." His eyes narrowed as he looked over the professor. "Listen, man, we know the pillars. Double Needles, we call them."

"You do? You know them?" Rempart could scarcely contain his excitement.

"Sure. But you're goin' way the hell out of your way. It'll take you over a day to walk to them. Why don't you use the creek?"

Again Rempart held out his all but useless map. "According to the map, they aren't near any creek, but miles inland to the north."

"Map?" Skinny Buck shook his head. "I never heard of no map of the Double Needles area. This whole wilderness is crisscrossed with creeks and streams that don't show up on no map, ones that only have water part of the year, flood you out, and then go bone dry. But this here creek"—he jutted his chin towards the water—"is a big one. It'll take you right near the Needles' front door. If you're sure that's where you're wantin' to go."

"They got a *rep-u-ta-tion* of being kinda hard to find." Big Kyle gave a knowing glance at his companion. Skinny Buck nodded.

"It's all right," Rempart said. "We're scientists."

No, we're not! Devlin wanted to shout. He had a bad feeling about this. Didn't Rempart have the brains not to trust those two?

"Ah." The two men nodded at each other as if Rempart's words explained everything.

"Now, you need to know," Big Kyle added, "nobody much goes to that area. You head out there and get yourself hurt, it's not gonna be good."

"I understand." Rempart beamed. "We'll be just fine, but if you could tell us how to get there—"

"Professor," Melisse warned, but he ignored her.

Big Kyle folded ham-like arms. "Tell you what, I'm Big Kyle Barnes, and this here's Skinny Buck Jewel. We worked this area all our lives, and I gotta say, the direction you're headed, the mountains and cliffs are too steep for you and these kids. If someone said they'd take you overland to the Needles you been snookered. It happens out these parts. Don't trust nobody. That's the safest way. But maybe we can help."

"You're right, Kyle." Skinny Buck said earnestly, then smiled at the group. His teeth were black from decay. "We ain't doing much but sittin' on our asses waiting 'til Saturday when we got a group for a raftin' trip down on the Salmon. If you'd like, we'll take you close as we can get on this here creek. It'll be easy. This creek's child play to float."

"I don't think so." Rempart said with regret. "The university has more time than money. We have no authorization—"

"We could get you close to those twin pillars in just about ninety minutes." Big Kyle's tone sounded smooth, encouraging. "It's an hour's walk from there, but it'll shave a day off your trip. You're talking some real rough country."

"A day?" Rempart was aghast. "It'll take another day? We've already wasted a day trying to get around the landslide. How much does it cost to hire you?"

Big Kyle scratched his beard and thought. "I'll take you for only fifty each. That's a cut rate, believe me."

Rempart looked over his students. "Can't do it."

"You sure?" Big Kyle scrounged through a duffle bag for an old flyer advertising their service and handed it to Rempart.

The students gathered near. The grimy, wrinkled flyer looked like it had been printed off a Word file on someone's computer:

White water rafting on the Salmon River!!
River of No Return thrills, chills, and no spills!!
Forty-years of combined experience with
Big Kyle Barnes and Skinny Buck Jewel!!

"I don't reckon you want to walk through the forests around here," Big Kyle added. "There's some strange things in them."

"Oh?" Rempart said.

"I got an idea," Big Kyle said as he looked over the group. "Since you people are involved with *ed-u-ca-shun,* and that's a good thing, and since me and Buck ain't busy otherwise, we'll take you for only twenty-five each. But no less."

Rempart and the students got together and emptied their wallets. A quick counting and sharing of funds, and they turned up enough money to save a day's travel.

Rempart handed it over to the guides. "Let's go."

ELEVEN

MONGOLIA

"Michael! Michael! Wake up! Wake up!"

Michael heard Jianjun's voice, felt his assistant's hand shaking his shoulder, felt air so cold it numbed his teeth. He opened his eyes to a blue sky.

He looked around amazed to be alive, then pushed away the sand that covered his body and sat up. Finally, he held his head, lay back down, and shut his eyes once more. The last thing he remembered he had been inside the *ger* drinking and then felt sleepy. A vague memory ... Lady Hsieh calling him, drawing him outside ...

He didn't want to think about that, about *her*.

Now it seemed an entire caravan had marched over his body while a yak dung fire burned in his mouth. *Airag* did that to a man. Opening one eye at a time, he tried again. "What am I doing here?" he whispered.

"Good question. You tripped over me leaving the *ger*. Woke me up." Jianjun's hair stood on end, his face pale, and his eyes blood shot. He looked as bad as Michael felt. "You were sleep-walking. I tried to talk to you, stop you, but you kept going so I followed. We both fell, I guess. At least, I'm assuming we fell, and that's how we got down here. Way down here. I must have been knocked out, or I was too tired to stay awake, because next thing I woke to the loud sound of my own teeth chattering. They're still chattering. It's freezing and—"

"Stop!" Michael pressed his palms against his aching head. "I get the picture."

He rose unsteadily to his feet and saw they were at the bottom of a steep drop. They were lucky they hadn't broken their necks in the fall.

After nearly thirty minutes and any number of tries, they climbed out of it. The sun was high, the sky clear, pale and ghostly, but the land ...

Sand and dust lay everywhere, covered everything, and had turned a grassy plain to a tan-hued ocean.

Michael stumbled toward the camp's sand-covered *gers* on legs that felt shaky and weak.

No smoke billowed from the chimney, and no one moved around outside. An unnatural, eerie stillness had settled over the area. As much as Michael wanted to convince himself that Batbaatar and Acemgul might yet be sleeping off the liquor, or that they had already gone to the dig site to see how much damage had been done, he couldn't. A foreboding took hold and refused to let go.

Somehow he found it within him to run toward camp, cautiously at first, then faster.

As he got closer, his steps slowed and faltered. Jianjun, right behind him, did the same.

Two low mounds of sand were on the ground near the *gers*. Looking at the size and shape of them, Michael's heart sank.

He went to one mound near the truck and with a gentle hand brushed away the sand. He shut his eyes, his worst fear confirmed.

Batbaatar.

Not far from him lay Acemgul's body, also covered with sand.

They'd been shot in the back of the head. Two executions.

Michael fell to his knees as he surveyed the horrifying scene, the startled, anguished death stares on the faces of men he had worked with for so many weeks, men who had become true and honest friends.

"What happened here?" Jianjun placed his hand on Michael's shoulder. "Why kill these men? These good men?"

Michael didn't reply.

"If you hadn't left, and I hadn't followed you," Jianjun said in a voice scarcely above a whisper, "could we have saved them? Or would we also be dead?"

The question remained unanswered as, angry and sickened by the senseless deaths, Michael gazed in the direction of the dig. No tire tracks or other signs survived the storm, yet a suspicion, one he prayed wasn't true, formed.

He went to the truck, Jianjun silent beside him. Batbaatar had covered the hood with a tied-down tarp before entering the *ger* the day before to keep sand out of the engine. When Michael removed the tarp and cranked the key, the truck came to life.

Michael drove straight to the dig site. The storm should have completely buried it, but as he neared, what he saw infuriated him.

Someone had been here. Someone had dug into the pit and cleared any sand that had fallen into it. No, not some*one*—removing that much sand would have taken a small army.

Wordlessly, he jumped from the truck, searching for any sign of who had done this.

He scrambled down the ladder to Lord Hsieh's tomb. Everything connected with Lord Hsieh had been removed, but that meant little to him.

He hurried down to the lower level, and half-slid, half-fell into Lady Hsieh's chamber.

The coffin was gone.

Raw fury cut through him like a razor. Who did this, and why? With those questions, he made a resolution. He would find her again. He would find her and learn what all this meant. He would do it, no matter what it took.

TWELVE

Paris

Despite herself, in the cold gloom of the Cluny museum, Charlotte became entranced by Nicolas Flamel's bizarre tale and continued reading.

Flamel was obsessed with learning the meaning behind the words and symbols in *The Book of Abraham the Jew*. He knew something about alchemy from other manuscripts and books he had copied, but none of them compared to the book he now possessed. He placed some pages he had copied in his shop window, seeking anyone who might understand them, but the populace scorned and laughed at him.

For twenty-one years he struggled to decipher the book with little success. At age fifty, he feared he would not live long enough to learn the book's secret if he didn't act.

He needed a Kabbalist scholar, but the Jews had been driven out of France by persecution. Many fled to Spain, to Malaga and Granada, ruled by Moorish kings.

Flamel decided to go to them. Carrying only a few carefully copied pages from the manuscript, he went dressed as a pilgrim with a staff and shell-adorned hat.

The Jews in Spain were suspicious of Christians, however, especially French ones dressed as pilgrims, and refused to help him.

Defeated, Flamel headed back to Paris when, in León, he met a fellow merchant who told him of an old Jewish scholar named Chanches. At first

Chanches eyed him warily, but once Flamel mentioned *The Book of Abraham the Jew*, everything changed.

According to Chanches, Abraham was the most venerable of all the sages who studied the Kabbalah. He lived in the Jewish sector of Alexandria in the first or second century A.D., and wrote in Greek. Centuries ago, his book disappeared. Legend had it the book had passed from hand to hand, always to the man destined to receive it. Chanches dreamed all his life of finding it, but had failed.

Chanches agreed to return to Paris to translate the complete text, but he died on the way. Once back home, Flamel and his wife Perenelle used what he had learned from Chanches to decipher the remaining pages of the book. It took him three years, and at the end of that period, he began his experiments.

"Oh, my God!" Charlotte murmured as she continued to read:

. . .following always my Book, from word to word, I made projection of the Red Stone, upon the like quantity of Mercury, in the presence likewise of Perrenella only, in the same house, the five and twentieth day of April following, the same year, about five o'clock in the evening, which I transmuted truly into almost as much pure Gold, better assuredly than common Gold, more soft and more plyable. I may speak it with truth, I have made it three times, with the help of Perrenella, who understood it as well as I, because she helped in my operations.

Charlotte stared at Bonnetieu. "The old bastard claims he actually created gold!"

"Yes," Bonnetieu said quietly. "People have debated whether or not to believe him for more than six hundred years. Yet he built shrines and even a children's hospital, all costing a great deal of money."

"He probably stole some gold and then made up this story to hide his crime." Dismay fueled Charlotte's rebuttal. Dennis hadn't wasted his time on this folly. "He was a scribe and a bookseller! How could he have managed to do what no one else could? Flamel's tale is no more real than Harry Potter."

"Perhaps," Bonnetieu said.

His condescending tone exasperated her. "After Flamel's death, what happened to *The Book of Abraham the Jew?*"

"That's the question." Bonnetieu gave a small shrug. "His wife died before him, and when Flamel died, his house and grave were ransacked. Whether the robbers were looking for the book or the gold, we don't know. No one found the book. Throughout history, we hear of it turning up various places. One of those was the American West. The story goes that a French monk brought it there after the French Revolution. But, as I've said, most people believe it never really existed."

Charlotte shook her head at the imaginative tale.

Bonnetieu squeezed her hand. "It's all nonsense, I'm sure. I believed in it once, I'll admit. The idea of a medieval sorcerer and his wife brewing gold held great appeal to an old historian like me."

She pulled her hand free. Somehow, his agreeing with her argument didn't make her feel better. She caught his gaze in her large, blue eyes and wouldn't let go. "Still, I can't help but believe this book is the connection between Dennis' investigation fifteen years ago and Mustafa's murder yesterday."

"That makes no sense," he insisted.

She removed the papers she'd picked up on Al-Dajani's desk from her shoulder bag. "I suspect Mustafa wanted to talk to me about these. I haven't had time to translate them yet, but maybe—"

He flipped through the pages and pulled out one, staring at it.

"Ah! This symbol is found in Flamel's manuscript," he said as he unlocked the display case and put on the white gloves he carried in his pocket. With utmost care he turned the ancient pages to the one with the same symbol. "There it is!"

Charlotte stared at it a moment. "What does it mean?"

"I have no idea. But Mustafa and I talked about it on the phone. Many years ago, a Danish scientist came here to view the symbol. Once he saw it, he became quite excited. He said it was also found in China and elsewhere. Then, he wanted to learn how to read old alchemical texts, so I referred him to Mustafa. A few days later, an American who claimed to be a friend of the Dane also arrived here with many of the same questions. I gave him Mustafa's name and address."

"A Dane and then an American, both interested in this symbol?" Charlotte was incredulous.

Bonnetieu simply nodded.

"Wait...are you talking about the professor, Lionel Rempart?" Charlotte asked.

"No, no, no. This happened *quite* a few years ago, twelve? Fifteen? I'm not sure. I don't remember the names, I'm afraid, but the American was obviously rich. That I do remember."

"It happened before Dennis came to see you?"

He thought a moment. "I must confess it's all rather fuzzy. My memory isn't so good anymore." His expression tightened. "As I recall, both the Dane and the American, their visits and their questions, interested Dennis."

"Did he say why?" she asked.

He shook his head. "Your husband was, I would say, close-mouthed. He explained nothing to me."

That described Dennis all right, she thought, especially as she realized he had kept all this from her. Those other men intrigued her. "Is it possible you've kept some records with their names—"

"Is that the Flamel exhibit?" a voice boomed. The words were in English, the accent American.

Bonnetieu thrust out his arm as if to protect the unlocked display. "No one should be out there!"

Charlotte shoved Mustafa's papers back into her bag.

"I told you already, *monsieur*, this area is closed to the public! You must leave, now."

"Tourists!" Bonnetieu said. "Excuse me, Charlotte, while I assist the guard."

She stepped out of the room and watched Bonnetieu as he went down the hall to speak to the brusque-sounding American.

The American was a big man, broad shouldered with a hard, chiseled face, short blond hair, and blue eyes.

With a start, she recognized him—the man who had pointed his gun at her in Jerusalem.

He noticed her. Several shots rang out in rapid succession. Bonnetieu fell.

Charlotte spun around a corner as a bullet slammed into the nearby wall. She pulled the Glock from her handbag and blindly fired back. Ahead of her narrow steps led to the ground floor. She ran down.

Guards shouted about the gunfire and the need to secure the building. Immediately, a terrified tour group tried to push through an emergency side exit, but a guard beat them to it and locked the door to prevent the shooters from escaping. The public panicked.

The museum rang with alarms, cries and shouts. People pushed and shoved against the emergency exit. A man lifted a young girl into his arms to prevent her from being smothered. A woman screamed when the crowd ripped her son's hand from hers. Several fainted from being pressed against the door unable to breathe.

When the guards re-opened the front entrance, the group turned and ran toward it. One woman fell and was nearly trampled. Charlotte watched, the gun hidden under her jacket. She didn't see the shooter. She suspected he had gone toward the main doorway and waited for her there.

She broke away from the crowd and started down a different corridor. Her mind replayed all that had passed. Al-Dajani. Bonnetieu. Her. Why?

At the end of the hall, a man stood looking off to one side. She noticed a wire from his ear to his jacket.

She quietly backed up.

Another alarm shrieked in the distance. The man turned and saw her. His hand whipped under his jacket and came out holding a 9 mm automatic. She whirled back to the crowd, pushing her way deep into it, bending low, trying to hide. The human wave carried her through the front gardens and out onto the street.

The chisel-faced blond man, taller than most, remained in the garden. Their eyes met, and he knocked aside others as he strode toward her. Part of her, cold and deadly, wanted to stay and fight. To kill this killer. But too many innocent people stood between them.

He didn't care. To her horror, he raised his gun. She tried to duck, to hide, as he fired. Beside her, a young man fell. Only then did she feel a painful, burning sensation on her arm.

THIRTEEN

Idaho

"We can move anytime," Big Kyle Barnes announced. The guides pulled the orange rafts away from bushes of red-tinged sumac and bulrushes, and shoved them into the water. "Three students and one teacher in each raft should work."

Rempart scowled at the ignorant guide's mistaken impression of Melisse's position, then turned to his assistant with a smile. "I can scarcely believe our good fortune at finding these rafts. I can taste success already. If this works out, Melisse, it'll make big news when we publish the find. You may be able to publish it with me. We'll see how things go," he announced with all the arrogance of a full professor holding a graduate student's future in the palm of his hand.

"I appreciate that, Professor." As she spoke, Melisse didn't look at Rempart, but watched Big Kyle and Skinny Buck check over the rafts.

"You look nervous," Rempart said. "Didn't you grow up in Montana? You should know about rafting. Besides, the guides said this is a creek. It's nothing to worry about."

She eyed the clear waters. "This so-called creek is already wide and we don't know how much wider it'll become downstream. We're close to the Salmon River. If we get on it, this little joyride will turn treacherous very quickly."

"You must learn to be adventurous, Melisse!" Rempart said with a laugh. "They said nothing about the Salmon. Let's get going."

Melisse knew much more about the Salmon River than Rempart ever imagined. It was known as "the river of no return" for a reason. It meandered from its source near Sun Valley, northeast toward Montana and the Bitterroot Mountains. There, it angled sharply westward and began a wild, tumultuous 420 mile journey that slashed directly across the entire width and heart of Idaho until it reached the confluence with the Snake River near the Oregon border. In the course of its fierce journey, the Salmon River forged a canyon deeper than Arizona's Grand Canyon with looming unscalable walls surrounded by dark, impenetrable forests.

The first white men known to attempt to navigate it were mountain men, four trappers for the Hudson's Bay Company in 1832. Two drowned and the other two lost their canoe and traveled overland, arriving three months later, naked, at Fort Nez Perce.

Forty years later, the Northern Pacific Railroad Company wanted a route from Montana across Idaho to Washington State and sent a party of twenty-five men and four boats under the direction of the railroad's chief engineer to survey the river. The group set out from Salmon City in July 1872, and didn't reach the Snake River until November. The engineer's summary of the trip concluded, "This survey down the Salmon River may, I think, be regarded as the most difficult instrumental survey ever made in the United States."

The railroad selected a different route, bypassing Central Idaho altogether.

To this day, the area remains a roadless, fiercely impassable no-man's-land in the heart of Idaho.

Now, Rempart and the guides gathered together the students, who were more interested in whining about having no cell service and being unable to text their friends than in what was going on around them, and ordered them into the rafts. The voluptuous Brandi, chubby Ted, and nerdy Vince climbed into one raft. Rempart joined them, while Melisse got into the second with scholarly Rachel, Devlin-the-jock, and his shadow, Brian. Melisse's nerves were tense. The Salmon River swallowed up proficient rafters and kayakers, even guides, with frightening regularity. Some said the Indians called it the river of no return because so many men who set off down it were never seen again.

The day grew chilly, so everyone put on their jackets and donned life preservers. They strapped their backpacks onto the raft to keep from losing them if the vessel overturned. Big Kyle took charge of Melisse's raft. She felt him ogling her as she settled into place and glared at him. He grinned, and then openly leered at Brandi in the other raft as she struggled to draw the sides of her life jacket together over her generous breasts.

Big Kyle gave everyone a quick lesson on rafting. "Listen up! If you get dumped into the water, lay on your back, feet downstream. Push off any rocks that come close, use your arms to paddle, and don't stand up until you can sit on the bottom of the creek and still keep your head out of the water. The worst thing you can do is try to stand where the water's deep and get your foot stuck in the rocks. It's a death sentence. And hang onto your paddle—it'll help others pull you to safety."

"That's right," Skinny Buck contributed.

"We're the captains," Big Kyle said. "When we say 'all forward,' you paddle. At 'all rest,' you stop. And at 'all back,' you back-paddle. Can your brains keep that straight?"

The students nodded.

Big Kyle set out first, pushing the raft toward the center of the creek. The swift current took hold and pulled with a sense of unstoppable momentum. Soon, the small beach disappeared. Creek banks, covered with vines and rock, dropped steeply to the water.

A red-tailed hawk lifted from a nearby tree with one slow powerful flap of the wings, then circled over the water before disappearing from view. Dark green foliage grew thick along the banks but beyond it, arid grassland lay punctuated by pines. The view, barren and harsh but beautiful in its desolation, stretched for miles.

They floated peacefully for a few minutes, then heard a churning sound up ahead. Big Kyle assured them that the rapids they were approaching were so weak and mild they scarcely deserved the name. Nonetheless, they were strong enough that Devlin and Brian whooped with excitement as the raft plunged headlong through the turbulence.

The raft coasted out the other side and the creek grew tame again. A doe raised her head, still chewing, then loped away, her white-tipped tail held high. Ahead, dead trees that had swept downstream were wedged between boulders, their roots and branches reaching out over the water. The debris split the creek in two.

"Lean left," Big Kyle shouted. "Left, left, left!" The raft buckled and swerved uncontrollably, then plunged through a clear chute of water, zipping unscathed by the tentacle-like brush. Nervous laughter rippled through the raft as everyone took deep breaths once more.

The creek widened and a beam of sunlight found its way through the pines to brighten a stretch of lavender covered banks. In the distance, craggy mountaintops touched a clear blue sky.

Melisse turned to look back. The other raft followed peacefully behind them.

Only after they drifted awhile did she begin to relax. She didn't trust these men, but so far, they hadn't lied. Ninety minutes, Big Kyle had said. She checked her watch. Only twenty minutes had passed.

The sheltered creek forked, and the raft floated onto a much wider body of water. She looked around and then sat bolt upright. The banks were far apart, and the water cold, deep, and fast. "We're on the Salmon!" she shouted, her voice tight, harsh.

"Just for a little while, lovely lady." Big Kyle gave her a broad smile and wink. "Then we turn off and paddle upstream to your pillars. Don't you worry none, sweetie. I won't let anything happen to you."

Melisse ignored him.

They entered a gorge. Sheer rock rose steeply above the river on both sides. Far overhead whitish gray lichen and eddy moss marked how high the water rose in spring when snow run-off reached its peak. Even though it was fall, the frigid water remained deep and treacherous. They could do nothing but hold on and hope they weren't tossed overboard.

The black granite walls of the gorge continued to narrow as the river carved its lonely course. The sun no longer reached them. No one spoke and Big Kyle's eyes took on a strange glint.

Melisse searched the banks for a safe landing point, but found none. The air had something different about it. Something that chilled her to the bone.

A strong current caught hold of the raft and carried it forward ever faster. The sound of thunder rumbled up ahead, but instead of stopping, the oddly familiar sound continued. Melisse looked downstream and saw nothing. Then she realized what she heard.

They were heading straight toward a waterfall.

"Beach this raft!" Melisse ordered.

Big Kyle glanced fiercely at her. "Where?"

The raft sped up. As the students realized what was happening, their screams mixed with Big Kyle's laughter as the raft plowed over the edge.

Half its length froze in mid-air before it tilted and nose-dived several feet into a hollow curve of water. A sheet of freezing water broke over them.

The raft didn't flip, but shot straight ahead. The river turned, but the raft headed toward the rocky canyon walls. The terrified rafters tried to paddle away from the deadly rock. Even Big Kyle's laughter ceased as his arms and shoulders bunched and strained to maneuver the raft sideways. They missed the granite by mere inches.

The river angled steeply downward. Its path cut one sharp curve after the other through the empty wilderness, causing the raft to buck, shimmy, and pick up more speed. Waves violently rocked them and showered them with spray. Kyle shouted orders, but the students were too petrified to do anything but hold on as the raft careened forward like a thing possessed.

Vertical granite faces lined the river banks. No safe landing existed.

Melisse peered over her shoulder. She no longer saw the other raft.

Around a bend, the river formed an eddy shaped like a huge, spinning bowl. Unable to avoid it, they pitched headlong into the abyss. The raft shot straight across to the wall of water on the far side. Its bow rose vertically up the side of the bowl and then flipped upside down.

Melisse sank deep. Despite the life jacket, the ice cold water seemed determined to hold her under. She somersaulted, helpless in the strong, swirling current. Fury filled her for not acting on her instincts, for doing nothing to save herself and the others from this disaster. Her lungs burned, but she wouldn't give in to the urge to breathe.

Darkness overtook her, her lungs about to burst, when the water churned her up and spat her into the air. Coughing and sputtering, gasping gratefully for air, a frenzied froth surrounded her. She turned in a circle, searching for the others. She saw Rachel, flailing wildly. Melisse grabbed her and held her head up as Rachel coughed and spewed water from her nose and mouth. Melisse gave Rachel's lifejacket a strong push in the direction of a small rock-filled bank. Rachel swam toward it. Melisse saw Devlin and Brian's heads bobbing as well as Big Kyle's. He held the tow rope for the raft.

Melisse's limbs throbbed from the icy water. She swam through her pain to the bank, crawled onto the gritty rocks, then struggled to sit up and look out onto the river.

Skinny Buck Jewell must have seen what had transpired because he amazingly avoided the eddy and steered toward the bank. He let Rempart and the rest of the students off to help their companions and then headed for Big Kyle to assist him in righting his raft. Devlin and Brian left the two experts to secure the rafts and swam toward the bank.

The students and teacher huddled together, shaken, wet, and freezing cold, all the while congratulating each other that they made it out alive and were on dry land. Then they looked out at the water.

The two guides, alone in the rafts, paddled rapidly downstream.

FOURTEEN

Mongolia

Michael and Jianjun fled the nightmare of murder and destruction at Bayan Ölgiy, and made a frenzied cross-country drive to Ulaanbaatar, Mongolia's capital city, in Batbaatar's jeep, stopping only for gas. Once there, Jianjun went off to find a way for them to leave the country without attracting unwanted attention.

Michael hadn't slept since Bayan Ölgiy. Whenever he shut his eyes, he saw the corpses of the men who had worked for him, who had trusted him. He'd failed those he should have protected. Again.

He was a child the first time it happened. Only ten years old. People around him, and later psychiatrists and psychologists, told him a child couldn't be expected to take care of his mother, couldn't stop an adult from doing as she pleased. Couldn't stop her from taking her own life. But he had been there, and no one else was.

His father never forgave him. And he never forgave himself.

His older brother, Lionel, ignored him more than ever.

Only one person ever looked at him with understanding, forgiveness, and love. And then she, too, walked out of his life. He'd gotten over it, eventually. But now, memories of the past rushed back.

He might not have slept on the trip across Mongolia, but he had thought a great deal.

He believed some secret arm of the government or shadow government had taken Lady Hsieh's coffin, and suspected that may have been why, after months of being told 'no,' he had suddenly been granted access to the dig site.

A team of soldiers or mercenaries would have been needed to remove the sand from the dig site and then steal the coffins. And clearly they had been ordered to not only remove the site's contents, but to eliminate everyone who knew of its existence. If Michael and Jianjun hadn't left the *ger*, they would be dead as well. Lady Hsieh, he was sure, had saved them. Somehow, he must save her.

An idea struck. Having left Jianjun, he hurried across Ulaanbaatar.

The city reflected its tenure under the Soviet Union's bleak rule. Old city walls had been pulled down so only fragments remained. Large open streets for trucks and soldiers ran where bazaars once stood. Colorful homes, shops, and temples had been replaced with grim quadrilateral Communist buildings. Since the Soviets had gone, a gloomy dust hung over everything.

Up ahead, he saw Gandan, short for the Gandanlegchinlen Monastery. It was the only place in Ulaanbaatar Michael genuinely liked. Tibetan style gold and crimson pagodas with pavilion roofs filled the skyline, along with a cloistered Buddhist university, and the Migjid Janraisig Süm temple, which held a one-hundred-foot, gold leaf-covered Buddha. Under communist rule, many of the Buddhist monks had been slaughtered, and all religion prohibited, including "ongoing reincarnations." All were back now.

Just beyond the monastery grounds, Michael saw the Natural History Museum. Four stories high and lining several blocks, it housed Mongolia's enormous collection of dinosaur fossils and more dinosaur eggs than any other place in the world.

Bitterly, he realized his find would have changed all that. How could dinosaur eggs compare to a perfectly preserved human?

The museum was the only place in Mongolia with a climate-controlled environment and instrumentation. If the government was involved in Lady Hsieh's theft, her body should be there. In a half hour the building would be closed for the night.

As Michael made his way through the cavernous site, he became surer than ever that Lady Hsieh had been brought here. She deserved better than to be shut up like some bizarre feat of early science to be studied, bits of her carved and diced and placed under a microscope. He wandered the halls and displays along with the few other tourists, but spent most of the time checking the museum's security.

He found a stairwell and when no one watched, ran down it to the basement where the laboratories were. He looked around until he found an exit, knowing that at some point he might need to make a quick escape.

Nearby he found a large, unlocked closet, and snuck inside. There, in total darkness, he waited for the buzzer to sound indicating the museum had closed for the day. He continued to wait for thirty minutes after that.

FIFTEEN

Paris

When the gunman fired into the crowd at the Cluny, complete pandemonium broke out.

Charlotte half-crawled, half-ran, her arm bleeding, to a side street. From there she found the Boulevard Saint Germain, hailed a taxi, opened the door, and jumped in.

The driver looked startled by her appearance. He began to say something about it, but she slid her hand into her purse, staring hard at him, letting him worry about what might be hidden in there as she gave him an address. He paled. His expression stark, he nodded, turned his back to her, and headed straight for the location she named.

She sank back against the seat as her thoughts swirled.

The Agency had done everything it could to comfort and take care of her after Dennis died. Dazed and grief-stricken, she hadn't questioned anything they told her or paid attention to areas he was investigating when he died. Over the years, whenever questions niggled at her subconscious about his death, she pushed them aside. It hurt too much to do otherwise.

Al-Dajani had gone back to look at what Dennis had been investigating. Now, he and Bonnetieu were dead. And their killers traveled internationally with ease, brutally shot bystanders, and organized cold-blooded murders in two secure facilities.

She knew of only one person who might help her. Years ago, Dennis introduced her to Laurence Esterbridge as an old friend and owner of an art gallery. Before long, she realized their true association.

Dennis's position was originally to work with Israeli intelligence, but it soon became apparent that Dennis was receiving orders and assignments from Esterbridge.

A few times she had traveled with Dennis to Paris. Often, he would meet with Esterbridge while she toured museums and other attractions, but on a couple of occasions, they dined together in an expensive restaurant, and once at his beautiful apartment on the top floor of a stately building on the rue Clement Marot.

She went to that apartment now and rang the bell. There was no answer. She waited, and as someone walked out the main door to the building, she slipped inside before the door shut and locked again.

She took the elevator to the top floor, and there, knocked on Esterbridge's door. When no one answered, she tried the doorknob. The door was not locked.

She went on alert and pushed the door open without stepping inside. The living room was directly in front of her and on the sofa she saw Esterbridge. He wore a stylish brocade smoking jacket. His impeccable hair was white now, with a carefully constructed wave over his brow held in place by a good amount of hairspray. An apparently forgotten pair of reading glasses perched low on his nose.

And a bullet hole marred his high forehead.

She stepped backwards and leaned against the wall in the hallway as she tried to catch her breath.

She wanted to tell herself his murder had nothing to do with her or Dennis ... but she couldn't.

She looked at the elevator, then opted for the stairs. Her head spun, and she felt faint from shock and pain from the gash the bullet had torn in her arm.

She went down to the parking area in the basement and waited, hiding, until she saw a woman drive in alone. She stepped in front of her and when the driver stopped, she pointed her gun and told the woman to get out of the car.

Looking ready to collapse with fright, the woman complied.

Charlotte ordered her to remove her coat and turn around. She did. Charlotte then hit the back of her head with the butt of the gun, and the woman fell, unconscious.

Charlotte put on the coat and drove out of the garage. She soon abandoned the car after wiping her fingerprints from the door handle and steering wheel.

At a pharmacy she bought bandages, alcohol and antibiotic ointment, then went to a department store where, in a women's restroom, she cleaned and bandaged her wound. That done, she bought and changed into a non-descript outfit, tossed the stolen coat into an outdoor dumpster, and then took the Thalys train from Paris to Amsterdam. There, she caught a flight to Washington D. C. People would be watching the Paris airport; people looking for her.

She did all she could to be sure no one followed her; all she could to stay alive.

SIXTEEN

Idaho

Shock and disbelief filled the students and instructors as the rafts glided away. They cried out; they shouted accusations and blame; they yelled and shrieked until their throats grew hoarse.

Not one of them noticed the eyes watching them.

Instead, they focused on the backpacks and gear lost. Food, tents, bedrolls, tools, supplies, as well as the satellite communication equipment remained strapped to the rafts.

Devlin cursed and ran along the river bank after the disappearing guides. Brian followed. The small beach area soon ended, replaced by rough, rocky land that sloped upward. As they climbed, the Salmon stretched in front of them. The banks grew steeper, and the brambles thicker. Soon, they gave up and returned to the others.

"It's all right," Rempart announced, to everyone's amazement. "They may have taken our things, but they also brought us closer to our destination than we ever would have been on our own. It's now up to us to find the 'Double Needles' as they called them and then get on about our business. I still have the maps." He patted his breast pocket. "We can catch fish and eat nuts and berries for a few days. Live off nature's bounty and all. We'll be just fine. Let's go." He waved an arm and headed north.

"Shit," Devlin said to Brian. "We lost our gear, we're in the middle of nowhere. We should go home."

Melisse eyed Devlin. "Scared are you? So we were robbed. Big deal.

We're almost at the site, but instead of doing the job, you want to go home. That tells me you aren't cut out for anthropology."

"She's right," Vince said, moving closer to Melisse as he adjusted his glasses higher on his nose. "I'm not giving up."

Melisse and Vince followed Rempart.

"Bitch," Devlin muttered, and then he and the others followed as well.

Evening arrived before they found a stream. By then, they felt so hungry that nature's bounty didn't look very plentiful.

"How the hell are we supposed to fish without hooks or lines?" Devlin glared at the water, hands on hips.

"The earliest people here," Rempart said, "had no metal hooks. You young people were raised in Idaho. I should think you'd know something about roughing it."

Devlin stared at Rempart as if the man was delusional, then he and Brian went off to find something edible.

They followed the creek and climbed a hill along its bank to a wide, flat area. To their amazement, it held several bushes with small round berries. "Hey, are these huckleberries?" Devlin took a tentative taste.

Brian plopped a berry in his mouth. "Whatever, they aren't bad."

"They're food. That's all I care about." The small berries tasted tart. Neither of them had ever eaten huckleberries from the vine, so they didn't know what to expect.

They planned to eat enough to stop their stomachs from growling and then pick the rest for the others. Huckleberries weren't usually found this late in the year, but they guessed the berries hadn't ripened by August as normal due to the high elevation.

A strange snort sounded nearby, causing them to stop and listen, but then all went silent again. "Probably just something small," Devlin said.

"Yeah." Brian plopped two more berries in his mouth. "Something very small."

They kept eating even though the sense of being watched grew stronger.

"Do you trust Rempart?" Brian asked after a long silence.

"Hell, no! He's an asshole," Devlin said.

"That's right." Brian chuckled, then took another mouthful. "The dumb fuck's going to get us all killed!"

"We should forget about the place Rempart wants to find and get the hell back home," Devlin said. "Stupid berries don't do it for me. I'm a meat eater." He pointed to his teeth. "I don't have these incisors for nothing."

They both laughed, trying to dispel the odd tension in the air.

"I think I ate too many of these." Brian made a face and began to rub his stomach. The berries had stained his hands and mouth purple. He'd been so hungry that he shoveled them in as fast as he could pick them. Now, though, he stopped and looked at the berry bushes carefully. "Are you sure these are huckleberries?"

"Didn't you say they are?" Devlin noticed his stomach started to ache, too.

"I think I'm going to be sick." Brian stumbled away.

"Don't you dare get sick anywhere where I can hear, see, or smell it!" Devlin said. "I want to keep my belly full, no matter what the hell I've just eaten."

Brian normally would have laughed, but instead he turned a bit green. His stomach started to heave, and he clamped his hand over his mouth and ran behind the bushes, back towards the ledge.

Devlin stood alone. He didn't like being here. They probably shouldn't have wandered so far from the others. But then, if they hadn't, they wouldn't have found the huckleberries. The berries were fine, he decided; they'd simply eaten too many, too fast.

"Brian?" he called. "Brian, are you okay?"

No answer.

"Brian?"

Devlin ran in the direction Brian had headed. He got there, but didn't see any sign of his friend. "Brian? Come on, is this a joke? It's not funny, Bri!"

He couldn't imagine Brian going to the edge of the hill they climbed earlier. Nevertheless, he went there and looked down. The bottom lay far below. He scanned the creek and the land along its banks. He didn't see Brian. He called over and over.

Brian wouldn't joke. He had never gone far from Devlin's side, and there was no reason to think he'd start now.

Devlin called and searched another couple of minutes. When he heard that same, strange, animal snorting sound as he'd heard earlier, he scurried like a scared rabbit back to the area that Rempart had designated as their camp.

SEVENTEEN

Mongolia

Michael opened the closet door and peeked out onto an empty, dimly lit corridor. Electricity was an expensive and valuable commodity in Mongolia, and the state didn't waste it.

He made his way to the laboratories and picked the old-fashioned door lock. He stepped inside when the overhead lights came on, bright and harsh.

Two men, one on each side, lunged at him. Instinctively, he crouched, deflected the outstretched arm of the first one, caught and twisted it so the man went head over heels. Simultaneously, he swung his leg around, bent the knee, and then straightened it, jabbing into the second man's solar plexus. The opponent was lifted into the air and then sprawled across the floor.

In a *shao-lin* stance, knees bent, hands guarding his heart and chest with fingers pointed upward, Michael poised for another attack.

"Stop, please!" a voice called. "We are not here to attack or arrest you, Doctor Rempart, but to see you safely from this country. Although with your martial arts knowledge, my men may be the ones who need protection." With that he barked orders in Mandarin to the two attackers, who struggled to their feet and backed away.

Michael remained on guard as a tall, lean Chinese, his head shaved, walked toward him from a side room. "I knew you would come here," he said, self-assured and impressive, "seeking your treasure."

"Who are you?" Michael demanded.

"Zhao Yin, Director of the Fourth Chinese Institute for the Preservation of Cultural Heritage under China's Ministry of Culture." With that, he gave a proud, slight nod.

Michael knew the top archeologists and historians in China staffed the Ministry of Culture, and its directors possessed serious pull in the nine-member Politburo Standing Committee, the CCP's inner circle. But right now, he didn't care. "Under international law, and agreed to by Mongolia, any archeological discovery becomes the property of—"

"None of that matters, Doctor Rempart," Zhao snapped. "The contents of a Chinese tomb are not Mongolia's to give away. I am here to assure their safe return to my homeland."

"You have them?" Michael asked.

Zhao's expression turned arch.

"Are they so valuable to China that they were worth taking two men's lives?" Michael practically spat the question out.

Zhao didn't react, didn't flinch. "My task was to be sure nothing happened to the artifacts." He withdrew papers from his breast pocket. Michael saw that he wore Buddhist prayer beads on his wrist. He also recognized that Zhao neither confirmed nor denied murdering Michael's assistants. "I have passage for you and Li Jianjun, nonstop, from Beijing to San Francisco." He handed the papers plus Air China tickets to Michael.

"Beijing? But how—"

"You will travel there on one of our planes." Zhao led Michael from the room toward an exit at the end of a corridor. "No questions will be asked. The Mongolians want you out of their country as much as we do. They don't want the mysterious death or disappearance of a famous archeologist to cause the foreign press to descend on them. People have been watching you, Michael Rempart, since you began your excavation. In fact, they helped pave the way."

"What do you mean? Who are 'they'?" Michael demanded.

Zhao's gaze was frigid. "Batbaatar was not who you thought. If you were successful, he was to make contact with people who wanted the contents of that tomb. He set up the skull and candles that made the workers run off. He wanted you alone, unprotected, so that his bosses could come and steal the findings in the tomb."

"I don't believe it. Batbaatar was loyal to a fault!" Michael said.

Zhao shrugged. "The radio equipment he used did more than pick up NESDIS. The Chinese government has been monitoring it for some time.

But the sandstorm made everything go wrong for those he worked for, which gave me and my men time to mobilize."

"It makes no sense," Michael said. "Who did he contact?"

"Someone who had enough money to bribe his way into Mongolia, find Batbaatar and others to do his bidding, and then plan to steal the contents of the tomb and remove them from Mongolia. That person has remained well-hidden ... perhaps by your own government."

"The U.S. government has no interest in ancient Han tombs." Michael grew more furious with each word Zhao spoke. "Besides, why should I trust you to tell me the truth? Especially when you've all but admitted your men killed Batbaatar and Acemgul."

Zhao smiled. "You really don't know what happened out there, do you? We believe someone from your country wanted to study Lady Hsieh. To determine if alchemy worked. They were the ones who raided the tombs, killed your men and should have killed you. After Batbaatar finished his part of the assignment, he needed to be eliminated, and Acemgul was merely an unfortunate witness. The mercenaries were to take the contents of the tomb. We stopped them as they were removing sand from the tomb, and they fled. We then continued the job. We didn't open the coffins until they were in a safe environment in the museum laboratory."

Michael sucked in his breath. "You must have some idea who was behind all this."

"My answer would only be speculation," Zhao said, then stepped out to the loading dock.

Michael followed. A truck stood at the end of the dock. As the doors shut, he saw large crates inside, crates the size of the coffins he had found.

Past the dock, a limousine waited for them. Michael saw Jianjun inside, his face scrunched with worry and fear.

Michael, Zhao, and his two bodyguards got into the limo. As soon as it drove off, Zhao said, "Now it is time for you to answer my questions. What was in the coffins?"

Michael wondered if this was some sort of trap. How could Zhao not know? "Lord Hsieh's skeleton and the beautiful Lady Hsieh," he said cautiously.

Zhao's dark eyes flashed with suspicion. "You saw Lady Hsieh?"

"Yes. Perfectly, incredibly preserved." When Zhao said nothing, a chill pulsated through Michael. "Didn't you see her? What was in her coffin?"

"Nothing but ash." Zhao's calm tone made his words all the more jarring. "She was gone. As she would have wanted. The symbol outside Lady Hsieh's coffin proved she was an alchemist."

"You're talking about the circle-and-triangular symbol?" Michael asked.

"Yes." Zhao drew in his breath. "Archeologists and historians laugh about alchemy. I wonder if they'll laugh now."

"You and I both know alchemy is no more than superstition," Michael said. "Whatever happened out there, wasn't supernatural. Someone opened the coffin and stole her body. We've got to find whoever did it."

As the limousine drove through Ulaanbaatar to a small, private airport on its outskirts, Zhao waited until Michael's anger quieted a bit, and then said softly, "History is filled with proof of alchemy working. It is we who refuse to accept what others saw with their own eyes." His fingers touched the prayer beads, one by one, as he continued. "During the Han dynasty of Lady Hsieh's time, a great warrior named Bo Yi Kao fought the barbarian hordes of the north, the Mongols. He possessed an invincible body that no spear, arrow, or sword could penetrate. A Chinese Achilles if you will. He bore a mark on his chest which became his crest, the same symbol as on Lady Hsieh's coffin. We call it the symbol of immortality. One day, an enemy archer struck him in the chest, on the black circle. Only then did Bo Yi Kao die. That was the only vulnerable spot on his immortal body."

"That's nothing but a folk tale." Michael had no patience for stories now.

"Yet someone paved the way for you to come here, to find Lady Hsieh's body."

"That's ridiculous. It was my idea to come to Mongolia," Michael said.

"Oh? Are you so sure your brother didn't begin it all?" The limousine stopped, and the driver opened the door for Michael and Jianjun to leave. Zhao didn't get out. "Remember that your government could have stopped you, or stopped the people watching you. They are more involved than you know. And so are others. The reason for their involvement is something you might ponder if you want to stay alive." His gaze shifted to the runway. "That small plane is yours. Once in Beijing, simply show the papers I gave you, and you will be granted passage. I suggest you do not tell anyone about any of this. Also, do not deviate from the plans you have been given and attempt to stay in Beijing. Such actions will not be healthy for you or"—cold eyes leaped to Jianjun—"your cohort."

The driver shut the door.

As Michael walked to the Cessna 172, he noticed Mongolian soldiers holding Russian Dragunov rifles with bayonets attached watched him. He decided not to argue about leaving the country.

But as he got into the Cessna, Zhao's words about his brother reverberated in his head.

EIGHTEEN

WASHINGTON D. C.

Charlotte's car was in the parking lot at Dulles International Airport. Only four days had passed since she'd left home, full of anxiety but also anticipation, to board a flight to Israel. As she got into the familiar old Taurus and started the engine, the mental and physical toll of the last few days hit her. She bent forward, her forehead against the steering wheel as unbidden tears fell. She felt alone, numb. Whoever was behind this had more money, pull, and knowledge than she. She should keep her head down, slink into the nearest corner, and fade into the background, just as she'd done for the last thirteen years.

She sat back, lit a cigarette and indulged in self-pity a moment longer. But as she did, thoughts of the men who had lost their lives filled her. And of Dennis. His death wasn't an accident. She knew it in her heart. Perhaps she had always known it.

Angrily, she stubbed out the cigarette. One person, right here in Washington, might be able to help her: Professor Lionel Rempart, George Washington University. She wanted to know more, lots more, about his visits to Jerusalem and Paris.

She used her cell phone to call the Anthropology Department at George Washington and asked for the professor, only to learn he was spending the year teaching at Boise State University.

She ended the call and stared at the cell phone as the adrenaline-and-emotion fueled burst of energy drained from her. She needed to reach

Rempart, but couldn't bring herself to do it right then. She would go home first. Recharge.

Home, what a comforting word.

Home was an old farmhouse on the outskirts of Alexandria, Virginia. When she had returned to D.C. after Dennis' death, she sold their Dupont Circle co-op and found a place in the country. She wanted quiet and couldn't bear the idea of living where she and Dennis had been happy together.

Being honest, she wanted more than quiet. She wanted to hibernate, unbothered by anyone. Thinking about the way she'd been living her life gave her pause. Where had the young carefree, gutsy woman gone? The one who married a man she hardly knew and had followed him half-way around the globe? The one who wanted to explore the world—both modern and ancient? How had she lost herself? Had she buried herself along with her husband?

When she walked into the house, she stopped a moment in the hallway, feeling as alien and incomplete as she'd ever felt since Dennis' death. She took a deep breath, then went straight to the closet where she had stored his papers.

The boxes were neatly stacked. She hadn't wanted to throw them away, nor had she ever gone through them. They were his life's work, all she had left of the fabulous mind of the man she loved.

She placed the top box on the floor and sat. Inside, she found a pile of small leather bound notebooks rubber-banded together. Dennis took notes about everything and would go through two or three such notebooks a year. With shaking fingers she pulled out the top one, the last he had used.

The dried blood on the cover and along the edges of the pages caused several to stick together. Dennis had carried it the day he'd been killed.

Black and purple spots danced before her eyes. She took several deep, ragged breaths before she opened it and looked at the familiar hard-to-read scrawl. A couple of pages had dates and times, appointments perhaps?

But a page near the end of the notebook, near the last words Dennis wrote, stopped her short.

This page was easier to read than most, set up as a checklist. It said:

Thomas Jefferson—OK
    Lewis & Clark—OK
    Others—OK
    PLP—OK

—OK
Idaho—??

She sat leaning back against the wall, needing to catch her breath, to think what it all meant. What was PLP? And why Idaho? And the strange symbol, again ...

A dark shadow passed outside the sheers that covered the living room window and then disappeared.

She put down the notebook and crawled to her purse for her Glock.

The sound of breaking glass came from the back of the house, then the side, then the living room. A device landed on the floor where she had been sitting a moment before, and burst into flame with a loud *whoosh!*

It caught the box filled with Dennis' papers and quickly moved to the draperies. An accelerant caused them to burn hot and fast.

Fire leaped around her. Whoever did this must have been watching the house, saw her drive up, saw her enter. She wanted to run outside, but didn't dare. More than one person could be out there waiting to kill her as she tried to escape. But if she stayed, she could die in the fire.

The farmhouse had a root cellar under the pantry. She threw her jacket over her head, clutched her handbag and gun, and ran to it. The smoke grew thick, and she had trouble breathing. She pulled open the cellar's trap door, then shut it tight behind her before she fled down the stairs. So far, the air was clear.

Aiming her Glock at the trap door in case anyone came after her, she used her cell phone to call 911. The crackle of flames told her the entire house was burning. All Dennis' papers were being destroyed. She couldn't help but wonder if she or those papers had been the primary target. Or both. She sat on the ground, keeping her head low as the ceiling slowly filled with smoke. Two minutes. Four. Five. Then the loud wail of sirens.

She waited until she heard shouts of firemen, and then crept through the spiders and other insects to a wooden ladder that led to the cellar door that opened directly to the garden, the one farmers used when loading the cellar with produce.

She slid back the heavy bolt lock and pushed upward. The door didn't budge. Years of non-use, plus dirt, leaves and grass covered it on the outside. Fear of being stuck here, of dying from smoke inhalation, nearly caused her to panic. She put her back to the door and used every ounce of strength to lift. It creaked, snapped, and then opened.

Still gripping the Glock, she peered out.

NINETEEN

Beijing

Jianjun waved the papers from Director Zhao as he dealt with PRC customs and immigration. His face grew red, and his voice higher and louder as the discussion continued. It wasn't nearly as straightforward as Zhao had led them to believe, but Jianjun's background along with his Beijing accent, the same as used by the governing Communist Party, served him and Michael well.

Michael stopped listening to the bureaucratic wrangling as he considered Zhao's words. If Zhao wasn't lying, Lady Hsieh's corpse must have disintegrated. But how had it happened so quickly?

Michael wondered how much his brother Lionel knew. That Lionel might be involved in something shady wouldn't be impossible to believe. Michael and Lionel were completely different, always had been, always would be.

Calls to Lionel's cell phone and Georgetown landline were unsuccessful, but the call to George Washington University yielded better, if unexpected, results.

Michael phoned Boise State University's anthropology department and received even more shocking news. Lionel hadn't checked in from his remote location, and all attempts to reach him had been unsuccessful.

Assurances were made that an electronic or technical glitch must be the reason, and that Lionel and his students were fine. They had supplies, a seasoned guide, and the weather was clear and warm. A search party had been dispatched. A group that size would be easy to locate, and they expected good news to arrive any moment.

Michael hung up on the garbled platitudes. Lionel was a desk jockey, not an out-in-the-field guy. He wouldn't know the right end of a tent. He had once mentioned Idaho to Michael in connection with the French alchemical book, and now he was missing in, of all places, Idaho.

It only took Michael a split second to make up his mind.

Time to go to Idaho

PART TWO

Idaho

TWENTY

DEREK HAMMILL SNORTED WITH DERISION WHEN HE SAW THE TWO supposed tough guys sitting at a bar in tiny Riggins, Idaho. The dark tavern's unpainted wood walls were decorated with posters and back-lit fixtures advertising beer and whiskey. A couple of dim amber pendant lights hung over the lacquered bar.

A former Delta Force major, Hammill had the wide shoulders and washboard abs of a weight lifter. He peeled off his sunglasses, revealing deep-set steel-blue eyes that peered coldly from narrow slits in a hard, lean face with a heavy jaw. Pale blond hair made his tan appear darker than it was. Hammill's men never referred to him by anything other than The Hammer.

A private jet had brought Hammill and the seven members of his team to the McCall airport.

It didn't take long for them to track the satellite phone stolen from the university group to Riggins, a few miles east of Hell's Canyon near the confluence of the main Salmon River with one called the Little Salmon. The halfwit who took it must have used it to call just about everyone he knew. The town was small enough that Hammill found his quarry in the second bar he hit. Simply dialing the number and waiting for the phone to ring once told him exactly which of the customers he sought.

Hammill took a stool near Skinny Buck Jewel and ordered a beer. He then motioned the bartender to refill Skinny Buck and Big Kyle's whiskey glasses. Small talk followed.

After a couple rounds of drinks Hammill convinced the guides to go outside with him to discuss hiring them for some private business. Big Kyle and Skinny Buck suspected that Hammill would propose something illegal, but that had never worried them before.

They sauntered down to the river and along the bank. Once there, Hammill pulled out a 10 mm Smith and Wesson 1076. Its bulk alone made it look lethal. He released the safety. Big Kyle and Skinny Buck stumbled backwards, ready to run. "I wouldn't do that," Hammill's words were soft, yet deadly. The two froze.

They continued on for nearly a mile to a remote, lonely spot sheltered by pines and thorny hackberry trees.

"The students and professor you stole the camping gear from," Hammill said, "where are they?"

"What students?" Big Kyle asked innocently.

Hammill didn't bother to respond.

Skinny Buck couldn't tear his eyes from the weapon and broke into a cold sweat. "We don't know!" he said. "They wanted off the rafts after they overturned. We left them on the river bank like they told us to!"

"Without their gear?" Hammill's face contorted with contempt.

"Put the gun down, man." Big Kyle shifted nervously. "No need for that. Who are you, a relative? Those kids forgot a couple backpacks, that's all. You want them, they're yours."

"Where did you leave the kids?" Their lies bored Hammill.

"Far from here," Big Kyle said earnestly. "On the main Salmon, up past the Middle Fork."

"Where were they headed?"

Big Kyle glanced at Skinny Buck and swallowed hard before answering. "Don't know."

"But you know where you left them."

"Sort of," Big Kyle said. "But it's far from here, and I'm sure they've moved on."

Hammill grimaced as another man appeared from the tree-lined bank. "Nose, good timing."

Brownley, aka Brown Nose or simply Nose, smirked. His hair had been clipped to no more than a quarter inch, his black mustache connected to a goatee that circled large, rubbery purple lips. He held an H&K G36 assault rifle across his chest, the stock nestled under his arm, and one hand on the trigger.

"They aren't being helpful," Hammill said.

Nose marched toward Big Kyle. Without hesitation he spun the H&K

around and drove the butt into Big Kyle's mouth and nose. Blood spurted, and the mountain of a man went down flat on his back, his eyes glazed as pain hit. Nose struck two more times.

"Wait! Don't!" Skinny Buck cried. "No need for that. They were looking for pillars! We can't take you there 'cause there's no such place! We left them on the banks of the Salmon. That's all. They were fine. Let us go, please, fellas. We didn't hurt no one."

Nose turned on him. After two hard blows, Skinny Buck howled like a baboon. His attempts to fight back were pathetic. His nose split open, and blood gushed through his mustache to his mouth and the sides of his face. He lay on the ground whimpering.

Hammill turned to Big Kyle now on his hands and knees. "So they're wandering around, and you can't help us."

Big Kyle's bruised mouth swelled, his broken nose, and cracked front teeth left his face unrecognizable, but he somehow managed to open his eyes wide and look innocent. "Maybe ... maybe I do have some idea where those pillars might be. There was talk, the kind that old timers tell kids. Don't go here. Don't go there. Bad medicine. Bad spirits. Weird, scary animals that nobody never seen before. Folks go there and are never heard from again. But it's all mumbo-jumbo. Not real."

"Where did they say those pillars were, these old timers whose tales you're just now remembering?"

"Way the hell out in the middle of nowhere. The central wilderness area. Nobody goes out there. Never have. That's the reason for the tales. Heard tell there are some plenty weird animals there, too. Big, dangerous things. Nobody's ever caught one, but those who survive tell tales that don't even sound real. That's why people stay away, even the Indians."

"You've got a reason for everything, don't you?" Hammill said.

"It's God's own truth!" Big Kyle insisted.

The Hammer grabbed Skinny Buck by the hair, lifted his head up off the ground and held a Blackjack hunting knife against his throat. Skinny Buck's eyes opened wide, and he made croaking sounds of terror. "I don't believe you."

"Tell him!" Skinny Buck croaked, wary of the sharp steel touching his skin.

"All I know," Big Kyle blubbered, "all I can tell you is, the professor wanted to go northwest from Telichpah Flat. To the pillars."

"That you say don't exist."

"I could be wrong! I could find them!"

"I doubt it." Hammill drew the knife in one slick slice across Skinny

Buck's throat, opening his carotid artery and jugular vein. Blood gushed out, splashing Big Kyle.

He crouched down, rocking and shaking so violently he could barely speak. "Please! I'll take you there. I'll find them."

Hammill shook his head. "Now you're lying to me."

Big Kyle cried hard now. "No! I swear it!"

Hammill said, "Nose, you know what we do to liars, don't you?"

Hammill walked back into the forest to the sound of Big Kyle's gurgled screams as the Nose pried open his broken mouth and cut out his tongue, leaving him to drown in his own blood.

TWENTY-ONE

On the flights between Washington D. C. and Boise, Idaho, Charlotte finally slept. Her emotional and physical exhaustion left her blissfully unaware of the news story captivating the area she headed toward.

She had snuck away from her burning house amid the hubbub of fire trucks, police, and nosey townspeople, made a quick stop at the bank to clean out her savings account, and then used cash to buy a plane ticket to Idaho. She might have been crazy to go there, but she had nowhere else to turn. Hiding and hoping that somehow, miraculously, this madness would end wasn't her style. The scum behind this had taken away her home, her sanctuary, and years ago, her husband. She had nothing left to lose.

For a brief moment, in Jerusalem, she remembered how it felt to live, not merely to exist. She remembered how it felt to love, to laugh, to care.

She refused to go back to the emotionless woman she had been, the one filled with bitterness. Bitterness be damned; anger filled her. Despite her exhaustion and fear, doing something to answer unspoken questions buried deep in her soul caused her to feel more alive than she had for the past thirteen years.

As she left the Boise airport, a startling *Idaho Statesman* headline caught her eye. Professor Lionel Rempart and a group of his students had disappeared.

She bought the newspaper, absorbed every detail of the story, and even then remained stunned by the news.

Dennis had often said if something was too coincidental to be believable, it was no coincidence. Lionel Rempart's disappearance was no accident, neither was the fact that he had come to Idaho, and that Dennis had learned Idaho was involved in all that had happened.

A grim rage spurred her to action. Many phone calls later, she found a car company willing, for a hefty deposit, to rent via cash instead of a credit card. At a local D&B Supply sports outfitter, she bought boots, warm clothes, an extra box of ammo for her Glock, and a map showing the way to the town the newspaper had named as the headquarters for the search operation.

An all-night drive over winding mountainous roads took her to Telichpah Flat. Only it wasn't a town. It was no more than a blip on a dirt road that ran along the northern bank of the Salmon River.

The Telichpah Flat General Store, a white clapboard building with a covered porch at the main entrance, seemed to be the only active business in town. A hand-painted sandwich board read "Temp Search Hqtrs In Back."

The back of the building also had an outside entrance. A Lemhi County Sheriff Department car and gray Ford F250 were parked beside it, and a large make-shift parking area had been set up. She approached a scene of barely controlled chaos with news trucks, vans, trailers, satellite dishes and communications gear. Beyond that, to the right of the store, she saw a permanently closed bar-restaurant, and a couple of houses. To the left, a trash dump that included two rusted trucks and six wagon wheels. Nothing but the river and darkly forested emptiness surrounded the town.

Welcome to Telichpah Flat. She parked at the edge of the town, lit a cigarette, and watched until the sun came up.

TWENTY-TWO

"Just keep him away from me!" Lemhi County Sheriff Jake Sullivan growled at his deputy as he pounded the stapler on his desk only to find it empty. Barrel-chested and muscular, he had close-cropped brown hair mottled with gray and receding at the temples. World-weary green eyes in a craggy, weather-beaten face missed little. They glowered now at the mounting paperwork around him.

He'd had it with the journalists, family members, university people, and miscellaneous busybodies who'd descended on Telichpah Flat thicker than flies on honey. His patience had been stretched thinner than string on a crossbow.

Two days before, he had received a call from the president of Boise State University informing him that a visiting professor, his graduate student assistant, six seniors, and their guide had vanished on a field trip to the national preserve. The U.S. Forest Service area station wasn't staffed for search and rescue, so the job went to local law enforcement. Although only a small portion of the Wilderness Area was situated in Lemhi County, since the university group had entered via Telichpah Flat which was, Jake got stuck with the operation.

Everyone from the governor on down didn't want their names connected with the potentially tragic situation and agreed the sheriff should take complete charge of the problem. It had rapidly turned into a very big problem for Jake Sullivan.

The college students' mysterious disappearance had captured the public's imagination. Human interest stories about them abounded. The fact that the professor's brother was Michael Rempart, the broodingly handsome archeologist that *People* magazine once called "a modern day Indiana Jones," added fuel to the media fire.

Phone calls, emails, and media reports, along with the usual flood of crank sightings, dubious eyewitnesses, and publicity-seeking, self-appointed best friends, bombarded Jake. At one point, he slammed down the phone before he realized the caller really was Katie Couric.

Not only did the students and professor's story intrigue the media, but so did the utter desolation of the area. Reporters and photographers descended on the wilderness, acting as if they had just discovered Idaho and had just learned that it consisted of not thousands, not hundreds of thousands, but millions of acres of barely charted virgin land.

They airlifted in satellite dishes and expensive gear to give them a few of the comforts of home. Jake expected to see a Starbucks open up any day now.

The university group's guide, Dan Hoffman, found himself the scapegoat for the disappearance. Cable TV talking heads bellowed that if any of the students or their teacher were found dead, he should be charged with negligent homicide for walking away from the group after the professor "allegedly" fired him.

A crazed psychic announced that Hoffman went mad and killed everyone as they slept. The story earned the main headline slot on *The Drudge Report*.

Hoffman led the search party to the place where he'd left the hikers and pointed out the direction the professor had insisted on taking. The road back to civilization was well-marked. Had the professor so desired, Hoffman insisted, he could have easily turned around and marched the students to safety.

The searchers discovered, as Hoffman had warned, that the trail Rempart wanted to take had been cut off by a landslide, the surrounding terrain too steep and slick for inexperienced students to traverse.

Dogs brought in to track the students revealed that they hadn't traveled over the landslide, but avoided the area completely via a circular route to the banks of Squaw Creek. The creek entered the Salmon River just above some treacherous rapids.

Once the news leaked, the press, in a caravan of news trucks and rented SUVs, demanded to see the area. Higher ups ordered Jake to assist. He'd be damned if he would let a bunch of tinhorns trample all over a spot that might have some significance later in his investigation, and took them instead on a teeth-rattling, bone-jarring, off-road ride for several miles along the Salmon River road.

Their relief when the ride ended vanished when they learned they needed to carry their equipment uphill to see the wild, frothing turbulence of the Salmon's Pine Creek Rapids. Once there, the sheriff pointed out that they stood on the exact same location as Captain William Clark when he decided he could not navigate the Salmon River and turned away to meet up again with Meriwether Lewis. In his journal, Clark described the river as *"almost one continued rapid...the water is Confined between huge Rocks and Currents beeting from one against another for Some distance below &c. &c. At one of those rapids the mountains so Clost as to prevent a possibility of a portage....The water runs with great violence from one rock to the other on each Side foaming & roreing thro rocks in every direction."*

The reporters and cameramen gasped at the dangerous flow and seconded Captain Clark's wisdom.

Jake then told them they would need to hike yet another two miles to reach the place where the students had disappeared along "Sego" Creek. He lied about the name to keep the politically correct off his back. Exhausted, cold, and miserable, the reporters chose to go no farther. All were quite happy to return to the relative warmth and safety of their rented trailers.

Since the trail went cold at Squaw Creek, Jake believed Rempart must have met with some rafters who offered to help him. Unfortunately, once on the Salmon River, the university group could have ended up just about anywhere along its banks, provided they survived the rapids. That meant the search area was considerably larger than originally thought.

Jake had no choice but to call in reinforcements even though he hated that so many people would be tramping through the pristine wilderness. Normally, except for the heart of summer, this part of Central Idaho stayed almost devoid of humans. Rowdy sportsmen from out-of-state were the biggest problem Jake faced, and he liked it that way just fine. The attention the disappearance received would cause many more people to learn about Idaho's national forests and perhaps decide to visit.

He didn't want to see any of this change. Born forty-eight years earlier in Salmon City, he had left as a young man for Los Angeles, only to crawl back to escape unwanted, regrettable notoriety. He found himself middle-aged, divorced, childless, and appreciating the beauty, peace, quiet and particularly the seclusion of the area. All of which were sadly lacking at the moment.

And now his deputy had just told him that someone from, of all places,

U.S. Customs, wanted to speak to him. How lost was this guy? Since no international border, seaport, or air terminal was anywhere near, Jake wasn't interested.

But Deputy Mallick didn't leave. Instead, he shifted from one foot to the other, staring at Jake the whole time.

"What?" Jake demanded.

Mallick seemed to swallow hard before sheepishly adding, "The Customs agent is a woman."

"Then what I said goes double, damn it! I'm busy. Send her to Salmon City."

He bent low over a drawer and rummaged through it for a box of staples when he heard a far different voice from his deputy's tenor. "And here I believed it when people told me Idahoans were friendly."

He looked up to see Mallick flee out the door as a tall woman approached. She carried herself stiffly, head high, expression stoic. Her coloring was fair yet wan as if she suffered from a weighty fatigue. She was dressed sensibly, but her clothes looked so new he expected to see price tags dangling from them. Something about her made him immediately suspicious. For one thing, most federal bureaucrats reeked of undeserved cockiness, and she didn't.

Extending her hand, she said, "Charlotte Reed."

He stood to shake her hand. She had a strong grip, her demeanor formidable. "What brings Customs out here?" he asked. "Are you with the border patrol or immigration?"

She turned as if to make sure the deputy had gone. "Neither. My job has to do with art smuggling and forgeries." She showed her credentials. "I also have a concealed-carry permit and"—she laid her 9 mm Glock 19 on the table—"I'm armed."

He studied her ID. It looked legitimate. "You're in Idaho now." He gestured for her to sit on a rigid wooden arm chair as he sat again behind his desk. "Concealed carry's not a problem. What brings you here?"

She put her gun back in her handbag as she took a seat. The sheriff had no love for Feds and regarded her with cold calculation. "We're trying to track down an ancient manuscript," she said. "An incredibly valuable manuscript. Lionel Rempart allegedly knows something about its whereabouts. I need to question him."

"Your timing is peculiar, to put it mildly." Jake wondered even more what her game was.

"I know he's missing, but I don't want to take the chance of him getting away." She seemed nervous. "I need to be there as soon as he's found."

"You've got more confidence in our success at finding him than most of those vultures camped outside." Jake gave a caustic grimace.

"Perhaps." Her fingers tightened on the arm of her chair. "What have you been told about Rempart's reason for going into such a remote area?"

He leaned back in his chair, hands clasped behind his head, elbows out as he studied her. Her story sounded like a crock of B.S., but for the moment, he played along. "Nothing useful. Just verbiage to cover their collective butts."

Her lips tilted wryly. "Some reporters are saying that since Rempart is an expert on Lewis and Clark, he must have come here because of them."

He snorted. "Idiots. Makes you feel warm and fuzzy about journalists, doesn't it?" He turned serious, yet continued to study her like a bug he'd just pinned to a whiteboard. "Look, Ms. Reed, people who study Lewis and Clark are fanatics, the sort who can tell you the phase of the moon on every night of the expedition from the time it started in May 1804 until it reached the Pacific in November 1805. But you've got to head a good deal north if you want to walk in their moccasins. Rempart knew they were never out where he went."

Moments earlier, Michael Rempart stood in the doorway behind Deputy Mallick, silently watching the exchange between the hard-faced local sheriff, and the pale, tense woman. The Deputy seemed loathe to interrupt, but Michael couldn't pass up the opening.

"The name's Rempart," he said as he moved around Mallick and strode into the room. He watched the sheriff's quick assessment of him. "Seems I'm in the right place."

Jake rose to his feet, a grimace covering his face. "You sure as hell aren't the professor."

Michael surveyed the former storage space, now search headquarters, as he dropped his leather duffle bag on the floor, and his Oakley sunglasses atop it. "I'm Michael. Lionel's my brother."

"I'm sorry, Sheriff," Deputy Mallick said, still hovering in the background. "I had to let him in to get him away from those news people. Apparently, he's some big deal to them. They're going nuts out there!"

"Son, you got a gun," Jake said with a scowl before facing Michael again. "You can leave a phone number or some way to reach you. We'll keep you apprised of any news."

Michael turned toward Charlotte. "Please pardon my interruption," he said with a slight nod.

"No problem." As Charlotte held out her hand, Michael heard relief in her voice, as if she might be glad that someone else would deflect the sheriff's bad humor. "Charlotte Reed, U.S. Customs."

"Customs?" Michael asked as they shook hands.

"It's a long story," she said.

Michael stared a beat too long as he remembered the Chinese director Zhao mentioning the U.S. government's interest in his dig. Was she part of that interested group of Feds? He then turned back to Jake. "I didn't come all the way from Ulaanbaatar to sit in a motel room. I'm here to find my brother."

Jake bristled at the tone. "Can't say I know or much care where Ulaanbaatar is. In fact, I don't care much about customs agents or brotherly love. Right now, I need to get back to work, so listen up." He strode to a large U.S. Forest Service area map taped to the wall. In brusque, no nonsense terms, he explained where the search teams were deployed. "We suspect the university group got on the Salmon River and headed to who knows where. There's nothing for you to do but wait."

"Hell, no." Michael spat out the words as he moved closer to study the map. "If that's where they've gone, I'm going after them. I've never met a river I couldn't run."

Jake took a deep breath, strained to remain calm, but each word grew louder. "We've already sent teams up and down the river. Did no good. It's the size, the number of inlets, tributaries, creeks. They could have turned off at any one of them. I'd invite you to look for yourself, but I'll be god-damned if I want another Rempart lost out there. As for Customs"—he faced Charlotte—"I don't give a rat's ass about it. If you have official business here, Ms. Reed, you go through channels like everyone else or, to me, you're just another civilian." He glared at them. "You two can leave now."

"I don't think so," Charlotte said, as she scowled back every bit as fiercely as the sheriff.

"I know my brother's ways and scientific methods," Michael said. "Look, he studies the western expansion in the U.S., which means he spends most of his time in small towns, museums, and libraries. Roughing it is a visit to a national park. He almost never goes anywhere that's in its natural state. I'm the one who does that."

"The way I heard it from the University," Jake said, "he was Daniel Boone and Kit Carson rolled into one. At the same time, the fired guide claimed Rempart didn't know which end of a horse has a tail. I should have known who to listen to." His mouth curled in disgust.

"When is the next search party going out?" Michael asked.

"Listen to me and get this straight." Jake was beyond exasperated with all the Johnny-come-latelies who kept showing up at his office door. "I've already got three search teams and two helicopters out there. There's nothing more for you to do. I don't know why either of you came all the way to Idaho, but you are *not wanted here.*"

As the sheriff's gaze turned to Charlotte, she said, "I told you my reason."

Jake grimaced. "Did you?"

She turned away from his steely green-eyed stare and looked at Michael.

"I'm here for my brother," Michael stated.

"And what else?" Jake asked.

Michael's jaw clenched. "I have no idea what you mean."

Jake reminded himself not to give in to his anger and annoyance. It wouldn't be "professional" as the County Commissioners warned him when they first offered him the job of sheriff. "As I said, if you'll both excuse me, I have search teams to coordinate."

Charlotte joined Michael at the map, and Jake used the time to cool down and study them.

Michael Rempart seemed an arrogant SOB with a reckless air that Jake found disturbing. Charlotte Reed was altogether different. She had a strained look about her, as if she held something deep inside, and a sadness to her eyes when she thought no one looked. Yet, he liked something about those eyes, an intelligence and—although she worked hard to hide it—a genuineness and warmth.

Not that such things mattered to him anymore. Not at this point in his life.

"One person," Michael said, interrupting his thoughts, "would be hard to find out there, even two. But this is eight, most likely all moving together, not going anywhere fast, having to light fires, eat, fish. They could be hurt. Dying. We've got to hurry. I don't see how you've failed to find them."

"I don't give a goddamn what you see." All his good intentions about his temper vanished. Jake drew himself up to his full height, still a good three or four inches less than Michael's angular, six-foot-two frame, but he wasn't about to hear his search tactics second-guessed. He knew this land—it was in his soul—and he knew how it could swallow up a person, and there was little anyone could do about it.

"Would you rather," Michael said, his tone cold, "I go to the press with some sob story about how the local sheriff won't let me help look for my beloved brother? Maybe Ms. Reed can do the same with the Feds, bring in a few more of them to crawl around Telichpah Flat. They'll make a fine addition to the mob already outside."

On the verge of telling them to bring it on, instead Jake regarded the two as they waited for his reaction. As he did, his irritation dropped to a simmering boil. He didn't know the reasons for the half-truths they tried to feed him, and he didn't trust either one, but he recognized the demons in their eyes. He'd been down that road before himself. They were haunted by ghosts and something more. Guilt? Regret? He shouldn't care, but for some reason, they made him curious.

Whatever was going on, it verified the bad feeling he'd had about this search and rescue ever since it started. Michael Rempart was right about one thing. Eight people should be relatively easy to find even in an area as enormous, rugged, and empty as the River of No Return Wilderness. He felt danger in this rescue, and the sense of danger grew worse, not better, every minute. He refused to allow the two of them to get hurt.

Just then, Deputy Mallick entered the room and walked directly up to him without waiting to be acknowledged, which was unlike him. His eyes were round and scared as he handed the sheriff a note. Jake read it and frowned. He glanced quickly, coldly, in Charlotte's direction. "I'll be goddamned. You verified this?"

"As best I could," Mallick said. His Adam's apple bobbed as he stepped back outside.

Charlotte went on immediate alert. She watched the sheriff put on a heavy sheepskin coat and tug a black Stetson low on his brow. With Wrangler's, brown pointy-toed boots, and the weather-hardened lines of his face, she had to admit that he looked like Hollywood's idea of an old-time cowboy star, but she found nothing about him in the least bit heroic. He was insensitive, overly brusque, and too much of a bully. She wondered what the note could have said that made him glare at her the way he had.

Jake walked to the door, but then stopped and faced Michael and Charlotte. "Sounds as if you two might be around a while. I suspect the few hotels and motels around here are booked solid, and it'll get a lot worse once all those Customs agents come here to help Ms. Reed. I've heard the CNN crew scored an Airstream trailer from the days of Nixon. Maybe they'll let you bunk with them for a few days in exchange for the big news scoop you plan to give."

With that, he stormed from the search headquarters and pushed his way through the press.

Charlotte glanced at Michael with stunned dismay. "My, but that went well."

TWENTY-THREE

Derrick Hammill was sour. His men stayed clear. From a ridge overlooking Telichpah Flat, the Leica Rangefinder binoculars gave him a clear view of Charlotte Reed entering search headquarters. Why in the hell was she here? He thought she was dead.

He hated the bitch.

She killed his man in Jerusalem. It was bad enough that he'd just missed eliminating her there, but then he lost her in Paris. When he'd been dispatched to Idaho, he'd been told some so-called pros would get rid of her in Washington D. C. Obviously, they'd blown the assignment. Or Charlotte Reed had more lives than a cat.

But now, with an M-107 .50 caliber long range sniper rifle, he could kill her when she left the office. Easy as target practice. He wouldn't, though. Not yet, anyway. Not while she could be useful to him. He lowered the binoculars.

He knew of only one reason for her to be here: Lionel Rempart. Her being here told him the university group must be nearby.

The bitch was lucky and smart, which was more than he could say about those two idiot river guides he'd wasted time on. And the sheriff wasn't much better.

Hammill had been sent here to find Rempart's group. Too bad he couldn't get more specific intel on where they were going. It wasn't as if there were street signs out here. Hell, few roads existed. He'd never been to a part of the U.S. as barren and desolate. He and his men had been monitoring all law enforcement frequencies, every bit of data the media sent to their newsrooms, and even personal emails into or out of the immediate area. At a moment's notice, if the right signal came in, they could triangulate a position and move out.

But not one bit of good data came in.

Something told him Charlotte Reed might be able to find the lost group before anyone else did. He would watch her, see if she had any success. Of course, if she gave up and tried to leave the area, he would be happy to assist in her permanent departure.

One way or the other, once he found the university group, Charlotte Reed would pay for making him look so bad.

He lifted the binoculars to his eyes once more.

TWENTY-FOUR

WASHINGTON D. C.

Li Jianjun used the long flight from Beijing to San Francisco and then to Washington D. C. to hack into George Washington University's computer system. Once in, he located Lionel Rempart's email, and from it sent a message instructing the anthropology department's office manager to allow "student John Lee" access to Rempart's office and his Idaho files.

By the time the plane touched down at Reagan National, Jianjun also managed to request a replacement GWU student body card, and to have it waiting for him when he reached the school.

A student covered the desk for the anthropology department's administrative office. After Jianjun showed his student body card and explained about Rempart's email, the student unlocked Rempart's office door and let Jianjun enter. She then stood in the doorway to watch.

Michael had told him to find out all he could about Lionel's interest in Idaho. So far, everything was working as he'd hoped it would.

Behind Rempart's desk, he found a box marked as meeting acid-free, lignin-free, chemically purified ANSI standards for paper preservation. Curious, he sank into the desk chair and opened it. The student heaved a sigh and shut the door behind her as she left the office.

Documents from New Gideon, a tiny Mormon settlement that existed for one year in Central Idaho filled the box. Jianjun dug through it, finding mostly notes about the weather, crops, grains, births, deaths, and lots and lots about God, until he pulled out a couple of diaries that presented a fascinating picture of how the small settlement came to exist.

Followers of the Church of Jesus Christ of Latter-day Saints, established in 1830 by Joseph Smith, were led by Brigham Young to the territory of Utah in 1846 after years of persecution, which included Joseph Smith's murder. They believed their sacred duty was to spread the word from *The Book of Mormon*.

In May 1855, twenty-seven missionaries headed north of their settlement around the Great Salt Lake to establish the Salmon River Indian Mission. The group averaged thirty-two years in age and came from ten states and two foreign countries. Most were married, and some were polygamists.

Their leader, a New Yorker named Thomas S. Smith, had no knowledge of the people they sought to redeem, but his ordination as president of the mission gave him absolute authority over all actions taken by the group.

The Bannocks gave the missionaries a friendly greeting, and escorted them to a crossroads and gathering place for many tribes, ones not always friendly toward each other, on the east fork of the Salmon River. There, the Saints, as the Mormons called themselves, established Fort Lemhi, named after a Nephite king in *The Book of Mormon*.

Jianjun paused long enough to ponder why a group who wanted to be known as Saints would build a place to spread the word of God and called it a "fort." Even after all these years, the ways of Americans were still strange to him. Very strange. Peculiar even. He continued his reading.

Two years later, Brigham Young visited the fort. What he saw convinced him that the valley would suit the Saints. He decided to send more brethren to "have what land they could cultivate." No one mentioned, however, purchasing the land from the Indians who considered it theirs.

As the first step in this expansion, after more Saints arrived at Fort Lemhi, a group of seven missionaries were sent many miles northwest to establish the community of New Gideon. They were quite alone in the remote outpost, but the tiny Tukudeka tribe made gestures of friendship by giving them some exceedingly strange gifts and warning them to stay away from certain areas.

Unfortunately for the Saints, the rapid colonization of their land outraged the Bannocks and several other tribes. Thomas Smith's complete lack of understanding of how to deal with them aggravated an already bad situation. In February 1858, the Bannocks and Shoshone attacked Fort Lemhi. They killed two missionaries, wounded five, and took all their horses and cattle. The survivors immediately fled back to Salt Lake City.

The diaries stopped there. Jianjun imagined as soon as the residents of New Gideon heard what happened, they also abandoned everything and returned to Utah. Many years later, according to Rempart's notes, gold prospectors stumbled upon the colony's remains. Its few surviving materials were eventually sent to the Smithsonian museum for preservation.

So far, Jianjun had found not one word about alchemy.

He looked around the office. It contained nothing about the weird science, but he did find a folder marked "Idaho." Inside he found a paper with "Smith Inst" and a couple of numbers. He made a note of the numbers.

He also found copies of letters written by a woman named Susannah Revere to President Thomas Jefferson asking what had happened to her fiancé, a young writer named Francis Masterson. Masterson had told Susannah he would be away for one to two years on a secret mission for the President. That was in 1804. He never returned. Susannah sent her first letter to Jefferson on December 20, 1806, and the last on May 12, 1824. She never married and never gave up hounding Jefferson for some explanation of Francis's disappearance.

Jianjun couldn't help but wonder if her fiancé simply changed his mind about marrying her. Susannah came across as a terrible shrew. He also wondered why Lionel Rempart cared.

The door to the office burst open. A severe looking middle aged woman entered. "What are you doing in here?" she demanded.

Jianjun stood and gave a respectful bow of the head. "Professor Rempart sent an e-mail explaining—"

"Professor Rempart has been missing for three days!"

"Missing?"

Her lips tightened. "Don't pretend you don't know. Who sent that email?"

"I don't know. Really. I mean, I received one from Dr. Rempart telling me to come here and find"—with relief, he clutched the letters in front of him and waved them at her—"the Susannah Revere letters. He said he would let the office know. So, here I am."

"Leave them!" she ordered. "Someone must be playing a trick on you. I know you students don't pay much attention to anything that isn't on Facebook or Twitter, but I would have thought you'd have heard about your professor! Come with me. We'll let the campus police sort this out."

Jianjun politely stepped into the hall as the office manager demanded. As soon as she turned to lock the door, he bolted from the building.

TWENTY-FIVE

As Devlin studied the expressions on the faces of the professor and his fellow students, he felt sick with the realization that no one had any idea where they were.

They had no supplies, shelter, food, or means to contact the outside world.

On the night of Brian's disappearance, it was too dark by the time Devlin gathered the group to return to the spot Brian went missing. No one slept that night. Devlin told them about the strange sounds he had heard right before Brian vanished. Most feared a grizzly had dragged Brian off and killed him. Devlin, however, knew that with a bear, some sign would have been found and Brian would have had time to call out for help.

Whatever lurked out here, it wasn't a bear.

At dawn, scared, sleepy and cautious, they returned to the area with the berry bushes. They might not be huckleberries, but they weren't poisonous, and were ripe and juicy.

"We've got to go right back and report Brian missing so people can come and help search for him," Rachel said as she ate. "Hopefully, he's alive. We've got to get help for him as soon as possible."

The others agreed.

They pushed forward and soon noticed the absence of small forest creatures and birds. They never even heard the sound of a leaf rustling in the breeze.

And then, to everyone's amazement, Rempart saw that the mountains and a nearby creek matched the shape of those on the hand-drawn map he carried. He insisted they follow the map, and told the students if they did so, it could be the answer to their hopes and dreams for the future.

Non-stop, exhausted, dehydrated and hungry, they forced themselves to trudge on as best they could.

TWENTY-SIX

A SWARM OF REPORTERS AND PHOTOGRAPHERS STAMPEDED MICHAEL and Charlotte as they left the temporary sheriff's station. Several called out, "Doctor Rempart! What can you tell us about your missing brother?" "Doctor Rempart, where did you go on your latest expedition? Did you have to abandon it to come here?" "Doctor Rempart, any chance that you'll get back together with Sonia Chavez now that she's won an Oscar for her role in *Fire Fight?*"

Charlotte froze as a flashback of the last time she was in a crowd overwhelmed her. Her breath came in short, thin pants. She searched the crowd for the assailant from the Cluny and feared the sound of gunfire.

Michael saw the stricken look on her face. She appeared close to passing out. "They're obnoxious, but they won't hurt you." He took her arm to pull her away from the media, and to somehow get to their cars at the edge of the parking lot. But the reporters swarmed, demanding to know who she was and why she was with Michael Rempart.

A black Chevy Trailblazer circled the throng and stopped behind Michael and Charlotte. The passenger door swung open. "Get in!" the driver ordered.

Michael hesitated. The stranger's appearance was eerie. He had a youthful yet deathly pale face, with whitish blond hair slicked straight back, barely visible brows and lashes, and black dots for eyes. Odd, cupid-shaped lips presented a slash of liver-red when he spoke. "What are you waiting for?" His voice sounded flat, nasal, yet commanding.

Good question, Michael thought. With his rental car hard to reach, and the woman beside him nearly hyperventilating, he decided quickly. "Let's go." He pushed Charlotte toward the SUV.

"No!" She pulled back.

"You rather face them?" Michael jerked his head back toward the reporters.

Her gaze held his a moment, then she got into the vehicle.

The Trailblazer careened out of the parking lot and sped along the Salmon River Road. The reporters tried to follow, but the driver extended the distance from the others by paying no attention to ruts in the dirt road or how badly his passengers were tossed about.

"Who are you?" Michael asked.

"Simon Quade. Consultant with the CIA. We'll talk later." His oddly hushed tone increased the tension in the SUV. Everything about him was out of place in this wilderness, from long, soft-looking hands, to an impeccably tailored charcoal suit, white shirt, black tie, and black dress shoes.

"You're right we'll talk, Mister CIA consultant," Charlotte said, breathing hard as if her earlier fear pushed her to a reckless defiance. "I've got questions—"

"I said later." The order was firm but not threatening.

Michael watched the struggle going on within her, and in that moment he knew whatever story she'd given the sheriff about U.S. Customs, and any paranoia he had about the government's involvement, had nothing to do with her being here. This was personal for her.

Quade glanced in the rearview mirror and drove even faster. Before long, he swerved off the main road and onto one that consisted of no more than two ruts for car or truck tires. Michael studied him. He was trim, his skin wrinkle-free, yet papery and nearly translucent, much like the skin of the elderly—perhaps because it was so excessively pale.

A couple of miles into the forest, Quade turned onto a gravel-covered driveway with a sign that read "U.S. Forest Service." The road ended in front of a small log cabin. Quade stopped the SUV beside a gray Ford F-250 parked to one side. A seething Sheriff Jake Sullivan filled the cabin's doorway as he stood feet apart, hands on hips. Michael's gaze met Charlotte's. Neither relished another confrontation with him.

Quade got out of the SUV and politely introduced himself.

"I was told the CIA wanted me out here immediately, and when I arrived the place was empty!" Jake's gaze narrowed with suspicion as he watched Quade, Michael and Charlotte walk past him into the cabin. He followed. "First Customs, now the CIA? What's next? A Marine Corps

Marching Band?" He took in Quade's thin build, his overtly expensive style of dress. "What the hell is this about?"

"Let's just say I'm the person they call upon when they require specialized knowledge," Quade replied. "There are none who can match me. That's not boasting. It's fact."

The cabin had a central room with a cheap brown vinyl couch, a square wooden dining table with four chairs, a kitchen area against one wall, and a wood-burning stove on the wall opposite. Two tiny bedrooms and a bathroom completed it.

Simon Quade stood apart from the others, his slender hands clasped together as he faced them. "I've brought you together so I only need to say this once. We want the same thing, but for different reasons." His sharp midnight gaze fixed on each person in turn. "You, Doctor Rempart, want to learn the story behind the Chinese tomb and the special being found there. You, Ms. Reed, must discover the truth about the past so that you will have a future. And you, Sheriff Sullivan, have a job to do, one you must succeed in for very personal reasons."

The three gawked at Quade, as startled as if he'd sprouted horns.

"What do you know about my past?" Charlotte's cheeks flushed hot, her mouth tight.

"Or mine," Jake roared. "What the hell is this? I don't have time for games. Your message said you had information about the university group. I don't know why the CIA is involved in something domestic, but I'll take help wherever I can get it. I said help. Not psychological bullshit. Where are they?"

Michael leaned against the door, arms folded, and waited. He not only wanted to find out how much Quade knew about the Chinese tomb, but why the government cared.

"To understand where the professor and students have gone, you've got to learn a little history," Quade said as he poured water into a tea kettle and set it on the stove. "About alchemy."

Interesting, Michael thought, even as he noticed Charlotte's body go rigid at the word. Alert, but not shocked. The sheriff was a different story.

"Alchemy! What the hell! Now, I'm definitely out of here." Jake put on his hat, ready to explode.

"Don't be so eager to dismiss it, Sheriff," Quade spoke quickly, but carefully enunciated each word. "There is a rich tradition behind alchemy. Think of it as a subset of chemistry, and in fact, much of what we learned of chemistry came about because of the alchemists. There is something to it."

He hesitated. "And you will need to understand as much as you are capable of. Will you listen?"

Jake looked skeptical, but after a moment, nodded. He dropped his hat onto a chair by the door.

Quade folded his hands. "Have a seat, please."

Charlotte sat at the table and Michael took the couch. Jake looked disgusted, but strode from the door to join Charlotte. She bristled and scooted her chair a couple of inches away from him.

Quade spoke slowly, carefully, as if to be sure they understood. "The basic belief was simply that everything in the world came from animal, vegetable or mineral matter, and since animals and vegetables grew and changed, it only made sense that minerals did as well. Just as carbon in the earth's crust could transform over time into coal or a diamond, alchemists believed other, baser materials could be made into gold if only they could find the right formula.

"But alchemy is much more than that. Many alchemists have attempted to transform much more important...things...than mere metals."

"Except that it doesn't work," Jake pointed out.

Quade met him with an arch look. "The acknowledged mother of Western alchemy, Maria Prophetissa, lived in Hellenistic Egypt around 200 B.C. She created and used laboratory equipment, including the double boiler still used in American kitchens. Since her fame has lasted, isn't it logical that her experiments were successful?"

"Santa Claus's fame has lasted, too." Jake radiated disgust. "That doesn't mean he's real."

Undaunted, Quade continued. "The Arabs of the Caliphate believed in alchemy, presumably because it worked, and from them, it went to Europe. There were a number of European alchemists. When Pope John XXII decreed against alchemy in 1317, a monk named John Dastyn wrote a famous defense of it. It's believed Dastyn was an alchemist and much of his gold ended up in the Pope's treasury. Edward Kelley created gold for the first Queen Elizabeth. Thomas Norton produced enough gold for Bristol, England, to finance the rebuilding of St. Mary Redcliffe Church. Thomas Charnock of Salisbury was successful, as was William Holway, the Abbot of Bath, and—"

"In other words, a lot of people no one has ever heard of claim to do something no one else can," Jake announced.

Charlotte nodded. "The sheriff is right. It's been proven to be a hoax. To say otherwise, is wasting our time."

"You have heard of Sir Isaac Newton, I imagine," Quade said. "He was one of the world's greatest scientists and spent over half his life studying alchemy. He got so far into it, he even predicted the end of the world. 2060. Or, to be more precise, he actually said the world would not end before 2060. I suppose people of his time found comfort in that. Now, not so much."

"Even great scientists can go bonkers," Michael said, unable to help but be amused by Quade's history lesson and the growing irritation it caused the other two in the room.

"Alchemy's problem lies in the philosopher's stone," Quade explained. "What it is, and how you make it. All texts agree that to perform alchemical transmutations, one needs a philosopher's stone, and most say it is red in color. But some say the stone is needed to begin any experiment, while others say it comes about at the end of the process. All difficulties with alchemy come about because of that one issue: what is the exact nature of the philosopher's stone?" With that he gave a small smile. "Tea anyone?"

They all turned him down, with Jake growing increasingly antsy at the time being spent here. Quade poured hot water into his cup, dipped in a bag of Earl Grey, and again began to speak. "Many ancient alchemical texts have been translated, but they make little sense to modern men. Everything is described in poetry and symbolism. One book, however, is different. It's called *The Book of Abraham the Jew*. It supposedly spells out how to create the philosopher's stone. It is, in a sense, the Rosetta Stone of alchemy."

"The what stone?" Jake asked.

"The key. The Rosetta Stone was found in 1799 in Rashid Egypt, and with it, linguists were able to understand how to read hieroglyphics. In a similar vein, using *The Book of Abraham the Jew*, modern man will be able to perform alchemical transmutations."

Jake leaned back, arms folded, legs extended. "I'm supposed to give a damn?"

"Let him speak," Charlotte snapped.

Jake shut his mouth, stunned, then looked at her as if she'd become possessed. A few minutes ago when Quade mentioned her past, she looked ready to murder the guy, and now she wanted to listen to the creepy jerk.

"Many scholars believe," Quade said eying them one by one, "that in the late 1700's, before the time of Lewis and Clark, someone carried *The Book of Abraham the Jew* to what is now Idaho."

"So, an old book about alchemy was brought to Idaho. I repeat, what does all this have to do with the missing students?" Jake demanded, with a quick but pointed glance at Charlotte.

"What he's saying," Michael explained, "is that my brother came here to find *The Book of Abraham the Jew.*" He then faced Quade. "It must be even more important than I imagined if the CIA is looking for it. How does this become an international incident?"

"Hold everything," Jake said, sitting up straight again. "You're telling me Lionel Rempart ventured out to a million-plus acre wilderness, high rugged mountains, unnavigable rivers, dangerous wildlife, to look for a book? That's the craziest thing I've ever heard!"

"People have been killed because of that book," Charlotte whispered, her face ashen.

At those words, Michael saw past the stiff demeanor, the glares, the tightly pursed lips, to eyes lined with the weariness of a woman who faced too much suffering and sorrow. He realized that with her shaken, heartfelt words this situation had suddenly risen to a whole new level. Jake must have seen the same thing because his tone became gentle. "I'm sorry."

She raised eyes that were deep, troubled pools. She said nothing, but seemed to call upon some inner strength as she again faced Quade. "Did you know Dennis Levine?" she asked.

"No." His gaze remained steady. She seemed to sink into herself a moment, then got up and went into the bedroom that had been designated as hers.

Charlotte sat on her bed trying to organize her thoughts when she heard a knock on her door. Her fingers wrapped around the Glock under her pillow as, ready to bolt, she called, "Who's there?"

"It's time to talk, Ms. Reed."

She let go of the gun and opened the door. Jake Sullivan stood in front of her. He was no taller than her, aging and husky, hair too gray, nose too broad, hands too large, square and hard, but he exuded a raw masculinity that surprised her. Raising her chin, she met his gaze. "Where are the others?"

"Outside. Quade wanted to smoke while they continue talking about that alchemy garbage."

"Come in." She found herself simultaneously intrigued and bemused to see him suddenly uncomfortable as he entered, leaving the door open. "What's going on?" he asked. "I'm not risking any more lives until I hear the truth."

She crossed to her backpack and took out a flask of brandy. She poured a little into an empty water glass and handed it to him. "You'll probably find this better than Quade's tea."

His eyebrows rose at the liquor.

"Consider it medicinal," she said. "You're wound tighter than a drum."

"Pot, meet kettle." He took a sip. "Very good."

"Even medicine should be quality."

"Brandy's nice, but I still want to know what's going on."

She sat on the bed, and he took the only chair in the room, a stiff wooden one. "As you suspected, it's not government business. It's my business, crazy though it may be."

"I somehow doubt it's crazy," he said with a slight smile.

He had a pleasant enough face, she thought, when he wasn't frowning or scowling. His large, green eyes seemed to vary between a blue green and a more mossy shade, depending on their surroundings. Right now, they shined an intense emerald.

She met his gaze and then folded her hands. In a concise, factual manner she gave an abridged version of the events that brought her here. "I want to find Lionel Rempart and ask him why"—she hesitated as the full impact of what she needed to know filled her and she struggled to prevent her voice from breaking—"ask him why that book has caused so many deaths."

"And why someone has targeted you as well." His face was grave with concern.

"I'm sure the answer is one and the same." Sad, resigned eyes met his.

"Thank you, Ms. Reed," he added, "for telling me all that. I'm sorry about your losses—your husband, your friends. It must be very hard for you."

"Your words are appreciated, Sheriff." With a small smile she added, "And please, call me Charlotte."

How much prettier a simple smile made her, he thought. He should leave her. He didn't like how difficult tearing his gaze from her face had already become. He reminded himself he'd just met her as he looked toward the door trying to think of a graceful way to exit.

Just then, the telephone in the main room rang. Jake went out to answer as Quade came through the front door. "It's a Forest Service line," Quade explained as he reached for it. "They set up special communications out here for me since there's no normal cell service."

He answered and immediately handed the receiver to Jake. "For you, Sheriff."

When Jake hung up, he felt shaken and forlorn. "A body's been found. It may be one of the students."

TWENTY-SEVEN

THE UNIVERSITY GROUP TRAVERSED A SHALE-LIKE MOUNTAINTOP WITH treacherous footing when Rempart fell to his knees, sweat running down his temples. Tears rolled down his cheeks. He said nothing.

The others stopped and stared at him, confused and worried by this sudden change.

He raised his arm and pointed at the valley floor. "Look!"

Below lay a wide, scrub-covered valley that seemed to continue on for more than two miles. In the center, the landscape rose to a single flat-topped hill, and on it stood two dark pillars. The two appeared to be the exact same height and width, and stood perfectly upright and parallel to each other.

"The twin pillars," Melisse said as she ran an arm over her forehead, wiping off the perspiration.

"I knew we could do it." Rempart brushed away his tears. His breath quickened as he struggled back to his feet. "We've got to get down there. We've got to check them out. It's an unbelievable find."

"Are you kidding me?" Devlin shouted. "It's a long way. We've got no food, no water. Brian is lost. We need help. We need to find people, a town, something. Anything!"

Rempart spun around to face him, his lip curled with contempt. "Do you intend to become an anthropologist or not?"

"We've got to get back," whimpered red-faced, chubby Ted. His reddish curls were wet and matted against his head.

"He's right," Vince said, pushing his glasses higher.

"What's wrong with you? Are you men or boys?" Rempart asked derisively. "Those pillars are what we came for. It'll be dark soon. We need to make camp, scout the area for food and water, and tomorrow act like anthropologists by going to those pillars. Only after that will we leave this area."

"Poor Brian," Brandi whispered to Rachel, but the others heard her.

"It's time we admit it: Brian isn't alive," Melisse answered.

Brandi began to cry.

"But the rest of us are," Vince said, his thin little body shaking with indignation. "And it's Professor Rempart's responsibility to get us home safely."

"Absolutely." Devlin's hands clenched into fists. "We don't give a damn about some old pillars. We want to go home now!"

The other students loudly agreed.

Flush with his fellow student's support, Devlin raised his chin high and squared off in front of Rempart. The professor was fairly tall, but his puny muscles were no match for Devlin's football player's build. "Are you coming with us, Lionel?"

Rempart's cheeks reddened at a mere student's use of his given name. "No, I'm not. Go where you want," he said bitterly. "Go straight to hell for all I care. I'm going to investigate those pillars. I expect this will be the last great archeological find in the continental United States, and I'll be damned if I'm going to give it up because of a bunch of whiners."

"Fine, then." Devlin turned his back to Rempart and addressed the others. "Let's go."

Melisse ignored him as she faced Rempart. "You've never told us why those pillars are so important."

"They are a key to history"—Rempart's voice rose with passion and eloquence in a way the students had never heard before—"a history only rumored and scoffed at until this discovery. Now, before our very eyes, we see that it exists. The man...or group...acclaimed as its discoverer will be right up there with the archeologist Alfred Kidder. Just as he garnered fame and wealth after finding the ancient, unique Navajo civilization he named the Anasazi, so will the discoverer of this. I will not walk away from it because of you slackers!"

At the mention of fame and wealth, the students looked from Rempart to each other, and several dropped their gazes to the ground.

"I don't care!" Ted fought back tears. "Don't listen to him. I want to go home."

"We all need to keep in mind," Rachel said in her calm, intelligent voice, "that we've already come this far. It won't take much longer to get to the pillars. Once we do"—she addressed Rempart now—"this should count for our futures, right? I mean, if we're the first, we're the discoverers. All of us."

"Well," Rempart demurred, "yes, I would say so."

"I guess we could even spend a little time here figuring out what they mean," Devlin added. "I mean, we can't discover something and then, when asked what it signifies, say we were too chicken shit to stick around and find out."

"But what if we stayed and someone else gets hurt?" Brandi stamped her foot, her face, eyes and nose blubbery. "I'm with Ted. I want to leave this horrible place!"

"Do we split up?" Vince asked. "Some stay, some go?"

"No," Devlin stated. "We've got to stick together."

"Vote?" Rachel suggested.

"I say we make camp now, and tomorrow morning we go with the Professor," Melisse said.

Devlin studied the teaching assistant a long moment, then joined her. Finally, so did Rachel and Vince, and then, reluctantly, Ted and Brandi.

Jake's fury built, took hold and twisted inside him as he pulled torn human remains from a creek. The boy's body had caught in some brambles near the bank. Given its condition, Jake doubted he'd been killed nearby, but most likely floated some distance before reaching the ranch of a local resident, Polly Higgins.

The water had washed away the blood, and before him lay a bloated body with gashing bite marks on its head and shoulders, and a gaping hole where the stomach should have been. The boy's shirt was gone, but wet jeans clung to his body, wedging a wallet in a back pocket. Jake pulled it out. A laminated Idaho driver's license with the name Brian Cutter confirmed his worst fears.

The possibility that Lionel Rempart and all his young, bright students had met a similar fate was all too real. Ugly memories of Los Angeles rushed at him as well, and the combination consumed him with anger and frustration.

He wanted to look for the college kids himself. Forget these nicey-nice search teams, high-tech equipment, and hourly reports in triplicate. He wanted to put his own boots on the ground. To hunt.

Could he have done more? Acted more quickly? Better? He tried to shake off the doubts, both past and present, but knew from experience that they'd return again and again, especially at night when he lay in bed alone. And then the nightmares when he slept. He had hoped Lemhi County, Idaho would be different. He'd been wrong.

He backed away when the county's on-call forensics team, a pair of retired San Francisco Crime Scene Unit investigators, arrived.

"Any thoughts on what happened to him?" Michael asked, breaking the silence that had surrounded the body from the time Jake placed it on dry land. He and Quade stood by the sheriff's side through all this, but Charlotte remained many feet away, a silent, worried, and upset observer.

"The evil spirits got him," Polly said. She stood with a shotgun in hand, a small, seventy-five-year-old woman in loose Levi's, a bulky insulated jacket, and Gortex boots. Three large shepherd mix dogs stood at her side. She ran the ranch alone after her husband died and her only son left for a less lonely existence. Ownership of her ranch had been grandfathered into the Federal wilderness area. "When I was a girl, my best friend Clara, a Shoshone, said her grandmother called it Nininbe. She warned us never to go west of Devil's Gulch. This here creek flows down from that area. Clara's granny used to tell us that Nininbe created thunder and attacked strangers, tearing their bodies apart. Those not eaten disappeared. That's why no one, no Indian, no whites, not even the Feds spend any time up in that area. They won't admit it, but they know."

"No spirit did this," Jake said. As a boy he had heard the kind of stories Polly talked about, but they were just stories.

"Have there been deaths like this before, Sheriff?" Quade asked. Being careful not to touch the body, he inspected the wounds.

"Not that I've ever heard."

"In the old days there were lots of stories." Polly gave the odd-looking Quade a once-over as if trying to decide exactly what he was. "Since the Feds took over and the gold prospectors are gone, nothing happens out here anymore. Except...let me see, when was that?" She tapped a bony finger against her lips as the others waited. "Ten years? I'm not sure. Six men, not your usual hunters and fishermen, came out this way. People talked about them up at the Telichpah Flat General Store. They wanted to know about some pillars, two pillars, that made thunder and lightning. Most folks didn't know. But the old ones, the ones who remembered the Indian legends, they knew and said nothing. The men, we heard, headed west. They never came back. They disappeared, just like that." She snapped her fingers.

"They could have gone straight through the forest, or got on the river and came out somewhere downstream," Jake said. "It'd be known if six men disappeared around here, and I've never heard about it. Excuse me." He went to check on Charlotte, to be sure she was all right after seeing the grisly discovery.

"Why do you say those men weren't hunters or fishermen, Mrs. Higgins?" Michael asked.

She shrugged. "Simple. They had no fishing gear, and the rifles and handguns they carried were a lot more firepower than anyone needed to take down a moose. Those who saw them said they looked like ex-military guys."

TWENTY-EIGHT

Washington D.C.

Jianjun stood in the night darkness outside Lionel Rempart's Georgetown townhouse and worried that breaking into it would be a challenge. Sophisticated electronic locks and security systems came to mind. A street lamp illuminated the front of the home, casting light on the doorway.

Jianjun didn't like the layout, but he had no choice. He hurried to the front door. Once there, his worries vanished.

In three seconds, he picked the simple lock in the doorknob with a tension wrench. The deadbolt would be more time-consuming, but to Jianjun's surprise, when he turned the knob, the door opened. The deadbolt had been left off.

It made no sense unless someone was home. Cautiously, he slipped inside, quietly shutting the door behind him.

The security alarm system had been disarmed. He quickly inspected the 1500 square foot home and found it empty.

Something was very wrong here. He couldn't believe Lionel would go away for months and not check and double-check his security system and locks. Someone must have beaten him here. Apparently, Michael wasn't the only one curious about what Lionel Rempart was up to. He again locked the deadbolt.

In the den, Jianjun found a number of books and papers on alchemy stacked on a desk. He understood why Lionel would not leave such things in his university office for other professors to see. He would have been a laughingstock.

Included were notes and a list of reference books suggested by someone named Mustafa Al-Dajani. Jianjun tried reading them, but they made his head hurt. He found equally obtuse notes about a book he'd never heard of called *The Book of Abraham the Jew* and a medieval alchemist, Nicholas Flamel. Finally, a name he'd heard before. He'd read *Harry Potter*.

Jianjun knew all this alchemy business would interest his boss. Michael had been enthralled by the subject ever since finding Lady Hsieh's tomb. Jianjun still got cold chills when he remembered how the mummy's eyes had opened. Man, but they had looked eerily alive. They scared him so badly he nearly flew out of the tomb without using the ladder. He shivered at the memory, then went back to reading Lionel's dull stash of materials.

A folder labeled Idaho was empty except for two items, a hand-drawn map and a letter from the widow of someone named Professor Thurmon Teasdale. The widow wrote that she was willing to give Lionel a copy of Professor Teasdale's Idaho map, although to do so troubled her. Jianjun wondered what that was all about.

The map named no cities or towns and gave no longitude or latitude, not even a scale.

Jianjun wondered if it could be a map of the Idaho wilderness area Lionel had gone to. If Michael followed it, would he be able to find his missing brother and the students?

Jianjun used Lionel's printer-scanner-fax to scan the map and send it to Michael with a short text about where he found it.

To his surprise, he received a text reply almost immediately.

One student found dead. No word on Lionel. Map might help. Pls ck into Charlotte Reed, ICE, and Simon Quade, CIA consultant. Background? Why here? Also rumor 6 paramilitary disappeared here 10+ yrs ago. True?

"No, no, no," Jianjun muttered as he plugged a thumb drive into Lionel's computer to copy his files. "I'm just finding answers to the first questions he asked, now he asks a whole bunch more. ICE agents, CIA informants, and paramilitary men. What the hell is going on out there? At this rate, I'll be stuck in Washington a month."

As the information downloaded, he went through Lionel's desk to see if anything interesting jumped out at him.

He heard a car door slam shut. Probably just some neighbor. He looked at the computer.

A key rattled in the door lock.

His hand hovered over the thumb drive to remove it as soon as the download finished when he heard the brush of the door against the carpet as it opened.

TWENTY-NINE

Michael printed out the map that Jianjun sent him using the Forest Service computer equipment made available to Simon Quade. Michael, Charlotte and Quade had returned to the Forest Service cabin, while Sheriff Sullivan went to Telichpah Flat and then to Salmon City to report the news of the dead student.

Michael placed the map on the table and Quade and Charlotte joined him in perusing it. "Very interesting," Quade murmured.

"Look!" Charlotte pointed to the center of the map. "Two pillars. Polly Higgins talked about two pillars."

Michael nodded. "Exactly. But this map gives no indication of where they are. There's not another landmark shown, just pillars, streams, and mountain ranges. For all we know, it's not even real."

"You said it came from Professor Thurmon Teasdale," Quade said. "He was a historian, an expert on the Lewis and Clark expedition and the American Northwest. If he drew it, it's got a high probability of being accurate."

"If so, we need someone who knows the landscape well, who would recognize the mountain range and where the river bends and curves that particular way." Michael wasn't ready to trust Simon Quade, but he accepted his expertise.

"Give me some time online with the map and the CIA's field charts," Quade said. "We're a bit better than Google Earth."

Michael nodded. "In the meantime, I'll go into Salmon City and buy some gear for backpacking. I'm going out there, wherever there is."

"I'm going, too," Charlotte said.

"Buy enough for three," Quade called, tossing his car keys to Michael.

Michael and Charlotte got into the Trailblazer. "Are you sure you want to do this?" he asked. "It could be dangerous. Besides, the law won't like it. The sheriff didn't exactly greet us with open arms."

She gave him a stern, fleeting look. "I suspect he's not as bad as he pretends to be. Also, I don't blame him. I'm sure the higher ups don't want anything to do with the disappearance, and he's the one stuck with it. He'll be the scapegoat in the end, no matter how it turns out. In any case, no one is leaving me behind."

Her cynicism surprised him. "I've never heard of Customs sending someone out to investigate a missing scholar," he said after a while, taking a quick glance at her.

She didn't look at him. "Oh?"

"What's the real story?" He watched her struggle with whether to trust him or not. "The search for Lionel and the students is personal for you. I'd like to know why. Is it something about Lionel? Were you seeing him?"

"Please." Disdain dripped.

He realized she wouldn't be open with him unless he confided in her, at least a little. "I'm here in part," he began slowly, cautiously, "because of a strange thing that happened to me in Mongolia. I'm not sure how or why, but I believe it's connected to my brother's disappearance. Last year, he asked me to contact the family of a Chinese geneticist who died some years earlier ..."

She stared at him, confused. "Go on," she whispered.

He told her about his excavation, finding the tomb, and that its contents were stolen. He didn't give any details about Lady Hsieh or the murders of his field experts. "This history interested Lionel for some reason. I contacted him to ask why and learned he was missing."

Charlotte inhaled sharply. "That's everything?"

He hesitated. "There's more, but ..."

"Yes?" she urged.

"It ... nothing."

She studied him openly, gauging his reactions. Finally, she spoke. "If you told me, you fear I might think you mad."

He could scarcely believe his ears. "What do you know about all this?"

She took out her pack of cigarettes. "Do you mind?" she asked.

He shook his head.

She rolled down the window, lit a cigarette and took a couple of deep drags before she said, "I said people have been killed. They were friends, and someone tried to kill me. More than once. That's why I'm here—to find your brother. To understand."

His mind raced to the deaths in Mongolia, and his feeling of dread when he learned Lionel was missing. "It doesn't make sense. Deaths connected to Lionel's search? I mean, strange occurrences happened in Mongolia, but it's a land of superstition ... and other things."

She found a piece of paper in her purse and drew a symbol on it—two interlocking triangles with two vees and a circle inside. "Have you ever seen this before?"

He looked at her in shock. "Yes. But how—"

"Where did you see it?"

"I found it in the Chinese tomb in Mongolia," he said. "On a sarcophagus."

Surprise flickered in her blue eyes a moment. "It was also found in France among Nicholas Flamel's papers, showed up in important papers in Jerusalem, and"—she hesitated then decided against mentioning her husband's name—"and on a paper I found with the word Idaho written beneath it." She drew in her breath then asked with a frightening intensity. "Do you know what it means?"

He hesitated as the full import of her words struck. "Some people in China consider it a symbol of immortality. It's apparently connected to alchemy."

The color drained from her face. She stubbed out the rest of the cigarette in the ash tray, then turned away from him, and studied the view from the passenger window.

"What do you know about it?" he asked.

"We should ask Quade about the symbol," she said instead of answering. "See what he knows."

"Do you trust him?" Michael asked.

"I don't know." After a moment she looked at him, unyielding, her manner infinitely sad. "Find your brother and ignore the rest. That's the smartest move." Her voice choked. "You don't want to die."

"This isn't only about my brother," he said softly. "Young university students are in danger. They need our help. They need *your* help."

She gazed hard at him as he drove, trying to understand him. In her field of work, she had heard of him before this, and knew his reputation as a person of intelligence and passion about his work—as well as a womanizer, someone who lived on the edge, and possibly a thief of international treasures, drawing Custom's unwavering suspicion at his every transaction.

His few comments about Mongolia and alchemy had shaken her. And yet, for some reason she trusted him. He held something back, but she sensed it was deeply personal, that it touched his core, either the kind of man he was or wanted to be. Despite that, his words rang true. Against her usual cautious nature, she found herself liking him.

"Do you know about the Danish scientist?" she asked.

He glanced at her quizzically. Something rattled in the back of his mind, but he couldn't bring it forth. "No."

She stared at the distant mountains, wondering if treating him as an ally would put him in danger. She didn't want to see him hurt, or worse. But then, she realized, simply being here searching for his brother did that, and he deserved to know as much as she did. "What I have to tell you will be in the strictest confidence," she said.

He agreed.

She glanced at her wristwatch. "I hope there's a diner or something in Salmon city. I haven't eaten in over a day, and it's a long story."

Sheriff Jake Sullivan also traveled to Salmon City where he met with the parents of Brian Cutter. Telling them of their son's death was one of the hardest things he ever had to do. As soon as the meeting ended, he called a press conference. He hated it, but had no choice in the high profile situation.

Only after all that could he do what he had wanted ever since hearing Polly Higgins' story about six missing men.

Lemhi County's law enforcement files were kept in Salmon, the county seat. There, what he found shocked him.

THIRTY

New York City

Jennifer Vandenburg, the chief executive officer of Phaylor-Laine Pharmaceuticals, entered her plush Dakota duplex after work and immediately rushed up the stairs to her daughter's white and pink, fairy princess decorated bedroom. "Felicity, sweetheart, Mommy's home."

The nurse stood and shook her head, then quietly left the room.

Felicity opened eyes that were too large and protruded too far from their sockets. "I missed you, Mommy. You were gone so long."

Vandenburg sat on the edge of the bed. She had borne this child, her first and only, when she was forty-three. Now, at fifty-five, with her hair colored blond, a face-lift, Botox, a strict vegan diet, and a very sexy personal trainer, she made sure she looked more like the girl's mother than grandmother. She bent low to kiss her daughter's forehead, careful not to apply too much pressure, careful not to touch the girl in a way that might injure her delicate bones and skin.

Vandenburg wanted to tell herself Felicity was better today, but it would have been a lie. Felicity's only hope was for someone to find a cure for Hutchinson-Gilford progeria syndrome. The doctors, hospitals, and specialists throughout the world were all hopeless. All incompetent.

Ironically, for the past ten years, Vandenburg had been CEO of the top pharmaceutical company in the world, with the most scientists, the most sophisticated equipment, and the most intelligent researchers. But they were years away from success.

When she first approached them she found that several of the scientists had never even heard of progeria. She would have relished firing the idiots on the spot, but CEOs didn't hold as much power as she once imagined.

She gathered her team, offered bonuses and made threats, but a cure continued to elude them.

Life couldn't be so cruel as to take her only child away from her. She had no one else. Her parents were a tedious old couple living in a condo she'd bought them in Florida. They never made the effort to understand or appreciate her. Her ex-husband was a screw-up and a cheat. All she had left were Felicity ... and the disease.

Hutchinson-Gilford progeria syndrome was a genetic anomaly caused by a de novo dominant G608G mutation in exon 11 of the LMNA gene. Vandenburg could scarcely believe that one simple mutation could cause her once beautiful little girl, who had seemed so perfect at birth and in her early months, to turn into an old woman almost overnight. At age twelve, she had the body of a ninety-year-old.

The doctors said she had at most six months left. Progeria children rarely lived past age thirteen.

Cruelly, the disease caused no mental deterioration. Felicity possessed the mind of a normal pre-teen, which meant she knew how different she looked from everyone else, from her strange, bulbous eyes, to a beaklike nose, to protruding ears.

"Did you bring me a treat, Mommy?" her daughter asked as she sat up. Her arthritis made movement painful, and her thin brittle bones made it dangerous. "I've waited all day for something delicious. My food is so boring!"

Vandenburg reached into her pocket. Her daughter had developed a love of Milky Way bars after finding one in her nurse's purse and tasting it. Her diet had been strictly monitored all her life, allowing her only the healthiest foods. It hadn't done one bit of good. All it meant was that Felicity would die without having eaten ice cream, cotton candy, peanut butter, or hot dogs.

Vandenburg unwrapped one end of the bar and handed it over. Just doing that felt like a major triumph against all the quacks who told her Felicity would never do anything normal, and that reaching another birthday would be a miracle.

Severe atherosclerosis was a common result of advanced Hutchinson-Gilford syndrome, and a heart attack or stroke would most likely cause her death. Vandenburg knew her daughter's cardiovascular, cerebrovascular, neurological, musculature and osteopathic status better than anyone else.

Sometimes she wondered why she bothered with anyone from the medical profession or scientific community.

She didn't believe in miracles. She believed in results. Her daughter would live, no matter what it took.

As Felicity opened her mouth to gobble down her third bite of the candy before swallowing what she'd already bitten off, she drew in her breath and the morsel caught in her throat. She began to choke.

She coughed, but the sticky candy refused to dislodge.

Vandenburg jumped to her feet and eased the girl forward, wanting to slap her back to force the candy out of her mouth, but feared that would cause a fracture—a broken back.

"Help! Kay!" Vandenburg screamed for the nurse, unsure what to do. "Help me!"

Felicity's tiny hands clawed at her mother, trying to get Vandenburg to help her breathe. Her desperate, primitive moves caused her strange little body to seem more abnormal and animal-like than ever.

Vandenburg backed away, fearful, heart-sick, but also repulsed.

Kay grabbed the girl and practically turned her upside down in order to dislodge the candy from her throat.

Once Felicity calmed down, Vandenburg left her with her nurse. In the living room, she poured herself a double shot of brandy, then sat on the sofa to ease the drumming of her heart, the jangling of her nerves.

Her fists clenched in anger. She hated that her plan, her only hope, was proceeding so slowly.

It would work, she promised herself. It had to!

She held her daughter's future in her hands. There was no time for anyone else to step in with a miracle cure. She was well aware of all the bad press about "big pharma" as many called companies like hers. How surprised they would all be when she succeeded in not only saving her daughter, but also others. A select group of others. Her plan would have a profound effect on the world.

Some might call her crazy, but she was all but certain it would work. After all, she had proof.

Soon, the world would be hers. And Felicity's.

THIRTY-ONE

First light cast a gray hue over the sky as Michael loaded a box into the back of his rented Cadillac Escalante. At the sound of a car engine, he turned and watched a truck careen up the gravel drive toward him, and come to a stop at his side. "Sheriff Sullivan," he said.

Jake got out. "Going somewhere, Rempart?"

"Why not? We now have somewhere to go."

"Are the two Feds inside?" Jake asked.

"Only Charlotte. Quade helped us pick up our rental cars last night, but didn't return with us."

"Where did he go?"

"I have no idea. Charlotte and I decided if he doesn't come back soon, we're going on without him."

"Great! That's all I need! A missing Fed!" Jake stomped into the cabin, Michael behind him.

Charlotte stuffed beef jerky into a backpack. Camping gear was piled by the door. She stopped as Jake entered and her body stiffened. "This is a surprise."

"But that isn't." Jake bellowed as he gestured at the gear.

"You can't stop us, Sheriff." Charlotte turned her back on him and continued packing.

Jake eyed her, then Michael. "I don't intend to. In fact, I plan to join you. The old lady's story about the six missing men was true. From all accounts, they went into the wilderness, and no one ever saw them again."

Suspicion gripped Michael. "How is it you didn't know about them before? That disappearance has similarities to this one."

"That's why I'm interested. They were well-armed, paramilitary types. Such guys are taught survival and how to take care of themselves. Before this, apparently everyone assumed those men had a reason to disappear, and going into the wilderness area was a means to do it."

"And now?" Michael asked.

"Now," Jake admitted, "I'm not so sure."

Charlotte shut her eyes a moment. She didn't like hearing him express doubts. He was a rock. Or had been. Just as quickly she grew irritated with herself and had no idea why she cared what he thought. Despite all that, she asked, "We've heard the superstitious reasons that cause Polly and old-timers to stay away from that part of Idaho. I'd like to know what you think, Sheriff. Why is the area so empty?"

"It's simple," Jake said. "No one goes out there because there's nothing to see, hunt or fish. For some reason, not even game animals are found there in any number. Guess they don't like the food. Who knows? But that's why no one goes. Everything else is just hearsay."

"I wouldn't be so sure," Quade said as he entered the cabin. They each did a double-take at his heavy shearling jacket, Wranglers, hiking boots, and wide brimmed cowboy hat. He removed the hat and put it on a chair. "A theory is that once away from the area, something makes people forget the details of what they see and experience, and they're left with a vague dream of an unnamed and unnamable fear. They rationalize the feeling by saying they saw nothing."

"I say it's time we find out what the truth is," Michael suggested. "Any luck with the map?"

"Not much," Quade said with disgust.

"What map?" Jake asked.

Michael showed it to him. "My associate found it in Lionel's files back in Washington D.C. Mountains, creeks, and two straight vertical lines annotated 'two pillars.' Does any of this look familiar to you, Sheriff?"

"No. And there are no pillars out in that wilderness, if that's what you're hoping," Jake said. "I don't know what the map is showing."

"How well do you know the wilderness area?" Charlotte asked him.

"I was born here."

Quade added, "But you left for twenty-five years, and didn't return until three years ago."

Jake's brows crossed. "So?"

Michael took over the questioning. "To become a sheriff so quickly, you must have had some law enforcement experience."

Jake didn't like being interrogated and particularly didn't like Quade or Michael Rempart knowing anything about him. Charlotte said nothing, but he felt her waiting for his answer. He took a deep breath. "Since all of you are so all-fired curious, I was a Robbery-Homicide detective with the Los Angeles Police Department."

Michael looked at him skeptically. "Why leave?"

Jake's eyes drilled him. "How about because I'd had it with the shit in L.A. and came home to get the stink out of my nostrils. The prior sheriff had a heart attack, and the county asked me to hold down the fort. He passed away, and now it's my job until the next election. Anything else you want to know?"

"Yes," Michael said. "Are you riding with us, Sheriff?"

Somehow, Jake knew it would come to this. He'd already left his deputy in charge, saying he was following a new lead. He glanced at Quade, who wore a smirk that Jake would have loved to scrub off his face, and Charlotte whose gaze was firm and steady. "Since my truck's been modified to handle off-road, looks like you folks should ride with me. Theories be damned. No evil spirits or anything else strange is out there. The only thing dangerous is nature itself."

"They're on the move. Roll out." Derek Hammill gave the order as he double-checked the safety on his 10 mm Smith and Wesson 1076, glad to have it near. He was a country boy, grew up in Alabama, and he sensed a strangeness about this area.

"Fuck this!" Nose shouldered his H&K assault rifle as he stared off to the left, his mouth a grim line. "Someone's out there, boss. I feel him watching us. I say we stop and give whoever it is a lesson."

"We've already checked!" Hammill's words came a little too quick, a little too loud. "Heat sensors don't give off anything big enough for a man. It's some animal. Forget it."

Nose had joked to the men about the river guides' delirious stories and old Indian tales about monsters and evil spirits lurking in the forest. Suddenly, the tales weren't quite so funny. The guys looked ready to blow up chipmunks.

As their leader, Hammill needed to steady them. He couldn't let nerves get in the way.

"We've got our orders. No delay. We've got to return with the objective A-SAP. Now, move it!"

❄

"There's a good reason nobody knows where it's at," Polly Higgins said when Jake handed her Thurmon Teasdale's map and asked if she recognized the landscape. "Nobody goes up there. I suspect this stream is most likely Cayuse Creek. It's plenty wide, plenty long, and wends its way west from Square Top Mountain. If I'm right, you'll have to head due west, some ten miles past Devil's Gulch, just like I told you."

Using ground area maps Quade had printed off of the CIA's database, they located the general area they should head toward. "Why don't we simply fly over and find the pillars that way?" Charlotte asked.

"As good as maps and technology are, there are a lot of things you can only find on the ground surveillance," Michael said. "Those pillars might be in the middle of a thick forest. They might look like tree trunks from the sky, maybe diseased ones that had lost their leaves and limbs."

"Michael's right," Quade said. "We need to go there. Ready?"

Polly walked with them out to Jake's truck. The Ford F-250 had traction bars, three-inch coilover shocks, and thirty-five inch all-terrain tires. The four of them had fitted it with tents, backpacks, medical supplies, and enough provisions to last a good ten days, even though they expected to be gone no more than three or four. If they found anyone alive, the extra food, water, and medicines would come in handy. Jake even included four Remington 700 rifles, plus magazines. He didn't expect to need them, but they were going into grizzly and wolf country.

"That's a might fine rig you got there," Polly said with a frown. "But it won't do out that way. Ground's too rough, too uneven. I'll give it twenty miles, tops, then you'll be walking, that's for sure."

Jake nodded. "We'll go as far as we can. I expect we'll be in for a long trek."

"I got horses you can use," Polly said, "but no trailers. You'd have to ride them from here."

Michael turned to the others. "That might be faster in the long run. Once we're in the area, we're probably going to have to go around in circles before we find those pillars—if they even exist. It would be a lot easier on horseback than walking. We'd cover a wider area quicker. Can all of you ride?"

Jake and Quade answered affirmatively. Charlotte's expression leaped from scared to worried to defiant. "I've ridden a camel in Egypt," she said. "I don't know if that counts, but tell me what to do, Michael. I'll manage."

Michael gave a half-smile. The city girl was clearly out of her league in this wilderness, and was frightened by it, but she had gumption he couldn't help but admire. "I suspect Polly has at least one gentle gelding that'll be good for a newcomer."

"Be careful with my kids," Polly said. "They're like family to me. Still, I can't help but think none of you should go out there. When people say there's something evil, they aren't joking around. You hear me?"

"Yes, ma'am," Michael said with a smile.

"Humph," was Polly's only comment as she led them toward the stables.

Michael stood a moment, breathing deeply and trying to shake an oppressive dread. He agreed with everything Polly had said. He could feel the evil out there, thick, heavy, smothering.

And it waited for them.

THIRTY-TWO

FRUSTRATED BY HER SCIENTISTS' LACK OF PROGRESS, JENNIFER Vandenburg had done some of her own digging, and to her surprise, she came across amazingly persuasive documents about a means to extend life.

In fact, the reason she came across such a bizarre subject was nearly as remarkable as the subject itself.

After she had been made CEO of Phaylor-Laine Pharmaceuticals, she grew increasingly curious about the man she had succeeded. The founder of Phaylor-Laine Pharmaceuticals, Calvin Phaylor, had been essentially fired by the company's board of trustees. Whispered rumors said Phaylor had lost his mind. She decided to see if his papers reflected that or if the board had, in fact, staged a coup. If so, she needed to be wary about them doing it again...to her.

When she learned PLP's computers kept records of everything, including personal emails and papers, she called up Calvin Phaylor's and read them.

She was shocked to discover his interest in alchemy. Perhaps the board was right, she initially thought, and the man had gone crazy.

But the more Jennifer learned about alchemy, however, the more convinced she became that there really might be something to it. All the men initiated into its arcana weren't gullible fools. Throughout history many people believed in its power, including most of the outstanding minds of their time—men such as Roger Bacon, Sir Isaac Newton, Carl Jung, and

Leonardo da Vinci. To be fair, she ought to include the bad with the good—Adolf Hitler.

If they had believed in alchemy, why couldn't she?

The alchemist would create a philosopher's stone and somehow end up with gold. The common man perceived alchemy as a sort of ATM for Krugerrands.

But the master alchemist, the true believer, did not stop there.

Jennifer's excitement spiked as she learned of this "higher" aspect of alchemy. It became, for her, an obsession—and a hope.

From pure gold, the alchemist could produce a "pill of transformation," a means for a man to achieve his ultimate self, his perfect self: a man who would not die but live forever in immortal splendor.

That was the alchemist's ultimate goal.

The ultimate goal of Calvin Phaylor.

And now, the ultimate goal of Jennifer Vandenburg. Stopping a person from aging would allow her daughter to live. She could not, would not, fail.

THIRTY-THREE

It took all the Hammer's willpower not to speed up, not to wrap his hands around Charlotte Reed's scrawny neck and demand she tell him exactly where she was going. Tempting as it was, he knew that the sheriff, and possibly the other two with her, would put up a fight. The pretty boy he recognized as Michael Rempart, but he was puzzled by the one who looked like a walking corpse. He looked like the type who'd pull the wings off flies and then eat their flightless bodies. Hammill didn't like going up against guys like that. Their reactions were never normal.

He decided to see where Charlotte Reed and the others, "the searchers" he called them, led him. That should be the fastest way to end this mission, then clean-up any collateral damage such as witnesses, and finally to leave this god-forsaken part of the country and get his fill of booze, broads, and a soft bed.

He watched through binoculars as Reed and her friends left the sheriff's truck at Polly Higgins' ranch and took off on horseback. "Hell and damnation!" He pounded the steering wheel of the Suburban before turning to Fish. "Looks like we get to play cavalry. We'll head over to the stables and see what's in it."

After the sheriff and his friends left, Polly Higgins went back to the house to cook biscuits and gravy. She wondered if she'd done the right thing telling

Jake and the others about the Indian legends. Pillars that created thunder sounded so frightening that no one in his or her right mind should want to go there. But then, the sheriff's companions seemed to be scholarly types, and from what little Polly had seen of that kind, they were never in their right minds anyway. Besides that, anyone with half a brain could see the sheriff was a might smitten with that Charlotte Reed, much as he tried to hide it. More than likely, she could lead him straight to the fires of hell if she wanted. Polly snorted, glad romance was no longer on her agenda.

Shadow erupted in barks, followed by Gretchen and Lolo. The dogs raced to the window to see what was outside. The scruffs of their necks stood on end, their barking loud and hysterical.

Polly grabbed her Mossberg double-barrel shotgun, chambered some buckshot, and went outside, shocked to see men in black running around her stables. She ordered the dogs to stay with her.

The obvious leader was blond and muscular, wearing sunglasses, a heavy black jacket with lots of gear dangling from a wide belt, black baggy pants tucked into heavy boots, and a black baseball-style cap. What in the world was he made up for, she wondered. Had war games come to Idaho? No wonder her dogs barked. She would, too, if she could.

He saw her and approached.

"Who are you?" she called.

"Major Derek Hammill, retired," the leader said, removing the glasses. A cold dread filled her at his flat, hard blue eyes. He stopped a few feet away. "We're investigating the whereabouts of Sheriff Jake Sullivan and some visitors. We understand you may know where he went."

She raised her chin. "Jake can go wherever he wants. This is U.S. Forest Service land, not military."

"Yes, ma'am," The Hammer said. "But he went off without saying where. Now his deputy needs him. It's serious, so we were called in."

She looked over Hammill and the others. There were a lot of them—six or seven, all moving around. All held rifles and looked like they had enough fire power on them to conduct a full scale war.

She had no choice and proceeded to explain, giving little detail, where the sheriff was headed.

"I take it we'll need horses," Hammill said. "Do you have more?"

"Nope."

The Hammer thanked her for the information, then turned to walk away. He glanced at a nearby man and nodded.

Instead of following Hammill, Bates drew his .44 magnum, turned toward Polly and aimed. She was too stunned to react, but Shadow did. The dog flung herself at Bates' throat, clamped down on his Adam's apple and tore.

He made a gurgling sound, his blood spraying into the air as he fell with the shepherd mix on top of him.

The Hammer spun around and fired at the dog, then moved closer for a shot at the old woman.

Polly raised her shotgun and aimed at Hammill as Gretchen and Lolo attacked. But she and her two dogs weren't a match for the mercenaries' deadly firepower. Bullets slammed into the old woman, jerking her body, her shotgun firing ineffectually into the air. Polly fell dead as her dying dogs whimpered beside her.

The massacre had taken only seconds.

The Hammer never left one of his men behind. He ordered the others to carry Bates with them. They would give him a warrior's burial.

He sent two of his men back to Salmon City to rent, buy, or steal three double-seat ATVs, and a rig to carry them out here. He'd leave the Suburban behind. Even though this meant a delay, four horses would be child's play to track, and the ATVs would easily make up the time lost.

THIRTY-FOUR

Lionel Rempart's chest nearly burst with pride, especially at the way his find had caused the obnoxious students to stare in silence. That morning, they had crawled down the mountainside to the secluded valley, and now marched closer to the pillars.

A perfectly shaped symmetrical mound of reddish-tan dirt, shaped like a pyramid with the top lopped off, stood over twenty feet tall and forty feet across. At the top, two granite pillars, charcoal gray in color, soared high into the sky. The pillars were stark, overwhelming, and frightening.

"We did it!" Rempart kept his voice hushed, as if in a cathedral, even as jubilation filled him. "It's not exactly Angkor Wat, but as close as we'll get in Idaho." He chuckled at his own wit.

Melisse shook her head, her expression unreadable.

"It's impossible," Rachel murmured, her brow lined with worry.

"No way," Devlin declared.

He had to admit that something eerie and surreal hovered over the area, making the small hairs on his arms stand on end. But he didn't care.

"Could this be how Schliemann felt when he found Troy?" Vince wondered, his voice hushed, nervous.

"Or Bandyopadhyay at Mohenjo-daro," Rachel added.

"Or what's his name who found King Tut," Ted said.

At the last, all went silent. The students all had learned about "the curse of the pharaohs"—that anyone who opened or desecrated a sacred site would die. They were also taught it wasn't true, but Rempart loved the way the story kept students in check.

A cold wind whipped through the valley, chilling him.

"You can see the pillars for some distance around here," he pronounced cheerfully, feeling magnanimous in victory, as the group walked toward the pillars, slower now. Merely waving the possibility of money and prestige had turned the students his way.

He intended to continue to use that tactic, and through it to put Melisse back in her place. His teaching assistant had become far too bossy, strutting around with her hard muscles and outdoor know-how. He couldn't stand her. "We'll make camp right beside them, and you'll always easily find your way back if you're tempted to wander off. Frankly, I wouldn't recommend going anywhere alone. Aside from the mountain lions and black bears you know about, wolf sightings are not unheard of in this area, and rattlesnakes."

"Just watch where you step and you'll be fine." Melisse snapped, no longer even trying to hide her irritation at Rempart. He gave a derisive snort.

No one spoke as they continued forward. Their earlier fatigue had vanished with the possibility of fame and fortune, but it returned now, four-fold. The air turned increasingly cold.

"A storm's coming." Devlin shivered, folding his arms tight against his broad chest for warmth, and peering at the darkening sky. "That's all we need! We'll have to work to keep a fire lit."

"At least rain water will be drinkable." Ted licked his pudgy, parched lips. They hadn't been near a stream or pond all day and shared the couple of waters bottles that hadn't been stolen.

"How do we capture it? Stand around with our mouths open?" Vince's normally wiry, jumpy demeanor grew more frenzied with each step.

"I'm ready," Ted replied.

A loud boom caused the group to freeze. The air felt still, yet the monoliths seemed to quiver before their eyes much as a desert seemed to ripple when heat rose off the ground.

"What was that?" Brandi whispered, her voice hushed and trembling.

"Thunder?" Rachel asked hopefully, although it didn't quite sound like thunder.

"Just the wind," Rempart said. "Keep going."

"We should go back to civilization and get equipment, supplies, and more people so we can do a proper study of the pillars and a search of the area," Melisse suggested. "There must be a deserted settlement nearby, a place where the pillars were made. I can't imagine anyone creating them elsewhere and then carrying them way out here to the middle of nowhere."

Vince tapped the face of his watch. The second hand had stopped moving. He shook his wrist and checked his watch again.

Devlin saw him and checked his own watch. "My watch stopped," he said softly.

"Mine's the same," Melisse said, wriggling her wrist. Then she looked at the sky. "I wonder if the pillars are emitting some sort of electro-magnetic charge."

"Electro-magnetic?" Rempart whispered. "That isn't good. Not good at all." He started toward the mound, then stopped, staring at the ground. Out of nowhere, lightning flashed, and then a sound like rolling thunder.

"That was no wind," Ted said nervously. "What was it?"

"I don't know," Rempart said, inching backwards.

"Not only is there the question of how those pillars got here," Rachel said, "but what do they mean? Nothing like them exists in the native populations. Who would have built them?"

Nervous excitement caused more speculation. Stonehenge. The giant heads of Easter Island. The Nazca Lines of Peru.

"We need to go up there," Devlin said. He shivered. "Inspect them. Take samples. Soil, scrapings, air. Plus whatever it is that made our batteries stop."

No one answered. Rempart took a step toward the pillars and stopped again. "The ground...it flickered!" he called out. At the students' startled, confused expression, he asked, "Didn't you see it?"

The students shook their heads.

"Must have been an optical illusion, a glint from the sun." He began, again, to walk closer to the mound, and then his steps grew faster. "There's some kind of carving at the top of each pillar! I can't make it out from this distance. This is miraculous!"

Another bolt of lightning lit the sky and thunder clapped, longer and louder this time as Rempart reached the bottom of the mound and began to climb up it.

"Professor," Melisse called. "Do you want us to join you?"

Foolish question, Rempart thought. Why would he want her near?

"What's wrong with him?" Ted asked nervously, watching the professor climb the mound without a word or glance back at any of them. Ted sat on the ground exhausted, his feet swollen, and his too stocky legs aching from the long trek.

"I want to see what's up there," Melisse said. She, too, began to climb.

All except Ted followed, ignoring another flash of light and boom of thunder. He watched the other students use their hands to make their way up the tightly packed, slippery earth. They quickly caught up to the slow moving professor.

Dark clouds gathered overhead, but it didn't rain. Only lightning and the raucous, near continuous claps of thunder.

When the group reached the top of the mound, oddly, irrationally, the thunder and lightning stopped.

"Be careful, guys!" Ted called, his voice sharp and edged with fear. "Hurry back down!"

The group moved toward the pillars, which were over thirty feet tall and stood about fifteen feet apart. No one said a word.

"Guys!" Ted yelled as loud as he could, trying to get their attention. Something was very wrong. He got up and hobbled closer to the mound. "Guys, what're you doing? Do you see anything up there? Why aren't any of you talking about it? Hey...*GUYS!!*"

Then, as he watched, the most incredible thing happened. They walked between the pillars.

And vanished.

THIRTY-FIVE

Washington D. C.

Jianjun sat with his back resting against multiple plush pillows on a king-size bed in a luxurious room at the St. Regis Hotel north of Lafayette Square and two blocks from the White House. He couldn't believe the time. He had slept sixteen hours straight. Although past noon, he ordered eggs Benedict from room service, ate breakfast in bed, and now settled in to work on his computer. After roughing it in a *ger* in Mongolia, and then traveling non-stop half-way around the world to get here, he owed it to himself. Ah, the good life, he thought as he patted the comfortable, lump-free, luxurious Egyptian sheet-covered mattress.

His gaze turned to the thumb drive holding files from Lionel Rempart's computer. Maybe "the good life" wasn't exactly the right term for this. He poured some tea from room service into the cup on the nightstand, set the laptop on his thighs and plugged in the drive.

The night before, he thought he was in big trouble when he heard a key in the door of Rempart's town house. It turned out to be a management service Rempart had hired to keep an eye on the place. He showed the guy his student body card and a copy of the e-mail from Rempart's server giving him authority to find some documents Rempart needed in Idaho. The property manager bought it, to Jianjun's surprise. Taking his thumb drive, and telling the manager that someone had failed to lock the deadbolt or to arm the alarm system, Jianjun quickly escaped.

After buying a burrito and chalupas from Taco Bell, which he'd learned to love while living in Seattle, he'd returned to his hotel room and crashed.

Now, he began to go through Rempart's files. He learned that Rempart's interest in Idaho and *The Book of Abraham the Jew* began over a year ago. Rempart apparently had met someone he called "JV" and liked what he heard. Two weeks after that meeting, he began writing down notes of their conversations. He didn't annotate the initial meeting, only referred to it in later entries.

Rempart's interest peaked when JV told him about a group of explorers who had been commissioned to secretly follow the Lewis and Clark expedition westward. Two young foreign students, Chou An-ming from China and Niels Jorgansen from Denmark, discovered the story of that "secret expedition" many years ago as they worked together on a term paper for an anthropology class taught by Professor Thurmon Teasdale.

Lionel Rempart had been stunned by this. It was a part of American history hitherto unknown. Clearly, the two students had no idea what an important bit of history they had discovered.As JV continued to feed Rempart new information, however, a change came over Michael's brother. *The Book of Abraham the Jew*, which he had initially ignored, became more and more fascinating to him. JV had talked about a man named Calvin Phaylor as having been the source of much of her information about all this. It sounded as if Phaylor was deceased, however.

Lionel had learned about *The Book of Abraham the Jew* during the time his brother, Michael, was in China. He wanted to know more about it—lots more. That was the reason he had asked Michael to track down the onetime "young foreign student," Chou An-ming, and ask what he knew about the book and alchemy.

At the same time, Lionel flew off to France and Israel to learn more.

Jianjun paused to think about all this. He clearly remembered meeting Dr. Chou's daughter, who insisted Chou knew nothing about alchemy, nor would he have wanted to. He had to wonder: was she purposefully lying, or did she really not know?

Jianjun found himself frustrated by the way Rempart's notes expressed few thoughts and gave no explanation of why Lionel suddenly started running around the world to learn more about the book.

He continued reading.

Finally, he came across the answer: the mysterious "JV" offered Rempart the sum of one million dollars if he would spend a year of his life searching in Central Idaho for *The Book of Abraham the Jew*. Jianjun had not seen that coming.

Here, Lionel did explain some of his thinking, wondering what harm it would do to take the money. If he found anything, he'd be praised by his peers; if he didn't, he'd still be a million dollars ahead. To make sure he wouldn't lose in any way, he arranged for a visiting professorship to Boise State University so he could use the school's money and students to fund his little field trip, along with paying his salary.

Cheap bastard, Jianjun thought.

Rempart's notes about all this ended in the middle of him getting ready to move to Idaho for the school year.

Jianjun ran some searches to find out more about the mysterious people behind Rempart's activities.

Calvin Phaylor, he learned, wasn't deceased, but merely retired. He had founded Phaylor-Laine Pharmaceuticals forty years earlier. When the company grew into one of the major pharmaceutical businesses in the world, Phaylor had it go public, and the hand-selected board kept him on as Chief Executive Officer until thirteen years ago, when they gave him a vote of "no confidence." Three years later, the position went to Jennifer Vandenburg.

Ah ha! The mysterious JV.

Jianjun soon sent Michael a long text message filled with information about the discoveries on Lionel's hard drive, from the secret expedition to Lionel's payment for searching for *The Book of Abraham the Jew*.

He also let Michael know that, so far, hacking into the federal government's personnel files, he found nothing about Charlotte Reed except that she had worked for ICE for over twelve years, and was now a GS-13. He could not find anything whatsoever on Simon Quade. Also, there were no news accounts of a group of men going missing in Idaho in the past twenty years. Whatever happened was kept under wraps or wasn't newsworthy.

THIRTY-SIX

THE HORSES MOVED BRISKLY THROUGH THE WILDERNESS AREA UNTIL they reached Devil's Gulch, some four hours after leaving Polly Higgins' ranch.

Charlotte quickly overcame her fear of the gentle gelding she had been given, but the empty countryside troubled her. She understood the dangers inherent in big cities with hordes of people packed close together, and she learned to be alert, careful, and cautious around them. Here, she had no idea what to expect.

The foursome followed a Forest Service fire trail along one of the Salmon's tributaries. The ground rose gradually from stands of lodgepole pines and Douglas firs with outcrops of granodiorite towering above the creek to treeless terraces and crumbling granite hillsides. As the miles passed, cliffs of metamorphic rock sprouted from buck brush and fescue. A few hearty wildflowers still bloomed before winter's freeze hit.

Most of Central Idaho had been formed by a mass of granite called the Idaho Batholith. A geologically active area, the landscape had been shaped by erupting volcanoes, melting glaciers, and severe earthquakes as recently as 10,000 years ago. Time hadn't yet softened the jagged peaks and ridges of the mountains or rounded their sharp edges, giving the landscape a spiky crispness.

Jake pointed out a family of Rocky Mountain bighorn sheep peering down at them from cliff faces. Several stood in spots that appeared unapproachable and impenetrable for any animal, two or four-legged.

Every so often, a rise provided a view of the endless, desolate mountains they were supposed to search. Charlotte admitted she'd never before felt quite as small and insignificant. Quade sat as if lost in meditation, the reins lightly held in one hand, his eyelids half shut, and his pink cupid lips upturned in a mystical smile, while Michael paid close attention to every detail.

A strange sense of eerie desolation pervaded the land. Even if the stories of "something bad" were completely false, Michael sensed why they had started. The cool breeze which had aided their journey throughout the morning suddenly stopped. Now, the air turned still, and not the faintest breath of wind stirred a cloudless sky.

As they journeyed ever deeper and higher into the mountains, the excessive loneliness of the area reminded Michael of the *kurgans*, a lurking disquiet of something that didn't belong. At the same time, the conviction struck that he and his companions were the ones who didn't belong there.

The land connected itself to Michael and drew him inexorably forward. The mountainous deer path they followed eventually opened to a sea of grassland. A single tree, now dead, stood at one side. Black crows lined a branch, peering down on them, while a lone golden eagle circled overhead. A fox started across their path, saw them, then turned and disappeared so suddenly it seemed to vanish into the air.

When they finally reached Devil's Gulch, they found it a barren indentation that looked like a quarter-mile wide strip of cat litter laid down between face-to-face cliffs. There, they stopped for lunch. Polly had sent them off with big roast beef and cheese sandwiches on homemade bread, telling them to save the beef jerky and dried packaged food until needed.

As Michael ate, he looked at his Iridium satellite phone and read the email from Jianjun. He then said to Charlotte, the sheriff, and Quade, "My associate found evidence that, if true, confirms that a secret expedition was commissioned by someone—we don't yet know who—to follow Lewis and Clark westward in hopes of finding *The Book of Abraham the Jew* out here. They failed, and now Lionel has been paid a lot of money to do the same thing."

"He was paid to do this?" Jake said with disgust. "To bring a bunch of kids out to this wilderness with no guide, no one who knows how to handle himself in nature when things go bad? How ironic that money seems to be the root of all the troubles here, and it doesn't matter if it's US dollars or some bullshit alchemical concoction."

❄

Ted's already weak legs gave out completely as he watched his companions disappear, one by one, as they stepped between the pillars.

Too frightened to move, he sat on the ground and waited, telling himself it was an optical illusion. They were all right. He would see them again.

One minute passed. Two. Five.

It had to be a joke of some kind, he told himself. A practical joke. He struggled to stand again, and then limped on tired, sore feet around the mound, praying he'd find all six of them waiting for him on the opposite side. They would laugh at him, the way so-called friends and classmates had done all his life. He didn't care. He'd rather be laughed at than stranded.

He circled the entire mound, but saw no sign of them. No sign of anyone. All his complaints about hunger and thirst, aching muscles and blistered feet, disappeared.

Something had happened at the top of that mound. It happened fast, too fast for them to call for help or do anything to save themselves.

If he went up there, the same would happen to him. He was no dummy. No way was he going to do that to himself.

He wanted to go home.

Besides, he was hungry. And exhausted. He had a lot more weight to lug around than tiny, anorexic Vince. Melisse's weight, on the other hand, looked like it was all muscle.

He hadn't even wanted to come on this stupid trip. "I want to know what Lionel Rempart's up to," his mother had told him. "So you're going! You can handle it for five days. You might even lose a few pounds, which would be good for you...unless you like being known as the Eric Cartman of BSU," she said, referring to the obnoxious fat boy on *South Park*.

His mother's slam made him hide his fear. "It'll be a waste of time," he muttered.

"As if you've got something better to do! Besides, if there's anything special out there, I'm not letting some Easterner claim all the glory."

In the end, she won. As always.

Ted's muscles ached, his feet were so swollen and blistered he could scarcely walk, and he was freezing. He wanted nothing more than to sit in front of a big fire. No one had even bothered to collect firewood yet.

He decided to wait. Soon, he told himself, soon they would come back.

But night quickly approached. He didn't want to be alone out here at night.

He had two choices, to find a way back home all by himself, or to go after his friends.

The thought of both filled him with dread, but no way—no way on earth—would he spend the night alone next to those pillars. If he headed east, eventually he would reach the north-south highway that ran between Idaho and Montana. How hard could that be?

But how many days would it take? And what would he do for food or water? And what about the animals out here, the wolves, bears ... and whatever took Brian?

He shuddered at the thought of Brian.

He didn't know anything about survival in this wilderness.

His stomach ached from hunger, and his mouth was dry. His friends weren't too far away, he told himself. And maybe they were waiting for him. They wouldn't leave him, would they?

Too frightened to stay put, he did the only thing he could. He walked toward the pillars. With each step, lightning flashed and thunder rolled.

He began to climb the mound. He got up about five feet, but slid back down again.

Finally, crawling on hands and knees, after about thirty minutes he managed to make his way to the very top.

Holding his breath, he walked between the pillars.

And nothing happened.

Everywhere he looked, everything appeared the same as before. And he was still alone.

Sad, miserable, scared, he slipped and slid his way back down the mound.

At the bottom, he shuddered as he looked out across the valley, at the high mountains all around. He had to find his way back home. Somehow, he would make it.

The area, he noticed, had developed a strange stench. A smell of decay.

He guessed he'd been too busy looking at the pillars to notice it before, but he wanted to get away from it now. It grew stronger quickly, making it almost hurt to breathe. He began to walk in the direction he hoped was east.

At the edge of the valley, the firs thickened, and the ground began to rise. Something flicked by up ahead.

His instincts told him to run, but what if it was one of the others? Or maybe even a rescue team? Earlier they had speculated that many people must be searching for them.

"Help!" he yelled. "I'm over here! Is anyone there? *Haaallooow out there!*"

No one answered. He must have been wrong.

Exhausted, he continued on. He would make it to the top of this mountain and then he'd be able to study the topography, determine the best route to reach civilization. Yes, that would do it. Everything would look better up there. He could see into the distance—maybe even find some hunters or fishermen. Anyone.

Something moved in the brush to his right. His heart nearly stopped. He faced there. Nothing.

He went faster, running, climbing, slipping, his breathing hard and labored. Maybe if he ignored it, it would go away, leave him alone.

The brush suddenly cleared. A full minute passed before he registered what he saw on the ground. A small pile of bones that had been picked clean were neatly stacked to look like a miniature ivory pyramid. What kind of animal stacked bones of its kill?

The skin on his neck prickled, and tears of fright filled his eyes. A rustle of leaves sounded nearby.

He ran, almost tripping over his own feet, his mind a gibbering, screaming mess. The only sounds were those of his footsteps and his panting.

Tears fell. *Please, please,* he prayed.

Something big, black, and fast streaked out in front of him.

He screamed. As he stopped, his feet slipped on the silty ground. He fell on his backside, but quickly scrambled up, eyes wide, head swiveling back and forth. He saw nothing, heard nothing but the sound of his wheezing. A burning pain filled his chest. And then he heard leaves rustling sharp and fast. Too fast.

This couldn't be happening. He let out a hysterical cry and forced leaden legs to run. He sobbed and shouted for help. Grunts and snarls sounded close behind him, loud and growing louder.

"No! Leave me alone!" he screamed.

His shoulder burst in red-hot pain. Unbalanced, he spun around, arms flailing. Except that he didn't see his left arm. He looked at where his left arm used to be, and then, horrified, he looked up at his pursuer. His mind snapped.

What little sanity remained, escaped in one high-pitched scream.

THIRTY-SEVEN

Washington D. C.

The Smithsonian Institute consisted of nineteen museums, 144 affiliate museums, and nine research centers in its public sector, but that wasn't the entire Institute by any means. Many of its 136 million objects, art works, and specimens were not displayed, but tucked away in special buildings and locations for only researchers and museum employees to handle and study. These were places the public and most of the Institute's employees knew nothing about.

On a hunch, Jianjun filled out the document request form with the information he'd found on Lionel Rempart's "Smith Inst" note and twenty minutes later a museum attendant brought him a box of materials. Success! He carried it to a carrel.

Opening it, he found dishes, rusted spoons, tools, knives, and penny nails from the failed Mormon community at New Gideon, Idaho. He wondered why Rempart would care about this old junk. But digging deeper, he found strange Indian trinkets and then an aged and battered bound journal with a thick leather cover.

He opened the journal and stared with amazement at the date—1806, a year after the Lewis and Clark expedition. And then at the name of the author—Francis Masterson. It sounded familiar ...

Then, he remembered the letters of Susannah Revere to President Thomas Jefferson asking what had happened to her fiancé, Francis Masterson.

A chill rippled down Jianjun's back.

The writing had turned so faint over the years, brown-tinged ink on age-darkened pages, and the formation of letters so curvy and embellished, that he was forced to read slowly, making out one word at a time. But as he read, the skin on his arms filled with goose-bumps.

Journal
Property of Francis Masterson
The Spring of Our Lord, 1806

All hope is gone. Evil is victorious.

In the time I have remaining I will, herewith, impart a tale so filled with Dread and Terror that my heart overflows with immeasurable Sorrow to tell it.

It began with the highest of Good Will and Promise and, on my part, great Excitement. I can only trust to Providence that one day this small account which I leave in a land of unimaginable desolation and Wildness, may be discovered, and that it will serve to warn others of the wickedness that may ensnare Good men.

Ours was to be a Secret Expedition, and we were, each and Every One, to keep our own Journal in accordance with our discipline. As the Journey continued, however, such writings lessened, and so I have taken upon myself the sad Burden to record a brief History of our group since I fear we will never meet our Loved Ones again this side of Heaven.

It all began simply.

President Thomas Jefferson, scandalous rumor to the contrary, was neither Rosicrucian nor Illuminati, but he had an understanding of the world beyond the ken of most men. He realized that there are Wonders on this Earth that Rational Science and the strange Beliefs of the Churched could not begin to fathom.

I beg your indulgence, My Future Would-Be Reader (if you do exist), as I recount some of the History of this time, for I have not the foresight to know how much of it has become common knowledge.

When Jefferson sojourned in Paris some years before his Presidency, he met a group of Occultists. It was our misfortune that Jefferson took little notice that Occultists often involved themselves in the Study of Evil. If he had, perhaps our adventure would not have come to this frightening condition.

He continued this association into his presidency. Among those

Occultists was a Medieval scholar who had studied the ancient practice of Alchemy. The man told Jefferson that one of the most important Alchemical texts of all time may have been brought to America by a Frenchman. The man, said to be a Seer and an Alchemist, ventured into the area the French explored, but which was now under dispute between the English and the Americans after the Emperor's sale of Louisiana.

Desiring the land, the text, and the Alchemist's gold (if it did exist), Jefferson contacted Ezra Crouch, a retired Captain in the Army of the United States of America as well as a student of Freemasonry and Rosicrucian history, to pursue the matter.

Captain Crouch learned that a French explorer had indeed discovered Pure Gold as well as Arcane and Magical materials and symbols near the Nez Perce nation. The Indians refused to touch it, insisting it ensured Death to anyone who did so. Included in the findings was a most peculiar Symbol:

Jianjun scarcely believed his eyes. The journal contained the same symbol Michael had found in Mongolia.

Jianjun continued to read.

Jefferson dispatched to the Medieval scholar a finely wrought drawing of the symbol. He foreswore mention of the Gold.

The man replied with clear excitement, saying the symbol was from the selfsame Alchemical text he had spoken of, the one that taught the sorcerer Nicolas Flamel the Art of Transmutation.

In Great Secret, Jefferson gathered our little group with Captain Crouch as our leader. We were given one Mission: to go to the locale where the Alchemical symbol had been found, and bring back all that was there, including the Gold.

He then organized the Corps of Discovery which would be led by Captains William Clark and Meriwether Lewis. Our duty was to follow them. Of course, it could not become General Knowledge that Jefferson was spending the Public Treasury for our Mystical adventure. Thus, we were dispatched in complete secret from everyone we knew and from all we held dear on this Earth.

I can little convey the excitement with which our most Remarkable expedition set out. My particular friend, Noah Handy, was well versed in the study of Astrology and the Heavens. He entertained us with Numerous stories about the Stars and their meaning. Reuben Hale was an older man, perhaps in his fifties, and I feared for his Health on this journey. He was a devotee of Medieval sorcery and knew a great deal about cures and potions. I found him amiable, but strange. I will confess to little amity with Orril and Asa Munroe, who were first cousins, and who professed to be practitioners of Mentalist Powers. They held themselves as Superior to me in every way simply because they were skilled Hunters and Frontiersmen. I found their constant prying about my Thoughts and ridicule of my Weakness as destructive to our mission and often wished they would leave the group. I feared their hearts were corrupted by Vice and Arrogance.

I shall admit, although I enjoy good health, I am not as physically strong as most men for I have spent the majority of my twenty-eight years in the pursuit of knowledge. I am a writer. I have published several books on the Occult, not as a believer, but as a scholar. The books sold only passably well in our practical America, but I have a devoted following in England. The public there are especially curious to learn of the beliefs and practices of the American aboriginals. Mine was to be one of the first learned books on the subject when we returned.

I shall not recount here, as we followed Lewis and Clark, of our troubles with the fiercesome Lakota Sioux, or of the hardships of our first Winter on the plains. Suffice it to say that without our Guides, Eli Borah and Miles Weiser, fine men with good knowledge of survival in the Implacable Wilderness, we would be long dead.

Instead, I shall proceed forward to the fateful day when Noah Handy peered through his spyglass and saw that Captain Clark was separating from Captain Lewis, who seemed to be in ill Health. By this time, we believed we must be near the Nez Perce land, for we had traveled far longer without falling off the edge of the continent than we had imagined was possible. We looked forward to achieving our Goal and returning Home.

I longed for Home. My own Susannah Revere, the truest, most honorable woman I have been privileged to meet, had promised her hand to me before I left Maryland. I vowed that after I returned, I would never again leave her side.

Upon Captain Crouch's order, we followed William Clark and his small band. I should have known, as soon as we entered this strange Land, that something was dreadfully amiss. The mountains, tall, and blood-red at sunset as a Beast's maw, stretched farther than I ever imagined they would, and were far more Barren and Inhospitable. We were at such an altitude the Air was thin and we struggled to breath.

If the land our Ancestors had found in the New World had been as empty and forbidding as this, with murderous aboriginals and monstrous, ferocious bears called Grizzlies whose roar caused men to fall to the ground quaking in terror, they never would have settled it, but would have fled back to England and kissed the ground with gratitude for their deliverance.

Our group was forced to lag some distance behind Captain Clark because we knew Scouts would travel between his camp and that of Captain Lewis. For the first time, we were unable to simply follow the trail the Corps of Discovery had created, because to do so would have placed us in the path of the Scouts. We were forced to blaze our own trail.

And that was our Undoing.

To keep clear of the Scouts, we traveled far to the South.

The second night, dry Lightning continued into the early morning hours, and we awoke to a Sky yellow with smoke. The forest blazed, and Fire progressed toward our camp with terrifying rapidity as if it were some great Hellish demon devouring all in its wake.

The next day, we traveled south to avoid the path of the rapidly approaching blaze.

We reached a deep canyon. The gorge precipitously yawned straight down and was impossible to descend. We were forced westward, following the gorge, and hoping to find a way across. Once the fire diminished, we would circumambulate back to regain Captain Clark's trail.

As we continued, however, hope of finding our way back to Clark diminished, and should the fire be burning toward him, we knew not if he would be able to return to Lewis, or if he would perish in the hellish flames.

That night we had recourse to prayer, a remarkable thing for men who had turned our backs on the One God of our fathers, and had in truth lived most of our lives in search of other, more Aesthetically pleasing, more Rational and Modern deities.

The Fire galloped at great speed with strength and endurance. We ran, but it pursued, jumping boundaries and heading our way like a ravenous monster in search of nourishment.

We crossed a wide creek only to watch in dismay as the fire vaulted over it. Was there no safety from this monster? We could see the crown of it, with flames higher than a hundred feet into the sky.

The blaze created a clime of its own. Furious temperatures sucked the heated air into a column where updrafts whorled smoke into a vertical cloud.

We could only shake our heads in frightful wonderment as we watched in helpless awe at the power of nature.

After four days, we wondered if it would ever end. By the eighth day, temperatures lowered and the moisture in the air increased contrary to the usually blistering dryness of this climate. With this change, the rate of combustion slowed.

The following morning, cloud edges had darkened to a gentle gray, and by noon, a steady drizzle had become a drumming rain. Trees and rocks grew cooler. By the next day, almost an inch of rain had fallen.

Like a giant beast that is spent, the fire burned itself out as we slept.

As the overhead lights flickered on and off a couple of times, Jianjun slowly returned to this time and place. The Institute was about to close.

He slid the journal into the fake bottom in his laptop computer case, the same secret compartment that held lock picks, key cards, SIM cards, and other tools of his trade. He returned the boxes of materials to the librarian, then calmly walked through security and out the museum doors. As he tried to put the pieces of a nightmare puzzle together, he wondered how the journal had been ignored. Had it been dismissed by hasty readers as crazed fiction? A frontier tall tale? And he wondered who else had read it.

THIRTY-EIGHT

Something was terribly wrong here, Michael thought as he perused the rugged terrain. The emptiness, untouched by man, seemed to go on forever.

The previous day the group found nothing that could lead to the pillars. At first light, they began again.

They stopped when they reached a location where the mountain dropped away. They couldn't see through the thick, high foliage to the bottom. Something about it seemed familiar to Michael, however. He had never been there before, yet it welcomed him.

"This is it," he said quietly. "We've got to climb down the mountain."

"What makes you say that?" Quade's dark gaze fixed on Michael.

"I don't know," Michael admitted.

Jake and Charlotte exchanged worried glances. "Good enough for me," Charlotte said. Jake nodded.

Michael led them forward as anticipation, hope and fear collided. The possibility that Lionel and the students were already dead, that he was chasing shadows, weighed heavily.

He realized the mountain's relentless steepness and treacherous footing would only increase the farther they went. They left the horses on a flat pasture near a small stream, removed the saddlebags and filled their back-packs with as much as they could carry, then crawled and slid down the mountainside.

Michael stared into the distance with both satisfaction and alarm. He stopped walking and pointed so that the others would follow his line of sight.

He heard Charlotte gasp in both surprise and disbelief.

In the center of a long valley stood two pillars, taller and more frighteningly unearthly than any of them ever imagined.

As they hiked toward the pillars, Jake found footprints among the crushed scrub. "Look at this! They were here! We're going to find them. I know it!"

Michael said nothing. He had somehow known he would find the pillars, had known they would find evidence that the university group had been here. He felt as if he had been led here by a force beyond himself, but by who or what, for good or evil, he had no idea.

It was ironic that he felt such a force. After all, he had turned his back on believing in such sixth senses, turned his back on everything other than the here and now, the real and concrete ... until Mongolia. There, everything changed.

"I've got to call this in," Jake said excitedly as he pulled out his satellite phone. "I want a search team out here pronto." He tried the phone. "Damn! There's nothing but static. I've never had that happen before. What could be causing interference way out here?" He walked back some distance to see if he could get a better signal.

Charlotte followed him. Michael couldn't help but notice that she tended to do that, as if she found being near Jake somehow comforting—and clearly, the sheriff didn't mind having her near. She called out, "Does it work yet?"

"No. For all I know, the damn thing's broken. But I've got backup." Jake dropped the phone back in its case and took out a satellite messenger, capable of sending a distress signal with the sender's location. But it was as dead as the phone.

"My sat phone's never failed me," Michael said as he took his out. Besides, he should have already contacted Jianjun, told him where he was, and asked him to be ready to send help if things grew any weirder.

But his device also refused to connect. The pillars had to be the cause. But why? What did they do? What was their purpose?

He put the phone away. They were on their own.

"Before we waste time with this technical junk," Jake said, "let's see if we can find those kids and give them food and first aid. After that, we'll figure out how to get a helicopter out here. The kids' tracks are heading straight for the pillars, so they might be camped nearby."

"It's too quiet here," Charlotte said.

"We will understand the strangeness as soon as we learn what's causing it," Quade stated in his usual emotionless, cerebral manner.

Michael, however, saw perfection in the symmetry of the straight, matching dark gray posts atop the pyramid-like hill. They reminded him of Miyajima in Japan's Inland Sea, where a tall vermilion gate, a *torii,* had been built so that at high tide water surrounded it. Beautiful and symmetrical, the *torii* was considered a gateway between the physical and spiritual world. A gate in such an unlikely location made it startling to behold. Just like the two pillars.

He saw footprints leading toward the pillars, but none away.

The air grew colder as he neared the pillars, and then a bolt of lightning streaked across the sky and a boom of thunder sounded.

"What was that?" Charlotte stopped short.

"It seemed to come from them," Jake said, looking at the pillars. He, too, froze in his tracks.

Once more, lightning flashed above the pillars and thunder rumbled.

"People nearing the pillars must create a displacement of air," Quade said, "like wind booming through a cave."

"Wait!" Michael held out his arms as if to stop them. "The thunder could be a warning to stay away."

"Now you're out in *Twilight Zone* territory," Jake declared. "It's dry lightning and thunder. Happens now and again, and I'm not letting it stop me from going where I please. Or from finding those kids. Ignore it. Let's go."

"All of you talk about the noise, but what about the lights?" Michael asked.

The others glanced at each other. "What lights?" Jake said.

"Those!" Michael pointed at the ground from the foot of the mound to the top. "Don't you see them? They're fantastic, like intricate Celtic knots all jumbled together, and yet, overall, they form a large-scale pattern, a definite pattern that works its way up the mound to the pillars."

"I sure as hell don't see any lights," Jake said, staring at him as if he'd lost his mind.

Charlotte and Quade moved a bit closer. He could tell from their expressions they saw nothing.

"I know what I see!" Michael hurried a few steps forward then dropped to the ground and scooped away bits of dirt, eventually ending up with a small hole. He sat back on his heels. "They won't go away. They aren't on the earth; they're *of* it."

"What you are seeing is an array," Quade said calmly. "It holds and focuses energy. However those pillars came to be here, they are held in place by energy. For some reason, you alone can see it."

"See energy?" Jake cast a beady eye on both Quade and Michael. "Sounds like witchcraft. Which, I hasten to add, I also do not believe in." He marched forward. Charlotte and then Quade walked close behind him, and eventually, Michael followed.

When they reached the foot of the mound, lightning flashed and thunder boomed every sixty to ninety seconds. Static electricity charged the air.

"Now, what the hell's he doing?" Jake muttered to Charlotte as he stared at Quade who sat cross-legged gazing up at the formation. Michael had walked away from them.

Charlotte shook her head, too stunned by the pillars to care about Quade. She stepped to Jake's side. "Remember how I told you I studied ancient Egypt? I hate to say it, but now that we're close, those symbols at the top are Egyptian hieroglyphics."

"You've studied hieroglyphics?" Jake rubbed his chin, looking at her with equal parts awe and befuddlement as a dopey grin spread over his face. "At this point I'm ready to believe anything. Can you read them?"

"Not without my books and dictionaries."

He turned back to the pillars. "So, now you're telling me ancient Egyptians, the guys who built the pyramids, were once here in Idaho?"

"No."

"That's good," Jake sounded relieved, as if he had feared for her sanity.

"The stones would be more weathered, and the ground much more reclaimed if the pillars were thousands of years old. They're much more recent."

"That's it!" Jake said. "It's a prank! Some college kids rigged this up. Maybe even as a joke on the visiting professor. Now, you're talking."

Much to her surprise in this crazy situation, Charlotte found herself smiling at him. "I should have said recent, *archeologically* speaking." A glimmer filled her eyes "They're probably no more than two or three hundred years old."

"Good God!" Jake groaned.

Michael hurried toward them. "There's a problem." He beckoned Quade to join them. "I walked all the way around the mound and I saw footprints going up, but none coming down or walking away from it."

"Impossible," Jake said.

Charlotte said nothing as she tried to understand all this.

"There's an explanation." Quade's tone was firm, all-knowing.

"What, they flew?" Jake put his hands on his hips. "I know the old legends talked about people disappearing, but I don't buy it!"

Quade peered up at the pillars. "If we want to find the students, we'll have to follow them." His frosty gaze turned to Jake. "The wisest move might be that you don't join us, Sheriff," Quade said. "We don't know what's on the other side."

"Other side of what?" Jake asked.

Michael answered. "That's what we need to find out."

"Are you the only sensible one here, Charlotte?" Jake asked.

His question churned in her mind. Sensible? If it was sensible to believe these pillars held answers about her husband, then she was. After thirteen years of not knowing why he had died, what he had pursued those last few weeks of his life, the answer seemed to be within her grasp. "I'm going with them," she replied softly.

Despite her words, she was afraid, and something told her the sheriff realized that. She looked away.

"I think you've all lost your goddamn minds," Jake yelled, far too gruffly. His eyes again found Charlotte's as he said, "I'm not letting you go anywhere without me."

Quade climbed up the mound first, Charlotte next, Michael, and then Jake. As they neared the top, the booms struck with less frequency rather than more, and then stopped completely.

The earth at the top was the same as the earth everywhere else on the mound. They found no hole that could swallow people up. Nothing.

And yet, they could not deny that footprints rose up to the pillars, but none descended from them.

"I'm going to walk between the pillars," Michael said. "But before anyone else does, you should realize there's a possibility you won't be able to come back."

"That's crazier than Quade!" Jake said.

"Maybe we tie a rope around Michael's waist," Charlotte suggested. "If something goes wrong, or he finds himself in danger, we can pull him back out."

"I don't believe that will work," Quade said. "Any link to this world will stop one from entering another."

"We can try," Charlotte said.

"Ropes aren't needed." Quade held Charlotte's outstretched hand as he alone stepped between the pillars. Nothing happened, and he came back to her side. "As I suspected."

"I can't believe any of you are serious about this!" Jake yelled.

"Are you ready?" Michael asked Quade and Charlotte. They nodded.

"Hell no! Not if we can't come back!" Jake thundered.

"We'll have to find that out on the other side," Michael answered. "It's what all scientists must do at some point."

"But don't you—" Jake began his question but didn't have a chance to end it as he watched Quade, Michael, and finally Charlotte step between the pillars and vanish.

"Oh, shit!" Jake muttered. Against his better judgment, he followed.

THIRTY-NINE

New York City

Jennifer Vandenburg stood at the window of her corner office on the PLP building's forty-third floor and looked out over Central Park. The lights of the city burned bright. She found Manhattan more beautiful at night than during the day.

She should have been home now, but she couldn't face being there. She couldn't face her own daughter.

Vandenburg had achieved much in her life, more than she ever thought possible. Now, if she could succeed once more, she would finally be happy.

She glanced at the clock. Her visitor was late.

The phone rang, startling her. On her personal line was the investigator employed by PLP's lobbying firm in Washington D. C.

"We found a student in Lionel Rempart's condo gathering information," the private eye announced without introduction.

"Did you check him out?" she asked, irritated at the bizarre intrusion.

"So far, all we know is his I.D. was a fake. We're working on it."

She didn't like the response. "Keep me posted." She hung up.

When Rempart and his students dropped off the face of the earth in Idaho, she immediately suspected him of something underhanded. He might have found the book and decided to keep it, or had gotten sick of the hardship of trekking around the woods. She had his home watched in case he went back there for something, such as his passport. Her plan depended on him being a reputable anthropologist, and he had taken her money. But she still didn't trust him.

If he couldn't be found in Idaho, and he hadn't snuck back home, where was he? Had something terrible happened to him and the students?

A tentative knock on the door, the one she had been waiting for, interrupted her thoughts. "Come in."

Milt Zonovich, Phaylor-Laine Pharmaceutical's first vice president, entered. He was a small man, with short gray hair, horned-rimmed glasses, and a nervous habit of excessive blinking.

Ten years ago, Zonovich had hoped to get the CEO position, but it went instead to the young Jennifer Vandenburg after she'd resurrected a chain of home improvement stores from the doldrums into one of the country's top retail businesses. She'd campaigned hard for the position and eventually the executive board offered her a fortune to make sure that Phaylor-Laine maintained its hold as the world's premier pharmaceutical company, despite numerous lawsuits stemming from side effects from the latest "super-drugs" that do everything short of curing the common cold, but have an unfortunate tendency to be fatal to a small number of the population.

Cure or kill...that was the question in twenty-first century medicine.

So far, Vandenburg had managed to keep the Phaylor-Laine name surprisingly positive in the mainstream press.

That didn't mean, however, that Zonovich either liked or respected her.

"Milt, thank you for joining me. Would you like a drink?"

He looked at the well-stocked bar against the wall, and his lips thirstily rubbed together before he forced himself to say, "No, thanks."

They sat on the sofa, one at each end. "Fifteen years ago," she launched directly into her reason for calling him, "the company began an inquiry into an ancient text on alchemy. Do you know about that?"

Surprise flickered across Zonovich's face.

Blink. Blink. "Yes. It was Calvin Phaylor's idea," he explained, then nervously bit his bottom lip before continuing. "He had an interest in many strange things he thought might provide possible pharmacological breakthroughs. It was a lark, nothing more. I think he hoped to spend some time in Idaho at company expense. He loved sports fishing, salmon, steelhead—"

"I'm curious about a team sent into the area," she interrupted. "The reports don't say what happened to them. That troubles me."

His blinking sped up, and he rubbed his chin. "Kohler. Thad Kohler. He led the group. They were supposed to be experts. All ex-military. Supposed to know how to take care of themselves in the wilds." He stopped speaking suddenly.

"I'm surprised you remember his name after all these years," she said. She not only knew about Kohler, but knew the other five names as well: Ben Olgerbee, Will Durham, Gus Webber, Sam Black, and Arnie Tieg.

"I remember only because the whole thing turned so very bizarre," Zonovich exclaimed, his voice too high now. "We never heard back from them. We made inquiries, did some searches. We couldn't do too much in the way of publicizing our activity—we didn't exactly want our stockholders to know that PLP paid to investigate alchemy." He laughed nervously.

Vandenburg didn't join in.

"The money we paid Kohler"—*blink, blink, blink*—"had been distributed by him to his team before they left. Some of the families made a fuss when the men didn't come home, but we pointed out that they were paid by PLP for work that wasn't, as best as we knew, accomplished. We compensated them out of the goodness of our hearts, I might add, and simply asked that they remained silent. There's not much more I can tell you."

"Was there any follow-up? Were all six men truly lost out there?"

"I'm sorry to say Mr. Phaylor wasted quite a few resources trying to find those men. As far as we could tell there was never any trace of them. Not anywhere." Beads of perspiration appeared on Zonovich's forehead. "How did you find out about all this?"

Did the idiot really think she would tell him? "Thank you, Milt," she said. "You've been most helpful."

"You aren't thinking of reopening that inquiry now, are you?" He glanced longingly at the scotch on the wet bar. "It's all nonsense, but with us pushing to get the FDA to approve our new 'healthy bones for all women drug,' rather than targeting only the post-menopausal group, we don't want to do anything to make them look askance at us. That pill will make us tens of billions of dollars. Maybe more. With no competition."

"Yes, I know," she said, trying to keep the bitterness from her voice. She had pushed the concept, trying to get the numbskulls in R&D to come up with something that would undo the damage Felicia's bones had suffered. All they developed was a way to maintain strength and suppleness in already healthy bones, not repair damage to weak ones. PLP would make it so that taking one little pill every day would enable thirty-year-old women to bounce up from falls like eight-year-olds. Unfortunately, it also had a tendency to destroy women's livers, but it would take a long time before that little side-effect was discovered, if ever.

She walked to her door and opened it. "Good-day, Milt."

He quickly exited.

FORTY

WASHINGTON D. C.

Jianjun couldn't shake the feeling he was being followed as he hurried from the Smithsonian back to his hotel room. He double locked the door, stretched out on the bed, took out Francis Masterson's Journal, and once more began to read. Soon, he was caught up in the early nineteenth century world.

I have never known such Despair. Noah Handy has often tried to cheer me by making my Horoscope and claiming my life will be a long one, but the good Soul's words do little to assuage me.

I have no faith in Astrology. No faith in anything anymore.

If there be a God, He has abandoned us in this Alien land.

The air crackles with Dryness that leaves my throat perpetually parched and sucks the life from my Skin. My lips flake and peel, and my fingers bleed.

After the Fire, we waited until fairly certain there were no more Hot embers to burn the horses' hooves, but they were too frightened to enter the Charred land, and in fact, we shared the beasts' trepidation. We endeavored to return to Captain Clark's trail, but the Signs used to guide us had vanished. The slate had been wiped clean, and all that remained were Compass, Sextant, and Stars.

Our mission had failed, for neither the symbol, nor Alchemical text, nor Gold were to be found in this wasteland.

How could we find our way? The forests had burned, and I write the word in plural for the burned Vastness went on as far as the eye could see.

Lost, with none but our Wits as guides, we continued Westward.

The mountains grew more steep and dangerous than I had before experienced, with Soil so loose that when a mule packed with necessary provisions lost his footing and rolled downhill into a stream and was killed, we were unable to go after it to extricate our Supplies or even to harvest the mule for food. Hail stones the size of robins' eggs pelted us, and rattlesnakes slithered everywhere. Voracious wood ticks converged to feast on both men and horses. At times we sweltered in heat, yet above us on the mountaintops lay ten feet of snow.

Sadness filled me, for I had never imagined such a contrary, hateful land, such a place of sudden senseless Death.

And, as happens when God turns his back on Man, the Devil enters with his minions.

After days of wandering, one morning we awoke with glittering Knives thrust in our faces. The hands that gripped them were those of fierce and loathsome Heathens. These were not the gentle Nez Perce whose women oft times marry hairy barbarians, as they call the French trappers. These were from some other tribe, one our guides knew not.

Six men, seven women, and ten children, all poorly clothed in Deer and sheepskins, yet well armed with knives, bows, and arrows pointed with honed Obsidian, appropriated our horses, mules, and supplies, and forced us to follow them.

Our guides labored to convince them our intentions were pacific, but that if any Harm befell us, more White men with powerful guns would descend on them and kill them all. Most were unconvinced by such Bellicose braggadocio.

Their regard for us changed, however, when we demonstrated to them use of our Rifles to fell big horn sheep. With that, we became instant friends and benefactors.

We spent the cold Winter with them, hunkered down in their wretched Wikiups and caves to guard against a stabbing, miserable cold. Food was scarce, and every night my Belly ached from emptiness. Worse was the ache in my heart when I thought of my own sweet Susannah.

To this day I envision her in her home, seated by a fire-warmed hearth, and I long to be with her. I wonder if she is still awaiting my return, or if she has already forgotten me and our Promise to each other. I should not doubt her, for she is as Faithful a woman as has ever walked the Earth, yet I do. Loneliness and fear have become my Companion and my Enemy.

In Spring we attempted to bid Farewell to the Heathens and be on our way. That was when we learned we could not depart.

The Tukudeka spoke of a Bad place, of Earth's thunder that swallowed men. We had no understanding of what new sinister dread they spoke of until they drew a figure on the ground for us.

We stared with shock and wonderment for it was the exact symbol that had inspired our President to commission this Journey. Had we now reached our Goal only to be thwarted by our inability to leave this place?

The Tukudeka said a white man, a Holy man, had come and used that symbol to create a place so frightening as one could not Bear to look at it without fearing he had succumbed to Madness.

Despite this warning, under the leadership of Captain Crouch, a stern man who had become ever more Harsh and Unforgiving, we vowed to reach the Goal we had been sent to achieve. We would escape, or die in our attempt. We were Free men, and would rather die than to live as prisoners against our will.

One night, a battering rainstorm raged. Knowing the gushing rain and shrieking wind would assure us from being heard, we gathered up such belongings as we could carry and crept away while the Tukudeka slept. Although we were not guarded, the horses were, so we were forced to flee on foot.

After a day's labored Journey, we discovered what the Red Men had feared.

As a mere Mortal, my paltry words can little express the Unnatural sight before us. Two massive pillars, perfectly round with strange symbols at the top, soared high into the sky, far taller than any building back home. Glowering mists surrounded their peaks. They stood atop a Pyramid the size of a three-masted schooner.

My knees quaked at the sight, for I immediately realized it was not anything of this World, but something surely created by the Darkest demons of the Netherworld. Tears sprang to my eyes.

Lightning bolts lit the Sky and Thunder sounded. I was sure those tall rocks had vision and watched us approach.

I tried to speak of my fear, of a sense of Evil enveloping me, but my voice shook so, I could not.

At that moment, our scout Miles Weiser, who had been at the rear of our party, ran to us shouting that the Tukudeka were riding toward us. All of us knew the Horrific fate of anyone who disobeyed them.

Captain Crouch ordered us to run for the pillars, for the Indians feared them and might not approach. Mr. Weiser refused, saying he must try to save Mr. Borah, the other scout who was lagging behind.

We approached the pillars. The storm had strengthened, and the pillars themselves seemed to be the source of Lightning and rolling Thunder, just as the Tukudeka had warned. Perhaps my words have an aura of Madness, and so they may, for ensuing events showed that it was not any known Reason that here ruled.

The Tukudeka appeared in the distance with savage cries and Murderous intent.

Captain Crouch shouted that we were to Ascend and stand between the stones, that there, the Tukudeka would not attack us, they would not risk the Magic they so dreaded. Orril and Asa Munroe, Noah Handy, and Reuben Hale did as ordered. I did not wish to leave my Captain's side, however. I believed he might fight to free the scouts, whom we feared would be tortured and killed. If so, I planned to assist him. He accepted my presence with a cold, almost angry, nod.

Our four Companions stepped between the stone pillars as Crouch had ordered.

As soon as they did, Stillness descended. Thunder ceased. I glanced at the sky, and then toward my companions, and, as God is my witness, the four were no more.

I fell to my knees, agog at the Madness that had occurred.

The Tukudeka also saw and turned and fled.

And now, as I remain here, I know my own Death fast approaches.

Captain Crouch and I have waited through the day and into the night at the foot of the looming mound that bears the pillars. He snarls dire Imprecations and strange Musings. Miles Weiser and Eli Borah have not found us, nor have our four companions returned. The first two are surely dead or will soon be. We know not if we will ever see the Others again this side of Heaven.

As we sit and await our fate, growing hungrier and thirstier with each passing hour, I have spent these daylight and moonlit hours completing here the woeful story of our Secret Expedition.

We will attempt once more to sneak past our Watchful pursuers this night and find safety. But hear this, if we do not Succeed, as Dawn breaks, we shall walk between the pillars of our own desperate Volition.

Here lies certain Death for us. There, we can only hope we shall not enter the mouth of Hell.

I shamefully admit I have lived my life without God. I did not want to believe in Him or His laws as I went about my days and nights enraptured with the Occult and the Other. And yet, now, in my time of greatest need, it is to the God of my fathers that I turn. I pray to Him, not for life, but for forgiveness for the foolish way I lived before I let Him fill my Heart.

The crescent moon is high, and Captain Crouch says we must leave soon. My eyes fill with tears as I end this Record of our piteous, forsaken Expedition. I shall enfold it in Sheepskin and secrete it under a boulder.

Someday, I pray it will be discovered. If Ezra Crouch, Orril and Asa Munroe, Reuben Hale, Noah Handy, and I, Francis Masterson, are never seen again, know that we were once Good and True men, working to serve our Country and our uncertain God. I bid thee farewell.

May a Generous and Almighty God have mercy on our souls.

Li Jianjun shut the small volume. It was four o'clock in the morning but he was wide awake. The story was so bizarre he couldn't help but suspect someone had a very grand imagination. A Mormon Jules Verne, perhaps.

But what if it was true? He remembered Susannah Revere's letters. They had looked legitimate. Was this the reason she had never heard from her fiancé, Francis Masterson?

He had to tell Michael about it. Michael would know whether to believe it or not. Jianjun had seen too many strange things since meeting Michael to dismiss anything out of hand.

He called Michael's cell phone, but as expected, the call wouldn't go through. He tried the motels and hotels in and surrounding Salmon City asking for Michael, and still no luck. He called the Salmon City police who connected him with the county sheriff's search headquarters where he talked to a deputy who said he last saw Michael with some blonde woman.

That figures, Jianjun thought. And to think, I was worried about him.

He shut off the light and went to sleep.

He didn't know that for the past few hours, once again, his every step had been watched and recorded.

FORTY-ONE

Earlier that day, Hammill had stopped his ATV at the top of the mountain ridge and looked at the horses Charlotte Reed and her fellow search team had used, but now had abandoned. "Damn it all!"

It had taken longer than he expected to find three double-seat ATVs in the Salmon area, and then they had to rent U-Hauls to get them out to Polly Higgins' ranch. Once there, it had been child's play to follow the tracks of four horses into the wilderness, and they quickly closed the distance between them.

But just as the horses could not descend the steep mountain, neither could ATVs. Hammill and his men got off them, then ran, slipped and slid down the mountain. The pillars surprised them, but they believed the pillars meant they were near the end of the mission, that they would soon find the university group. Exhilarated, they jogged toward the pillars, but stopped when Charlotte Reed and the others came into view.

Hammill and his men dropped to the ground and watched.

Lightning flickered, then a strange rumbling thunder echoed through the valley although the sky remained clear. The men grew nervous, but Hammill kept focused as the searchers began to climb the mound.

He watched the searchers at the top as they stopped and talked, then saw a strange pirouette by Charlotte Reed and one of the men. He picked up his sat phone to give an update on his success at finding the pillars.

His sat phone didn't work, which made no sense. He smacked it against his palm then tried again.

"Aw, fuck!" Crawford, aka Crawfish, aka simply Fish muttered.

The Hammer looked up just in time to watch as, one by one, the searchers walked between the pillars and disappeared.

He nearly dropped the expensive communications equipment. "Holy shit!"

FORTY-TWO

NOTHING HAD CHANGED, AND YET EVERYTHING HAD. THE FIRST THING Michael noticed was that the tracks that had been going up the mound, were now going down it. They were on the other side; they had crossed over, but to what, he didn't know. Quade's mouth uplifted in a tiny smile while Charlotte and Jake stood still. They spoke not a word; their eyes said it all.

Michael turned slowly. The distant trees looked the same as those before, and the mountain ranges hadn't changed. Yet, the very air felt different, heavy, almost sandy.

Jake broke the silence. "It can't be," he said, looking down at the footprints. "I don't get it."

Even the phlegmatic Quade sounded excited. "It is said that the first and greatest alchemist, Hermes Trismegistus, used his alchemical powers to create a portal between worlds—in alchemical terms, to create a transformation."

"That's crazy," Jake said.

"Is it?" Quade asked. "Look around you. Open your eyes."

"Quade is right," Michael said. "The pillars are simply a visible part of the phenomenon. Their rumbling, thunderous sound is a warning that you're approaching an altered reality."

"It makes no sense," Jake insisted. "It's wrong."

"I'm going to try to go back," Charlotte announced as she walked through the pillars. Nothing happened. She remained in full view of the others. She then entered the pillars through the opposite direction with the same results. She went through forwards, backwards, around the pillars and then through. She even walked backwards between them. Nothing worked. "It's all right," she said, trying to project strength. "When we need to, we'll figure out a way."

Jake nodded at her even as the full impact of all seemed to build within him. "We knew we were going to have to find our own way back, and we will. But first we follow those tracks going down the mound. The students are here, alive, and we're going to find them."

Quade, Charlotte and Jake climbed down. Something held Michael back. He took the red stone from his pocket, the stone he had lifted from Lady Hsieh's lips. He had kept it with him since that day, feeling that somehow he would see her again. The color radiated even more vibrantly than before. "Lady Hsieh," he said softly, "are you here?"

A flock of crows circled the pillars. Caws, too loud, created a wall of noise. Then, a shadow. He put the stone back in his pocket and slid down the mound to the others. "Something's near, watching us. We've got to be careful."

A low growl sounded. They froze.

"What was that?" Charlotte asked.

"I don't know," Jake said, drawing his Smith and Wesson 327, with a five-inch barrel, eight round, .357 magnum. He was more comfortable with it than the Remington strapped on his shoulder.

Michael and Charlotte chambered their rifles.

"The beasts here could be different from those now in Idaho," Quade said. Even he sounded tense now. "We don't know what era this 'world' is from, how long it's been here, how the beasts evolved."

The creature shrieked now, louder, and a heavy musty odor wafted near.

"I think," Charlotte said, her voice small, "it's coming closer."

They backed away from the sound, then turned and quickly put some distance between themselves and whatever hid out there. They walked on a slight upward grade when Jake cried out. Horror on his face, he slowly moved toward some bushes.

One Adidas sneaker with the foot still in it lay before him, along with tufts of curly red hair. More gnawed and scattered remains were near.

Jake found torn clothing and an I.D. to confirm what he knew as soon as he saw the hair color.

They dug a shallow grave and buried as much of Ted Bellows as they could find.

FORTY-THREE

WASHINGTON D. C.

Jianjun sat in Starbucks, a grande mocha latte and cranberry-orange scone in front of him as he tried once more to reach Michael by phone and text. He kept getting "out of range" messages. That was the first time it had happened with a satellite phone, but he knew it was theoretically possible. He tried not to worry, telling himself that Michael was simply in a canyon where the satellite waves couldn't reach.

Jianjun would try again soon, but in the meantime he did further investigation of Phaylor-Laine Pharmaceuticals, Jennifer Vandenburg, and Calvin Phaylor.

He learned that Vandenburg's only child had progeria syndrome, a rare and fatal disease. In the archives of the *Wall Street Journal, Financial Times, Forbes* and *Bloomberg,* he read about Calvin Phaylor's sudden fall from glory. Those reports led him to the archives of the *New York Times,* and a fifteen-year-old article entitled "Death Stalks Group Seeking Answers to Life."

He read that Phaylor and PLP had sponsored an International Symposium on Genetics in Medicine to bring in top scientists from around the world. Two of them, Dr. Chou An-ming from China and Dr. Niels Jorgansen from Denmark, had died tragically the day before attending.

Jianjun nearly jumped out of his chair. Finally, a connection! He got himself a Frappuccino with whipped cream to celebrate and continued reading.

To calm the People's Republic of China's suspicions about Dr. Chou's deadly accident, the FBI investigated. Jianjun suspected Interpol and the CIA were also involved. Nothing was found according to news reports, but it was the beginning of the end for Phaylor. A year later, he was put on administrative leave for fiscal irresponsibility, and a year after that, he was dismissed. A search for a new CEO began. Milton Zonovich acted in the position, but eventually the board selected Jennifer Vandenburg.

From what Jianjun had read about progeria, Vandenburg would have known there was a problem with her daughter by the time she became CEO of the world's largest pharmaceutical company. Under her leadership, PLP launched some initiatives that had to do with genetics and stem cell research. Nothing helped Vandenburg's daughter, however.

Jianjun hacked into PLP's administrative and email records, but could find no inside information.

Both Jennifer Vandenburg and Calvin Phaylor lived in New York City. Time to schedule another trip.

FORTY-FOUR

From the moment Melisse stepped between the pillars, everything felt out of kilter. She tried to tell herself nothing had happened, but she couldn't ignore the way Ted Bellows had vanished from her sight. One minute he was at the bottom of the mound looking up at them; the next, he was gone.

The university group had scrambled off the mound and huddled together fearful and awestruck. Some insisted nothing had changed for them, and that it was Ted who had somehow disappeared, not them. The argument was far from resolved when they heard a loud, eerie shriek. They ran from the mound and the pillars.

They clung close to each other as they desperately made their way eastward, the direction they hoped would lead back to Telichpah Flat. They felt guilty about leaving Ted, wherever he was, but were too scared to stay near those unearthly pillars. All they wanted to do was go home. Not even Lionel Rempart argued about it.

Hungry and tired, they eventually stopped. They gathered wood for a campfire. Melisse and Devlin still had their metal canteens, so they at least could boil water to kill the *giardia protozoa,* an intestinal parasite that lived in the area's streams and creeks.

The moon was high when the forest erupted in a series of howls. They weren't the shrill cries of coyotes, and the group wondered if they were wolves.

"Does anyone have a gun?" Brandi asked.

When no one answered Devlin said, "I think the only one who did was fired."

Rempart tried not to think about stories he had heard of strange creatures found out here. "Any wild beasts are much more afraid of you than you are of them," he announced, hoping to quell fears by platitudes. Unfortunately, his voice shook.

"How does he know?" Brandi loudly whispered to Rachel.

"Everyone, get some sleep," Rempart ordered. "We have a long day tomorrow."

The students glanced at each other, every one of them too nervous and fearful to move until Melisse said, "He's right."

As the sun began to rise, Melisse awoke.

She unclipped a tracking device from the inside of her cargo pants pocket. The green light wasn't blinking. It looked dead. The tracking device kept tabs on where she was, so that, if the situation grew dangerous, she could be rescued. She suspected the electro-magnetic transmission that had stopped her watch had shorted the device.

The others still slept. She crept to the shelter of some trees. In another of the many pockets of her cargo pants she carried a phone. Dire emergencies only, she'd been told. This qualified.

The state-of-the-art phone looked like a Blackberry, but the watertight lead-titanium alloy case shielded it from everything short of a nuclear blast. It up-linked to a constellation of 66 low earth-orbiting satellites that blanketed the globe. Its high capacity Iridium battery used a solar charger to avoid any downtime.

It was as dead as the tracking device.

"What are you doing?" She jumped and spun around to see Vince approach. "I wanted to make sure you were okay," he said. "What's that? A phone?"

She put the phone back in its case and shoved it in her pocket while saying, "Phones don't work out here." He might be a nerdy little weakling, but he knew electronics. A high tech sat phone would cause questions she didn't want to answer.

She hurried back to the camp where others were stirring. Hunger had caused them to wake early.

"Shouldn't we go back to the pillars to see if we can find Ted?" Brandi asked. "First Brian, now Ted! I'm scared!"

"Ted probably couldn't climb up the mound," Devlin said. "I doubt we'll find him."

"I don't get it." Brandi began to sob. "I don't understand where we are! What's happening to us?"

The others started walking, leaving her behind.

Melisse soon noticed that Brandi wasn't following them. As much as she hated to, she went back to find her.

Brandi stood in a half crouch, looking all around and seeming all but frozen with fear.

Melisse marched closer when she smelled a foul odor. Leaves rustled; a twig snapped.

She put her hand at the back of her waist under her jacket and sweater and gripped a Beretta M9 semiautomatic pistol. It was warm against her skin, the familiar handle oddly comforting in this peculiar environment.

"Come on," she ordered Brandi. "Move it!"

"It's here," Brandi whispered.

A flash of movement. Melisse spun left, toward the brush, gun in hand.

A low growl rumbled, and then a strange beast, well over a hundred-fifty pounds and shaped like an enormous brown weasel stepped into view, its long snout in the air as if trying to analyze their scent. Then it rose up on its back legs, as tall as Melisse, its eyes yellow and malevolent, its claws long and glittering as if made of gold.

She had never seen, never heard of, anything like it. Trying hard to quell her shaking hand, she raised her gun. The beast's growls grew louder, fiercer, as if it knew what a gun could do. The lips curled and a snake-like forked tongue lashed out at them. Shocked, Melisse nearly dropped the Beretta. In a surge of pure muscle, the monster leaped.

Two hands on the gun, Melisse fired, hitting its shoulder. The beast seemed to pivot in mid-air, and her second shot missed it altogether. It ran for the cover of the brush.

She fired once more.

She heard the crackle of dead twigs behind her this time. She spun around, her gun again poised to fire.

"Stop! Don't shoot!" Devlin shouted.

She lowered the handgun as the whole group approached.

"Where did you get that firearm?" Rempart demanded.

"What were you shooting at?" Devlin asked, seeing the ashen pallor of her face.

"It was a...a mountain lion," she whispered, placing the gun in the holster at her back. She couldn't possibly have seen what she thought, and Brandi was too hysterical to contradict her. "It came at us."

Rempart looked ready to contradict her, but then caught himself. She wondered how much he knew about all this? "Why didn't you tell me you had a gun?"

Asshole! Melisse glared furiously at him. "What difference would my gun have made to you? At least I had one, or Brandi and I would be dead!"

"Perhaps I should be the one to hold it," Rempart said, his chin raised.

"Only if you can take it away from me."

Rempart backed away. "Let's get away from here." He turned to follow the students who were already hurrying away from the scary location.

"Yes," Melisse murmured. "It isn't dead. It might return."

Melisse took Brandi's arm and pulled the girl forward, irritation at Rempart momentarily blocking the shock and terror of facing that horrible creature. She dragged Brandi along, hoping to catch up to the others soon. But then she saw that everyone had stopped. *Run,* her mind cried. *Why didn't they keep going? What were they waiting for?*

Then she saw. They stood at the edge of a cliff, the descent too sheer and steep to climb down. There was nowhere to go but back, where monsters waited.

FORTY-FIVE

New York City

Jennifer Vandenburg quietly walked out of her daughter's bedroom, leaving the door open so she could hear if Felicity called her. The girl slept. Finally.

In a comfortable seating nook in her master bedroom, Vandenburg drew in several deep breaths, then settled back in a pale green wingback chair, a lamp table at her side. She was running out of time. Rempart still hadn't been found. She had arranged everything so carefully: Rempart, the sabbatical in Idaho, the field trip, even the maps. She had thought of everything, yet, she had nothing to show for it.

Her thoughts turned to the paramilitary group Phaylor had used years earlier. Was this strange disappearance the same as happened to them out there?

If trained military men couldn't survive, how could a professor and some students?

No! She refused to think that way. Her plans would work.

Some might have thought her crazy, but she had proof that she was right, and she clung to it like a talisman.

Years earlier, Calvin Phaylor had tracked down a bizarre set of bones found in Central Idaho. No one could identify exactly what sort of animal they had come from—some unclassified creature which made it easy to denounce the find as a clever hoax. But one thing no one could denounce was the scientific evidence that the bones had no normal age degeneration.

The cellular degradation seemed to have slowed down substantially. It was as if the creature had barely aged over the years, as if it could live almost forever.

As if it could be immortal ...

That find began Phaylor's obsessive interest in the area, an interest that led to his downfall and her rise.

Even now, after all she had learned, the rational part of her mind shouted that alchemy was bunk and a sham. But at a much deeper level, the concept that since everything in the physical world changed and developed, such change could be controlled, seemed right. Not only that, it was logical, and, dare she say, scientific. Since change could be sped up or slowed down, if slowed, life would naturally be extended, perhaps forever.

Her daughter's illness was living proof that change, the aging process, could be sped up. And if that was the case, then of course it could also be slowed down.

She lacked only the key to that change—a philosopher's stone. The book in Idaho explained how to create one, and therefore how to perform the change to save her daughter. Once she had that book, no one could stop her.

She would get the book. For Felicity's sake.

And, as the full ramifications of immortality struck her, she smiled. For Felicity's sake...and for her own.

FORTY-SIX

Rachel, the quietest but also the brainiest of the students, was the one who noticed a cleft in the cliff face. It sloped in a way that, being careful and using muscles they didn't know they had, the university group managed to descend.

They reached a flat clearing and were congratulating themselves when Rempart decided to make camp. As the oldest and least fit of the group, he felt ready to drop. He didn't even help gather firewood, but lay down and soon snored almost as loud as the beastly howls from the forest.

The others built a fire as Devlin and Melisse began to carve wood into sharp fishhooks. The others joined them and soon began braiding grass to form fishing lines and weaving strands of grass into nets. Their empty stomachs and the chill in the air focused them on their predicament. If they couldn't find their way out of here, once winter set in and the snows came, how long could they last?

Constantly sorrow over Brian, a nagging fear for Ted, and worry over strange creatures and dangerous landscapes hung over the group.

"I think it's time for a new plan," Vince said, pushing up his glasses. "We've got a long way to go. The weather is turning cold. I say we stay put and build ourselves shelter, find food, and store it to get us through the winter. It could snow any day. We've already woken up to frost. If it snows, and we aren't prepared, we'll die."

"Don't say that!" Brandi pressed clenched hands to her temples and began to cry.

The students turned quiet, fighting their own tears.

"We don't have time," Devlin said, "to find or prepare enough food to make it through the long winter. Once heavy snows hit, the mountain passes won't open until late April or May. That means we'll be stuck here five or six months. I'm not ready for that. We need to keep moving, to hurry."

"No way!" Vince clenched his fists. "Don't you know the dangers out there? Am I the only one who's ever heard stories of this area? About ghosts and old Indian tales of bad things and of people simply disappearing? That's what happened to *us*. It's time you faced it."

Rempart, awakened by the bickering, turned to Vince. "You've heard that?"

"It's a *wilderness*," Devlin ranted. "People get lost in the wilderness. What else is new?"

"There's something seriously wrong, and we need to stay put until we figure out just what's going on," Vince countered. "We can make it safe to stay here. We'll survive this if we all work together."

"I'm not staying, Vince," Devlin announced. "Who wants to travel with me?" He glanced at Rachel and she nodded.

"That's crazy!" Vince shouted. "You'll get yourselves killed!"

"Stop it!" Rempart ordered as he rubbed his eyes. "I've listened to both arguments. It's not likely we'll be rescued if we remain in one place in this god-forsaken nothingness. The only prudent thing to do is to head south right now. Surely, we'll find a major roadway before long. There, we'll find help."

"What if you don't?" Vince cried. "What if there's nothing out there?"

"You're being silly. We must all concentrate on making this work. Be positive, and get a good sleep," Rempart stated, lying back down and turning his back on them. "We'll start out fresh tomorrow morning."

"Who made you king?" Vince shouted. He stood, hands on hips, and faced the others. "What's wrong with you people?"

"Don't be so stubborn," Melisse snapped. "Trying to save ourselves is well worth any potential risk."

The others agreed with her.

Vince's face flamed at his idol's rebuke. "Like hell! You'll see." He stomped away from the camp, angry and embarrassed.

"I guess I should go get him," Devlin offered.

"Leave him alone," Melisse said. "He can't rush off simply because he doesn't get his way. I suspect he'll realize it soon enough."

❄

Vince was furious that the others didn't know better than to take chances with winter weather. He'd once been stranded in it as a child. His uncle thought it would be fun to drive out to Silver City, an old mining town south of Boise deep in the Owyhee Mountains. People were warned not to try to reach it in winter, but the interesting and colorful town was worth the trip.

The sun shone that day, the snow bright, white, and beautiful. They were high in the mountains, the frost-covered dirt road a narrow ribbon whose flatness and width were the only things that distinguished it from the rest of the sparkling white landscape. About five miles from their destination, the weather changed. Out of nowhere, ominous dark clouds gathered, and the wind kicked up, harsh and loud. They hadn't thought it would snow that day, but they were wrong. Thick, wet globules of snow and hail pelted the car and made it impossible to tell what was a road, and what was not.

The car went into a slide. Fortunately, it slid toward the hillside and not the drop-off since guardrails were unknown in most of rural Idaho. The car hit a snow bank. Every attempt to get it out caused the wheels to spin, wedging the car even deeper.

Vince, his uncle, and two cousins decided to walk back toward the paved road some fifteen miles away. Since no one inhabited Silver City in winter, no help would be found there.

They were pretty sure they would see a car coming their way before long. But they didn't. No other fools were on that road.

Even as a child Vince was small and somewhat weak, and soon he was exhausted. His mom had dressed him warmly, but he'd forgotten to take the mittens she'd put out for him, and even keeping his hands in his pockets, his fingers were soon numb.

One of his cousins wore light sneakers, and his toes became frostbitten.

By nightfall, Vince's mother had grown worried and called the sheriff's office. A deputy found the nearly frozen foursome about seven miles from the paved road.

Vince never forgot how cold and scared he'd been as the sun had sunk lower on the horizon, and he knew that night would be colder and lonelier than anything he'd ever experienced. He'd had nightmares for weeks thereafter.

He didn't know what was...

A sound, something indefinable, all but beyond hearing ...

He jumped to his feet and turned in a complete circle.

Nothing was there. At least, nothing he could see in the darkness.

Vince was no fool. He hadn't wandered so far away he couldn't see the glow of the campfire through the firs. Mrs. Norton hadn't raised her son to be an idiot, even though she had raised him alone when his father took off with another woman when Vince was only six years old.

He thought of a wolf, a bear, or mountain lion, or whatever had carried off Brian, or the monster Brandi swore attacked her and Melisse.

Vince assured himself he was simply nervous. Perhaps a tiny night creature made the sound. A jackrabbit. Maybe a badger or a beaver. Nothing dangerous would venture close to a campfire.

In fact, maybe he should return to camp.

But once there, how could he convince the others not to try to walk back to civilization? If they got caught in a blizzard, it would all be over.

Silence settled around him. Maybe he should simply tell them about his Silver City experience and remind them how quickly weather in the mountains could change. They all knew it. Well, maybe not Rempart who didn't seem to know anything except what he read in books. But perhaps none had ever actually experienced it.

Melisse was the smartest, the most experienced of the lot. She would listen to him. She had to.

Just then, two shapes moved toward him in the darkness of the pines. The moonlight behind them gave him an idea of their outlines, upright, like great hulking gorillas, or Sasquatch, or men.

They stopped, held perfectly still, and stared at him.

FORTY-SEVEN

MICHAEL, JAKE, CHARLOTTE, AND QUADE MADE CAMP. AFTER THE shock and horror of what had happened to Ted Bellows, they searched for footprints and found several that probably belonged to the university group. The footprints headed east. With renewed hope they followed them until it grew too dark to see. Eventually, they each fell into a restless, troubled sleep.

It seemed he had scarcely shut his eyes when Michael awoke to the lute-like sound of a *sanxian*. The melody sounded beautiful, intriguing. He had to see ...

Quietly, he left his small tent and sleeping bag and walked toward the gentle music. Moon and starlight in a cloudless sky lit the way. Instead of dry, brittle ground, a lush green garden of low grasses, moss, red peonies, and a mulberry tree spread before him.

With wonder, he continued on. Mist swirled around a pond filled with lotus pods, and by the bank, her back to him, a woman sat on a low bench and lightly strummed a *sanxian*. She was slender and wore an emerald green Chinese robe. Gold ribbons and mother-of-pearl combs held her long, heavy hair in elaborate coils.

He approached, but the setting made no sense. No placid waters or thick foliage existed in this high, arid land. And it had been night, but now sunshine warmed the day.

Was this heaven? If so, he was sorry he'd stopped believing in it.

The woman turned his way. He knew her at once.

"Come sit by me." She gave a small bow of the head as she gestured toward a small, second bench nearby.

He didn't recognize the words she spoke, yet by the time they reached his ears, as if the mists themselves possessed the power to translate, he understood. When he answered in English, the same translation seemed to occur. He sat at her feet. They were tiny, but had not been bound. That practice came many centuries after the Han dynasty. He was thankful she had not been made to suffer. He felt big and clumsy beside her, but her warm smile eased his awkwardness.

She had a teapot and two Chinese cups at her side. She poured him some tea. He thanked her and took a sip. He tasted it, smelled it, felt its warmth as it slid down his throat. He then set the cup aside. His gaze never left Lady Hsieh. She stared back at him in equal wonder.

"I'm dreaming," he said after a while. "That's the only explanation. But it's a pleasant dream." He smiled, as she did. Once again, a sense of connection with this woman, deeper and more profound than anything he'd ever known, jarred him.

"It's not a dream, but for you, it should be," she said softly. "I'm not of your world. And yet, you are the only one who can set me free. You have begun, but there is more work to do. Dangerous work."

She placed her hand lightly on his forearm. He covered it with his. The skin of her small, delicate hand was softer than the silk she wore. He felt its warmth. "You are real. I can touch you," he said. "How can that be?"

"You've been searching for me. I heard your call. It made me happy," she said shyly. She spoke as much with her eyes as with her lips. He felt lost in them, the fine lashes, the thin feathery brows that lifted and drew him closer with each word.

She pulled her hand free, but remained leaning towards him. He noticed the scent of peonies. "After you accomplish your work here, Michael, you must find your way back. That is where you will find what you seek. There is nothing here for you."

He could read the sorrow in her eyes and it filled his heart with profound sadness. "What is this place?" he asked.

"It is a place where time meets."

"This makes no sense."

She clasped both his hands with hers. "My grandmother taught me the ancient instruction that the alchemist Li Chao Kuin gave to the Han Emperor Wu Ti. I learned to transform the powder of cinnabar to a yellow gold that gave prolonged longevity. With such longevity I lived among the blessed *hsien*—beings—of the island of P'eng Lai. There, I could not die. That is the Chinese way of alchemy."

He shook his head. "I don't understand any of it."

"I don't expect you to," she said with a smile. "But you should know that I did wrong. What is existence without life? Without love? It is torture." Her dark brown eyes seemed to read his very soul. He had never seen anyone so beautiful. He felt her loneliness because it matched his own. "Be careful," she pleaded. "There are those who would stop you."

"Stop me from what?"

She dropped his hands. "From destroying this world. Destroying me."

Stunned, he refused to listen to such madness. "I would never hurt you."

She studied him as if committing to memory every inch of his face. Her tender gaze filled with regret. "How remarkable that you were the one who woke me from my immortal sleep. You are a good man, with a good heart, and"—she blushed—"very pleasing to look at. I wish ..." She stopped and sadly shook her head, unable to go on, to say what filled her heart.

This is madness. He fought against his too sudden, too strong feelings for her. *She's not real.* And yet, he wanted nothing so much as to touch her again, to hold her. "Tell me everything," he whispered.

She turned as if hearing something that only she could hear. "Time cannot be out of step in this way. It brings too much disorder, too much danger." She faced him with an intensity that reached his very core. "When the time comes, follow your intuition. It will save you. I'm sorry, so very sorry."

The image shimmered then faded, and he found himself standing alone on a scrub-covered hillside in the middle of nowhere. The moon set just beyond the mountaintops. He felt empty inside. Destroy her, she had said. He would as soon destroy himself. "No," he whispered, then louder. "No!"

Charlotte slept lightly and awakened suddenly. Whether because of a noise outside her tent, or the sudden quiet of the two owls that had been calling and answering all night, she didn't know. She rarely dreamed, yet in this place, she'd done nothing but dream of the dead.

Thoughts of the men who had been hunting her, who had killed her friends, jarred her into action. She took her gun and crept to the opening of the tent where she peered through the slit.

And saw Michael.

He acted arrogant at times, even cocky, with his intelligence and the successes he'd had, but it was almost as if he were putting on a show, a strong face to the world so that people wouldn't see the real Michael. She could sense that he held locked inside a deep sorrow, perhaps because she had done the same for so many years. Where she had burrowed into a mundane life to avoid facing all she had lost, he did the opposite. He seemed to seek danger in his travels, as if he used them as a means to run from his troubles, or perhaps, to run towards them. And he seemed to do so with little care or concern for the dangers he would face. Perhaps, she thought sadly, even welcoming them.

She wondered if he would talk to her.

Michael heard his name. He turned to see Charlotte standing outside her tent.

He spoke quietly so as not to wake the others as he approached. "I couldn't sleep. Strange dreams."

"You aren't the only one," she admitted. "You're trembling."

He wasn't aware of that until she mentioned it. He felt half frozen. She took his hand to draw him into the warmth of her tent. He knelt because the tent was small, and she touched his forehead to check for a fever.

"I'm not sick," he said, yet felt oddly comforted by her touch, her concern.

She sat, cross-legged, and he did as well, then she placed the back of her hand against his cheek. "You feel like ice. Get into the sleeping bag. You've got to warm up or you might become ill." She had him lie down and eased a corner of the bag over her cold feet and legs.

"What were you doing out there?" she asked.

He didn't answer the question—he wouldn't know how to. Instead he asked, "Do you believe any of this, Charlotte? A vortex to another time, another place. You're the realist. I want you to tell me I'm dreaming and none of this is real."

His words surprised her, and she studied him before speaking. "You're as much a realist as I am, Michael. Why do you say that?"

"I'm not sure." He stopped himself from saying all he wanted to, how, usually, he felt only emptiness, as if he was adrift and didn't know how to stop himself. But here, he had found an anchor ... and he doubted it was real.

Cold, she slid further into the unzipped sleeping bag with him, turned onto her side, bent her elbow into position and rested her head on her hand. "Tell me what's troubling you, Michael," she said. There was nothing sexual about her actions; she was merely seeking to understand his troubled mood.

"Do you know what it's like to feel empty inside?" he asked. "To wonder why you go through each day?"

"Yes," she admitted. "But I'm surprised to hear you say that. I would have thought you have everything—money, fame, an exciting profession that takes you all over the world, and I'm sure more women than you know what to do with. What more could you want?"

He answered without hesitation. "Perhaps ... to not feel hollow?"

Her blue eyes met his, and she nodded. She understood.

He remained silent, however. As much as he wanted to open up, he couldn't. He wasn't that way.

No longer was he trusting, able to "share" or to bare his soul. Once he had been, but no more. Once, he knew a woman—or thought he did—the two of them had grown up together. She knew his family, knew how cold and unfeeling it was, how everyone in it had ignored the youngest child—the boy named Michael. Only with her could he share his deepest secrets and reveal his wildest dreams.

And the way they had ended still haunted him.

He had loved her, but it hadn't mattered.

After that, women seemed to come and go in his life. He'd been "in lust" often enough, even to the point of contemplating marriage, but his instincts told him "happily ever after" didn't exist for him. Deep-in-the-heart-and-soul love was as alien to him as the galaxy of Andromeda. So he kept traveling as far and as fast as possible ... but he couldn't outrun himself.

Charlotte waited, her expression trusting and empathetic. What kind of fool was he? He opened up to a figment of his imagination, and wouldn't talk to this compassionate woman who had been through so much he should have been the one offering her comfort, rather than vice versa. Sometimes he disgusted himself. He forced himself to speak.

"I've tried to fill my days with people, possessions, places to go, and things to do," he whispered, "but nothing has worked out the way I expected. Or perhaps I simply expected too much."

"You never talk about your home, or your family," she said.

He thought about "home." But where was home for him? He had a house in California he never visited. It was a storage dump and mail drop, not a home at all. He had filled it with valuable possessions from his trips, and paid a housekeeper, gardener, security experts, and a bookkeeper to assure everything ran smoothly in his life. And for what? "There's not much to talk about."

"What's odd," she said softly, "is being here. This place is filled with ghosts. It has a sense of the Other. I suspect that appeals to you, Michael."

"The spiritual?" He scoffed. "I don't believe in 'the spiritual,' whatever that is." Thoughts came to him of Lady Hsieh. *Or, I didn't,* he thought.

The expression on her face told him she wasn't convinced. "Sleep, Michael," she whispered. "It will help."

"I may be able to now." He got out of the sleeping bag. "I'll give you back your bed."

She stepped out of the tent with him.

"You're a good person, Charlotte," he said. "Thank you."

He turned to leave. "Michael," she whispered. He turned, and she put her arms around him in a quick hug, then eased back and brushed her hand against his face in a gentle stroke. "Anytime you want to talk, Michael, I'm here."

"I know," he whispered.

With that she nodded and went back into her tent.

To his surprise, he found himself oddly comforted by the somber but understanding woman. He got into his sleeping bag and fell into a fitful sleep dreaming of the sound of a *sanxian.*

FORTY-EIGHT

Derek Hammill and his men camped near the pillars. He kept someone on guard the entire night so that if and when the four searchers reappeared, he could follow them. But they didn't reappear.

It was morning. Decision time.

They could stay here and fail in their mission, or continue on.

Hammill was no fool. He and his men had seen the students' tracks as well as the searchers'. They saw that all the tracks went up the mound to the pillars, and none came back down. What the hell was up there? Where did they all go?

His men were spooked. It had been simple to get someone to stand guard. No one could sleep. He heard them talking among themselves about the pillars, the lightning and thunder around them and nowhere else, the strangeness of the area.

He had tried to make outside contact, to request direction. Should they follow or not? But his sat phone had crapped out. He believed the same static or electricity or whatever in the hell caused the damned pillars to vibrate and make noise had also knocked out communications.

He could walk back until the phone worked again, but who knew how many miles that would be? He suspected they would have to climb the mountain, get out of this valley. That would take hours.

If, after all that, he received an order to continue on between the pillars, the searchers would be so far ahead they might be difficult to track.

Following fresh tracks was one thing; following those more than a day old required a lot more skill. Even now, it would take a while to catch up.

No, Hammill reasoned, he didn't have time to go back for instructions. He had to make his own decision.

People didn't disappear into thin air. Something up there simply couldn't be seen from ground level. The men were nervous, but they were seasoned fighters, and had done enough wet work for PLP that they couldn't stop now.

He stood. "We're climbing up there, and we're going through. We will not abandon the mission."

FORTY-NINE

MELISSE AND DEVLIN INSPECTED THE AREA WHERE VINCE HAD GONE to sulk the night before. He had run back to camp howling, screaming, and blithering that human-looking monsters had stared at him and wanted to kill him. Or eat him. Or tear him limb from limb.

The two found no tracks or signs that anyone or anything had been out there.

The group broke camp and hiked for two hours before they spotted a creek. They stopped. Hunger made them weak. They had little hope of catching fish with their wooden hooks and grassy lines, but they needed to try.

Rachel and Brandi searched for nuts, roots, and berries. Rempart and Vince found firewood. Devlin and Melisse fished.

Devlin had fished many times with his father. Now, slack-jawed, he looked down into the creek. Suppressing a whoop of joy so he didn't scare the fish away, he cast his line.

Salmon and steelhead trout were anadromous fish. Born as freshwater fish in the headwaters and tributaries of the Salmon River, they made an eight hundred mile journey down the Salmon to the Snake River, the Columbia, and the Pacific Ocean. After living as ocean-faring fish for one to three years, depending on the species, they found the mouth of the Columbia River for the reverse journey upstream, climbing more than 7,000 vertical feet in altitude, to arrive back at their spawning grounds as freshwater fish once more.

With the introduction of dams on the Snake and Columbia, the fish faced eight dams over the course of their journey. It took phenomenal strength to make it past the dams and then leap against the current, far more than any human could manage. Before the dams were built, salmon nearly choked the Pacific Northwest streams. Despite "fish ladders" and other aids to migration, few fish now survived the journey.

Wild salmon and steelhead had disappeared altogether from many waterways.

Or so everyone thought.

Here, the fish were plentiful enough that even without decent hooks, lines, or bait they were biting. A stack of fish quickly formed.

"Any thoughts on what this place is?" Devlin asked after a while.

"Not really," Melisse replied.

"I think it's some sort of glitch in time and space. Like the Bermuda Triangle."

"That's original," she said sarcastically.

"You got a better idea?"

"Yes. Stop scaring the fish."

He concentrated on his line and soon had his eye on a big steelhead circling near. Thoughts of grilling it over an open fire made him salivate. He sat still, hoping it would go after his bait, when he noticed something shimmer downstream, on his side of the bank. He stared a moment. "What the hell? It looks as if the ground is moving."

"You're dreaming." Melisse concentrated on snaring one of the largest trout she had seen that day. The wooden hooks required a well-timed sharp snap of the wrist. "Got it!"

Devlin stood. "Whatever it is, it's coming this way. Fast!"

Melisse glanced where he stared as she pulled in the fish. She stood. The very earth seemed to ooze toward them. Her eye followed the hump in the ground from off in the distance, forward, toward her and Devlin just as she saw something jump at her.

A large black bug landed on the leg of her cargo pants. Another on her boot. Then two. Three. A dozen. She swatted at them, trying to get them off her.

Devlin jumped back. "What the fuck!"

Melisse smacked the bugs from her boots in an effort to keep them from crawling up under her pants legs. "They're like some kind of giant beetle." At that moment, the line she continued to hold went lax. Where a long, plump trout had dangled moments before, she now saw a skeleton covered with bugs.

"The fish!" Devlin yelled. As he spoke, the beetles covered their food supply, devouring the fish in seconds, and continued toward them.

"They're flesh eaters!" Melisse cried. "Run!"

They ran, yelling, toward the camp. At first the others thought they were making some kind of unfunny joke. But then, they watched the earth become a gelatinous, oozing mass that seeped toward them.

Rempart stared as if he couldn't believe what he saw. "Impossible! Dermestidae, or flesh-eating beetles, are small and slow and like damp, moist environments. This isn't the climate they live in."

"Whatever they are, you'd better not let them swarm you!" Melisse shouted.

Everyone ran, swatting at the biting, stinging creatures.

"We can't outrun them," Devlin shouted. "We've got to get in the creek. Don't stop!"

The creek water moved rapidly, and they couldn't tell its depth. They had no choice but to jump in. The ice cold water reached their waists and the strong current knocked them off their feet. They tried to go straight across, but the current pulled them downstream. They clutched any large rocks or boulders they could find to prevent being swept away. Devlin grabbed hold of Rachel, the lightest, who was having the most difficulty fighting the water's strong draw.

From the opposite bank, someone threw a rope at them. "Grab hold, lads," a voice said. "And ladies." Despite their shock, they gratefully followed the order.

One by one they were towed from the water by two men wearing faded camouflage clothing. The men had neatly trimmed beards and hair, and looked to be no more than thirty years old. Strangely, each carried a long bow and a quiver of arrows.

The men hustled the university group away from the banks, then scoured the water. The beetles had stopped at the creek's edge and faded back into the land. "Water is too fast for them," the second man said. "Fine and clever thinking to hurl yourselves into the flow." He smiled pleasantly. His accent, like the first man's, sounded odd and unrecognizable.

Rempart and the students stared at the strangers, scarcely able to believe what they saw, even as they shivered from cold, exhaustion and fright.

"Come along now," one of the strangers said, looking back into the trees. "We must hurry. This is not a safe area come nightfall."

"Who are you?" Rempart asked.

"The name is Sam Black, and this is my cousin, Arnie Tieg. The village is not far."

"Village?" Rempart asked, looking from one to the other and then at Melisse. "Are you saying there's some sort of town out here?"

"Let's go," Sam Black said.

"Wait!" Rachel cried. "Where's Devlin!"

FIFTY

Alexandria, Virginia

Jianjun got out of the taxi he'd taken from the Van Dorn Metro station. A small white and yellow house, complete with a manicured lawn and flower beds, stood before him.

Michael had never contacted him, despite the quantities of information he had sent about the pillars and their history, PLP, and Jennifer Vandenburg. Jianjun was tempted to pursue the PLP angle by going to New York City to talk with Vandenburg and Calvin Phaylor, but he hesitated to do that without checking with Michael first. Also, a line of inquiry near Washington D. C. needed to be followed before he left the area.

Anthropology Professor Emeritus Thurmon Teasdale had created the map Jianjun sent to Michael. Obviously, Lionel Rempart considered it of great value, but Jianjun could not figure out why, nor exactly what area it covered. He needed more information.

He tracked down Professor Teasdale's widow. He took a deep breath, walked up to the front door, and rang the bell.

Lurline Teasdale was an elderly woman who readily spoke with Jianjun and didn't ask him for credentials or anything else to prove who he was. Instead, she warned him against looking into the "secret expedition" that had followed Lewis and Clark. She was convinced that her husband's interest in their story had somehow brought on his death.

"That discovery excited Thurmon beyond anything I can remember," she explained over cups of tea and a platter of sugar cookies as they sat in her cozy living room. "He gained access to an old journal in the Smithsonian. There had been rumors about such an expedition, but never before any proof."

"So he believed it was real," Jianjun probed.

"Absolutely! "</p>

"And this all happened about fifteen years ago?" Jianjun asked.

"Good gracious no. It happened over thirty years ago, back when Thurmon was a young professor. A couple of his anthropology students found the journal. They were foreign students, I believe, and quite interested in the Mormon culture, which foreigners tend to find rather exotic. In any case, the students thought the journal was fiction, but Thurmon believed it all quite true. There were too many details that corresponded to other information Thurmon had. For example, the journal writer spoke of the woman he loved. A young woman spent her entire life sending letters to Thomas Jefferson asking him what had happened to her fiancé. When Thurmon told me that I found the story so very touching and sad, I'll admit it made me cry for her, poor dear."

Jianjun nodded and said nothing. The thought of a woman's tears—any woman's—made him nervous.

Mrs. Teasdale also told him that Thurmon had spent several summers in Idaho back in those days, seeking the pillars described in the journal, and any signs of the lost Mormon settlement. He had no success, and eventually he ran out of money to pursue that particular project. He gave up his dream until about fifteen years ago when an extremely wealthy individual contacted him about his early studies. That person convinced him to create a map of the area he had explored.

Thurmon did so, but where that area was, Lurline had no idea.

Thurmon had been quite excited about getting back into that line of study, but only one day after completing and delivering the map, he had a heart attack and died.

Men often have such heart attacks, she had to admit, yet Thurmon never had any hint of illness.

"Tell me, Mr. Li," she said, her gaze clear and sharply intelligent, "what really brings you here? I haven't spoken to anyone about Thurmon's map since Professor Lionel Rempart came here last year to ask for a copy. Now, I learn on the news that he and his students are lost in Central Idaho."

"We're trying to find them," Jianjun admitted. "I had hoped you could help."

She apologized that she had no further information, and soon after, he thanked her for her hospitality and left.

He felt like someone who had been handed pieces of a jigsaw puzzle. All the pieces might be there, but he couldn't yet fit them together, and had no idea of what it would look like when finished.

FIFTY-ONE

"Fuck!" Fish said, his one expression for all situations. He kept an AR-15 on his shoulder. "We didn't sign up for this."

Having led his team between the pillars, Hammill kept his expression neutral. But Fish had it right. The military had a term for it—FUBAR—fucked up beyond all recognition. He refused to admit it to his team though. Not to anyone. Not yet, anyway.

At least he didn't have to worry about admitting it to his boss since every piece of electronic equipment they had was DOA. PLP's piss-poor intel had put his team at risk. When he saw the four searchers disappear between those pillars, Hammill should have turned around and headed back to Salmon City. Back to broads, booze, and a back rub. Instead, the whole team followed, and now they were in trouble. Including him.

PLP had sworn nothing was dangerous here. Nothing "weird."

Weird, his ass. This was fucking unbelievable.

By habit he kept checking the sat phone, but it had crapped out even before they went through the damned pillars.

Maybe this was the long lost redneck version of Atlantis.

"Fish, I need a perimeter," Hammill ordered as soon as they had descended the mound on which the pillars stood. "I want to know what the hell this is."

The PTT didn't work either, and they had no idea why not.

"Fuck," Fish said, which meant, "I don't know either."

Hammill found footprints heading east, back to the area they'd come from. If they belonged to the students, they might manage to save themselves.

It wouldn't be bad, he thought nervously, if he and his men ended up at Telichpah Flat to discover that this mission was over. They'd have made a hell of a lot of money for a few days out in the bush. Damn good for a bunch of bullet sponges.

Soon, though, he and his men noticed something was wrong, although they couldn't quite put a finger on it. They told themselves that they must be a little off their direction. Hammill tried to use his compass, but the needle went around in circles. And the GPS had bellied up along with their sat phone.

FUBAR.

FIFTY-TWO

DUSK FELL AS THE UNIVERSITY GROUP REACHED WHAT ONE OF THEIR strange rescuers, the one named Sam Black, had called "the village." Upon first hearing the word, Melisse's heart had leaped. People and civilization. Electronics. Means of communication. But then, as the group stepped out of the forest, and she caught her first glimpse of it, her excitement died.

The land directly in front of them had been cleared for the distance of a football field before reaching a ten-foot high wooden fence with stakes at the top. Visible above the fence were only a single large building and what looked like a guard tower.

Melisse hoped this wasn't a trap. Rempart and the other students had immediately trusted Black and Tieg, and treated them like saviors. Melisse wasn't so sure. Also, her thoughts kept turning back to Devlin. Rachel swore he had helped her grab the rope to be pulled to safety, but then she lost sight of him. The rocky creek bank offered no tracks or other solutions. Black and Tieg seemed to think they had pulled him out of the water, and that he purposefully hid. If so, their looks implied, he would be sorry. They had refused to spend more than twenty minutes searching for him for fear of being caught outside the village at night. To do so, they claimed, was a death sentence.

As they entered the village, Melisse saw how small it was. The two-story building and guard tower were in the center. Located around them like numbers on the face of a clock stood six small log huts at the 2, 3, 4 and 8, 9, 10 o'clock points. At 12 o'clock were animal pens and a stable, and at 6 o'clock were a large storage shed and a couple of outhouses. All the structures were made of logs. They had no glass windows, only shuttered openings and doors. The walkways were not paved or cobbled, but what appeared to be hard-packed gravel.

Four men came out of the bleak central building. All had a military bearing although they had long hair and beards. Their baggy-legged camouflage clothing was clean, but old and patched.

Six huts, six men. Melisse scanned the area. Where were the women? The children? Normally, a village meant mail delivery, telephone lines, and radio reception. But that didn't seem the case here. Right now, she'd settle for a dirt road to civilization.

A man with an air of authority stepped forward from the others. His brown hair, gray hair at the temples, had tight waves, and his heavy-lidded eyes looked as if they'd seen all the sorrows of the world. "I'm Thaddeus Kohler, the mayor of this village. I bid you welcome."

"Mayor?" Rempart said, standing straighter. "Then you must be a man of law. These are a group of students and I'm a professor. Please help us get back to civilization—"

"Are we not civilized?" Kohler interrupted, arms out, palms upward.

Rempart gawked.

"Who are you people?" Melisse demanded. "And what is this place?"

Kohler gave her a long, lingering gaze, as if simultaneously surprised, amused, and impressed that she would speak up so boldly. "We are simple villagers. Nothing more." He asked their names and then introduced his companions, a jaunty, smiling Gus Webber, a youthful and serious Will Durham, and one he called the elder of the group, Ben Olgerbee, although he couldn't have been much over fifty.

"What village is this?" Rempart asked. "How did it come to be here? Do you have telephones, or other communication with the outside world?"

"As for your last question, I'm afraid not." Kohler's face was stern. "As to the first, we found the village empty when we arrived."

A look of dismay passed between Rempart and Melisse. "We simply want to get home," Rempart said. "I'm sure there's a huge reward for anyone who helps us return. Can you do that?"

"The only true reward," Kohler said, his eyes blazing and his voice low and rumbling, "is an eternal one after a life well spent. Now, please join us for supper."

They called the large central building the "community house." The inside consisted of two rooms, a gathering room on the first floor and an upstairs sleeping loft. A long wooden table and six chairs stood in the center of the gathering room. Several work tables lined the walls and atop them were a variety of old tools and strange implements. Animal furs were piled in a corner, and pottery bowls and dishes had been stacked on primitive shelves. A large fireplace and hearth held crude pots, and cooking utensils. On a grate, a kettle of stew cooked. Rempart and the students were so hungry, they were nearly brought to tears at the aroma.

A ladder led to the loft which had both shuttered windows and a door that currently opened to an eight-foot drop and gave Melisse an idea of how high the snow piled up here in winter.

Everything was rustic and ill-formed, which was a surprise given that each man wore an expensive, modern firearm on his hip. It seemed as if the university group had fallen into a well-armed Dark Ages.

The men brought extra chairs and stools with them. The university group sat on one side of the table, and five of the village men on the opposite side. Ben Olgerbee kept watch in the tower while the others ate. Melisse could see the villagers truly believed that something dangerous was out there. Not only, as Sam Black and Arnie Tieg had said, did dangers lie outside the village at night, apparently the inside was also unsafe if unguarded.

Thaddeus Kohler, the supposed mayor, stood. His companions bowed their heads as he muttered in low, sonorous tones, "May Almighty God grant us blessings for that which we are about to receive, and we give Him thanks for bringing these people to us."

Something about the prayer caused a chill along Melisse's shoulders. The feeling passed quickly, however, as Will Durham dished out the rabbit stew, and Rachel carried a bowl to each of the diners. They served flat, hard bread with it. The stew tasted delicious. Even Brandi ate without complaining.

No one spoke until the meal ended.

"Want something to help wash down your supper?" Gus Webber asked with a grin, holding a jug toward Rempart. He explained that they distilled wild tubers to make the liquor. Melisse watched Rempart take a sip and gag, much to the amusement of the villagers. When the jug came to her, she found it as potent and raw as pure alcohol. The village men's reaction to the moonshine made it clear that drinking a good quantity was part of their evening ritual.

The villagers attempted to be friendly, but Melisse saw something cold and calculating in them, especially in the way they looked at her, Rachel and Brandi. Clearly, they hadn't been around women in quite a while.

The only one who didn't make her uneasy was Will Durham. His gentle brown eyes regarded the university group with a compassion that seemed genuine, but also sad. She wondered why.

"Maybe you can tell us now, Mr. Kohler," she began as the jug took a second trip around the table, "how you and your men came to be here, and why you have made this your home instead of leaving?"

Kohler glanced at his men, one by one, as if to gain their agreement before he spoke. Several nodded. "We arrived here over a dozen years ago. No matter how hard we tried, we were unable to return to our land, to our own people. This is a strange place with unnatural creatures the likes of which we have never before witnessed. We watch the pillars in hopes that one day, someone will come through them who understands them, and will be able to lead us back."

"My, God," Brandi blurted out in distress, then clasped her hands to her mouth.

"Surely," Rempart said, "you aren't suggesting we're trapped here."

"We've tried everything, but the pillars do not change. They are unmoved by our plight."

"You make them sound as if they're alive," Rempart said with a nervous chuckle.

"Aren't they?" Kohler stood. "It is time to retire for the night. Durham, take the two men to the stable and make up bedding for them. The women will sleep here, *alone and undisturbed.* Tieg, tell your cousin he must guard more alertly than usual tonight, for we have precious newcomers to protect." He glanced at the women. "I leave it to you to clean up after Mr. Olgerbee, who is now in the guard tower, has completed his supper. All must work here."

With that, he and the other men left the community house.

This was a strange land, filled with strange noises, Michael thought, as he and the others made camp after another day of wandering.

A guttural sound caused him to stop setting up his tent, every nerve alert. A banshee-like shriek made his blood run cold. What was out there? Whatever it was had been following them. At times he noticed a musty smell. At other times, a sharp, acrid stink. The air would turn thick, as if it were humid, but without moisture.

And beyond all that was Lady Hsieh. Was she real, or was he going mad? He couldn't tell anyone about her. Not Charlotte, who was the most sympathetic but the most realistic. Certainly not Jake, who would definitely want to send him to a looney bin. Not even Quade, who had the most understanding of this unnatural state, but seemed strangely devoid of human understanding or empathy.

Quade bothered him more and more as time went on. The man watched and thought. He explained theory, but offered little explanation of what was happening here. Quade knew a lot more than he said.

Michael didn't trust him.

FIFTY-THREE

Melisse didn't know what to make of the village men. They treated her and the others well enough, except that Lionel and Vince were forced to sleep in the stable.

The first full day, the villagers taught them to dig up a small round root, a sort of primitive parsnip, and mash them so that they could be dried as meal for the winter. The village men seemed to be planning for them to remain through the winter and needed to increase the amount of food stored. It also meant the village men didn't plan to kill them ... at least not all of them, and not right away.

Today, they were separated, and all given a variety of chores.

Melisse grew tired of shelling beans and stepped out of the community house and looked around. "Mayor" Thaddeus Kohler chopped wood some distance away. The close-mouthed man aimed to intimidate with his stern, military bearing. She decided to see what she could find out from him.

"Do you think we'll have time to get out of these mountains before the winter snows hit?" she asked when she reached his side.

He stood his ax on end as his gaze raked over her. "Why would you want to try? It could be dangerous."

"We want to go home."

"Not a good idea." He returned to chopping.

"We just need some food, some warm clothes," Melisse said. "We had bad luck and our things were stolen. Perhaps you can tell us how to get out of here."

He slammed the ax into the stump of a tree trunk where it stuck. "You aren't going anywhere," he said brusquely.

"Are we prisoners?" she asked.

His sharply angled face crinkled into a grotesque smile. "You don't have to be. There's nowhere for you to go. The sooner you get used to it, the better off you'll be." He continued chopping.

She put her hand on his arm. "You're not getting off that easily. What is this place? Why can't we find anything we've known—no towns, no highways?"

"I don't know what you're talking about."

"Of course you do! Tell me!"

He looked down at her hand with a smirk, as if he found her toughness amusing.

She drew back her hand, and couldn't hide the bleakness in her voice as she added, "We went between two pillars and our world changed."

His formidable presence bristled, but then his eyes met hers. The temptation struck to turn and run from what she saw there—a deep all-consuming coldness coupled with understanding almost beyond human ken—as if he knew so much about the world and life that he no longer cared.

"So it did," he muttered. "I must remind myself how frightened all of you must be. How peculiar you must find all this and find us."

He fell silent. She struggled to remain and speak to him. "Have you been here long?"

His jaw clenched. He looked at her a long while before he spoke. "Yes, more than thirteen years. My men and I were sent here on a mission and have been unable to go back."

She sucked in her breath. "Thirteen years?"

He nodded.

"What...what kind of mission?"

He shrugged. "Scouting. Nothing special. I was a major in the Army, retired—"

"The U.S. Army?" she blurted.

"Yes. Why?"

She almost said something about his accent. None of the men here sounded like Americans, although their accents weren't "foreign-sounding" either. "Just curious. Please continue."

"I saw this as a way to pick up some easy money. Central Idaho—severe climate, worse topography, grizzlies, maybe even a wolf pack or two—and then home. I could handle it. Or so I thought."

She nodded.

"You?" he asked, his eyes like gray flint.

She told him how Rempart and the anthropology students had become lost, how she was on a mission to find them ... "and then home," she added. He found it within himself to smile as her words echoed his.

"Did you build those cabins?" she asked.

"No. We found everything here. I suspected this is what we were sent to find. I heard rumors of some expedition years ago—around the time of Lewis and Clark—that got lost in this wilderness. They must be the ones who built the cabins and lived here."

"And then?" she asked.

"I don't know. No graveyard, if that's what you're asking," he replied. "Maybe that means they got out, that they found a way home. For their sakes, I hope so."

"That's a nice thought," she said. "But doubtful. Or do you have proof?"

A strained, fierce look came over him. "Proof? You question me?"

The sudden change in him startled her. "I simply want to know—"

"Enough! What is of more interest to me is the here and now." He stepped closer to her, at once threatening and something more as his voice turned soft, cold, and deadly. "For example, I know that you and your friends need us far more than we do you. If you died at this moment, it wouldn't affect us one bit. And you could die or disappear in an instant." He snapped his finger. "Like that."

Her eyes widened at the sudden implied threat, and he gave his cruel, skeletal smile again. "Also," he continued, his hand swiftly clasping her jaw and lifting so her eyes met his, "I'm all that stands between you three females and some of my men giving into their baser instincts. I suggest you keep that in mind as well."

He walked away.

His words, his threats, worried her. And apparently, the village men had no more idea of how to leave here than she did.

But she knew how to keep warm in a storm, to build snow shelters, and to use her flint to burn combustible materials. Sacks of dried meal were in the storage building. If she stole one or two sacks, she could make it last long enough to get out of the mountains to lower, warmer climates.

If she got away, and somehow, miraculously perhaps, managed to find her way out of this strange land, she could return with help to rescue the others. She felt confident she could do it, and equally sure Lionel and the students could not.

That night, Melisse used the pretext of going to the outhouse as a means to reach the storage hut. She first wrapped thick fur blankets around herself in the shape of a hooded robe to keep warm, and then used a smaller blanket to make up a knapsack in which she put a sack of meal plus knives, flints, candles and anything else she could easily carry that might be helpful, and set out.

The village men guarded their guns and rifles well, so those she couldn't steal.

She headed east.

She traveled slightly over an hour when she heard something following her.

A beast, tall as a man, but hairy, its fur the color of flesh, appeared in front of her. The nose was flat, the eyes spaced far apart, and the ears small and pointed. Long claws and even longer teeth looked sharp and frightening. When it snarled, its teeth appeared a dark yellow, and dripping with some sort of mucous. The eyes were sharp and eerily intelligent.

She pulled out a long knife. She had been trained in hand-to-hand combat; she could handle it. Another beast appeared behind her.

Then a third, a fourth, a fifth.

She had expected to encounter one beast, and to fight it off, but not an entire pack.

All were large and misshapen. Some were tall and walked upright; some walked on all fours. Some had six legs, insect-like, yet furry as mammals. Others didn't seem to have fur, but instead a hard shell. Strangely, all had some part of their body that glittered like gold.

One snarled and roared hungrily, and soon all the others took up the cry. The forest shook with the sound.

They moved forward, their eyes fixated on her, poised to spring.

She heard a loud *thwack!* The forward-most beast fell with a long arrow piercing its brain.

The others fled as a volley of arrows flew at them.

Kohler, Durham and Tieg stepped out from the brush, long bows in hand.

Melisse stared at Kohler and the others who had saved her. They must have followed her closely and knew those creatures were out there. "Those beasts," she said, "they look like mutants of some sort. What are they?" She started towards the one that had fallen.

"Stop!" Kohler hurried toward her. "They're diseased. Keep away, or we may not be able to save you if you become infected."

Melisse froze. "But ... it looks like its claws are made of gold!"

"You would be wise to forget about them," Kohler warned. He pushed her to walk in front of him toward the village.

They walked in silence back to the community house.

Once there, Kohler's face twisted into an ugly, brutal grin. "I don't blame you for trying to escape," he said. "If I were somewhere I didn't want to be, I'd be doing the same thing. Unfortunately, my understanding does not equal my forgiveness. You must, of course, be punished for your crime."

A chill went down Melisse's back, but she said nothing and entered the building alone.

FIFTY-FOUR

GOMEZ KEPT HIS AR-15 ON HIS SHOULDER. HE WAS ON NIGHT patrol. Alone. The Hammer sent him out to keep watch so the others could get some sleep. Tomorrow night would be his turn to sleep, if he could.

He doubted it. This place was too screwed up. The Hammer wouldn't admit it, but Gomez sensed that even he was on edge.

A heavy, musty odor drifted toward him, damp earth mixed with something decaying. Perhaps, he thought nervously, perhaps the smell of death.

The scent grew stronger. Everything in him wanted to run back to the others, wake them, and tell them something was wrong. Instead, he took a deep breath. He needed to check the perimeter, control the situation, neutralize the danger. Only after that, if he still believed a threat lurked, would he disturb the others.

The last thing he needed or wanted was anyone mocking him for being scared.

A dark blur passed in front of him.

He jumped. *I'm just seeing things.* Of course these surroundings looked dark and mysterious. Probably just some large branches of a tree blowing in the wind, he told himself.

Except that no wind blew.

He had spooked himself, that's all. Nothing was out there.

Again, a dark blur whistled by, eye level. His blood ran cold. The thick, heavy stench ventured so close he tasted it with every breath.

He gripped his rifle tighter and shifted it so he could quickly aim and shoot the way he'd been trained to do. Maybe he had been wrong not to warn the others. Slowly he backed toward his comrades. Something neared him, closing in. He couldn't hear it; he couldn't see it. But he knew it lurked there.

The world seemed to slow down, so slow he could almost see it spinning on its axis. A sharp pain touched his neck, then something red and warm splashed in front of his face, every individual droplet visible. He lifted his hand to his neck, touched the torn, jagged skin. Blood. Too much blood.

Long, sharp claws ripped through his clothes, through his skin from chest to groin, piercing and slicing. As he watched his stomach torn from his body and lifted into the air, he opened his mouth, but no sound came. He fell to the ground, silently praying for the mercy of death.

No one said a word.

When their companion hadn't woken them at the end of his night patrol duty, they went in search.

Now, the Hammer and his men looked down at the body and wondered what could have done that to a man. After they buried Gomez, they walked away from the grave.

"This is wrong, man." Nose spat out the words. "This is so wrong."

"Fuck," Fish muttered, which meant he agreed.

"It had to have been a grizzly," Hammill said. "Nothing unusual. Nothing supernatural. We increase our patrol. No one goes it alone. We watch each other's back."

A twig snapped.

They pulled their guns and aimed them in the direction of the noise. They aimed at each other.

Hammill took out his nyala hunting knife, strong, sharp, and brutal. Whatever was out there, whatever did that to Gomez, wasn't going to get away.

Nose found a blood trail. Hammill led the group as they hunted it, following it deep into the forest until the smell told them they were near.

Hammill saw it first, and his courage nearly gave out at the sight. The creature looked more apelike than anything he had ever seen in the Americas. The possibility of this being the infamous Sasquatch flashed through his mind before he dismissed it. For one thing, it was no bigger than a man. It had to be some kind of bear.

He motioned his men to stand still, to stop talking.

It turned at that moment. With a roar, its mouth opened, baring fangs.

Hammill's grip tightened on the knife. The creature leaped, and he felt its fangs dig into the arm he raised to protect himself.

He stabbed at the monster's gut, twisted and ripped upward. He didn't want to think he heard his own voice screaming, joined by his men as they unleashed all the fear and anger they had held inside since entering this strange land.

Blood squirted onto his face, his hair, his hands, and he didn't know if it was his own or that of the creature as his men joined in the frenzied attack. They also used knives. They stabbed it over and over. They wanted it to suffer. They wanted to kill it in the same way that it had slaughtered Gomez. Still, it fought hard.

Then the creature slumped down, its life gone.

None of the men looked back at it. They didn't know, and didn't care to know, what it was. They dragged their leader away to flush his bites with antiseptics, sew him up, and try to ignore the panic-stricken dread that consumed them all.

FIFTY-FIVE

MICHAEL REACHED THE SPINE OF A HIGH, JAGGED RIDGELINE, AND then dropped down to lie flat on the ground. He motioned for Charlotte, Jake, and Quade to do the same as they crept to his side at the edge of a cliff.

Charlotte gaped in wonder at the scene below.

Beyond the sheer drop she saw a clearing, and within it, a fenced compound. It appeared to be a grim, bleak place. The smoke came from the chimney of a tall, central building. A figure sat in a tower beside it. She wondered what he guarded against.

"I saw a man and woman carry firewood into the compound," Michael said. "The man appeared middle-aged, wavy brown hair streaked with gray. The woman was tall, fit, with short blond hair."

"Could be Melisse Willis," Jake said. "But the man wasn't one of the missing."

"She didn't look or act like a prisoner," Michael said.

"Women's looks can be deceiving," Quade murmured, causing Charlotte to give him a quick glance.

"I don't think it's a good idea to let them know we're here until we learn more about them," Michael said.

The man in the guard tower left it, but no one replaced him.

Jake pointed out that a split rock face below them formed a deep crevice, one he might be able to climb down. "This is a good opportunity to scout around. I don't want to lose it. I'm going down there."

Charlotte went with him to the point of descent. She stared into the steep, vertiginous, and narrow fissure. "You could get stuck in there," she said. "I should go first, and if I get into trouble, you'll be able to pull me out."

"That's crazy," Jake countered. "No way I'd let you do that!"

Let me? Her anger flashed. Hands on hips, she said, "If you get stuck, you big oaf, who would rescue you?"

"And you could break your damn neck," was his retort. "What do you know about mountain climbing?"

She was stumped a moment. "I've climbed pyramids."

"Whoop-di-do!"

God, but he's infuriating!

"She's got a point," Michael offered as he peered through his rifle sights at the compound. "If you two go in that direction, Quade and I will head north, circle around, and see what's on the other side of that village."

Jake nodded, then glanced at Charlotte. "All right, we'll both go. But if they capture us, Michael, we'll give you a sign only when we're sure they can be trusted. Until then, be wary."

Jake looped a rope around Charlotte's waist. As he tied it securely he tugged on it, drawing her toward him. She ended up only inches away, and too aware of his nearness. Their eyes met and held before he broke it off and tested the strength of the knot he had made. He next looped the rope over his own waist, chest and shoulders, in effect, binding the two of them together. He made sure his jacket cushioned the rope, intending to use his body as a brake in case she fell.

He wore gloves, but she removed hers for the climb, not trusting them to grip the rock sufficiently tight. She walked toward the crevice. It created a wind tunnel and an icy breeze struck her, numbing her fingers and chilling her face. She steeled herself, but her breathing came fast and urgent as she carefully eased herself over the edge of the cliff. She was scared, but hoped not to show it as she looked back at him. Despite the worry that lined his face, he gave her a nod of assurance. She felt flustered and at the same time warmed, which was good because the very next moment she stepped out onto nothingness.

The loose, spongy ground let small rocks roll under her foot and clatter against the cliff as they dropped. She shifted left and breathed easier when the ground felt solid once more. Slowly, she descended, trying not to think about the sharp pain in her cold hands.

She put her foot onto a slightly jutting boulder that appeared secure. Almost immediately, it broke free under her weight and tumbled down the cliff. She, too, dropped, but the rope tightened. Jake, she thought, reassured, yet wondering what kind of insanity possessed her that she volunteered to dangle more than a hundred feet off the ground and trust her life to a man she'd just met.

She scrambled her feet to find solid footing and clung to the cliff face as the boulder plummeted straight down taking smaller rocks with it. Charlotte held very still a moment and wondered if the people in the compound heard the noise. The angle of the crevice made it impossible for her to see the compound or surrounding area.

From the top of the cliff, Jake could see the compound. He was staring at it. After a wait, he gave her a thumbs up, then nodded and gestured downward.

"So far, so good," she muttered to herself, then drew in her breath and took another step. The next boulder held. Then another. Suddenly, her footing gave way and once more she dropped straight down the slope until she jerked to a stop, the rope tight around her chest as it caught, bunching up her jacket with it. She felt smothered by the rope and jacket. She was just about to tell Jake to relax the tension of the rope and allow her to climb the rest of the way to the bottom when she saw something coiled just below her foot. "Jake! Stop! Don't let me slip!"

He strained to hold her in place. "What is it?"

"A rattler," she gasped.

"Shit!" He braced himself.

"He's leaving," she said. "Give him time."

Just then the rope that had been wedged against her jacket, slid up and over the material. She dropped down in a sudden, jerking movement, before the rope caught again under her arms. The rattler lunged, fangs protruding. She cried out.

"Charlotte!" Jake yelled. The rope relaxed and fell past her, followed by a cascade of large and small rocks. Suddenly, Jake slid past her then somehow managed to stop himself and scramble up to her side, his face stark. "Where did he get you?"

"I don't know. I saw him spring at me, but I didn't feel anything. There's no pain. He must have hit the sole of my boots."

He helped her climb the rest of the way down to the ground where he immediately wrapped his arm around her waist and ran with her to the shelter of the brush. She sat as he checked and double-checked her legs and ankles, and fortunately found no bite marks.

They then lay face down on the ground, and scooted forward to a spot where the brush was thin, where they could view the compound. For both to see, they had to move close together. There, they remained absolutely still and watched for any sign they had been spotted. Being that close to Jake, Charlotte heard his breath, felt his heartbeat. Her senses came alive, and it had nothing to do with the danger they faced.

At the compound, all was as it had been.

As soon as she determined they were still safe, she eased herself away from him.

"Wait here," he said. "I'll scout around."

"No." Charlotte grabbed his arm. "I'm going with you."

His anger flared. "Listen, I could scout a hell of a lot faster without a citified Fed tagging along worrying me."

Her cheeks burned at the words, even as she realized their wisdom. "Since I'm such a bother, go. And good riddance!"

As quickly as his fury came, it seemed to vanish, and he gave her a jaunty grin. "Wish me luck?"

"Humph." She folded her arms and settled back further into the brush to wait.

Jake had barely taken a half-dozen steps before he stopped. Two men stepped out from behind a hillside, their rifles aimed at him and the brush where Charlotte hid.

FIFTY-SIX

Their captors led Jake and Charlotte to the community house where they faced Thaddeus Kohler. Four men stood behind him. Melisse, Rachel, and Brandi stopped placing clean dishes, forks, and platters of food onto the table to stare at the two strangers.

"Who are you?" Kohler asked.

"Jake Sullivan, Sheriff of Lemhi County," Jake said. He gestured toward the women. "I've been trying to find those students and their professor."

"And her?" Kohler's gaze drifted over Charlotte with curiosity, from her straight blond hair, along her thin, angular body, now held stiffly rigid, to her heavy-soled boots.

"She's my deputy," Jake said. He moved closer to her, clearly protective. "Charlotte Reed."

Kohler's gaze moved between Jake and Charlotte. "I see." He continued. "Who are the others?"

"What others?" Jake asked innocently.

"We are not fools, Sheriff Sullivan," Kohler said. "The two men who travel with you, and the men following you."

Jake and Charlotte glanced at each other. "Following us?"

Kohler gave them an icy smile. "We suspected you did not know."

"You're right," Jake said, his jaw tight. "There's a reward for rescuing the students. Some damn fools might want it for themselves." He gazed hard at Charlotte. "Are they Feds? Friends of yours?"

"Don't be silly," she said with a sneer.

"Where are the rest of the students and their professor?" Jake asked Kohler.

"I am the one who asks questions here, Sheriff," Kohler said. "But there is no reason to keep from you that Lionel Rempart and Vince Norton are quartered in the stable."

Jake did a quick count in his head. He already knew the fate of Ted and Brian. That left Devlin Farrell unaccounted for. He faced the women. "Are you all right?"

"We're well enough," Melisse said. "Except that we don't know how to return home. Apparently, neither do they."

At Melisse's words, a chilling thought came to Jake. He faced Kohler. "You still haven't told me who you are."

"My name is Thaddeus Kohler."

Jake recognized the name of the paramilitary team leader who had disappeared some thirteen years earlier. But as he eyed the men behind Kohler, a couple of them looked too young to have been here that many years. "How long have you been here?"

"Thirteen years," Kohler replied.

At Charlotte's sharp intake of breath, Jake met her eyes. She, too, understood who these men were.

"What is this place?" Charlotte asked.

"I wish I could explain it." Kohler shook his head. "But I cannot."

"We'd like our guns back," Jake said. "We need to be able to protect ourselves."

"You will, as soon as we're sure we can trust you."

Jake braced himself, his eyes narrow slits as he coldly regarded Kohler.

Kohler's face grew taut. "Tieg, show the sheriff to the stable. The female 'deputy' will remain with the women."

Jake looked ready to argue, possibly to fight, when Charlotte put her hand on his arm and nodded. He hesitated, then nodded in return and went with Tieg.

Kohler waited as his men left the community house and then turned to follow them out when Charlotte stopped him.

She handed him her last pack of cigarettes. "I'm sure some of your men will enjoy these. There's no reason for us not to be friends, you know."

Kohler took one out and smelled it, then broke off the filter. Charlotte stuck a match and lit it for him.

"I want you to know," she said, "that if you have any information about what's going on here, and if it's in any way connected to the Egyptian hieroglyphics on the pillars, I may be able to help. But I'll need more information. A starting point."

"Egyptian what?" he asked.

"Writing."

He nodded. "We didn't know. The symbols were strange to us. None of us has ever seen Egyptian writing."

"I see," she said. Nevertheless, his words surprised her.

His haughty presence seemed to bristle as if he recognized her surprise at his lack of knowledge, but when his eyes met hers, her breath caught. She hadn't seen such emptiness since the day she caught a glimpse of herself in a mirror shortly after Dennis' death.

"I'll think about that 'starting point' you mentioned." With that, he left.

Charlotte considered herself a good judge of character. As much as she wanted to trust Thaddeus Kohler, she could not.

FIFTY-SEVEN

New York City

Jianjun got on the Acela Express in Washington D.C., and three hours later stood outside Penn Station. His worry about Michael grew, and if this silence continued, he might have to go to Idaho himself. He knew nothing about the place and wondered if people there considered chop suey to be Chinese food.

New York City was a welcome detour.

He took a cab to an Upper East Side address, and exited it in front of a tall, narrow limestone building. He walked up the steps and rang the bell. A woman dressed in black gave him a haughty once-over. He introduced himself as Michael Rempart's assistant and asked to speak to Mr. Phaylor. If Calvin Phaylor was as interested in alchemy and events in Idaho as Jianjun believed, using Michael Rempart's name would open the door for him.

The housekeeper left him waiting in the entry. It must have been beautiful once, with black-and-white marble tiles on the floor, elaborate raised-plaster designs on the walls, and a wide carpeted staircase up to the living quarters. But the carpet was frayed, and the walls in need of fresh paint. Dim lights and lack of furniture left the room devoid of warmth. Shutters barred the outside from view.

The housekeeper returned and offered Jianjun a choice between the stairs or a small elevator in a back corner. He took the stairs. The housekeeper heaved a sigh and slowly climbed up behind him.

On the second floor of the home, she showed Jianjun to a large living area and left him alone. The room was even less well lit than the foyer and furnished in dark Victorian antiques covered in green and black velvet. Heavy damask drapery framed the windows. Jianjun nervously sat on the edge of the sofa. The place was right out of the Addams Family, with the housekeeper a female version of Lurch.

Ten minutes passed before the double doors opened again. A male nurse pushed Calvin Phaylor's wheelchair, an oxygen tank attached to it. The once strong founder of PLP appeared rail thin, his skin tight over a six foot tall frame. His white hair was baby fine, long, and fly-away. The nurse stopped the chair a few feet from Jianjun, then quietly slipped out of the room.

Jianjun jumped to his feet, bowed, and introduced himself.

Watery blue-gray eyes fixed on him. Phaylor flicked his fingers impatiently toward the sofa. "Yes, I know who you are. Sit! Sit! Is Michael Rempart in Idaho? Have you talked to him?" Phaylor asked, then reached for the oxygen mask and breathed deeply, as if those few words had cost him.

Jianjun sat as told, then answered the question. "Dr. Rempart is there, but I haven't heard from him recently."

Phaylor's lips tightened. "What do you want from me?"

"Any help you can give. I know you've looked into what went on in Idaho centuries ago, and what is out there now."

Phaylor frowned and Jianjun knew he was going to lie. "I'm not sure—"

"*The Book of Abraham the Jew*," Jianjun said quickly. "Alchemy."

He had Phaylor's full attention. "I see." He wheeled himself to the bar. "Move this crap off me," he ordered, pointing at his oxygen tank. "I want a smoke and a drink."

Jianjun took the tank from the chair, closed the feed valve, and carried it to the far side of the room. He hoped the tank was well sealed.

Phaylor poured them each a single malt Scotch. Jianjun rarely drank any alcohol other than beer, but took it nonetheless. Phaylor told him to carry both drinks as he rolled toward the elevator. They rode up to a roof deck facing the East River.

Phaylor removed a cigar and matches from his shirt pocket. He seemed to enjoy the feel of the brisk wind against his grainy skin. He lit the cigar, clearly relishing the taste. Jianjun placed the drinks on a patio table and sat.

"Alchemy is just a dream, you know," Phaylor said, keeping his gaze fixed on the impressive skyline even as his voice took on a wistful quality.

"Having spent time with Dr. Rempart, I believe there may be more to it," Jianjun said. "Much more."

Phaylor attempted to laugh, but instead wheezed. "In that case, I must congratulate Dr. Rempart. Few young computer whizzes like you have any tolerance for the paranormal."

Jianjun simply nodded, wondering how Phaylor knew about his computer skills.

Phaylor continued. "I have learned a lot about alchemy, including how to interpret *The Book of Abraham the Jew*. If you've found me, I'm sure you know that the board took my company from me, and put that interloper, Jennifer Vandenburg, in my place. She's not a bad person, but she shouldn't run anything more complicated than a McDonald's franchise."

"I see," Jianjun murmured.

"No, lad, I'm not sure that you do. I've lost everything because I believed I could find something that would be of value to mankind. I have no family. Never married, no kids. My company was my life, and now it's gone." He eyed Jianjun a moment. "I know what a brilliant archeologist Michael Rempart is, all the treasures he has found. If he is seriously searching for *The Book of Abraham the Jew* I am more than willing to assist. I have books, records, which may help."

"Yes, my boss is very serious about finding the book, as well as locating his brother, Lionel Rempart."

"Lionel," Phaylor frowned. "That's right. I almost forgot about him. Tell me, does Michael Rempart know much about his family's history?"

"His family's history?" The strange question surprised Jianjun. "Not that I've heard. Why? What do you know about it?"

"Nothing of importance." Phaylor's eyes narrowed before he forced his mouth into a smile. "Why don't you stay here while you're in New York? This house has several guest bedrooms. Olga can freshen one up for you, and I'll send books and manuscripts on alchemy for you to read. You'll find them fascinating."

Jianjun doubted it. Despite feeling nervous about staying here, it made sense to do so. "Thank you. I would like that. Very much. Yes. Thank you."

Jianjun wheeled him to the elevator. Olga waited with his oxygen tank when the elevator doors opened on the third floor of the mansion. She frowned at the smell of tobacco and scotch. As Jianjun watched Phaylor instruct his housekeeper on the guest accommodations, he wondered if he'd regret accepting Phaylor's offer to stay.

FIFTY-EIGHT

MICHAEL AND QUADE LOOKED DOWN FROM THE TOP OF THE CLIFF where they hid. They had witnessed Jake and Charlotte's capture and had since received no signal from Jake or Charlotte that things in the compound were all right.

"Let's circle the compound," Michael said. "View it from all sides."

To stay out of sight, they made a wide arc through brush and pine forests until eventually they reached the compound's west side. There, they noticed an area where the ground had been trampled.

"The beasts?" Quade asked, walking toward the low-lying scrub where broken stalks lay flat on the ground.

Michael stooped low, peering at the dirt. "Not unless they're wearing shoes. It must have been men from the compound. Let's see where they went."

They continued on slowly, carefully. None of the landmarks they had used earlier remained visible to them, and they felt disoriented.

In the distance, they saw a large object on the ground. It looked like some sort of animal. Michael half expected it to wake up and run or attack. When it didn't, they moved closer for a better look.

Blood covered the ground. The creature lay face down and looked more like a bear than anything else, but not quite. It had been stabbed multiple times.

Michael turned it over.

The monster had a long snout with enormous fangs, and white skin under a brownish-gray coat. As he looked closer, he saw a symbol made up of bluish-red vein-like lines just above the stomach—the same triangle-vee-circle symbol he had seen in Lady Hsieh's tomb.

And now it marked this creature.

"What in the world?" Michael exclaimed.

"It's a chimera," Quade said, his soft hands clasped as if in prayer as he stood over it. "It's an animal made of components of other animals, possibly including humans. Some people believe that when the alchemist moves beyond gold to being god-like, in other words, moves from creating the perfect metal that will not decompose, to the perfect man who will not die, their earliest attempts often do not work. There are various names for the beasts that result—some are called chimeras, which are more animal-like, and homunculi, which are more human."

"Human? An alchemist, here, involved humans?" The idea appalled Michael.

"Homunculi were little humans created in a flask," Quade explained. "They were often discussed by medieval Arabs. Whether they actually created homunculi is unknown, but they certainly wrote as if they did, and I see no reason for them to lie. They even debated whether it was moral to use the fluids of these 'little men,' as the word means, to cure diseases in normal men. It's much as we will someday debate cloning humans for the sole reason of taking the cloned being's body parts. Is it moral and ethical, or is it simply good science? All of this, chimera and homunculi, erode the boundary between the artificial and the natural."

"This is our proof, then," Michael said with a shudder. "An alchemist was at work here, and may still be."

"Yes," Quade nodded, ever emotionless and scientific. "There are things at work beyond mortal understanding."

"But look at the way this beast was killed." Michael stood and then backed up as the full realization struck of the sight before him. "It was killed with knives and anger. Great anger." He peered into the dark forest and wondered what other strangeness lurked within. "We should get away from this creature, back to where we can keep an eye on the compound," he said. "The forest has eyes. I can feel them on us."

They no sooner left than the creature awoke. It slowly struggled to its feet, then stared with curiosity after the two men who found it.

FIFTY-NINE

THAT NIGHT, RACHEL GOODING HURRIED BACK TO THE COMMUNITY house from the outhouse, her head filled with both hope and despair after hearing Charlotte's tale of the search party trying to rescue them. Sam Black suddenly appeared on the pathway.

"I need a woman to warm my bed tonight." He slurred his words as he looked her up and down. "You'll do."

She backed away. He smiled. "You can't outrun me, missy."

"Get out of here, Sam!" Will Durham stood in the doorway of his hut, his gun pointed at his fellow villager. "You're drunk."

"I've had my fill of liquor," Sam said. "It's something else I'm craving now."

"You heard the Captain." Will stepped between the two. "The women are to be left alone."

Sam spat on the ground. "Until he wants one himself." He tried to sidestep Will, but Will pushed him back.

"You'll have to go through me, Sam."

"These whores aren't worth fighting amongst ourselves!" Sam shouted as he backed away. "Hell, there's others. And them that's not so scrawny."

Will took hold of Rachel's wrist and whispered to her, "Come inside with me until he's gone."

In her relief to escape Sam, she did as he said. Not until he shut the door behind her did she realize she might have gone from the proverbial frying pan into the fire.

"I won't hurt you," Will said. "But go out there now and someone might. If not Sam, then Arnie or Gus. Maybe Kohler himself. It's been a long time since any of us have been around women. Some of the men, clearly, have forgotten how to behave."

"But not you?" she said, a mocking jeer to her voice.

"I don't force women."

"Oh? You're irresistible, are you?"

"To one, I was. The woman I love. You're safe with me."

That stopped her, and she nodded. The room had a small cot-like bed, one chair and a desk-size table.

"Take the bed. I have work to do." Will picked up a chip of obsidian, sat on the chair, and began to sharpen it.

She sat on the bed's edge, unsure of him or any of this. She watched him work.

The accuracy the villagers could achieve with bows and arrows amazed her. She saw the hateful Sam Black take down a Canadian goose in flight the day before. "Why do you do that?" she asked as he finished one and picked up a second. "You have guns, why bother with bows and arrows?"

"When the bullets are spent," he said, "the guns are worthless. The arrows can be fashioned by us, and this way we can always eat."

"I see," she said. He continued to sharpen the stone and said nothing more.

"Have you really been here thirteen years?" she asked.

So many seconds passed before he answered she thought he wasn't going to. Then their gazes met, and she saw sadness in his that struck her. He seemed every bit as unhappy to be here as she was. Perhaps just as trapped in his own way. Whatever it was, she felt she may have found a kindred spirit.

His hands stilled. "That must seem an infinite amount of time to one as young as you."

She studied his face. Up close she saw that despite the beard, his skin was youthful. "You aren't exactly old, you know."

His gaze flickered toward her then away. "I've always been plagued with a youthful demeanor." He gave a shy, almost embarrassed smile.

She wondered if he and the others were part of a military or special operations mission that had gone bad. It would make sense if all this was classified, and would explain the secrecy surrounding this place. Fear for her situation and a hope that Will just might tell her the truth, emboldened her to ask, "Are we in danger here? Should we be afraid of you? All of you?"

His response wasn't what she'd hoped for. "There is evil here. It isn't our fault, but it has happened. If you can get away, it will be better for you."

"What do you mean?"

He put down the obsidian, his face harsh yet desperate. "I'll protect you, Rachel. I'll do whatever is in my power to protect you. But I may not be enough."

"My God, Will!" she cried, frightened by the change in him.

He clasped his hands together and stared at the floor as if realizing he had said too much. "I'm sorry that you and the others are caught up in this."

"What is it?" She was near tears. "What's going on here?"

"It's more than I know, and what little I know, I can't explain," he said. "But I can tell you this. I wasn't always this way. I was a good man once, loved by a kind and gracious woman. I gave all that up and came here, and nothing has ever been the same."

"Why did you come?"

"Why did *you*?" he countered. "I suspect for the same reasons—adventure, something new, interesting, and with thoughts of what it might mean to my future to have had this experience, something few people could even imagine."

"To beef up the résumé," she said.

He chuckled. "You have an interesting way with words," he said.

She looked surprised. "Not me—you're the one with the odd accent. Where are you from?"

"I can't say."

"Can't or won't."

"Won't," he replied firmly. "Don't worry, Rachel. I won't let anything happen to you." To her surprise, he reached out and gave her hand a reassuring squeeze. He kept his touch light, and he withdrew it after only a moment. The brief encounter forced her to realize how cold the Professor and Melisse were, how completely self-centered Brandi was, and how very afraid and alone she felt. She responded to Will's touch with a mixture of gratitude for a simple kindness, and something more.

"You're trapped here, aren't you?" she asked with sudden insight. "Just as we are."

"I have no idea," he said, then firmed himself, "no idea what you mean."

"I'm so sorry," she said, "for us both."

His voice dropped as he swayed ever so slightly toward her. "If the chance arises for you to escape, do it, Rachel."

"Come with us," she said. "Let's leave, all of us together."

"I wish I could."

"You can," she pleaded. "You know this area so much better than the rest of us. You must have some idea of what to do, which way to go. Help us, please." She placed her hand on his arm, and he covered it with his own. His fingers and palms were callused from hard work. As she looked from their hands to his face, she felt his fingers tighten ever so slightly before he pulled his hand away and picked up the arrowhead.

"Let me think about it," he whispered.

She nodded.

"It's quiet now, outside," he said. "I suspect the others will soon be asleep. It's my turn to keep watch all night. First, I'll walk you back to the community house. Don't worry. I'll make sure you're safe."

He held her hand as he led her back.

She went straight up to her pallet without a word to the others. She didn't want to answer their questions about where she had gone for so long or why Will Durham had been with her.

She lay down, exhausted. With Will's assurances of her safety echoing in her mind, for the first time since this madness began, she slept peacefully and deeply.

SIXTY

As Michael and Quade watched the compound and scouted the area that night, they found more peculiar tracks of chimeras. Strange animal noises, some guttural, some howls, and some high-pitched shrieks made it difficult to relax, let alone sleep. Michael kept watch while Quade slept for four hours, and then they reversed roles. He wondered, however, if he dared sleep.

He shut his eyes and hoped for rest, hoped to stop his mind from racing. A sweet perfume slowly filled his senses. The same scent of peonies that had risen up from Lady Hsieh's tomb.

He opened his eyes. She knelt beside him.

"You will find a copse of pines to the east. Go to them, Michael," she whispered. He sat up and reached for her, but she was gone.

Quade sat about twenty feet away, his back to the supposed sleeper.

Quietly, Michael stood, picked up his Remington 700, and walked east. In the starlight the trees looked like a massive nothingness, a void, but he kept going. Once he reached them, he continued forward another five-hundred feet, blackness all around him. He was ready to turn back, convinced he had been dreaming, when he saw a flicker of light.

He crept close. Around a campfire, five men slept.

He jerked backwards and bumped into something.

"Quiet!" Quade whispered. "I followed, curious about where you were going. How did you know they were out here?"

Michael made no response, but stared at the men in sleeping bags. The firelight showed them to be young, clean-cut, big and burly. Beside them were M107 sniper rifles. Military grade.

"Any idea who they are?" Michael asked fiercely. Shades of Mongolia, when government troops moved in on his dig site, killing and stealing, came to mind.

"No," Quade said indignantly. "They aren't government."

"Then they're contractors. Mercenaries."

Quade opened his mouth to ask why he thought that when Michael shoved him to the ground.

The shot was wide, but close. Michael fired back while Quade flattened himself.

The sleepers were immediately up and armed, their movements fast and efficient. Professional.

Quade and Michael ran back through the trees, shooting at their pursuers, but knew there were too many of them, too well-armed and well-trained for the two of them to last long.

The pines provided some shelter, but they quickly reached the edge of the copse. The ground was barren after that. They could do nothing but keep going, the night darkness their only friend.

They timed a run-and-shoot, ducking behind thick tree trunks, knowing if they went much farther they would have no shelter. They stopped, determined to hold their ground.

A bullet struck Michael in the upper arm. It bled heavily, indicating the brachial artery must have been hit. He clamped down hard on it. With only Quade able to shoot, the snipers moved in.

"This way!" a voice called. Two men armed with only bows and arrows were near. They crouched and gestured at them to run to the hillside.

Michael looked over the area. If they climbed up that hill, they would be exposed.

"Hurry!" the second man said.

They had no choice.

Quade fired shot after shot as he and Michael ran. At the same time, the two strangers kept their arrows flying fast and deep into the trees. Michael and Quade reached them.

Instead of a suicidal uphill climb, one of the strangers pushed them into what looked like a small crack in the mountainside. Michael bent down in the low, narrow space and soon reached a dug-out stairway that descended to a tunnel.

Torches lined the walls, providing light. The last man into the tunnel pulled a rope, causing a slab of rock connected to an intricate pulley system to slide over the opening, hiding the steps from the outside world.

"The name is Will Durham," the youngest of the two said. "This is Gus Webber. We shall lead you to safety."

SIXTY-ONE

Michael and Quade followed Durham and Webber through a tunnel into the village and straight to Ben Olgerbee's cabin. There, Olgerbee cleaned and dressed Michael's gunshot wound. A poultice he smeared over it numbed the pain and stopped the bleeding,

Kohler arrived and immediately began to question Michael and Quade.

"Who are the men shooting at you, and why?" Kohler demanded.

"We don't know," Michael replied.

"We watched them follow you for some time," Kohler admitted.

"We never imagined anyone would follow, considering where we are," Michael said.

"So, you know where we are?" Kohler said, his voice dismissive, mocking.

"Not exactly."

"I have a good idea." Quade muttered, then stared at Kohler without expression.

Kohler stared back. The tension in the room grew.

"Do you know where the shooters are now?" Michael asked as he put his shirt and jacket back on.

Kohler's gaze broke, and he faced Michael. "They are watching our village. We thought their presence had to do with you, but obviously not, since they were quite willing to kill you. The only surprise, therefore, is that they didn't kill you sooner."

"So it seems," Michael said calmly. "They're well-armed, but you only have bows and arrows. That diminishes our chance for success."

"We aren't worried," Kohler said. "Once their bullets are gone, they will be no more dangerous than children. Our arrows fly true, and we have a great store of them."

"Why? Who or what were you fighting before we came?" Michael asked. "Was it those strange creatures that lurk about, or something else?"

"Those creatures are not like any you have known," Kohler said, "for they have cunning and trickery such that is almost human. They resent our living here, and if we did not look out constantly, they would attack and take all that we have."

"And kill you?" Quade asked.

"Without mercy," Kohler responded.

"Interesting."

"Dangerous is a more apt description," Kohler said with a scowl.

Just then a ruckus sounded at the door. It burst open. "Michael! It's really you!" Lionel Rempart hurried toward his brother. Jake followed, as did the dark-haired, pale and sickly young man Michael knew must be Vince Norton.

Lionel stopped a few feet before Michael and went no further, as if unsure of how to greet him.

"Good to see you alive," Michael said. "You had me worried." He got to his feet, equally self-conscious. Too many years had passed without them seeing each other...or their father. Too many years of Lionel turning his back on Michael, and Michael deciding it best to have nothing to do with his family. Lionel's wild eyes, his gaunt features, and quivering hands stunned and alarmed him. Michael forced a smile. "I came to get you out of here, but I seem to have made a mess of it."

"You came through the pillars?" Lionel asked.

"Yes."

"Did you try to go back through them?"

Michael nodded. "It didn't work."

"And lights," Lionel said, his eyes wide and unfocused, "in front of the mound with the pillars...did you see any such thing?"

The question surprised Michael, but he decided against revealing too much. "I saw something out there. I'm not sure what."

"Then I'm not crazy!" Lionel cried, relieved.

Kohler's gaze fiercely zeroed in on Lionel. "What lights are you talking about?"

Lionel grew nervous. "Well, I...I saw lights around the mound that holds the pillars, and on the ground before it. They were there just an instant. The students didn't see them, but Michael did! Thank God!"

"I'm not sure—" Michael began.

"Can you describe them?" Kohler interrupted.

"Just some strange lines in complex configurations," Lionel said. "They quickly vanished, but I know what I saw."

"And you?" Kohler faced Michael.

Michael wondered about Kohler's reaction. "I never saw anything like that."

A voice shouted from the doorway. "It's a sign!" Ben Olgerbee pointed at Lionel. His gray hair stood wildly out from his head, and his eyes bulged as he walked into the room. "He is the one! He sees what we know must be there, but we cannot see. God has sent him to us! He will lead the way."

"Enough! There will be time to talk later," Kohler said, as he looked from one brother to the other. "Now, it's time to eat." Kohler led the newcomers to the community house for breakfast.

SIXTY-TWO

OUTSIDE THE COMMUNITY HOUSE, CHARLOTTE AND RACHEL GROUND what appeared to be a primitive corn or maize into meal. Rachel looked around to see if anyone watched them, then held a forefinger to her lips in a sign of "quiet" and motioned for Charlotte to follow her.

"You've got to talk with Will Durham," Rachel whispered.

She led Charlotte to a cabin and opened the door without knocking. "Will?"

"Come in," he said. The lit fireplace warmed the air. Rachel and Charlotte sat side-by-side on the bed while Will took the chair.

"Rachel tells me I can trust you," Charlotte said.

"We aren't bad men. It's just a matter of strange things that have happened." He looked sheepish, knowing how weak the confession sounded.

"Charlotte has a theory about this place," Rachel said. "That's why I wanted you to meet her. You've been here for years. Maybe with her theory and your practical experience you two can come up with a way to get us out of here."

"You have a theory?" Will asked. "Based on what?"

"There's a scientific explanation," Charlotte said, then admitted, "of a sort. It sounds crazy, however. I'd rather hear what you've experienced."

"I haven't experienced anything beyond not being able to leave. You say your explanation sounds crazy, but I say there's nothing that would surprise me. Not after what I've been through. If you can help, please..."

"You need to understand," Charlotte began, "that I was a student of ancient cultures in the near and middle east. That's where we find the earliest records of ... of alchemy."

"What?" Rachel said.

Charlotte found Will's lack of surprise both interesting and alarming.

"An ancient alchemical symbol was found in this area. I can't help but wonder if Lewis and Clark may have been looking for it—"

Will jumped to his feet, his face white. "No. Not Lewis and Clark. It was a secret expedition ... a secret expedition sent to follow them."

"How do you know that?" Charlotte asked.

He opened a drawer from the wooden desk and from it pulled some thin sheets of bark with writing on them. "I found this here," he said. "A journal, written by a member of the expedition named Francis Masterson. His words are horrible. Horrible to contemplate or to believe. Yet, I do believe them."

Charlotte looked at the bark sheets. The writing was awkward and the ink splotchy.

"I've had years to decipher it," Will said. "It is lengthy, but explains much. If you'd like, I'll read it to you. I've read it so often over the years I almost know it by heart."

"Please," Charlotte said.

Will moved closer to the fire. As he read, Charlotte could all but envision Francis Masterson himself sitting in this very cabin and writing this strange account ...

I, Francis Masterson, once turned my back on God. Now, I live with His back turned on me.

Madness or even Death would be welcome over all that has transpired, but I am too weak, too cowardly, and too afraid to face my Maker by my Own hand.

I have previously penned an arrogant discourse on our Secret albeit Failed Expedition under our beloved President Thomas Jefferson, in which our small collection of scholars and occultists foolishly braved this Vast and Unknown Land. If that discourse is ever found and read it will truly be a Miracle, and this one, doubly so.

But I am a writer, and as long as the last, small shard of the miserable Soul once known as Francis Masterson remains, I will record what has happened.

Lest anyone unfortunate enough to stumble upon this Discourse be tempted to dismiss it as Fiction or the child of a fevered, tortured mind, let me assure you on the grave of my own sweet Mother that every word is True. I call you Unfortunate because, if you are reading this, you, too, may be trapped here. If so, I pray with all my heart that you have more success than I and my ill-fated companions at freeing yourself before Despair and Derangement overtake you.

It began when Captain Crouch and I crossed between the pillars to flee the Tukudeka who were fast upon us with their spears and poisoned arrows. When we crossed, we found ourselves to be in the same place as we'd been previously, except that the Tukudeka were no longer threatening, and the thunder and lightning had ceased.

Our companions, Orril and Asa Munroe, Noah Handy, and Reuben Hale, stood before us like ghosts. The four had not dared move, so frightened and so astonished were they as Captain Crouch and I walked between the pillars and appeared before them as if by magic.

Fear overtook us all. If this place held safety from the Tukudeka, what else did it hold? The Rational mind could not explain it. Mr. Hale called it Infernal, and that word took hold of our thoughts and refused to leave. Dread of this unknown Region had so crippled our bones that they turned weak and we fell to the ground.

We huddled together and considered going back through the pillars, but if we did, we must again face the Tukudeka. That way lay certain Death, and here, an uncertain Future.

We ran away from the pillars. As we traveled, Mr. Handy noticed smoke rising in the distance. At first we feared another fire, and our instinct was to flee as fast and as far in the opposite direction as we could. We were despondent, hopelessly lost, but then Captain Crouch saw that the smoke wasn't moving. It remained a single white plume wafting high into the sky.

Had we found some means of help?

We approached cautiously. Three watched our flank while Ezra Crouch, Noah Handy, and I went forward to scout the reason for the smoke.

As we neared, we heard the most unearthly screams. The thought of them even now sends shivers down my spine and chills my soul.

Inching closer, we heard a drum and deep, guttural chants, not the song of the Aboriginal, but fiercer, more primitive, even, dare I say, animal-like. It inspired such all-consuming terror within me that my very skin prickled. But through it all, even worse, were the screams, sobs, and a litany of pleadings in an unintelligible, mumbled rush. Only as we neared, could I comprehend the word, Dieu, cried over and over.

We concluded that a French trapper had been captured and was being cruelly tortured. Oft times the most one can do in such circumstances is to pray that Death comes quickly.

I believed we would run as far from this wretched place as possible when Captain Crouch appealed to our qualities as Honorable men.

I shall confess that I have never worried about my portion of manly Virtue. Yet, it is an expression of man's essential weakness and insecurity that when another challenges his Manhood, he immediately puffs and primps himself up like a peacock and declares that he is willing to confront the World if need be. Captain Crouch led us closer. Using his spyglass, we soon reached a point where we could see what was occurring.

A white man had been stripped of his clothing and tied spread eagle on the ground. He was being ruthlessly jabbed with knives or burning sticks, not to kill, but to provoke so much Agony that his eyes had rolled back in his head and his mouth frothed. He emitted such bone-chilling shrieks that I could not reckon how anyone without a heart of stone could do anything but end the poor man's suffering.

Captain Crouch bravely crawled closer while Mr. Handy and I separated. I hid in a thicket, my back to a pine trunk so no one could sneak up behind me, which was my fear. I'll admit that as I held my rifle, my hands shook.

The Captain shouted to the Heathens to free their captive. They surely were Tukudeka, but—as God is my witness—they had covered themselves, head to toe, so completely and expertly in animal skins and feathers that they truly looked like unknown monsters, even more frightening than the Heathens we had escaped.

To our surprise, at the Captain's order, the warriors ran. We had no doubt that as soon as they realized how small our numbers were, they would return.

Captain Crouch cut the ropes that bound the victim, then pulled the pitiful Soul to his feet and wrapped him in a nearby blanket of hides.

The Frenchman was weak and dazed. I moved forward then, making myself frighteningly Visible as I wrapped my left arm around the fellow's waist and held him close to help him flee this area. Captain Crouch took up the man's sack of belongings while keeping his muzzle aimed at the thicket through which the Heathens had fled.

We feared that they would pursue us, especially when we heard the forest fill with the most Eerie and Mournful shrieking and inhuman howling imaginable.

With the help of the Munroe brothers and Reuben Hale, we were able to craft a sling to carry the Frenchman, which was a blessing since his body was so slippery from blood it was nearly impossible to hold on to him.

We found a location upon which we could secure our safety and there dressed the Frenchman's many cuts and burns as best we could. Some areas of his body required sutures, which I found myself unable to watch administered, and am loathe to describe in any detail here for fear of the Nightmares it will bring back to mind. There were many times I thought the poor Victim would be in a better state if he simply had died.

The next day he developed a fever and became quite delirious with it. Only a few times could he speak with any degree of rationality. Strangely, what he said when he was supposedly rational often sounded more of Bedlam and Madness than when gripped by fever. When the fever passed, he insisted on dressing. Among his belongings we saw a remarkable red stone, a pendant, on a long gold chain. He put it around his neck and then hid it from our view.

In his lucid times, we learned, to our amazement, that he was a holy man, a French abbot named Gerard Rombert de Fontainebleau. He said that at the time the French revolution ravaged his nation, Anti-clerical sentiment abounded amidst the rabble and their leaders. To save himself, Abbé Gerard escaped to Spain. Among his treasures was a book passed to him by his father, a book of Great value about Alchemy, called The Book of Abraham the Jew.

Dame Rumor soon whispered about the curious book, causing others to covet it. Gerard fled to Egypt. There, he discovered the Land of Pharaohs where Hermes was said to have explained alchemy to the world in his Emerald Tablet. Gerard learned the true meaning and value of the book he carried with him. As long as he could remember, he had Intuition and Sensibilities that others did not possess. Because of it, he had turned to the Church, thinking he was saintly. Instead, in Egypt, he learned that he was quite the opposite. There, he gained a sense of the potential power of his new calling.

He continued East, eventually reaching Cathay where he gained the trust of Taoist priests who taught him the Dao Zan which brought an understanding of his precious book beyond his wildest imagination.

His association with so many Ungodly persons caused the Jesuits in Cathay to harbor suspicions against him, and the Mandarins to do the same. Once again, the abbot found himself in danger, and took flight. He traveled by ship across the Pacific to the New World.

Supplied with the various tools of Alchemical Arts, he joined a group of fur trappers traveling inland. One night as they slept, he headed into the mountains. Alone, he almost died of starvation that first Winter, despite a store of gathered food. The Winter was cold beyond belief. He oft longed for his beloved Paris.

Throughout this time, his studies of his Miraculous Book continued.

Using the vast store of information and explanation he had gleaned from his days in Egypt and Cathay, he created a Philosopher's Stone, the stone he now wore.

With that stone, he told us with a sly wink and a smile, the world of alchemy opened to him as a flower's petals to the sun. I must admit to a sense of unease at his demeanor.

He stopped his story there, although we knew his tale was far from over.

Quickly, his strength returned. He showed us which plants were edible in this land, and at times prepared most delicious stews for us. We were, for a time, content to be alive and free of the Tukudeka. But eventually, a natural longing for home overtook us one and all, and despite the ease of life with the Abbé, we grew unhappy and angry, and demanded to find a way to leave.

Now that we wished to leave this place, he told us we must hear the remainder of his story.

In Egypt, he had learned of Hermes Trismegistus' greatest achievement. The great Hermes had created a portal between the mortal world and the Land where Pharaohs live for all eternity. The abbot proclaimed that he had become consumed with the desire to enter that portal, to live with the gods. He saw that as his Destiny, the reason for all the travel, trials and tribulation that befell him. To open that portal, to enter it, would allow him to live forever.

I stared at him, scarcely believing the words I heard. Immortality! It was too Unnatural to contemplate, and I shrank back from the abbot in horror. Something in his eyes chilled my blood and made me wonder if we had erred in saving this man's life.

He relayed that he had built an altar, and then continued for three more years using his Stone, his Book, and his studies. To survive, he created gold and occasionally traveled to trading posts to purchase supplies. He killed any Trapper who attempted to follow him to steal his gold, and soon word got out that he and his gold were Evil. He relished that and built upon it. As a Sign of Evil to ward off thieves and Heathens, he used the alchemical symbol of immortality with triangles, a circle and vees. To my Horror, I realized that his symbol and his gold were the reasons our Good Expedition had been sent to this Wretched place.

He continued with his attempts to contact the Portal of Hermes.

And one day, he succeeded. The Earth shook. Lightning filled the Sky over his altar and Thunder crashed. The Tukudeka ran to him to see what was happening, as the ground swelled into a perfectly shaped pyramid, and two magnificent pillars, inscribed with letters from the Gods themselves, dropped from the Sky onto its flattened top.

All stared in Wonder and Awe. Three Tukudeka warriors, swaggering and brave, climbed to the top of the pyramid. They inspected the pillars, but when they stepped between them, one by one, they vanished.

Their women and children lamented for them, and amidst wailings and affirmations to find them and pull them back to safety, crossed the threshold of the pillars and also disappeared.

The Tukudeka were furious, and told Gerard that if he did not return their brethren, he would be killed by being roasted alive, one small portion of him at a time. The Abbé tried, but could find no way to retrieve the lost warriors. He cared little about them in any case, and desiring nothing more than to join the Pharaohs and Hermes the Great, he gathered up his Alchemical tools and his marvelous book and flung himself between the pillars.

To his astonishment, despite the ancient Egyptian letters on the pillars, he was not in Hermes' World of the Pharaohs, but in a separate world build on Gerard's own experience—a world familiar to him. Fool that he was, to think the Dark Power of Alchemy would allow otherwise!

Wearing the Philosopher's Stone, ingesting bits of the vast quantities of gold he created and stored away, and using the knowledge of alchemy he gained in his travels, he divined for himself the state of immortality.

He exulted in it and lived happily for a while. But then, he found it took a great deal of work to prepare food and shelter for the long winter.

Several more Tukudeka had crossed over to rescue their brethren and became stuck in this world. Generally, he hid from them but one day, he set a trap and captured one. He soon realized, however, that a Human was both too intelligent and too wily to be trusted. He had learned that transformations were possible in alchemy, and not only of base metal to gold.

With his alchemical powers, he practiced on captives, creating them into confused but docile creatures, some mixed with birds, some with coyotes, some with bears, all with a variety of talents in hunting, fishing, and hauling that Gerard could use.

Finally, he enjoyed life. His creations provided companionship and would do his bidding. But slowly, they changed. They realized their own strength, and instead of loving and serving him for granting them Eternal life, they came to hate him. They wanted freedom and to be changed back, but he knew not how.

He had to run from them. To hide. To spend his days constantly moving. Even in Winter, he would starve and freeze, but he would not die.

In time, this Immortality became repugnant to him. His years of training as a man of God seeped back upon him, and he realized he was being punished for having abandoned his God, and for turning instead to Evil.

Creating this place, destroying and transforming the bodies of the Tukudeka, was surely Evil.

Man, he learned, was too small and too ignorant to tamper with nature. We lacked sufficient knowledge of the interconnection and balance of all things. Even with the best of intentions, most often, man will harm Nature, seldom can he mend it, and never can he perfect it. The man who attempts to usurp the creative power of his Maker, will create a monster in its place. And that was the Abbé's legacy.

In despair and sorrow, he gave up running from the Creatures trapped here with him. He allowed them to capture him and faced their Judgment. He told us he expected to die from all they subjected him to, but he did not. He remained alive and suffering.

Crying to Heaven now, he proclaimed that he welcomed Death. He only prayed to be spared the Fires of Hell for his dreadful deeds, and that someday he might serve his Penance and kneel at the feet of his Beloved, Jesus Christ, and plead for his Divine Mercy and Forgiveness. He said his last act would be to destroy the Stone.

At this, Orril Munroe cried, "No! Never!" He grabbed the stone, wrenching it from the Abbé's neck. Why, he asked, should a sick old man deny him gold and eternal life? With it, Orril raged, he would find a way to escape to the real World, take the abbot's gold with him, and use the Stone to create more.

As Mr. Munroe held it, the magnificent stone glowed with shifting colors amidst subtle transformations in shape. The Stone became a living agent of Change, and I sensed it had Intellect.

I could feel myself being drawn to its Unnatural power. All that made me Francis Masterson seemed to fly from my mind, my body, even my Soul, and I came to Desire the Stone beyond all Reason. I looked upon Orril and the Abbé with hatred and knew I would willingly kill to possess the beautiful red object.

And as I felt, so did the others. We were near to blows, or worse, when Captain Crouch turned to the abbot and demanded he create five more Stones.

The abbot said that would take many months, and the faster, easier route would be to divide the one we had into six pieces, for each would be as strong as the whole. Even as I rejoiced at this news, it crossed my troubled mind that we contemplated blasphemy, that we were creating an Idol that was Sacrilege itself.

With little heed to the Priest, we immediately took out his tools and used them to chisel the Stone into six equal parts. When we finished, however, the

Stone lost the strange aura it had possessed, and seemed no more than a common red rock. Seeing that, all six of us pelted the frail abbot, for he had Tricked us into believing him, and caused us to destroy that which we most coveted.

We demanded he create another Stone. The abbot refused to yield, but called up his God to give him Fortitude to withstand our fury, and offered his suffering as Penance for having once believed that he, a decrepit excuse for a man, sought to elevate himself to the level of God.

Desire for a Philosopher's Stone drove us beyond the Realm of Madness. We believed that the Stone was our only means to leave this Unnatural Land that Sorcery had created, yet that was but a small part of our Desire.

With it, we would have Gold and Power. Also, as we had seen with our own Eyes, with the Stone's magic we would not die.

The torture the abbot suffered at our Hands was worse than that of the Tukudeka, but no matter the cruelty we bestowed on him, he would not yield. If we came to fully command the Stone, if we unleashed it on an unsuspecting World, he believed the Harm would be Irreparable. Once he managed to escape, but we tracked him and caught him near the Great River that runs through this area. The effort cost him, and finally, the Power of the Stone he once wore dissipated. At our hands, the abbot died.

We hurled his body into the fast and treacherous River.

Guilt filled my soul, and with it came a quiet, desperate Madness. He was a Holy Man who had lost his way, but who, I believe, had found Repentance.

As for our pitiful but murderous Expedition, we had destroyed the Philosopher's Stone.

Thus, we are doomed to remain here, and here, we shall die.

The tale horrified Charlotte and left her sick at heart. If true, if the very creator of this blasphemy could not leave it, how in heaven's name could they? Were they all doomed here? Jake, Michael, the students ...

"May I borrow this?" she asked Will. "I'd like my companions to read it, to understand."

Will covered the manuscript with sheepskin and handed it to her. Soon, she and Rachel returned to the community house.

When they retired for the night, Charlotte couldn't sleep.

Eventually she gave up and snuck out of the community house and quietly crept to the stable, careful to stay in the shadows. Jake must have heard her footstep, or the opening of the stable door because he stood up as she entered.

"What happened? Are you all right?" Large, strong hands brushed the hair that had fallen to her face, touched her cheek, her jaw. "They didn't hurt you, did they?"

"I'm all right, but you must read this." She handed him the papers, her voice tremulous. "It's beyond belief, yet has the ring of truth."

He took the papers. "You're shaking."

She tried to pull herself together, to hold her chin up. "It seems so hopeless, Jake."

He put down the papers and put his arms around her. "As long as we have breaths to take," he said, his voice strong, "we have hope."

She saw his determination and fortitude, and placed her hands on his shoulders. Her gaze drifted from eyes that were the deep green of pines, to strong sun-burnished cheekbones, a straight nose, and sensitive mouth. How had she ever thought him cold and heartless?

As she looked at him, his eyes darkened, and neither could look away.

"Who's there?" Lionel cried. "What's going on?"

He woke the others with his shout. Charlotte turned and fled back to the community house.

SIXTY-THREE

New York City

Jianjun awoke feeling as if he had spent the night in Dracula's castle. The massive bed's wooden headboard reached nearly to the ceiling, its ornately carved panels reminiscent of gothic architecture. Dusty purple velvet drapery hung over the windows, blocking all sunlight. Flocked green, gray, and purple floral wallpaper covered every wall.

A six-foot wide, eight-foot tall dark mahogany wardrobe dominated one side of the room. Jianjun was afraid to look inside. Anything could be hiding in there. He drew open the drapes. A gray, drizzly overcast sky only added to the eeriness. Moments later, the housekeeper wheeled in a lavish breakfast of eggs, sausage, kippers, waffles, cold cereal, orange juice, coffee, and tea. A few minutes after he finished eating, she delivered over a dozen books on alchemy in Egypt and China, as well as discussion papers on Nicholas Flamel and Hermes Trismegistus.

Her timing made him feel spied upon. He rubbed his arms to ward off an eerie chill.

Instead of reading, he went looking for Phaylor or his nurse, but failed to find anyone, not even the seemingly omnipresent housekeeper. He discovered that the elevator would not stop for him on the house's third floor, but only on the first with its entryway and garages, the second or main floor, the fourth with his guest bedroom, and the roof garden. When he took the stairs, he found a locked door blocked access to the third floor as well.

He knocked on it, but no one answered.

Finally, he gave up and returned to his bedroom to spend the day trying to understand the basic tenants of a confusing mishmash of ideas about turning base metals into gold, and humans into immortal beings. No wonder sane people considered alchemy crazy.

In the evening, he sat alone in the dining room, eating a feast of grilled red snapper, roast beef, coq au vin, vegetables, one hot and one cold soup, and several salads. Everything about the meal seemed both elaborate and wasteful. He had eaten his fill when the door to the dining room opened. Calvin Phaylor entered, wheeled by his nurse. Jianjun jumped to his feet.

"I hope you enjoyed the meal," Phaylor said. "Please sit."

Phaylor's nurse brought out a decanter of cognac and two crystal glasses, and poured them each a drink. "I'll be fine for now, Bob," Phaylor said.

The nurse left, shutting the door behind him.

"Michael Rempart's adventures in Mongolia were quite fascinating," Phaylor said. "Dr. Rempart managed to do what no one else has. Find a Han tomb outside of China, and find someone who had once successfully practiced Chinese alchemy. Did your boss ever learn where or how Lady Hsieh's body disappeared?"

Jianjun was stunned. "How did you learn about all that?"

Phaylor grinned, shrunken gums making his teeth appear overly large and wide-spaced in his skeletal face. "As you saw by the books I sent you, my interest in alchemy is deep and has existed for many years. Some years ago, I traveled to China."

Jianjun nodded and said nothing.

"Recently, certain acquaintances there, men who work with Director Zhao from the Ministry of Culture, informed me of the loss of Lady Hsieh's body. It was most unfortunate. She would have provided science with indisputable proof that alchemy works."

"Or that the early Chinese knew a scientific means to preserve the body," Jianjun said, ever practical. He remembered Director Zhao's comment that wealthy, influential people, if not the US government itself, engineered the theft of the tomb contents. Phaylor, he was sure, had been one of those people.

"If anyone could learn alchemy's secret, it would be Michael Rempart," Phaylor said. "I'm absolutely certain Michael Rempart's fame is what caused Jennifer Vandenburg to choose his brother Lionel to find *The Book of Abraham the Jew*. I'm sure she expected Michael to step in and help his brother."

Jianjun couldn't comment right away because he was too busy mulling over Phaylor's mention of Vandenburg "choosing" Lionel Rempart. "Jennifer Vandenburg?" He tried to sound surprised. "Is she involved?"

Phaylor chuckled. "Don't pretend you haven't figured that out. If there is anything to alchemy, who could better benefit than a pharmaceutical company? Vandenburg could give the alchemical formulas to her company and perform wonders. Creating gold would be well and good, of course, but imagine the rest of it. What if alchemy truly can lead to a life that continues so long a person feels immortal? And what if PLP distributed the means to provide that immortality? How valuable would such a 'medical discovery' be?"

Jianjun wanted to kick himself for not putting that together sooner, but at the same time, as the implications of it struck, he looked at Phaylor with growing horror. "It would be priceless," he murmured. "Absolutely priceless."

Phaylor gave him a wide, ugly smile. "Exactly."

SIXTY-FOUR

LIONEL SAT ON THE FLOOR OF THE BARN, HIS BACK RESTING AGAINST A wall. He was alone except for Vince. Somebody or something had awoken him. His brother, the Sheriff and that spooky-looking Simon Quade had all left the barn to go outside and talk. He wondered what they were up to, and why he hadn't been asked to join them.

He also wondered why the villagers allowed the women to stay warm and comfortable while they treated him no better than a farm animal. He couldn't help but suspect the women offered the villagers all sorts of favors.

He noticed the way Thaddeus Kohler ogled Melisse. He wouldn't put it past her to take advantage of Kohler's interest. Enough coeds had played such little games with him. They knew what it took to raise their grades.

Even that sniveling idiot Brandi Vinsome had come to his office after hours a couple of times and practically threw herself at him to convince him to take her on this field trip. She had hinted without subtlety that she would provide him a most pleasurable excursion. What else would have convinced him to select her over capable applicants?

Once on the field trip however, she ignored him. So much for her promises and gratitude. Little bitch!

He sighed heavily. He couldn't think about women now.

Vince's loud snores interrupted his thoughts.

The boy had been abnormally quiet ever since his fright the other night when he ran caterwauling back to camp. Rempart didn't even want to think about Devlin and the possibility of another dead student. He rubbed his throbbing temples. Already he feared being forced to kiss his career goodbye after this abominable disaster. He would never live it down.

Tenure provided his only comfort. If they tried to fire him, he'd sue. How could he have known any of this would happen?

He felt sick to his stomach. He lay back down and covered himself with smelly animal hides. All in all, he was glad the villagers had taken them in, even if he did have to sleep in a barn. The villagers suggested they not attempt to leave the village walls. Dangers lay beyond them. In the pens beside the stable were wild boars and sows, ducks and wild turkey whose wings had been clipped so they could no longer fly, and surprisingly tame big horn sheep and mountain goats. Lionel felt like one of the animals...but at least he was safe.

If only he better understood what he encountered here, he might feel less nervous about the place.

The sheriff had told them the men here had disappeared thirteen years ago; he said he recognized their names from official reports on their disappearance. Lionel found that hard to believe considering how young some of them looked. Or, maybe, this place was the Fountain of Youth, too.

One thing he did know. The ancient tools, utensils and such all around here had to have been left by the secret expedition that followed Lewis and Clark.

Many months ago, when he first read the journal of Francis Masterson at the Smithsonian with all its talk about people disappearing into the pillars, he assumed Masterson had gone mad. But now, he learned the tale was true. The expedition's men must have built these log huts and the community house, trying to make this forlorn land habitable.

He wondered what had happened to them. Did they find their way out, or did they die here? He shivered. And what about the strange creatures all around them? Where had they come from? His thoughts returned to rumors of bones of odd creatures found in this part of Central Idaho. Maybe he should have investigated further, although any rational man would have expected they were a hoax. But if bones of those creatures from this side were found in the real world, there had to be a way to go back, a way to go home. A kernel of hope built inside him.

Getting back...back to his home...his studies...his coeds...

Happy thoughts lulled him back to sleep.

SIXTY-FIVE

Early the next morning, before dawn, all six of the village men entered the community house, their faces grim.

They awoke Charlotte, Melisse, Rachel and Brandi and ordered them to dress and come down to the gathering room.

After a long silence, Kohler spoke, his voice deep and troubled. "We have tarried long enough." He cast cold eyes on Melisse. "You have done wrong."

"She didn't mean any harm," Rachel said in a high and quivery tone.

Kohler glared at her. "She stole our food and supplies; she is a thief. Are you saying you are as well?"

Rachel shook her head, then meekly stepped back into the shadows, too afraid to stand up bravely, and too embarrassed and ashamed by her fear to look at anyone.

Charlotte glanced at Melisse, who shook her head waving Charlotte off.

"Bring the criminal forward," Kohler commanded.

Melisse glared at Kohler as Sam Black and Arnie Tieg each grabbed one arm. She easily pulled herself free of them and marched on her own to stand in front of Kohler, her chin high and defiant.

"You are bold," he said, a hint of approval in his voice.

She made no reply.

Kohler slowly marched around Melisse eying her as she stood alone. "I've given this great thought. It is not right to flog a woman as I would have done to one of my men. Nor is it manly to use a woman in a conjugal way as punishment—much as that would have pleased several in this room." He gave a studied, distasteful glance at Black and Tieg.

No one spoke.

"There are other means, however." He walked up to her. She never flinched as he unzipped her jacket and dropped it from her shoulders to the floor. She wore a turtleneck with a flannel shirt over it, multi-pocketed cargo pants, and hiking boots.

He said nothing but looked at her shirt and top and nodded.

Her face a mask of disgust, she removed the shirt, and then pulled the heavy turtleneck over her head, revealing a tight knit camisole. Her breasts were full, her waist small, and a flat abdomen disappeared into loose-fitting trousers. Every man, including Kohler, made a sharp intake of breath at the sight.

"Stoke the fire," Kohler ordered, then glanced toward the large fireplace in the room. Ben Owens went over and did as commanded.

No one moved as Kohler took an iron poker and placed it in the fire. He waited a minute, then used a wadded cloth to pick it up. The tip glowed as he walked toward Melisse.

"This is barbaric!" Charlotte cried. "What's wrong with you?"

Arnie Tieg approached her, knife in hand. Her protests stopped.

Brandi whimpered "No," as tears filled her eyes.

The other men crowded near, expecting Melisse to run.

"Hold her," Kohler ordered.

As they tried to grab her, she fought. She knocked Gus and Sam out of the way with ease. The elderly Olgerbee hung back, as did Will Durham who looked sickened, but didn't interfere even when Rachel begged him to stop this outrage.

Finally, Olgerbee and Will joined Gus and Sam. Together they wrestled her, face down, to the floor. While the others held her, Kohler knelt on the ground, straddling her hips. Angered by the struggle, he gripped her camisole and ripped it open to expose her bare back. Then he gasped.

"What is this?" he whispered.

Scars from lashes and burn marks crisscrossed her back. His fingers lightly touched the puckered, tortured skin.

She turned her head to look up at him, but made no reply.

"Who did this to you?" he asked.

"What does it matter? It's your turn now, it seems."

He tossed aside the poker then moved off of her. He grabbed her arm, made her sit up and turned her to look at him. The other four stayed close, ready to act if she lashed out or tried to run. She gripped her camisole to cover herself.

"I want to know!" Kohler demanded.

"I was with a couple of men doing recon in Afghanistan when we were captured by the enemy. The men were killed. Fortunately, our unit found me—saved my life."

"You were in combat? A woman?"

"Why so shocked?" she said bitterly. "It happens."

He held her gaze. "How long were you a prisoner?"

Without flinching, her tone filled with disgust, she replied, "Four days ... three nights."

His jaw tightened with anger, but something in his eyes told her he understood exactly what she was saying. He stood. "Leave her be," he ordered the others. They didn't move. "Damn it, did you not hear me? I said, leave her be!"

They hurried out of the room.

After one last glance at Melisse, Kohler also left.

SIXTY-SIX

UNAWARE OF WHAT TRANSPIRED IN THE COMMUNITY HOUSE, Michael, Jake, and Quade met outside the stables, out of hearing of Lionel and Vince. Quietly, Michael read the Francis Masterson paper to the others.

Masterson's account stunned Michael. No wonder his brother had dropped everything to come to Idaho to search for this place, to find out if any of the information was true. He would have done the exact same thing.

"These papers explain everything," Quade said.

Jake shook his head. "It's got to be some wild yarn."

"Do you believe it?" Michael asked.

"Yes, the story is true," Quade said. "I read Francis Masterson's first journal. The Smithsonian stored it among the remnants of a small, failed Mormon settlement called New Gideon. I assume the Tukudeka probably found it where Masterson hid it before crossing through the pillars, and that it later fell into the hands of settlers. If the settlers had found the pillars, they surely would have mentioned them. In any case, the journal chronicled the Secret Expedition before Masterson stepped between the pillars. Most likely, people assumed it to be either a work of pure fiction, or the wild scribblings of a madman. These papers and this place prove he wrote the truth."

"Even though I'm standing right here," Jake said, "I still find it hard to believe."

"I don't," Michael said. "It fits with a discovery I made in Mongolia."

He briefly told them about opening the tomb of Lady Hsieh and her practice of alchemy—but left out the fact that he believed he later saw and spoke to her.

Still, Jake looked at him as if his *mentis* was not very *compos*.

"More importantly," Quade said, "these papers tell not only what became of the Expedition, but also Abbé Gerard."

"You've heard of him?" Michael asked.

"The surprise is that you haven't," Quade said with a strange, secretive smile. "You didn't see it, did you?"

"See what?" Michael asked.

"Abbé Gerard's family name was Rombert, pronounced in the French way, Rohm-*berrr*. But it wasn't always French. The abbot was actually a descendent of Edward Kelley, who was either one of the greatest alchemists of all time, or one of the greatest con artists. What we know about him is a mixture of rumor, legend, and truth, and no one can be sure which is which."

"What does he have to do with any of this?" Michael asked.

"It's a long story, but one well worth hearing. Edward Kelley was believed to have been born in Ireland in the 16th century. A thief and swindler, early in life, his ears were sliced off as punishment. He fled to England and managed to find himself a wealthy, well-educated sponsor, an older man named John Dee.

"Dee had spent his life studying the supernatural and amassing a large library about it. When he met Kelley, who claimed to be clairvoyant, a psychic, Dee believed him. He even brought Kelley to the court of Elizabeth I."

Clearly warming to showing off his erudition, Quade wore a sly smile as he continued. "At one point, Kelley even convinced Dee the angels spoke directly to him, and wrote down what they said in a made up language he called Enochian. Dee became so much under Kelley's influence that when Kelley suggested they swap wives for the good of the angels and man, Dee agreed." Quade smirked. "By the way, history tells us Dee's wife was much prettier than Kelley's, and also that Mrs. Dee had a child some nine months after Kelley's escapade with her, something which apparently made Dee rather unhappy. But that still wasn't enough to cause John Dee to end their association."

"This is important, why?" Jake asked impatiently.

"Kelley's interest moved to alchemy," Quade said with a nod. "Using books and materials from Dee's vast collection, including *The Book of Abraham the Jew*, which Kelley kept for himself, he claimed to have learned the secret to creating gold, and apparently demonstrated it several times at the English court.

"Emperor Rudolf of Bohemia heard about this and wanted some of that gold. He invited Dee and Kelley to his court. They went, sans their troublesome wives. They had a problem, however. Once in Bohemia, Kelley apparently lost his ability to produce gold. He begged the King for more time. Dee, who wasn't a complete fool, fled back to England, while Kelley found himself a new patron named Vilém Rozmberk. This Rozmberk managed to protect Kelley from the emperor for some time, and spent a fortune on Kelley, in hopes of being repaid through Kelley's gold-making acumen. Kelley's only success, however, came when he convinced Rozmberk's daughter, Anna, to marry him...prior wife notwithstanding.

"Kelley spent lavishly, and his extravagances financially ruined Rozmberk. Finally, the emperor lost all patience, and sent Kelley to prison where he eventually died from complications after breaking both legs trying to escape.

"Kelley's wife grew fearful that the Emperor's wrath would fall on her and their young son. She fled Bohemia, taking *The Book* with her. She knew its value, and that an alchemist could use it to make gold for their family. It's said that her son, also named Edward, inherited his father's psychic ability, plus some of his less noble traits. He, too, became an alchemist and a confidence man.

"Also, you should know that Anna didn't take Kelley's name as hers. The man had been a scandal, and she wanted nothing to do with him. Since Rozmberk was an awkward name, she changed it to Romberg.

"During a period of anti-Semitism in France, the family changed their Jewish-sounding name to Rombert. Despite the name changes, Edward Kelley's bloodline continued, and each generation of males was said to possess psychic abilities. Some more, some less."

A chill rippled through Michael at these words. He wanted to tell Quade to stop; at the same time, he wanted to hear the rest of Quade's peculiar tale.

"The Abbé Gerard Rombert was one such descendant. Growing up, he thought his visions and understanding of future events were caused by the Devil. Because of that, he joined a monastery hoping the psychic powers would go away, but they didn't. In the monastery, he was drawn to ancient writings about alchemy. He owned *The Book of Abraham the Jew*, passed on to him by his father as a family keepsake."

"History tells us that Abbé Gerard Rombert de Fontainebleau, with his special book, left France after the French Revolution broke out. In his travels, he met men who knew much more about alchemy than did the Catholics in France. He asked questions, read books they gave him, and soon, a new world opened up to him—much as you have read in these papers."

"Fascinating," Michael said.

"Yes, but there's more," Quade said. "His name."

"What do you mean?"

"Over the years, as the descendents of Anna Rozmberk and Edward Kelley traveled to different countries, including the U.S., the Rozmberk name changed in various ways, to Rombart, Rembart, even *Rempart*. They are all from the same root. You, Michael, and Lionel, are descendants of Edward Kelley."

As much as Michael had been sure that would be the upshot of the story, he feigned disgust. "That's ridiculous."

"Is it? I have seen your 'intuition,' which is nothing more than a modern, unthreatening term for psychic abilities. Why were only you and Lionel able to see the array of lights when none of the rest of us could?" Quade asked.

"That's going too far," Michael said.

"Michael's right!" Jake groaned. "This is giving me a headache."

"The bottom line," Quade said, "is that alchemy got us here, and is needed to get us out. And we just happen to have a descendant of the alchemist Edward Kelley to help us."

"The con man, you mean," Michael said with a sneer.

"That's where I have a problem," Jake said. "It's simply too much of a coincidence."

"What, you don't find it a happy chance that Lionel and I just happened to come to Idaho?" Michael folded his arms in disgust.

"Clearly, it is no coincidence," Quade said. "Whoever is behind this has done a lot of investigating. That person knows about your family. The information I gave you is available to many people. Someone has connected the story of Edward Kelley and his descendants to the Rempart name. It stands to reason, given your notoriety, Michael, that once someone began putting this together, such connections would be made. In a way, it may also explain why both brothers have a professional interest in the anomalies of the past."

Michael shook his head. "No. I suspect Lionel was chosen because of his field of study, and his connection with George Washington University."

"Not really." Quade's small cupid-shaped lips curled in a smile. "Masterson's journal is in the Smithsonian. Any scholar could have read it. No, it took someone with a special affinity for the promise presented in *The Book of Abraham the Jew,* and an affinity for alchemy itself, to throw all caution to the wind and come on this journey. That there happens to be two of you makes you an even better fit."

"If it was a matter of finding a descendent of Edward Kelley, there could be hundreds of people to choose from," Michael argued.

"Or few. Or maybe none except the two of you." Quade pursed his lips. "Genealogical lines die out all the time. People die young, die in wars, in famines, or simply die without issue. The remarkable thing after so many centuries is to find any offspring at all."

Despite his protests, Michael knew everything Quade said was true. He knew it before he raised the objections. Quade's story answered questions about himself, about his strange intuitive ability. "What about Edward Kelley?" His voice was soft, resigned. "Where did he get his psychic abilities?"

"All we know is that he came from Ireland. Many people believe Kelley wasn't his real name, so we'll never know. Personally, I wouldn't be surprised if his ancestors didn't include Hermes Trismegistus himself." He stared at Michael a moment. "It makes me wonder what your father is like. Of course, that's none of my business."

Quade's last comment churned in Michael's mind.

William Claude Rempart was frightfully intelligent, but seemed to exist on a different plane, almost a different dimension.

Michael always suspected that oddness had a lot to do with his mother's death.

They lived on a large estate and she fell from the balcony of a third floor study onto a brick patio. Michael watched her fall to her death. Fall? Or jump? Whichever it was, Michael stood and watched ... and did nothing to stop her.

Her death had been ruled an accident, but Michael had doubts about that determination.

His brother, Lionel, was ten years older and had been away at Yale at the time.

Their father, who had never been very practical or down-to-earth, became even more withdrawn. Some said his wife's death drove him mad. Others said he caused her death, with dark hints of murder or driving her to take her own life.

Michael ended up being raised by nannies. The family housekeeper alone gave the young boy love and compassion. The housekeeper and her little daughter were once Michael's whole world, and then they too were gone.

After his mother's death Michael spent years trying to convince himself that he didn't care anything about his parents or their troubled lives, but he did. He sometimes wondered if he wasn't more his father's son than he wanted to admit.

Voices and movement beyond the stables warned them the villagers approached. "You're right," Michael said to Quade. "It is none of your business."

SIXTY-SEVEN

New York City

"Mr. Li," Jennifer Vandenburg said as she held out her hand and welcomed Jianjun to her office. The large windows and magnificent view stunned him. "Your call intrigued me," she said as she stepped behind her ebony and chrome desk and offered Jianjun a seat.

"Thank you for seeing me." He sat in the black leather arm chair facing her and then told his carefully made-up story. "It has come to Dr. Michael Rempart's attention that you were his brother's benefactress for his Idaho trip. He needs to learn as much as possible about the trip to help him find Lionel."

A flicker of what seemed like anger showed for an instant before she regained her composure. "If I had, I wouldn't be keeping it from the authorities, would I?" Vandenburg smiled sweetly.

"Except that you don't want the public to know about your interest in alchemy."

"Alchemy? I have no idea what you're talking about."

"But you do," Jianjun said coolly. "It's why you sent Lionel Rempart to Idaho."

She stood, arms folded, and walked to the window. Jianjun noticed her cell phone on her desk. He scooted his chair as close as possible. He palmed his own phone and punched in the spy monitor access code. The system would locate her phone and lock onto it, accessing her future usage. "Professor Rempart," she said, "was quite interested in following Lewis and

Clark. Many people, I'm sure, contributed to his investigation. PLP donates to many educational causes."

"We know about *The Book of Abraham the Jew*," Jianjun said.

She faced him with a cold smile. "And you aren't laughing? I am. I know Lionel Rempart went off on a tangent about that book and alchemy, but I never believed such a book existed, let alone was lost in Idaho! If that was the real reason for Professor Rempart's expedition, I'm sorry I authorized one penny to him. The last thing I expected was for him to drag along a bunch of students and then get lost. It's a horrible tragedy. I pray every day for their safe return."

"How did you, or PLP, become involved with Lionel Rempart?" Jianjun asked. He leaned back in the chair and casually slid his hand and cell phone back into his pocket.

She studied him for a long moment before she answered. "The professor sent us a proposal asking for assistance to find the site where a secret expedition that had followed Lewis and Clark had lived and died. I found it interesting. Nothing more."

"I understand many unique and useful drugs have been discovered by studying ancient herbs and medicines," Jianjun said.

Vandenburg frowned. "If you think we were expecting to find medicine used by those adventurers, you are completely mistaken. Besides, drugs today are mostly synthetic, produced after decades of research and experimentation."

He stood. "I'm sorry to have bothered you."

She walked to the door. "Yes, well, I'm sure PLP is one of many who contributed to Professor Rempart. Considering the terrible turn this has taken, I do not expect my name or that of PLP to be associated in any way with Rempart, his disappearance, or his strange pursuits. Do I make myself clear?"

Jianjun nodded and left.

SIXTY-EIGHT

THAT AFTERNOON, MICHAEL WAS ALONE AT THE STABLES. EARLIER, the village men took the others away to work. His arm felt much better already, and he wondered about the poultice Ben Olgerbee had used.

In the distance, he saw Ben Olgerbee walk by.

The word "wizened" came to mind to describe Olgerbee, a small, thin man who walked with a stoop, his chest concave. Wizened cheeks. Wizened hair. Wizened...Michael thought of a similar word. *Wizard.*

Something made him decide to follow the man.

Past the stables, near the fence that circled the village, a trap door lay flat on the ground. Olgerbee opened it and descended steep steps, then lit a torch and shut the door behind him.

Michael waited until he thought Olgerbee might have walked away, and then opened the door and hurried into the dark, narrow tunnel. When he shut the door behind him, he saw only a faint bit of light in the distance.

Michael hurried to catch up to Olgerbee, whose torch led him through a dark, narrow tunnel away from the village. Michael grew increasingly more claustrophobic with every step. Fifteen minutes passed before they stepped out of the tunnel near a steep, rocky rise.

Tucked away behind tumbled boulders along its base was the entrance to a cave. Olgerbee went inside.

Michael waited. He expected Olgerbee to come out any moment. When he didn't, Michael inched closer.

He didn't expect to be able to see much at all in the darkened cave, but to his amazement, torches fastened to the stone walls lit the way.

Michael crept along the wall until the tunnel opened to a wide room.

Olgerbee sat on the ground, eyes shut as if meditating. Before him lay pure gold nuggets. Numerous nuggets. Piles of them. A fortune in them.

Idaho had seen a few gold strikes, but most had been mined out. Michael saw gold the size of one and two inch river rocks, smooth as eggs and oval shaped. He couldn't even imagine where such gold had been found. It must have been from some river to have been worn so smooth, but he'd never heard of panned gold being that size.

"Who's there?" Olgerbee cried. As he roused from his golden reverie, he glanced about in suspicion.

Michael didn't move in hopes Olgerbee would assume the sound came from one of the many creatures that walked the forest and caves.

When Olgerbee stopped listening, Michael quietly backed out of the cave and hid near its mouth to wait for Olgerbee to leave.

He didn't have to wait long.

As Olgerbee headed back to the village, Michael snuck into the cave.

Alone, the gold looked even more wondrous, the quality and quantity more unbelievable, than he'd imagined.

He truly understood why people considered it the most perfect of all metals, and why, in every civilization, it had been valued and often used in worship.

A small golden box lay in the back of the cave. The box, about one cubic foot, reminded him of a tabernacle—where Catholics house the consecrated host—with doors that opened from the front to reveal the contents.

A simple hook and eye clasp with no lock held the double doors shut. He opened it.

Inside he found an old, grimy bowl made from some thick metal, possibly iron. He lifted it out. It felt heavy, the inside coated with a sooty substance, and looked quite poor and cheap among all this gold. Why someone put it in a place of honor was anyone's guess. It had a slightly sulfuric odor.

Under the bowl lay a book. He picked it up and felt it grow warm under his fingers.

Charlotte had told him about *The Book of Abraham the Jew* saying Nicolas Flamel described it as being bound with a cover of brass and written on some sort of delicate rinds.

He opened the heavy metal cover and found that the leaves weren't paper or parchment, but could well be rinds of some sort.

The first page had greatly faded writing on it, a very stylized script that formed words in classical Greek. Michael had studied both Greek and Latin.

Upon the first leaf, written with large albeit faint gold capital letters, he read, "*Abraham the Jew, Prince, Levite...*"

His heart began to pound. This was it ... the book that had been rumored about for centuries, argued over, sought. And here it was.

He carefully turned a fragile page, fearing the material might crumble in his hand.

Some pages were filled with writing that would take time and effort to translate. Others were painted with symbols—the god Mercury, a Caducean rod with two serpents, an old man with an hour glass and a scythe, flowers, dragons, griffons, a rose tree, a king, infants, mothers weeping at the feet of soldiers, and on and on.

None of it made sense and Michael understood why a Kabbalah scholar would be needed to explain it.

Time passed quickly. He put everything back the way he had found it. He knew he had to get back before anyone realized he was gone and where he had been. Yet, here, in his hands, he had held the knowledge that men sought for several millennia.

Walking away from it was difficult.

SIXTY-NINE

Thaddeus Kohler sent Brandi and Rachel to the community house to prepare lunch for the village men, but left Melisse alone in the field where the women had dug tubers all morning. The day was crisp and cool, but Melisse's cheeks were flushed and a sheen of perspiration covered her skin from the effort of digging into the hard ground. He stood before her.

"You must hate men for what they did to you," he said, feet wide and hands on hips.

She looked up at him and then stood, rubbing her hands against her cargo pants to brush away the dirt. It didn't surprise her to see him, not after the way he'd looked at her in the community house that morning. "Those men were the enemy. I hated them—and we killed them before we left the area."

"So you don't hold such brutality against my sex?"

"Yours isn't the only sex capable of brutality." She thought about how much to tell him, how useful it might be to have him as an ally. Very useful. "I hold nothing against men. In fact, I have a child. A daughter. Age five."

His brow lifted. "And a husband?"

She let her gaze slide over him slowly. She'd known better looking men...and worse. It wasn't the first time she used a man's weakness to survive. "I have no husband," she said. "As for the father, I don't know where he is. We didn't get along all that well."

He regarded her curiously. "Why?"

She met his gaze steadily, and when she spoke, her voice sounded husky. "He was weak. Too weak for me."

He took the iron spade from her hand. "Do you think to lull me with your tempting words and sultry looks and then put this blade between my ribs as I come to you like a lamb?"

She took back the spade and then tossed it on the ground. "You're no lamb, Kohler. And my thoughts about you were far different from that. But now"—she shrugged one shoulder—"I've changed my mind."

She walked away, but when she reached a stand of aspen, he stopped her and held her arm. She let him.

"You claim to like me now?" He adopted a mocking jeer.

She stepped backwards, deeper into the trees. "Like you? All I know is that I don't trust you."

He smirked and moved closer. "How can you not trust me? You've seen these men. I'm the one who controls them ... so far."

Disgust filled her face, and her next words were calculated. "So far? And here I thought you were strong."

She raised her chin as if daring him to come nearer. He took up the dare, so close she could feel his breath meet hers. Then, as if his hand had a will of its own, he reached out and touched her cheek, her neck, her collar bone. "I saved you," he said, his voice a raspy whisper, "from the beasts, from a branding, from the others. And now, it is I who has become a prisoner."

"A prisoner?"

"To you, woman! My own men mock me for my weakness."

"You lie," she sneered, and placed her hands on his chest. "Everything you say is a lie. You feel nothing for me."

He gripped her upper arms. "Am I lying now?"

"What will your men say?"

"They mean nothing. You want this as much as I do."

"I don't."

"Then why is your breathing heavy, your heart racing?" His hands spanned her waist then jerked her hips tight against his. "If you truly wanted me to walk away now, I would know it."

She placed her hands on his shoulders. "I despise you."

"As I do you. And I could have killed you time and again, but I didn't. Tell me that's a lie, too." He kissed her ear, her neck, but as he sought her mouth, she turned her head from a peculiar smell, almost of decay, that seemed to emanate from him. His hand went to her breast. "Tell me," he said.

She ran her fingers through his hair, then gripped and pulled it tight enough to inflict pain, enough to heighten his desire. "We both lie," she whispered.

He emitted a deep growl and pushed her to the ground. He hovered over her and unbuttoned her shirt. She did the same to his, but had only opened two buttons when his gold necklace with a red pendant stone slipped free. "What is this strange jewel you wear?"

Shocked, he drew back.

"Is it a gift from a lady friend?" she purred. "Or something you stole." She took the stone in her hand. It felt warm and began to glow.

"No!" He jerked it away from her, sitting up as his eyes leaped from her to the stone. His face filled with conflicting emotions of desire and horror.

"What is it?" She demanded as she sat up.

"Nothing." He stood and re-buttoned his shirt, hiding the stone once more. "Get back to the community house. You need to help the others prepare supper."

He turned toward the forest, then stopped and faced her again. "This, between us," he said, "it's not over."

She remained seated on the ground, puzzled over what had just happened.

SEVENTY

"How long are we going to wait?" Nose threw his dried jerky on the ground. They had spent another night doing nothing but watching and waiting, and now the morning was nearly over, the sun high in the sky. "I'm tired of sitting on my ass. This food is for shit. I say we go in, kill those weirdoes with the bows and arrows, find what we need, and get the hell out."

Hammill frowned; he didn't like his men speaking their minds that way, but he wasn't surprised. The men felt spooked, and that made them angry. "Okay, hot shot. Tell me how we get out."

"Right back the way we came," Nose said. "I'm sure there's a way."

"Fuck," Fish said, which meant he agreed.

"And if the plan craps out, then what?" Hammill asked. "You think those bozos stick around with their thumbs up their asses because they like it here? No one lives this way by choice. Think with your head, man, not your stomach or your dick. We'll wait."

He didn't admit to the others, but he thought that since Charlotte Reed got them here, she should be able to get them out. He didn't want to take the chance of killing her. He didn't like being superstitious, but he was. She had become a totem to him. She'd stayed alive in spite of his best efforts. There had to be a reason for that, and he saw it now. To kill her would be unlucky. To keep her alive would bring him luck. And they needed luck.

His conviction was confirmed when his scout gestured for him and the others to see what was going on.

Hammill watched two of the villagers lead Charlotte Reed and Lionel Rempart away from the village. Hammill and his men followed silently. Hammill suspected his men also carried a silent hope that Charlotte Reed would show them how to leave this hell hole when the time came.

When the villagers reached the pillars, they stopped. Hammill saw a confused expression on Charlotte's face. Next, he watched as Lionel Rempart lifted a cloth away from some big, elaborate book. He and Charlotte kept looking from the book to the pillars. With a jolt, Hammill realized the book had to be the one he'd been sent here to steal. But now, he couldn't take it. Not if it held the key to getting out of this place.

If it did, however, the key wasn't working because Charlotte and the professor kept shaking their heads. Finally, they sat down on the ground, the book in front of them, and seemed to pore over it.

Hammill hoped his men didn't feel the same sinking sensation as he did, or he'd have a mutiny on his hands, one that could be dangerous even for him. He'd have to act before that happened. Maybe if they captured Charlotte Reed and placed a knife against her scrawny throat, she'd be inspired to get all of them home again.

That was what they needed to do.

Charlotte and the book, together. Why wait?

But what if he was wrong?

"How am I supposed to know how to open the gateway?" Lionel whispered to Charlotte as they sat at the top of the mound facing the pillars with *The Book of Abraham the Jew* on a cloth before them.

Earlier, after breakfast, Kohler had stood and spoke to the group. "I know the interest some of you have in the ancient book of alchemy found here."

At their stunned look, he said, "Yes, we have found the ancient book of alchemy, but reading it is impossible for us." His gaze pin-pointed Lionel and Michael. "Yet, all of us believe it holds the key to our escape from this place. Since Miss Charlotte Reed is a student of Egypt where much of the information from the book stems, and Professor Lionel Rempart also has studied this area, Mr. Olgerbee will allow the two of you to access the book. We will watch and protect you as you go to the pillars and attempt to open the gateway. May the Almighty God guide your endeavors and bring you to success."

Shortly afterward, Olgerbee and Sam Black escorted them to the pillars and stood guard as they studied the book.

Lionel looked around nervously. He didn't like the way Olgerbee was glaring at him. He leaned toward Charlotte and whispered, "If these people are depending on me to get us out of here, we're in big trouble. You've got to come up with a way, Charlotte. Tell me the hieroglyphs on the pillars say how to open them so we can all go home again."

"I know *how* one reads hieroglyphics, but that doesn't mean I've memorized all the combinations of symbols and their meanings," Charlotte said quietly. "To read them, I need reference books and dictionaries."

A large bat-like creature jerkily flapping its wings swooped down over Lionel's head. Lionel ducked and Sam Black let loose an arrow that struck the strange bat. Lionel stood stock still, petrified, as the creature flew off with the arrow protruding.

"Well, I'm afraid we don't have any Egyptian dictionaries," Lionel whispered, more nervous than ever. "You'll have to figure it out without them. I need you to do it quickly."

The appearance of the winged creature so stunned Charlotte, it took a long moment for Lionel's words to penetrate. "I doubt what's up there explains much of anything," she murmured. "Something about them handing over this book so easily makes me wary. And don't forget that somewhere out there are men who shot at Michael and Quade. We don't know who they are, if they're here to find the students, the book, or why they attacked."

"Whatever we do," Lionel said, his face rigid with determination, "When we find our way back, *The Book of Abraham the Jew* goes with us."

SEVENTY-ONE

New York City

Jianjun arose and dressed early. He found Phaylor's house creepy. Calvin Phaylor ranked high up on the creepy scale as well. The guy looked like a cadaver on wheels.

Jianjun refused the huge breakfast, settling for tea and toast, then set up his computer.

He found that hacking into Phaylor's computer security system was child's play. Phaylor's bank and credit card data provided a plethora of information about his activities over the past few years. Two of the findings surprised Jianjun.

First, four satellite phones, all with New York City prefixes, regularly contacted Phaylor. Jianjun couldn't tell where the calls originated, but satellite phones only made sense in remote locations. He suspected Phaylor had bought and given out the phones.

Second, Phaylor had been interested in the recent murder of the curator of Paris' Cluny museum, and in Jerusalem, of a shooting involving a security guard, a paid assassin, and a scholar of ancient Egypt. Phaylor had also queried the name Laurence Esterbridge several times without success. Jianjun's heart practically stopped when he learned that the Israelis were looking for an American woman named Charlotte Reed in connection with the murders.

She was the woman Michael had asked him to check on. A security camera had caught her driving away in the dead scholar's car. Who in the heck was she? Was she a killer, out there with Michael?

He dived into his computer to search for more information on her. He learned that her Virginia home had been fire-bombed some days earlier. Despite both the Virginia and Israeli police trying to find her, she had not been located. Reports speculated that she torched her home to destroy evidence of her wrong-doings and went into hiding. The only other information Jianjun found about her was a marriage record between her and someone named Dennis Levine. When he searched for information on Levine, he found he was a State Department employee who had died in a terrorist attack in Jerusalem some thirteen years earlier. The date struck Jianjun. A lot seemed to have happened between thirteen and fifteen years ago. This background made him suspect she might not be the crazed murderer the press made her out to be. In fact, she might have been a victim.

What did it all mean, and why did Calvin Phaylor care?

After having learned so much about Charlotte Reed, he searched for more information on the other person Michael had mentioned, Simon Quade. When his usual personal data searches yielded not so much as a birth certificate, he went into the CIA's data base. After coming up with nothing, he tried their human resources. Consultants were fingerprinted, and of course always had IRS payment and withholding forms on file. Strangely, he found nothing at all. The name had to be phony, which made Jianjun more curious than ever. But without more information, he was at a standstill.

Searching for six men lost in Idaho some twelve or thirteen years earlier turned up only rumors and denials of same. Everyone involved agreed that six paramilitary types went through the area. Jianjun turned up their names, starting with their leader, Thaddeus Kohler. He found evidence of the men's existences before they went to Idaho, but nothing afterward. As one local said when asked if he thought they had disappeared in the wilderness, "Of course not. They left, that's all. They weren't exactly the type to drop in to say 'so long.'" Another standstill.

The men could be dead, but he found no evidence of that—no death certificates or insurance payouts. Their families all refused to say anything about the men, which made Jianjun immediately suspect that someone had paid for their silence.

Something was seriously amiss.

He then turned to his cell phone to see what information the spy monitor had picked up on Vandenburg. He found a long list of phone calls, but a quick check revealed all to be work or home related.

He turned back to Calvin Phaylor's files but, again, nothing new jumped out at him.

Time to go to Idaho, he thought, even though he hadn't yet figured out what he would do once he got there. Also, he had grown increasingly nervous about Michael. The news reported that the sheriff went on a "secret mission" to try to find the students. This happened right after authorities pulled the body of student Brian Cutter from a river. Few believed the "secret mission" story, which caused speculation that whoever killed the student had murdered the sheriff, or that the sheriff himself wiped out the entire university group and fled after one of the bodies turned up.

Jianjun didn't know what to think, but Michael had been with that sheriff, and now he could no longer be reached.

SEVENTY-TWO

New York City

"I want to go home, Mommy. Take me with you, please!" As Vandenburg stood to leave, Felicity's small, clawlike hand grasped hers, her grip amazingly strong. "I hate it here. I want to go back to my own room. Please, Mommy!"

"I'll see what I can do." She kissed her daughter's forehead and yanked her hand free, then she turned and hurried from the room with a quick goodbye to Kay. Felicity's kidneys were shutting down. If the girl went home now, she would be back in a day, anyway. The fools of doctors said the end was near. Vandenburg refused to allow it.

Outside the hospital, her limo waited.

She gave an Upper East Side address, and the housekeeper showed her to the living room of what had been one of the most beautiful homes in New York City, but now appeared old and neglected. Just like Calvin Phaylor, she thought.

Phaylor entered, his wheelchair pushed by his male nurse.

"Hello, Calvin." Vandenburg smiled sweetly. "Good to see you."

"No, it's not, and you and I both know it. Where are your new products? You can't ride on old ones forever, you know. What's wrong with you people? Have you no talent left in the firm? No imagination? Don't think you can make my company fail, not while I'm alive!" The nurse handed him the oxygen mask, then left the room. Phaylor breathed deeply.

"We're doing all we can to protect all you created. But that's not why

I'm here." Vandenburg paused a moment. She felt pressure build behind her eyes and turned her head so he wouldn't notice if she lost the fight with tears. She worked to control her voice. "My daughter doesn't have much time left. My people in Idaho are still missing. It's long past time for you to tell me everything. I need to find the book that tells how to create the philosopher's stone and use it before it's too late!"

He gave a snort of derision.

"I've toyed with going to Idaho myself," Vandenburg said. "Even announcing to the world what we're looking for, and how much I'll pay to whoever delivers *The Book of Abraham the Jew* to me. How does one billion dollars sound? People will laugh, until I succeed. With it, Felicity will live. It's her only chance. Her last chance!"

"How touching." His insincerity reeked. "You're damn right people will laugh. Even more will laugh as the board of directors carts you off to an insane asylum." He eyed her with contempt. "It's not your money. Wasn't even mine, as I found out. And if by some crazy circumstance, you did find the book, the government would step in and take it from you."

"No, they won't! I'm going to find it," she said. "One way or another. I came to you for advice, but if you have none—"

"Oh, I have advice, all right. Allow your daughter to die in peace."

Jennifer stared at him, hate filling every pore. "Never."

"I tried to find the secret of alchemy for myself." He wheeled himself to the bar and poured a Macallan single scotch malt. She refused a glass.

"I was one of the five richest men in America, and I was getting old and sick. This would be a way to beat death, or so, I thought." He sipped the scotch, smacking his lips with pleasure. "I threw all my money, time, and effort in it, and my reward was to be kicked out of my own company before I destroyed it. And I would have. What's a mere company compared to immortality?"

"My plan will save people from pain and suffering," she said, her voice growing more excited with each word she spoke. "But they're going to have to pay for it. We can't solve the problem of death only to have people starve from overpopulation. Only certain people, the right people, will have access to my elixir for immortality. And I'll be the one to decide who that is."

He chuckled, but just as quickly his smile vanished. "You think knowledge from the book is what you want. But it won't work. It'll drive you mad and destroy everything around you."

"Come with me to Idaho," she said. "You know where the pillars are. We can find them. We'll bring Michael Rempart's assistant with us. I'm sure he knows a lot more about all this than he'll admit. Plus, most importantly, I'll bring my daughter."

Phaylor just stared as her.

"Together, we'll get the book ourselves!" she continued. "We're waiting for people to return to us with the book, but we don't know what they've found out there. What if they not only found the book, but have learned how to use it? What if they're stealing it from us *right now*? We can't wait! We've got to go out there and see for ourselves. You've always wanted to be immortal. Show me the way."

"Why should I do anything for you?" His eyes were flat and cold, his skin wrinkled as a lizard's. "And as for your daughter, do I look like someone who gives a damn?"

Her body stiffened with outrage. She would make him pay for those words. She realized how frail he was, how little effort it would take to squeeze the life from his skinny neck. She reined in her anger as a better plan began to form.

She strode out of the living room, but before leaving glared back at Phaylor. "I look forward to the day when you do the world a favor and die."

The nurse, who had been seated in the hallway by the elevator, didn't look surprised at her anger. She guessed the old man treated all his guests equally graciously.

The open elevator waited for her.

As soon as she got off on the ground floor, she phoned her first vice president, Milt Zonovich. "Milt, I'll need the company jet to fly me to Sun Valley, Idaho, as soon as possible. And get a helicopter ready to meet me there. One big enough for a hospital bed."

SEVENTY-THREE

MICHAEL DIDN'T GO TO THE STABLES TO BED DOWN WHEN THE OTHER men did. Instead he stood at the fence around the sheep and goats, his foot on the bottom rung, and thought of the young people, the students, caught up in this madness, the dangers not only from the chimeras but also from the village men.

The village men had confiscated taken their guns and rifles. Now, he understood why. If they had them, they would be tempted to use them on Kohler or anyone else who threatened the students. Too many of these kids had already died.

Michael tried not to think about that, and not to think about the strange history Quade relayed of his ancestors. Psychics and alchemists? Charlatans most likely, and yet, he had known and seen things that this world had no answer for. If he had such abilities where had they come from if not his forefathers?

He couldn't think of that now. Instead, he did his best to concentrate on the silence all around, but his mind wouldn't allow him such peace.

The scent of the forest changed from that of firs and brush to a one much more floral and aromatic. He knew what was coming.

His body tensed, torn between the need to see her, and wanting to run from what was unnatural and wrong. He turned to force himself back to the stables.

"Michael."

He froze. It was a voice, but not a voice. The sound came from inside his head.

He shut his eyes. *This is madness.* When he opened them again, she stood before him.

Was this insanity, or was he seeing more of the reality and complexity of the world than he ever thought possible?

She stood in front of a shimmering garden of white and rose pink peonies. She wore a simple, long-sleeved dress, the color of the sea, with a Chinese collar and frog fasteners across the bodice and down one side. The thick braid of her hair hung to her waist, a plain style for a woman of her position, yet on her it looked regal and elegant.

"Lady Hsieh."

She glided toward him. "I could not stay away and leave you to this danger."

Joy along with sadness filled him. "I'm glad you didn't."

Her eyes traced his face. "You must destroy all this. In doing so, you will free yourself."

"And you?" He stepped closer.

She shook her head. "No, but there is no other way."

"There's got to be."

"I'll try to explain." She took his hand and led him away from the stables toward the fence that circled the village. He followed in silence until she stopped. She dropped his hand and kept her back to him. Head bowed, she began to speak. "After I performed my magic, using the ancient practice my grandmother taught, I achieved what I thought I wanted." She shuddered. "But I learned that immortality only means great loneliness...eternal loneliness, not heaven or hell, but nothing. A vast, empty wasteland. Only when I was freed from the alchemical spell, could I go on to the true afterlife, a place that's home, that's a comfort to the soul."

She faced him then, her eyes like black pools. "I left it to return here. To warn you. You can't allow this world to continue or allow the evil here to spread. You must stop it."

"How can I do that?" He caught her hands in his and held them to his chest.

She shut her eyes as a tremor rippled through her. "All I know is that you will understand when the time comes. You will do what's right. It's the only way. You're a good man, Michael. There is still much for you to do in your life. Follow your instincts, trust them. Only in them will you find the fulfillment you crave."

"Only if you come with me."

She looked toward the heavens. The moon appeared as a narrow sliver in the dark sky. "I cannot."

He cupped her face. "Why do I feel this bond with you? More than ever before in my life, from the moment you opened your eyes ... I won't leave you. I can't." He clasped her arms.

She shook her head. "I wish I had known you when I was a part of the world, your world. I'm not the only one you have ever loved. I know that, and so do you. The other one ... her life is not what you imagine. Find her."

He shook his head. "She's nothing to me."

"She did not betray you."

He winced, surprised the memory still hurt. He didn't want to open that wound ever again. He had learned that lesson well. "Whatever did or did not happen, it ended long ago. She was part of my past. But you are my present, and I want you to be in my future. You feel the same, I know you do."

"Because between us there is no pretense. It is pure...what? Feeling? Intuition?" She smiled at him. "My dear Michael, for you this is not enough. You have a generous heart, one that should know true love one day, and I hope and pray that you will. But first, you must find a way to leave this place, and then to destroy it."

"Destroy it?" He wrapped her in his arms. She took his breath way. "How can I, when you're here?"

Tears filled her eyes as she looked at him. "You must do it before it kills you. If you hesitate, you will die. There are forces that will try to stop you and make it impossible for you to escape. You must not let them win!"

"I'll be all right," he whispered, as he wiped a tear from her cheek.

"I'm breaking so many rules, so many laws to have spent these few minutes with you."

"Don't say that!"

She began to walk away, but he spun her around so they were face-to-face.

Instead of fighting him, a haunted look came over her. She lifted her hands to his shoulders. "My name is Lin," she whispered.

"Lin." He molded her to him. She was so real, in every way, it hurt his heart to think she would ever leave him. "Stay with me. Find a way."

She tilted back her head to look up at him. Her fingers lightly touched his scratchy beard, his eyes, his brows, as if she wanted to memorize not only his look, but how he felt, everything about him. "It is impossible, Michael. I should not even be here now. But for one moment I wanted joy. I wanted to know how it felt to look at a man and to know passion, to know love."

Her arms circled his neck. She stood on her toes as he bent his head and their lips met. He lifted her, holding her, as she kissed him the way she had never kissed a man before, feeling passion, desire, and joy.

Breathless, she drew back, breaking his hold. Her gaze never leaving him, she stepped backwards, once, twice. "Now, I do."

"No, wait," he said as he reached for her.

Her gaze filled with despair and longing.

And then she was gone.

SEVENTY-FOUR

New York City

Jianjun paced back and forth in his bedroom. He was quickly running out of time and patience, but didn't know what to do next. He checked on the spy monitor to see if Vandenburg made or received any interesting calls. He was stunned to see that she had phoned Calvin Phaylor the day before. They talked for six minutes. Next, she made and accepted no calls for two hours, followed by a five-minute call to Milton Zonovich at 6:30 p.m. He wondered what had happened in that two-hour interval.

He used his laptop to access Calvin Phaylor's phone log and saw that Zonovich called Phaylor at 6:35 p.m., right after he talked to Vandenburg.

It didn't take long for Jianjun to tap into Zonovich's phone records, to see who else the man talked to. He never expected what he found.

If the calls meant what he thought, he needed to quickly set several complex steps in motion.

He worked on his plan for the next two hours, careful to cover his trail. If he was wrong, his actions would leave a lot of people plenty pissed off.

Then he left the house.

He went to the Starbucks next door to Vandenburg's apartment building, and with a grande breve in front of him, he set up his laptop. Using the spy monitor to clone Vandenburg's phone, he synced it to her computer via Wi-Fi. As he suspected, she hadn't bothered to password protect it.

Such a trusting soul, he thought, and proceeded to download her computer files to his hard drive. Most of her files, including emails, were remarkably short. He opened the files, one by one, then scratched his head.

What had happened to all the information that should have been there? All the stuff about Idaho and alchemy?

Some information was there, but not in nearly enough detail. He missed something important. Could she have a second computer? One his cell phone couldn't locate?

He needed to go to her home, scout around, tap into her personal home wireless system and see everything she had available.

He gulped down the rest of his breve and went into the men's room of the coffee shop. He was thin enough that he could fit through the window. He found himself in an alley behind Vandenburg's apartment building, the exit for its parking garage. He waited until someone drove out of the garage distracted. An older woman on a cell phone provided his opportunity. As the garage door opened for her, he snuck past her into the parking facility, then got on an elevator with another patron. She started to complain, but he smiled, bowed, and acted very foreign. That went a long way with certain overly politically correct types who tried hard not to offend.

He got off on Vandenburg's floor and rang the doorbell. She would be upset that he had gotten past the doorman, but he had a speech ready.

No answer.

He rang again. From what he'd read, her daughter had a full-time nurse. Someone should be home.

After another ring and a longer wait, he took out his lockset and picked the front door lock. The deadbolt wasn't on, and neither was the alarm system.

He told himself he shouldn't be nervous about it. He could search for another computer, go through her files, do whatever it took to discover how much she knew, then leave.

He walked into the plush living room and froze.

There, on the floor, lay Jennifer Vandenburg. The marks on her throat, bulging of her eyes, and still-wet foam on her lips told him she had been strangled ... and not very long ago.

He backed away, ready to turn and run. But before he could, he felt something hard jab into his back. He didn't need to see it to know it was a gun.

SEVENTY-FIVE

Charlotte listened with amazement as Melisse relayed her strange experience with Thaddeus Kohler and the glowing red stone he wore.

Charlotte put the description of the stone together with the manuscript Will Durham had given her. Then she went to Kohler.

"We need the philosopher's stone," Charlotte said. At his startled look, she continued. "I'm sure you have found the six stones that were left here by the men of the Secret Expedition. I need them. Now."

"How do you know about such things?" he asked.

"I read about it before coming here and put it together with an interesting tale from Melisse."

Kohler's jaw stiffened while Will Durham gave her a slight nod to show gratitude she hadn't spoken of his role in this.

"What makes you think a philosopher's stone would do you any good, if such a thing existed?" Kohler asked. "Or that you would know how to use one?"

"Everything in alchemy starts with the stone. *The Book* states that. Lionel and I can spend years trying to make one, just as Nicolas Flamel and his wife did, or we can start with one that already exists. I suggest the latter."

Kohler nodded. "What would you do with them?"

"Take them to the pillars. We would put them together, touching each other, *The Book* indicates that if we heat the philosopher's stone, a special gas will be released. Lionel and I have collected some cinnabar, which can be found throughout this area. We will mix it with the stone and see what happens."

"You have cinnabar?" he asked, both skeptical and surprised.

"Yes." She knew Jake and others could find her some red rocks. "Give us the stones, and we'll do the rest." She held out her hand.

His gaze hardened. By now, the other villagers were listening, and all appeared equally reluctant to part with their precious stones. "We'll go with you," Kohler said. "So we can see this for ourselves."

"Five men have gone with Charlotte and Lionel to the pillars," Michael said to the others. "This might be our chance to get away. Only Arnie Tieg is still here somewhere."

"He's probably in the guard tower," Jake said, "watching us."

"We have to do something about that," Michael said.

It took some convincing, but they got Brandi to go alone to the guard tower. She stood at the bottom and called up to Arnie. "Hello?"

"What do you want, girl?"

"Nothing."

"Then don't bother me! You've got work to do. Two plump rabbits to prepare for our dinner, and meat to dry for the winter. Get busy! They'll be hungry when they get home."

"But...I can't. I mean, I can, but...it's too much for me to do alone! I don't want to skin them, or touch all that inside stuff," she wailed. "It's too disgusting!"

"What do you mean alone? Everyone is in the community house."

"Not anymore. They went into the tunnel and told me I'm too much trouble to go with them!" She began to sob loudly. "They said I should stay and cook. But I can't!"

"The tunnel!" He ran down the stairs. "Those bloody—"

As he reached the bottom of the stairs, and turned to run toward the tunnels, Michael stepped out from the side of the community house. Tieg noticed the movement and spun toward him just as Michael swung a thick piece of firewood against the side of his head.

He dropped like a stone. Jake helped Michael bind and gag him.

"I did good, didn't I?" Brandi all but danced with excitement. "I always wanted to be an actress."

"You did just great," Michael said, causing her to beam with pride.

"Take the kids and run," Jake said to Quade and Melisse who had been watching from the community house. "Michael and I will try to find our weapons. If we can't, at least you'll have a good head start."

"We'll go, as we agreed," Quade said.

"If you find a Beretta," Melisse said. "It's mine. Those bastards took it from me."

Charlotte and Lionel had been in on the plan, and knew they needed to string out their deception as long as possible to give Michael, Jake, and Quade time to find the weapons and escape with the students. Both of them took frequent rest stops and complained about fatigue and aching backs and hips as they walked the four miles to the pillars.

Charlotte and Lionel climbed the mound with the villagers and sat in a circle. The prior night's heavy rainfall left the ground damp, but the morning was warm and sunny. They then announced that they needed a small campfire and descended the mound.

Finding dry twigs took time, but eventually, they gathered enough to build a fire.

Once the fire blazed, the five men placed their philosopher's stones in a clay pot, and placed it on the fire. Kohler added in Arnie Tieg's to complete the six pieces that made up Abbé Gerard's original stone. Each of the six pieces had been set in gold and made into a pendant. "The gold will melt if the fire grows hot enough," Charlotte said, "and then the stones will all touch again."

"Where is the cinnabar?" Kohler asked.

"I've got it. I'll use it when the time comes. Now, we must read." She opened *The Book of Abraham the Jew* and began reading the ancient Greek aloud. She was unsure of the meaning or pronunciation, but no one could call her on it if she was wrong.

"I want to see the cinnabar now," Kohler insisted, "before this goes any further."

Charlotte didn't want to do it, but she removed the four small rocks Jake had found in the stream.

"That's not cinnabar. They're red pebbles," Kohler said.

"Have you seen cinnabar before it's removed from its natural setting? I have, and this is it," Charlotte said as forcefully as possible. Most people had no idea what the mercury sulfide ore looked like, or even that it most often resembled brick red quartz.

Kohler looked suspicious, then nodded. She felt a flood of relief. He didn't know. She continued to read from the book.

When she hoped enough time had passed, she stood and threw the fake cinnabar into the fire while she continued to read aloud. She expected nothing to happen. She planned to put on a sad face and tell Kohler and the other villagers that her plan failed.

But a few seconds later, the philosopher's stones began to glow. The village men gasped in awe.

"It's working!" Lionel shouted. "We did it! The gateway is going to open!"

Charlotte's mouth dropped open; she couldn't speak.

The villagers let up a cheer. Just then, Arnie Tieg came running toward the mound, waving his arms. He carried two full quivers of arrows, as if he expected a battle. "Don't trust them! It's a trap! The others escaped!"

"No!" Charlotte cried.

A shot rang out. Ben Olgerbee fell. More shots followed. A bullet hit Gus Webber next. The others scrambled and rolled down the mound to find cover. Charlotte peeled off her jacket and used it to pick up the crucible with the philosopher's stones and then followed Lionel who had paused to pick up the book.

Then they ran, slipping and sliding down the mound. Charlotte was surprised her friends had decided to attack the village men. That hadn't been a part of the plan. She would find out later what happened—if , somehow, she and Lionel could find a way to escape the villagers.

"Damn!" Michael said at the sound of gunfire as he and the others hurried through the pine forest toward the pillars. "High-powered rifle fire. It's got to be those mercenaries."

"The sound seems to be coming from the direction of the pillars," Jake said.

"Yes, but who are they shooting at? And why now?"

They were already moving fast, but hearing gunfire, they began to run towards the pillars. They had spent the two previous hours searching all the huts and the tunnel for the weapons taken from them and Melisse. They almost gave up but decided to do a more thorough search of the storage shed. There, they found the weapons in a barrel filled with wild onions.

Before they left, they saw that somehow Arnie Tieg had freed himself of the ropes they used to tie him. They had no idea how he had managed it, but he was gone. No one doubted he would head straight for the mound, which meant Charlotte and Lionel were in trouble.

And now, not only did they have to fear the village men, but the mercenaries as well.

The gunfight would surely be a blood-bath since the village men had only bows and arrows.

But almost as quickly as it began, the shooting stopped, and the land became eerily quiet.

Charlotte and Lionel no sooner reached the foot of the mound when Derek Hammill stepped between them and their escape route. He flashed them a smile more threatening than friendly. "I knew you could get us out of here. And you've got the book. A two-fer! Our lucky day!"

Charlotte immediately recognized Hammill from both Jerusalem and Paris. Her gaze riveted on his; her stomach knotted. "Who are you?"

"Who we are isn't important," Hammill said.

Lionel glanced at her, worried and confused. "What's going on?"

"The only thing for you to worry about is how to get us out of here. Go back up to those pillars."

"I'm not going anywhere with you," Charlotte said.

Hammill laughed. "Oh, I wouldn't be so sure of that, Charlotte," he said. "You don't want us to kill your friends, do you? All we want is the book, and to go home again. You give us the book and open that 'gateway' as you call it, and we won't hurt any of you. We're quite reasonable. We aren't killers. You can trust us."

"Like hell." She sneered.

"Down!" Nose shouted and fired into the trees.

At that same moment, arrows flew toward the mercenaries. The village men were fighting back.

Bullets and arrows flew at each other, cracking rocks, snapping brush and tree limbs, and ricocheting all around.

Charlotte and Lionel ran in the opposite direction from the village men, and also away from the area the mercenaries ran toward.

"This way!"

Charlotte turned at the whispered sound. She saw Michael with Jake behind him. They both carried rifles.

"We've got weapons and supplies, plus some of Ben Olgerbee's magic poultice in case anyone gets hurt," Michael said, glancing towards the mound where the fighting raged on. He handed her the poultice for safekeeping, and she zipped it shut in a jacket pocket. "Quade is leading the students to a creek. They'll wade through the water, head south, and wait for us. Let's get out of here!"

Michael knew that whatever happened, Lionel would never let go of *The Book of Abraham the Jew.* He never felt so happy to be right about anything as he did then. He found a plastic rain poncho in his backpack and wrapped the book carefully in it so it would stay dry even if it fell into a creek or pond. Lionel wanted to carry it until he felt how heavy the rations and rifle magazines made the backpack. He quickly agreed to let his brother have the honor, although his face contorted as he released the book.

Charlotte put all six philosopher's stones around her neck and tucked them under her shirt while everyone's attention was on the book. She found she couldn't bear to part with them.

SEVENTY-SIX

New York City

Jianjun lay in the trunk of the car driven by Bob, Calvin Phaylor's nurse. He tamped down his fear with the belief that if Calvin Phaylor wanted him dead, Bob would have killed him in Vandenburg's apartment, the same way Bob had killed Vandenburg. The nurse was simply following Phaylor's orders, but why did Phaylor want Vandenburg murdered?

As fit his logical, computer-like brain, he laid out the facts.

Point A. Years ago, Calvin Phaylor learned about the Chinese and Danish scientists and their discovery of the Mormon settlement documents including Francis Masterson's Journal. That started Phaylor on his findings about alchemy and Idaho. That set everything else in motion.

Phaylor would have quickly realized the possibilities: *The Book of Abraham the Jew,* alchemy, immortality. He then needed to eliminate the two men who knew most about it so he could take it over himself. The hard part would have been to get the Chinese scientist out of China. PLP's international symposium on genetics provided the perfect cover.

Getting rid of the Dane had been child's play in comparison.

Point B. Vandenburg seemed to know nothing about the recent murders in Paris and Jerusalem. Calvin Phaylor must have been behind them as well. He had used Vandenburg, manipulated her because of her daughter. He let her find out all about Idaho and the Secret Expedition. She provided him with the perfect cover, while he hid behind the scenes. Through her, he got the right people involved, people like Michael and Lionel Rempart.

Phaylor wanted Michael and Lionel involved, but why? What was special about them? That, Jianjun wasn't able to answer.

Point C. Phaylor knew what happened in Mongolia, not because he had been told by a member of the Chinese government, but because he was the one who had *paid* for the information, *paid* for Batbaatar's help, and *paid* to have him killed so he wouldn't warn Michael and confess all he knew.

Phaylor must have also been the one who sent people to steal Lady Hsieh's body. She would have added to his research, to his means to find a way to become immortal. That explained why getting permits to allow Michael into Mongolia to dig was initially very difficult, but suddenly became easier, too easy in hindsight, than Jianjun ever expected. Perhaps Phaylor's money helped pave the way there as well.

Phaylor might also have sent someone to follow Lionel and Michael in Idaho, perhaps to steal *The Book of Abraham the Jew* from them as soon as they found it. Jianjun wondered if that was why Michael was missing now. Was his boss, his friend, already dead?

Jianjun refused to consider that possibility.

At this point, Vandenburg had become a liability to Phaylor. She spent time and money, became far too invested in the results, and expected to own a part of them. She probably found out things Phaylor didn't want her to know. Phaylor was close to everything he wanted and wasn't about to share.

The car stopped, and Jianjun held his breath with fear. All other questions vanished from his mind, replaced by only one: *Was he a dead man?*

SEVENTY-SEVEN

Quade and Melisse urged Rachel, Brandi and Vince to move as quickly as possible through the brush and rocky uneven land toward the stream Quade and Michael found several days earlier. Brandi chattered nonstop about how nervous she felt when she lied to Arnie Tieg, and how she had skillfully managed to fake crying for his benefit.

They halted, wide-eyed, at the sound of gunfire.

"It's far from here," Quade said, trying to reassure the students. "The pillars are in a valley, and sound reverberates and echoes in these mountains. We're fine. We've simply got to keep going."

"What do you think it is?" Rachel asked. "Michael and Jake rescuing Charlotte and the professor? Or—"

"We can hope," Melisse's firm tone cut her off and discouraged anyone from voicing other possibilities. "Now go on. Hurry!"

The group ran. The gunfire stopped for a while, but then started up once more with even more shots.

When the group reached the stream, they waded into the water to hide their tracks.

At first they barely noticed the cold as adrenaline and fear pumped through their veins. They slipped, crawled, and lurched their way for nearly a quarter mile before their feet and legs grew so cold and numb they were forced out.

On dry land, they limped from the banks, their feet going from being numb to burning, making every step agony. Once sheltered by trees, they stopped. They didn't dare build a fire for fear it might give their location away to someone they didn't want to find them.

They huddled together, mute, cold, and frightened.

Michael, Jake, Charlotte and Lionel reached Melisse, Quade, and the students an hour later. Together they searched until they found a sheltered area to build a fire and discuss what to do next. "Someone's paying a bunch of real bad asses to hunt us down," Jake said as he and the others huddled barefoot beside the campfire letting their shoes and socks dry off. "Who are those professionals with their high-tech weapons?"

"I've seen their leader before," Charlotte said. "I watched him kill someone in Paris, and he tried to kill me there, as well as in Jerusalem."

"You think he followed you here?" Jake asked. "Why?"

Charlotte shook her head. "He wouldn't say who sent them or who they're working for."

"Whoever they are," Michael added, "they'll be coming this way soon. Both Gus and Ben Olgerbee were shot, and most likely are dead. The others won't be able to stop them for long. We've got to keep moving."

"We should go to ground that will give us some advantage," Charlotte said. "Straight up steep, slick, mountain slopes. Their weapons are heavy. They'll slow them down over time."

Michael glanced her way, impressed at how quickly she learned out here.

"There's one other thing that gives us some advantage," Michael said.

"What's that?"

"The mercs are missing their shots far more than highly trained pros should. I can only guess it has something to do with an imbalance of the air, or a magnetic pull, or who knows what, emanating from the pillars. Bullets aren't flying straight. It's something I suspect the villagers take into account for the flight of their arrows. If you fire your gun or rifle, remember that the bullet's trajectory will curve slightly toward the pillars, and aim accordingly."

The others nodded, glad to hear that something leveled the playing field in some small way. Though exhausted and chilled, they stomped out the fire and headed for the jagged gray cliffs that loomed above a wooded ridge.

Finally, they reached the top, and all lay flat, hugging the ground and breathing heavily. Michael sat up first. He scoured the horizon for any sign of their pursuers. Rachel handed him a roll of bread and a piece of goat cheese. "I took some food before we left," she said as she handed some to the others as well.

They all felt much better, even a little optimistic, with food in their stomachs. The students sat near and listened to the discussion of how to proceed.

"It may be possible to negotiate with them," Lionel said. "They don't want to be stuck here anymore than the rest of us do. They said that."

"They aren't to be trusted," Charlotte murmured.

"Until we know who they are, we'll have no idea how to negotiate," Michael said. "And I'm sure one of us knows a lot more than he's saying." His gaze drilled Simon Quade.

Jake also looked at Quade for an answer.

Quade's small smile upturned his red cupid-bow lips. "I'll tell you, but you won't like it. About fifteen years ago, Phaylor-Laine Pharmaceuticals began engaging in strange activity that caught the attention of several government agencies. PLP looked into alchemy."

"PLP?" Jake said, incredulous. "A big company like that studying alchemy? I don't think so."

Charlotte perked up at the name mentioned and stared at Quade.

"We assumed they wanted to find a way to create gold," Quade said. "If they could, they wouldn't have to worry when their latest wonder drug killed or crippled a bunch of people. They could easily pay off all lawsuits."

"As usual, follow the money," Jake said with disgust.

Quade faced Charlotte. "Since your husband was the best scholar the CIA had in ancient Near and Middle Eastern studies, he investigated Phaylor Laine's interest in *The Book of Abraham the Jew*."

Her jaw tightened, and her face showed how difficult it was to hear her husband spoken of so coldly.

"Someone placed the bomb that killed him," he continued, "under an empty table behind him. It was detonated by remote control and was far more sophisticated than the nails-in-a-pipe bomb terrorists were using back then."

Charlotte blanched. "You're saying he was targeted?"

Quade nodded. "A Chinese and a Danish scientist had both been invited to attend a PLP symposium in New York City some fifteen years ago. Both men were murdered. The CIA investigated the deaths. Dennis was a major player, working under a man named Laurence Esterbridge. We believe Dennis may have learned, or was very close to learning, who was behind their murders, and that's why he was killed."

"I thought you didn't know my husband!" she cried.

"I didn't. But I knew 'of' him. After his death, due to my rather extensive knowledge of alchemy and other paranormal phenomena, the CIA brought me in as a consultant." He paused a moment as if to give them time to absorb what he'd said. "We maintained a monitor on PLP's CEO back then, Calvin Phaylor. He sent a well-armed, well-equipped team to this area, but we soon lost them. Soon after that, everything stopped. We don't know why. All we could tell was that someone pulled the plug on the project."

He looked around to make sure he had all their attention before he added, "Several months ago, everything began again. Lionel Rempart's activities caught the CIA's attention. Some documents, some very high-up phone calls, and I found myself involved once more. Here I am." Quade glanced at the others, and then his cold, black eyes fixed on Lionel. "Here we all are."

Lionel looked pale. "I ... I did receive a grant from PLP, specifically from the current CEO, Miss Vandenburg. But big companies offer lots of support to educational and scientific groups. That's where we get most of our funding. I did nothing wrong."

"You were paid to bring us out here?" Vince said. "To put us in danger?"

Lionel opened and shut his mouth a few times, but no words came out.

Michael stood. "We had better get moving. It's too dangerous to stop here for long."

They began to hike once more. The ground, which had been bare rock, now turned sandy and began to slope downward. They kept their steps small so they wouldn't slide.

After a while, the ground leveled out a bit, the group came together once more. As they did, Jake's anger boiled over at the strange CIA consultant.

"Hold everything, here! Missing military men, dead scientists, big bad pharmaceutical companies," he said, drawing everyone's attention. "It sounds too much like the *X-Files* on steroids. I don't believe a god-damned word of it."

"It makes perfectly good sense, Sheriff," Quade said. "Someone at PLP has to be behind the mercenaries. PLP wants the book, and will do whatever it takes to get it. I suspect they thought Charlotte knew more than she does, and wanted to get rid of her. After all, her husband nearly cracked the case, and who knew how much he told her."

"So, who is behind it?" Michael asked.

"I'm not sure about the original perpetrator," Quade began, "but the only one with the resources and power to do all that's been done now is the CEO, Jennifer Vandenburg."

"No," Melisse said. "It's not Jennifer."

The others stared at her.

"Since it's confession time," Melisse continued, "Vandenburg is my boss, my real boss. I'm ex-military and now work security for PLP. I've been one of Jennifer's personal bodyguards. She's spent money and resources on this strange adventure and, yes, she wanted the book, but she didn't send any killers out here. She sent Lionel and then sent me to keep an eye on him. She knew I grew up in rural Montana, knew I could take care of myself out in this wilderness. She didn't trust Lionel."

"What? You? But you're a graduate student!" Lionel said indignantly. "You know anthropology!"

"Not exactly. I know enough to agree with whatever you say about it. Some well-placed dollars got me a fake résumé and onto your team, that's all," Melisse said. "The men shooting at us were not sent by Jennifer Vandenburg."

"Then who..." Jake fell quiet as a strange creature slowly approached the group. It looked like a cougar, but was the size of a tiger. "Christ!" he murmured under his breath, reaching for his S&W magnum.

To their left, a gold-colored grizzly with a human-shaped head appeared, and to the right, a monster that seemed to be a cross between a tarantula and a five-foot long lizard. Its tongue flicked out at them. The beast began to move toward them, closing them in.

Melisse pulled the Beretta from her waistband. "Do we dare shoot? The sound will give away our position."

The beasts charged as a single entity.

"We don't have a choice," Michael yelled as he fired.

The animals veered away from the gunshots. Three other creatures appeared, equally strange combinations of wolves and bears and snakes and lizards. As Michael, Jake and Melisse held them off, Charlotte and Quade led the students and Lionel downhill, running fast. Large, smooth rocks filled the ground. Vince's foot slipped and wedged between two of them. He fell onto his backside. Rachel, who had been ahead of him, stopped to go back and help him pull his foot free.

A creature that looked half-bird and half-cougar swooped down. Rachel screamed, tried to run and fell. Quade threw himself atop her to protect her. The flying beast swerved from them. Melisse shot it, but that didn't stop the creature as it soared high.

The other beasts continued their attack.

Jake went to help Vince, but a bear-like creature pounced on him. He fell backwards, his hands on its throat, holding its fangs away from him.

An arrow hit its chest, then another. More arrows flew.

The village men had arrived—all six of them. They stood at the top of the hill, shooting their arrows down to where the beasts attacked. The creatures shrieked with anger as arrows drove them back into the forest.

Michael and Jake glanced at each other, stunned that Ben Olgerbee and Gus Webber were not only alive, but able to join in the fight. They were last seen shot, looking as if they were dead or dying, and lying atop the mound.

"How can they be here?" Jake said.

Michael shook his head, as confused as the sheriff.

"Troublesome fools!" Kohler shouted, as he marched his men a little way down the hillside toward the students. "I told you to trust and listen to us!"

In the distance, they heard a low rumble. They glanced toward the sound, but saw nothing.

Vince, his foot still caught, held up a hand for help. Kohler nodded at Arnie Tieg who removed a long, heavy knife from his belt. Vince must have seen something in Tieg's eyes because he cried *"No!"* as Tieg swung the blade hard at Vince's neck, nearly beheading him.

Brandi screamed.

Rachel grabbed her and pulled her farther downhill, away from the village men. She couldn't stop screaming.

Jake and Michael, stunned, raised their weapons and aimed at Kohler. Behind Kohler, the other villagers stood with their long bows and arrows poised and ready.

"That is what happens to those who disobey!" Kohler roared. "Now, give us back the philosopher's stones, and come with us, or more of you will meet the boy's fate."

The students and their would-be rescuers stared at each other, too scared and heartsick over Vince to move, but also unwilling to go along with the murderous villagers. The villagers appeared fearless, Kohler unwavering.

Time stood still, and the roar grew louder.

A roiling sheet of water, several feet high, appeared uphill from them. It bore down, crashing and raging.

"Flash flood!" Michael shouted, his voice tight.

To the north and south of them the mountainsides sloped steeply upward. The village men turned and ran back to the hilltop as Michael and the students exchanged panicked looks near the bottom of a deep, flat, dry gully.

Signs of earlier floods surrounded them, floods that had torn through at speeds that ripped away trees, shrubs, and loose rock. The prior night's rainfall followed by warm weather must have melted snow at higher elevations and triggered the massive run-off.

A wall of water hit and knocked them off their feet, tossing them as they were a child's toys. Michael tried to reach Rachel and Brandi but his outstretched hand clutched at nothing as the rushing wave gripped and sucked him into the downhill torrent.

Snared by the unrelenting strength of the icy wave, he tumbled and spiraled wildly. He struggled to find the surface of the water, then strained to keep his head above the current, to gulp air before his lungs burst.

The current hurtled him down the mountain as if he rode a twisting, turning water slide. It knocked him painfully into objects that had held their ground. Up ahead, he heard the distinctive splash of a waterfall. He fought to reach the bank, to do something to help the others, but the relentless flood held him tight, pulled him under, then tossed him over the edge of the fall.

He sank deep, and the rapid flow carried him forward, arms and legs thrashing as if they belonged to someone else, before the water reached a wide, flat field. There, it spread out. The roar dimmed, finally quieting into nothing more deadly than a shallow pond. It took a moment before Michael realized he had stopped moving.

Gasping for breath, his heart racing, he crawled to his feet. Bruised and exhausted, he looked around.

He reached Charlotte and helped her to the bank.

"I'm okay," she murmured as he went back out to help Jake with Brandi and Rachel. Last of all, Michael dragged Lionel from the water. His brother was blue-gray with cold and shivered uncontrollably.

"We need to warm him up!" Michael said. "And the rest of us as well."

In a sheltered area they built a fire. They pulled off their jackets and heavy outer clothes, and draped them over branches set up near the fire as make-shift drying racks.

"Oh, hell," Charlotte said, shivering. "My gun's gone."

"I dropped the rifle somewhere up there." Quade pointed up beyond the waterfall.

Jake and Melisse still had their handguns. Michael sighed with relief that the water hadn't swept away his rifle or the backpack with *The Book of Abraham the Jew* carefully wrapped in it. The flood had taken everything else.

"Our things could be anywhere," Michael said. "Still up on the mountain, under the waterfall. To find them, we'd have to go back toward the villagers."

"It's hopeless," Jake said, shivering as if half frozen, weary and discouraged. "With only a Beretta, an S&W revolver, and one Remington with no additional ammo, how the hell are we supposed to hold off the villagers, those crazy creatures, and a bunch of well-armed killers?"

As evening fell, their outer garments dried enough to put them on again, Rachel, a Mormon and the only church-goer in the group, said a prayer for Vince. Although the others were not believers in the way Rachel was, each felt comforted by her words.

They stayed in the sheltered area to rest, recover their strength, and deal with the shock and despair of losing their young companion before they moved on. They needed all the strength they could muster to face their enemies.

Later, Charlotte offered to take the first watch. Sleep wouldn't come easily to her. It never did, and would be especially difficult after Quade's words about Dennis. Her life with Dennis, and his death, would replay over and over again in her mind.

As others fell asleep around the fire, she moved a short distance away from its light to stare with vigilance into the darkness. Despite her heavy heart, she remained alert to any strange noise or movement.

Her mind replayed the horrors of the day, and she shuddered at the memories, at how close to death she and her friends had been.

Facing death, she realized how much she wanted to live. Truly to live. Not here in this never-never land. Not the stern half-life that had made up her days since Dennis died, avoiding all emotion. She wanted to feel whole again.

Even her work gave testament to complacency. She had left her doctorate program and returned to the U.S., expecting her time as a Customs agent to be temporary, something to do until she got her life together again and saved enough money to finish her Ph.D. But somehow, one year drifted into the next. For a while, she continued to study on her own, but soon stopped even that. She drifted. Sitting in this strange, surreal world, she realized that simply wasn't enough.

She heard a rustle and tightly gripped the rifle Michael had lent her, ready to use it.

"It's only me. Thought I'd help keep watch for a while," Jake whispered as he sat down close beside her. "I couldn't sleep. I kept remembering how I just stood there and let them kill that boy." He frowned, his eyes troubled, questioning.

"We all did," Charlotte said. "No one expected such cruelty. It tells us we were right to run, and we've got to keep going. Somehow, we must get the others home."

"You're right. I'll do my best," he promised, not speaking the rest of his thought, 'or die trying.' "This place has me spooked."

"You and me both," she said, giving a tentative but understanding smile.

"But I'm the cop. I'm supposed to be able to handle these things."

"You're a man, too," she said. "A very caring man, I think."

The gentleness of her words seemed to touch him, but just as quickly, his expression changed, his mouth a thin line, downturned at the corners. "I never should have gotten you into this, Charlotte." He cast his gaze forward toward the darkness of the brush, toward potential danger. "I never should have allowed you to come on this search. I'd ask if you could ever forgive me, but 'ever' sounds pretty trite right about now. I'm sorry."

His concern surprised her, and even worse, it sounded so heartfelt sudden tears threatened. She hated such weakness and forced her face, her whole body, back to its usual reticence. "I would have found a way out here, whether you agreed or not, Sheriff. Even if I had to follow you. You heard Quade. My husband died because of this. I had to find out why, and exactly who was behind it."

"It must be hard, bringing it all back. I'm sorry you had to learn this way about your husband's death."

"I've done my grieving." She kept her voice hard, firm. "Thirteen years' worth. In an odd sense, I'm relieved to finally learn the truth. I often blamed myself for what happened."

He looked at her quizzically.

She couldn't meet his eyes. "That afternoon," she said softly, "Dennis asked me if I wanted to go out with him. I was working on some research of my own and turned him down. I always thought that if I'd gone with him, he wouldn't have been at that café. He would have been safe. He would have lived." She fell silent.

"They might have waited for another time, another place," he said. "Or killed you, too."

"I know that now." She took a deep, shuddering breath. "Still..."

"Don't do that to yourself, Charlotte," he cautioned. "It's easy to blame yourself even when you really couldn't have prevented it. Or to feel guilt that you weren't also a victim. It paralyzes you. Believe me, I'm a master at that. It's no way to live."

Her pale face masklike, her gaze riveted in the direction of the mountains.

As he watched her, he understood how deeply she hurt. If he was a softer man, a more caring sort, he would have put his arms around her and offered comfort. But he wasn't. He didn't know how. Instead, he faced the mountains as she did. He couldn't see them in the blackness of night, but they were etched in his mind. "The land out there," he said, "It's majestic." He wasn't good with words, but that one seemed right to him. "The vistas go on forever. High mountain ranges, one after the other, interwoven by blue rivers and clear streams. I found peace and beauty in the land around the Salmon River. It was exactly what I needed at a time when I couldn't see beyond the chaos and ugliness all around me."

She nodded. He stopped then, embarrassed. Who was he to offer advice? Not when, at one point in his life—when his marriage had gone down the tubes and his job turned beyond ugly—he almost gave up. He remembered studying his own gun, feeling the cruel temptation of the finality it offered, and wondering why he bothered to struggle, day in and day out.

He had scared himself with such thoughts and soon left Los Angeles where he'd become so mixed up that trivial things—like cars and promotions and possessions—had seemed important, and important things—like marriage and lasting love—trivial.

Back home in Salmon City, he had somehow managed to gain perspective once again. Maybe because it was simply more natural, more real, than the concrete and crime that had made up his days, he finally came to feel alive again, even more so near Charlotte. She was troubled, unnervingly wary, meticulous to a fault, overly critical, and with more brains, beauty, and refinement than any one person should possess. And she knew her way around weapons. He'd never met anyone like her before and felt like a teenager with his first crush. No fool like an old fool, he thought.

He wanted to take her mind off the past. She was only in her 30's with a bright future, if and when they got out of this place. "It's good to see you and

Michael together," he said abruptly, trying to sound as if he were doing nothing but making small talk.

She faced him. "What do you mean?"

"Two scholars and all." He cleared his throat. "You two seem right together. Might even last after we get away from here."

"Michael ... and me?" She regarded him with confusion. "Are you also a part-time match-maker, Sheriff?"

"I've seen the two of you together, how well you get along. I even, uh, spotted him leaving your tent early one morning," he confessed. "I'm not surprised. He's well-educated. Smart. Good looking."

"Interesting," she murmured.

"Interesting?"

"Because, while I think the world of him, our relationship isn't the way you imagine at all. He came to my tent for conversation and companionship, nothing more." She studied him, and he couldn't help but notice her cheeks redden a bit as she said, "Besides, he's not my type."

That took him aback, along with a twinge of something that felt a lot like elation—except that it'd been so long since he'd felt anything like that, he scarcely recognized it. Then, fool that he was, the wrong words spilled from his lips. "What is your type?"

She tapped her fingers thoughtfully against her chin, and to his surprise, said, "I'm not sure I remember."

He smirked. "Yeah, I know what you mean."

Her brow wrinkled, but she couldn't hide a small smile as she added, "I do believe I've always had a weakness for law and order types."

He gawked as his mind considered how to interpret that.

As silence stretched awkwardly between them, she murmured, "My husband was one."

Ah. "I see. Law and order and a scholar. He sounds perfect for you."

She seemed lost in thought. "Before meeting Dennis, I'd always gone out with academic types, scholars. Dennis' involvement with the CIA was a bizarre aberration to me. Yet, I learned to have nothing but admiration for men like him, like you, for your bravery, sense of duty, and commitment."

He didn't know what to say.

She rubbed the knee of her slacks a moment, and then asked, "Are you married, Sheriff?"

He swallowed hard. "I was. Divorced now. No kids. I spent too much time on the job. My wife got lonely and met someone who was 'there for her,' as she put it. She got what she had always wanted. Two kids, a nice home in Ventura, and a husband who isn't me."

Although he had tried to keep his tone light, the way she regarded him made him fear she had heard the pain in his voice at what he regarded as his failure, his blame.

"And so you're now living alone in the mountains of Idaho?"

"Yes, but it could be worse," he replied. "I could still be in L.A."

She nodded. "Can't say I disagree."

"Then you're a little cracked yourself. Most people thought I was flat-out looney-tunes to leave all that glamour and sunshine for this cold nothingness."

She watched him "Why did you leave?"

"I quit the force."

"Why?"

He dropped his gaze. "I don't think ..."

"Try me," she said.

A long moment passed before he spoke. "It was a hostage situation. Kids at a small private school in Bel Air. Three gunmen entered a classroom of first graders and threatened to shoot them one at a time unless they were given ten million dollars. For some of the parents that was pocket change. Higher ups decided to go along with the demand and grab the gunmen as they left. I headed the team tasked with making the capture. But something went wrong with the money drop. All hell broke loose and when it ended, two kids and the gunmen were dead. I still have nightmares about it. Guess I always will. Just like the parents of those little kids who died."

"I'm so sorry. Knowing you, even as little as I do, I can't help but suspect the blame wasn't yours, despite you taking responsibility for it." Her voice was barely a whisper as she murmured, "Violent men and innocent kids."

"Ironic, isn't it? I came all the way to Idaho to get away from those memories, and now this." Agony seared his words before he turned his head away.

Awkwardly, she placed her hand on his shoulder. "You don't always have to act tough, Sheriff."

He stiffened at her touch. "I don't," he said with a forced chuckle.

She withdrew her hand. "But you do, until you allow someone close enough to see beneath that gruff exterior."

Surprise, then caution, then a bittersweet sadness flickered across his face. "It requires trust," he said, "something I seem to have grown out of."

"You can trust me," she whispered.

He didn't move, but listened to the sound of their breathing. "I know."

Then, inwardly cursing himself as a fool, he forced his gaze to the rifle and picked it up. Looking only at the weapon he said, "It's your turn to get some sleep. I'll take over the watch now."

She nodded. "Yes, you're right." She waited and then rose to her feet. "Good night, Sheriff."

He watched her move nearer the campfire and settle down to rest. She told him he could trust her, and in thanks he sent her away. That just might have been the dumbest thing he'd ever done in his life.

"Good night, Charlotte," he whispered so only he could hear.

SEVENTY-EIGHT

"Should I give him more propofol?" Bob asked Phaylor.

"No. I want him lucid when we reach Idaho." Phaylor gazed, bored, out the window of the Cessna Citation X. They neared the Montana-Idaho border, but he only saw a cloud bank below. They would be landing soon. He squeezed the bridge of his nose wearily.

The nurse nodded, then leaned back in his seat.

Phaylor had decided to go to the twin spires himself. The two teams of mercenaries he sent out there, plus the university group Vandenburg sent, had been able to find them, so he should be able to as well. Once found, however, why did no one leave them? Was the world they offered so wonderful men chose to stay? Or did they die? He needed to see it for himself, to learn the answer. He was close to death, so he didn't fear going there the way a young man like Bob might. But he needed Bob's help. Promises of unimagined wealth bought Bob's loyalty.

When he finished this, if he survived, Phaylor would take back his company. With his newly created gold, he'd buy back the stock and make the company private once more. He couldn't wait to get rid of Milt Zonovich and fire that entire stupid board of directors.

With his plans in place, Phaylor-Laine Pharmaceuticals would become so wealthy it truly could have world domination. And he would be at its helm forever.

He would create his own empire, and soon, his own world. One world order. And all his.

Chinese alchemists used a term, *lien tan*, or "pill of transformation." His pharmaceutical soul liked that. Whatever means delivered immortality, he would market it as a pill. Also, he would make it clear that one pill alone would not help, but a pill needed to be taken every year—a placebo, of course, but who would know that? And who would risk challenging it? Yes, that way, money would continuously flow into PLP's coffers. He already planned his contracts with American billionaires and oil rich Arab sheiks. Immortality wouldn't come cheap.

Jianjun opened his eyes and fought to clear his head. "He's going to kill you, Bob, as soon as he doesn't need you anymore. You know that, don't you? Think about it. How could he leave you as a witness to murder and kidnapping and everything else he's planning? You would have too much power over him, too much knowledge. I know you aren't smart, but at least you should have some sense of self-preservation. Even a slug knows enough to try to get out of danger."

Phaylor chuckled. "I'll make you so rich, Bob, I have no worries. You'd never tell because you'd lose your fortune. Don't listen to him."

Bob smiled. "I don't. But I'll be glad when he's dead."

"You are a fool!" Jianjun shouted. "And a killer. Security cameras monitored Vandenburg's building. Are you sure you avoided every one of them? They'll see you entering her apartment and then taking me out of there at gunpoint. They'll know who the murderer is."

Bob's face flushed. "It won't happen!"

"You know it's true. You know the old man set you up," Jianjun raged.

Bob punched him in the mouth. Jianjun's head snapped back, and he tasted blood. The sound echoed through the plane.

Phaylor chuckled, but a phlegm-filled cough got in the way of his enjoyment.

All were quiet as the plane began to descend. They landed at an airfield near Sun Valley. There, they would transfer to the helicopter Milt Zonovich ordered soon after his talk with Phaylor.

The Cessna no sooner landed, however, when armed Blaine County deputies, Idaho State Police, and Homeland Security officers surrounded it.

The pilot opened the plane's doors.

The lead deputy boarded the plane, followed by others. He quickly drew his gun. "Drop your weapons," he ordered.

"Weapons? What is this?" Phaylor demanded. "There must be some mistake. I'm Calvin Phaylor! Do you have any idea of my influence? My power?"

Officers placed Phaylor and Bob under arrest.

"John Lee?" the deputy asked, untying Jianjun and noting his bruises. "Are you all right?"

"I am, now," Jianjun said. "Yes. I am fine. Very fine. So, Homeland Security sent you?"

"That's right, although their intel said you might be here or you might have been murdered. Glad to see it was the former, and we're able to free you."

"Thank you!" Jianjun exclaimed, giving himself an inward cheer that his plan had worked. After discovering that shortly after talking to Phaylor, Milt Zonovich ordered a Cessna out of Teterboro, New Jersey, and then chartered a helicopter in Sun Valley, he put two and two together. Phaylor planned to go to Idaho to find the gateway himself. Jianjun feared Phaylor might decide to take him along to help.

For that reason, he wrote a number of carefully worded and completely untrue emails filled with buzz-words and scenarios sure to excite terror specialists. He then sent all of them to his most reliable first cousin, Waymon Li. He asked Waymon to release them to specific people in Homeland Security if any four hour period passed and Jianjun hadn't sent him a text that he was alive and well. Fortunately, his cousin watched the clock.

"With all the bigwigs who have homes in this area or come here for vacation," the deputy said, his face beaming, "we've trained for situations like this, but this is the first time we've actually used it! Pretty exciting, I must say. We heard that you're the son of some muckety-muck in China. No need for this to become an international incident."

"I am much relieved to be rescued." Jianjun stood and bowed many times while trying not to chuckle over what his father, who worked as an accountant in Canada, would think of this story. "Very relieved, but I must go, now."

"I don't think so. We've got lots of questions, like why kidnap you? What were they planning to do? Also, considering who we just arrested"—he looked over at Phaylor—"I'm sorry to say Homeland Security is going to need a lot of answers."

"Of course," Jianjun said with a nod. If the authorities were confused now, just wait until they found Jennifer Vandenburg's body. Having used the police to free him from Phaylor, he needed to escape them. He wasn't worried. Given all he and Michael had been through over the years, doing that would be a piece of cake.

But after that, how was he going to find Michael?

SEVENTY-NINE

"Until we come up with a way to protect ourselves," Michael said when the group gathered after a restless night, "we're sitting ducks if they come after us."

"Sam Black and Arnie Tieg had rifles when they first picked us up," Melisse said, "and they had ammo clips. One day they headed northeast from the village with the rifles, and when they returned they no longer carried them. I saw some caves out that way when Rachel and I were picking tubers. I'd look there."

"Give me directions to find the spot," Michael said.

"I'll join you," Jake added.

"We should all go," Charlotte suggested. "I don't like the idea of splitting up."

"No," Jake told her a little too quickly, a little too abruptly. "It's going back near the compound, back to danger."

"It's best if you, Lionel, and Quade put your heads together with that book and the philosopher's stones and look for any hint on getting us out of here," Michael added, then looked hard at Quade, as if to say he knew Quade had a lot more information than he shared so far.

"I should go with you, Sheriff," Melisse offered.

"Michael and I can handle it," Jake said. "I'd rather you stay and protect the others. If this camp is attacked, you'll be most useful here."

"I know what you're doing, Sheriff." Melisse held her head high. "Don't cut me out. It's my job to go into danger."

"I understand that," Jake said. "But you may be needed right here."

He didn't know how prophetic his words would be.

By late afternoon, Michael and Jake still hadn't found the cave with a stash of guns. They hadn't found any cave at all.

"Should we give up?" Jake asked. "I'm worried about leaving the others alone all this time."

"There's only about an hour more of daylight," Michael said. "We should take advantage of it. In any case, it'll be dark before we get back to them."

"You're right," Jake said. "If we can only find those rifles, we'll be a credible fighting force."

"Bring 'em on," Michael said with heavy irony.

"Careful what you wish for."

"That's the story of my life, damn it."

Dusk fell as they continued their slow, cautious search. Jake glanced back to tell Michael it was time to give up. A red laser spot danced on Michael's chest—a high beam from a rifle scope.

Jake lunged and knocked Michael off his feet as the high piercing sound of a rifle shot whizzed by. A rock Michael had been standing in front of shattered.

A half second later, multiple rounds of rifle fire sounded.

Dirt and debris exploded around them. Jake groaned as he and Michael scrambled for cover.

"You're hit!" Michael stared at the gaping wound on the sheriff's thigh. Jake had seemed invulnerable to him.

They dropped to their stomachs and rolled into a dry creek bed offering a slight depression in the contour of the land. There, Michael fired back with the Remington, while Jake used his knife to cut and tear off material from his shirt to make a tourniquet for his thigh. The bullet had missed his femoral artery or he would have quickly bled out.

Gunfire stopped altogether for few moments. Then shots came at them from three new positions.

Jake drew his Smith and Wesson. With dizzying agony he balanced on his good knee, his wounded leg outstretched. Waves of blackness swept over him as he fired blindly at the enemy. As he struggled against passing out, each wave became more difficult to fight. "I don't know how much longer I can hold on," he murmured.

"Don't give up now, Sheriff!" Michael gripped his shoulder, his words harsh. "Concentrate on all who need you. Charlotte, Melisse, Lionel, Rachel, Brandi,"—he saw movement and shot at it—"even Quade and me. Hang on!"

Jake nodded, determined. More gunfire sounded, and the two began to work their way backwards, away from the heavy assault, finally making a labored run to a more secure position behind a cluster of jutting rocks.

Jake reached shelter, but the effort cost him. The adrenaline rush that propelled him to safety abandoned him, and he slumped over.

Michael aimed his weapon in the direction of the attackers' oncoming sounds and fired wherever he detected sound or movement, desperate to hold their position.

Volleys of gunfire came at him with such force and frequency that he found himself pinned down, unable to leave the security of the rock face to return fire. Not that it mattered. He had so little ammunition left, the fight would soon be over.

EIGHTY

The first glow of sunrise peeked over the mountains. Melisse had kept watch all night while the students, Charlotte, and Lionel slept in a relatively secluded and secure culvert. Melisse guarded the group's south flank and Quade the north.

Anxiety and a sense of hopelessness gripped her. The night before, as the group hiked, they heard the sound of high-powered rifle fire in the distance. They assumed the mercenaries found Jake and Michael. She prayed the two located the cave with weapons before that happened. But when the men didn't return by nightfall, dread became despair.

The small group pushed on. They had managed to hide from both the mercenaries and the villagers for a day, but she doubted their luck would hold out much longer.

Something moved not far from her.

She crept cautiously toward the movement, then lay down flat in the scrub and waited.

Two strangers approached dressed in black tactical gear and ball caps. They carried semi-automatic weapons. The mercs.

Three bullets remained in her Beretta.

She waited.

The men crept closer, but she still didn't act. A head shot would be the best way to stop them, but the hardest to make. She weighed her options. She didn't relish the thought of dying out here, not when she had so much to live for. Thoughts of her pretty little daughter, Marianna, came to mind, but she pushed them aside. She had no time for them now. The possibility of sidling back, out of the killers' view, waking Charlotte and the students and running appealed to her, but it wasn't possible.

Heart pounding, she watched the mercs. They stepped into the open now, just as the sun peeked over the horizon, casting a whitish-pink aura over the land. They crouched, careful. She hadn't moved for a long while so they had no idea she was there.

The sky was too beautiful for anyone to die under, she told herself.

Then, her training kicked in. She aimed, adjusted as she remembered Michael's caution about bullet trajectories, and fired.

She hit the first man in the middle of the forehead. He dropped, instantly dead.

The other man ran as she turned the pistol in his direction. Her shot went wide.

He fired as he ducked, but his foot caught a rock and the split second he wobbled caused his spray of shots to go wild.

As he fell, she aimed a little to the left, calculating that he'd catch himself and correct in the opposite direction. She squeezed off her third and last shot. He fell.

She'd beaten the odds.

Adrenaline rushing, she waited three full minutes. She heard and saw nothing more, so she crept toward the dead mercs to take their weapons. She assumed Quade and Charlotte woke the students and set them running at the first sound of gunfire. She would have to move fast to catch up to them, but the mercs rifles and anything else useful they might be carrying would serve them all well.

She reached for the first merc's M-107 when a rapid burst of firepower roared. Bullets tore at her back and side, knocked her sideways, and spun her around.

She fell face up, looking at a pastel sky, at the start of a beautiful new day, before her eyes no longer saw anything at all.

EIGHTY-ONE

THE EVENING BEFORE, DEVLIN FARRELL STARED DOWN AT THE EMPTY village. He wondered what the villagers had done with his classmates and the professor. He hoped the empty village meant they escaped.

He heard gunfire.

As more proof that he'd gone completely insane, rather than running away from it, he ran toward it. Maybe if he found the shooters, he would find his classmates and the professor.

He last saw them the day two strangers pulled them out of the creek when flesh-eating beetles attacked. After the experience of being duped by the river rafters, he decided to watch the strangers before putting himself under their control.

Devlin watched them lead everyone into some sort of compound where the men and women were separated. Something about the place, those men, seemed wrong to him.

He had a knife, but no other weapons. As he watched two men who carried rifles, bows and arrows, he decided to follow them. To his surprise, they tossed the rifles into a cave. It made no sense to him. Why treat good weapons that way?

He went to the cave after the men left. There, he found six HK-91 rifles, plus a few magazines. He had grown up hunting with his dad and was a crack shot. He silently thanked his cousin in the army who once showed him how to release complex safety mechanisms. He took two rifles, as many magazines as he could carry, and left.

Armed, he considered going to the compound to rescue the others. But then what? Alone, he could travel fast, find help—real help. As an athlete he trained for strength and high endurance. He decided to head south. Driving himself relentlessly, he found a safe spot to cross the Salmon River. From there, he reached the Middle Fork, and traveled along it. When the banks of the river became too high, steep and dangerous, he moved inland. But he would always find his way back to the river, clutching the hope that he would turn a corner and come across a gathering of friendly people.

But he didn't.

He found hot springs to soothe aching, weary muscles. He saw shooting stars and, once, the aurora borealis to keep him company through long, desolate nights. He experienced torrential cloudbursts and brief, near hurricane-force winds. Twice, he backed away from a grizzly who was mercifully more interested in its forage than in the tall, two-legged creature that feared it.

Despite everything, he would not stop. Memories of his friends, especially of Brian who he was sure had died, and of Rachel, who he hadn't given much thought to at all when she was near, but he now realized had more spunk, brains and courage than most men he knew, drove him on.

Past the Middle Fork, he trekked southward, until he recognized the headwaters of the Salmon River near the town of Stanley. He'd been to Stanley many times. Small and rustic with crystal clear air, whenever he was there he felt as if he were at the top of the world with the beautiful, jagged snow-capped Sawtooth Mountains in the distance.

From Stanley, continuing south, he would reach Sun Valley.

But there was no Stanley. The area looked as if the place had never existed.

With that, he knew his quest was hopeless. No sign of civilization at all was found. For all he knew, he was dead, and this emptiness some kind of purgatory. Or worse.

He turned back toward the village to rejoin the others. They were all he had left in the world, and he would do whatever it took to see them again, to have companionship, to end this aching loneliness.

And then, the strangest thing happened. It only took a day for him to reach the pillars. He shivered as a thought crossed his mind, a thought he didn't like one bit. The pillars appeared to be the center of this new, unreal universe. He had heard about curvatures of time and space in a physics class. It made no sense to him then and still didn't. But he was back.

He went straight to the compound, only to find it empty.

His debate over which way to go ended when he heard gunfire.

He hurried to the area from which he heard the shots fired. To his amazement, he had never seen any of the individuals involved in the shootout before, two on one side, and three on the other. He had no idea who they were, or why they were fighting.

The two were losing the battle. He crept near them.

One, trying to encourage the other, had to shout over the sound of automatic fire. Devlin heard him give the names of his friends...Rachel, Brandi, Melisse, Lionel...

He knew which side he belonged on.

He crawled around to the far side of the larger group of shooters. One sniper hid behind a tree. Devlin snuck behind him, aimed, fired, and immediately ran.

The sniper fell to the ground, dead.

Devlin snuck up behind the other two shooters and fired again.

The two apparently thought they were surrounded and ran.

Devlin followed them far enough to make sure they weren't going to backtrack, and then made his way to the two strangers. "Don't shoot!" he called as he neared them. "I'm on your side."

"Who are you?" Michael held his rifle aimed and ready.

"It's okay," Devlin called. "You know my friends. Trust me!" He stepped into the open, put his rifles on the ground and raised his arms high.

Although his face sported a full beard and his hair was shaggy, Michael recognized him from posters and news reports. "Devlin Farrell," he said as he moved out from behind the sheltering rocks.

"That's right," Devlin said. "But who are you? And who were those guys shooting at you? And why?"

Jake had passed out from the gunshot. Michael used his knife to remove the bullet and his shirt to wrap and bind the wound as he explained as much as he could to Devlin. Devlin told him how he'd purposefully separated himself from the other students to find help. He then told of the stark emptiness of the land around them.

As much as Michael hadn't wanted to believe what he heard, Devlin's story made sense.

Michael then briefed him on all that had happened with the students and villagers.

While Devlin stayed with Jake, Michael headed back to the man who had been shot to search for IDs or anything to give a clue as to who he was. He was young and hard-muscled, but carried no identification. His phone and walkie-talkie were completely dead. Michael took his rifle, ammo, and knife.

After Michael returned, Devlin went at night, alone, to the cave where the villagers had hidden their rifles and picked up the remaining four, plus clips.

The three set out at dawn. Jake's wound and blood loss forced them to travel slowly. Michael and Devlin had to support him as he half-walked, half-dragged himself while using a tree limb as a crutch.

When they heard gunfire a little later that morning, they sped up as much as possible while still keeping themselves under some means of cover. An hour passed before they neared the culvert where the others had camped for the night.

There, they found Melisse's body.

Their elation at finding Devlin alive and having gotten away from their attackers, sank into nothing.

Not far from her, two mercenaries lay dead. "Melisse did this," Michael said. "She gave her life to protect the others."

They found no sign of Charlotte, Quade, or anyone else, and Michael's fear grew that they were dead or captured.

"We'll track them," Michael said with determination, finding where grass and weeds had been trampled. "We will find them."

"They've got to be alive," Devlin murmured.

The sight of Melisse lying dead, the need to find the others, spurred the men forward.

Michael abruptly halted. He shot out his arm, stopping the other two, then pointed at a bush. Jake and Devlin aimed their rifles at the shrub. "Come out now, arms up," Jake bellowed, "or we shoot!"

They heard the sound of crying and lowered their weapons. They knew who it was. One student, at least, still lived.

Fish and Nose returned to Hammill's camp. "We had two of them pinned down when others showed up. We don't know how many and they were armed. They killed Dogman."

The Hammer's jaw clenched. His team was now down to Fish, Nose, and him. "I want vengeance. Those bastards have a lot to pay for. And they will."

EIGHTY-TWO

The sound of nearby gunshots woke everyone, shattering what little spirit and hope remained in the university group.

"Oh, God!" Rachel cried, and turned toward the sound. Without weapons, they couldn't help Melisse.

"Move it!" Charlotte said. She slipped the backpack with the book over her shoulders. "Leave everything else. Now! Go! Run!" She hoped Melisse could hold off the shooters long enough for her to get the students safely away.

Before long, Brandi gave out. She cried, and tried to keep moving, but her body simply didn't have the strength. Her legs buckled, her muscles quivered, and she gasped for breath.

Charlotte and Quade tried to help her, but Brandi was too tired and too heavy for them to handle. She slowed the group down, endangering everyone.

"She can't go on," Charlotte said. "I'll stay with her. They won't kill us."

"No, please. I'll try," Brandi wailed.

"It doesn't matter," Lionel whimpered. "We're all lost."

"It does matter!" Quade insisted. "Only Brandi stays. These men won't waste a bullet on her. Out here and alone, they'll consider her already dead. They'll continue past. If you stay, Charlotte, they'll threaten and eventually kill her just to get you to cooperate with them. When Michael and the sheriff return, we'll come back for Brandi."

"You can't leave me," Brandi shrieked. "I'm scared! You know what they did to Vince."

"Then keep quiet so they won't find you!"

They shoved a hysterical Brandi behind some bushes and covered her with brush, then hurried away. They lost so much time with her that they were forced to push on at a punishing pace.

Soon, Lionel felt the effects of the altitude, the cold, and the food and sleep deprivation. His fifty-one-year-old soft professor's body had been driven harder than he thought possible. Charlotte noticed he was near collapse.

She took Lionel's arm and let him lean on her as he limped along, slipping and sliding on the grade. He was too tired to speak or protest.

When a half hour passed with no more gunfire heard anywhere, Charlotte didn't know what to think. If Melisse had stopped the mercs, why hadn't she called out to the group? Or caught up to them?

Charlotte had a good idea of the answer.

But also, where were Jake and Michael? She hated to contemplate the possibilities, her fears too terrible to bear.

She knew better than to hope. Whenever she did, her life took a turn for the worse. She no sooner thought that than Lionel stumbled and fell. She tried to hold him up, but he needed to sit.

"You and Rachel keep going," Charlotte said to Quade. "Keep her safe."

"If Brandi could stay alone, so can I," Lionel gasped. "Leave me."

"No, I won't!" Charlotte said. "They're getting us through attrition. No more!"

Quade nodded and led Rachel away.

Lionel bent forward, breathing hard, and tried to stop his light-headedness. Before long, they heard Rachel scream. Lionel straightened, his face white with fear.

EIGHTY-THREE

Quade and Rachel had barely gone an eighth of a mile when Kohler and the other villagers stepped in front of them. Rachel screamed. They tried to run, but Webber and Tieg caught them and tied their hands behind their back.

The villagers led them back along the trampled deer path Quade and Rachel had already walked and found Lionel sitting alone on a felled tree.

"Where is everyone else?" Kohler demanded.

Lionel looked around. Charlotte was gone. "Dead. Running. I have no idea," he replied wearily.

"We'll go after them," Kohler said, then turned to Sam Black. "Black, take these three back to the village. When we return, we'll teach them what happens to people who run away."

About halfway back to the village, Quade slipped his thin hands free of the ropes that bound them. He stuck his foot out and tripped Rachel. As Black reached over to pick her up, Quade wrapped an arm around his neck, forearm pressing the carotid artery. He pushed Black's head and neck forward with his other arm, and slowly lowered him to the ground as he lost consciousness. Quade followed that with one quick snap of Black's neck, killing him.

Lionel and Rachel stood frozen with shock at the ease with which Quade acted.

"Let's get out of here!" Quade ordered.

"Which way?" Rachel cried. "It's not safe anywhere!"

Quade hesitated only a moment. "Back to the pillars."

Michael, Jake, Brandi, and Devlin marched single-file along the ridge of the mountain following the tracks of their friends. They stayed above the timber line, the land bare of foliage.

Each time they came to a bend in the trail, Jake worried that they would find their companions' bodies. He hated his own weakness from the gunshot and pushed himself in defiance of his injuries and exhaustion. He hated that he hadn't been there to protect Melisse and the students. Hated that he'd failed. Again.

And Charlotte—he couldn't let himself think about Charlotte.

They moved fast, but even Brandi kept up. He suspected she didn't dare mouth a single complaint for fear she'd be left behind again.

Before long, they came to a well-trampled spot. Clearly, a confrontation took place here. But they couldn't tell what happened next. Footsteps seemed to go in all directions.

"Where are they now?" Jake asked, sitting to rest his painful leg.

"At least they weren't killed." Devlin said as he sat down. He wasn't injured, but the constant travel and food shortages had taken their toll on him.

"Let's hope not," Michael added. "Sometimes, I wonder if all of us aren't already dead, stuck here forever."

"Dead?" Jake whispered. "What are you talking about? That's goofy talk. There's a way out. There's always a way out. Don't go defeatist on me."

Michael's stern expression offered little room for argument. "Unless this is Hell. *The* Hell. If I understand my theology correctly, if you're bad enough to have been sent there, there's no exit. Even Sartre, an atheist, in his own way believed that."

"Theology?" Jake looked skeptical. "I didn't think your taste went that way."

"It doesn't," Michael said. But perversely, a passage that he read long ago by St. Augustine came to mind: that the restless heart of man could only find rest in God. He wondered why he recalled that here, now. Everything about Augustine's faith was contrary to his nature. Yet, he remembered how he felt the first time he visited the Gandan monastery in Ulaanbaatar. He had found peace there, despite knowing that particular place was not one he would ever fit into. But it possessed some quality that he welcomed and felt welcomed by. Michael shook his head at the memory and forced his thoughts back to the surreal world that trapped him and the others. "We should get moving again. We've got to assume there is a way out of this place, and concentrate on finding it, and finding our friends."

Devlin helped Jake struggle to his feet. As Jake despondently looked at the emptiness before them, he muttered, "That's the spirit," in desperate hope that his words would encourage them.

Something caught Brandi's attention, and she lifted her gaze. She cried out.

A large, winged creature peered down from a rocky ledge, ready to pounce. Devlin fired. His shot disintegrated its small head. The body tumbled from the precipice to their feet.

Brandi squealed and backed away as Michael ran with Devlin to see the creature. It had an eagle's wings, but a huge badger's body. Long, treacherous claws were made of gold.

"We've got to get away!" Jake shouted. "The mercs and villagers will know we're here now."

They turned to run, only to see Arnie Tieg and Gus Webber strutting toward them, crossbows in hand. "We already know you're here," Tieg said. "Drop your weapons! You four can join your friends back at the village. We have a special get-together arranged for you there."

Charlotte ran. Earlier, as soon as she heard Rachel scream, she assumed it meant Rachel and Quade had been captured. Whether by the mercs or the villagers, she didn't know, but whoever it was would be looking for her and Lionel next. Allowing herself to be captured would do no one any good.

She turned off the path they had been following to plunge into the low-lying briars and leafless, prickly brush that covered the mountainside. She ran downhill to find shelter, to somehow find Michael and Jake and warn them what lay ahead. Together they might be able to rescue the others. She refused to allow herself to imagine that Michael and Jake had been captured or killed.

Suddenly, the ground turned silty, the rocks loose. The backpack with the book kept shifting, throwing Charlotte off-balance. After several slips she found it necessary to keep one hand on the ground, balancing like a three-legged stool, to avoid rolling down the mountain.

A cold breeze began with small gusts, but soon gathered strength. She stopped and listened. The desolation around her frightened her. The wind made the only sound. No triumphant hawk's cry, no gentle chirps, not even an owl's hoot was heard. Something ominous crept near, some essence that held an unknown terror.

She had no weapon. The wind increased, and brush blew like straw.

Something darted before her; a blur. She almost convinced herself that she had imagined it, but then she smelled the creature's stink, the scent of decay. Of death.

Lionel slowed down Quade and Rachel as they made their way toward the pillars. Quade was convinced that if any of the others were alive, they would head there. The pillars offered, after all, the only gateway out of here, the only logical place to go. Rachel agreed, although Quade scared her. She sensed something about him that felt impure, evil almost. She ached at the loss of her friends. She even missed Brandi, poor silly Brandi, who once confessed that she only came on this field trip because she heard Devlin would be on it. Devlin never gave her a second glance. And he was gone, too. It was all too much.

Lionel fell.

"Please," Rachel said, trying to help him up.

He shoved her away. "I'm too tired. Get away from me!"

Anger filled her. Her friends died out here, and this hot-shot professor was a fraud and a failure.

Quade stepped up to Lionel and without expression clamped steel-like fingers onto Lionel's shoulder and lifted. Lionel cried out, but the look on Quade's face so frightened him, he quieted and began to walk once more without comment or complaint.

Tieg and Webber brandished their crossbows as they moved toward Michael, Jake, Brandi and Devlin. Gone were the villagers who had given them a shelter and food. These men were killers.

"Jake's been shot," Michael said, turning his back on the two and winking at Jake. "He can't walk, can barely stand. He needs help."

Jake crumpled to the ground on cue. Michael bent over, acting as if he were trying, but failing, to get Jake to his feet again.

"Leave him!" Tieg ordered, marching forward. "I said, step back!" He reached out to pull Michael away.

Michael kicked the crossbow from Tieg's hand and as Tieg lunged for it, gave an uppercut to his jaw. He spun and kicked Webber in the stomach. Devlin immediately joined the fight, while Brandi cheered them on, once hitting Webber's back with a rock when he stumbled too close to her. Webber and Tieg soon lay unconscious.

Charlotte scrambled back up the hillside, away from the scent of the beasts. As dangerous as the villagers were, the chimeras were worse. They were killing machines without reason. Her heart pounded and her legs quivered as she pushed herself beyond endurance. The rocky slope caused her to slip and fall, bruising her knees and scraping her hands. The wind kicked up, howling now. She felt like it held her back, blowing dust, grit, and her own hair over her eyes, making it hard to see.

Up ahead, she heard a low rumbling growl. She stopped. A bear-like creature stepped into her line of sight. It, too, stopped and stared at her a long moment before it rose up on its hind legs with an earth-shaking roar.

She had no way to fight it. She slowly backed away, but black, intelligent eyes watched her. At any moment, it would charge. She had seen what such beasts had done to Brian Cutter and Ted Bellows.

She refused to pull her gaze from the monster as she slowly backed away. She smelled its musty, thick scent, and heard its heavy, raspy breathing as it watched her. It rolled its broad shoulders while its massive head swayed from side to side, readying itself to attack. She wasn't about to give up. Not while she had hope. She couldn't outrun the beast. The mountain was steep, rocky, and dangerous. Loose rocks, earlier, had given way under her weight, and were even more likely to roll under the weight of the creature if it tried to follow. There was only one way out.

She plunged down the hill, running, but soon lost her footing. She fell, slid and rolled, unable to stop herself.

Michael, Jake, Brandi and Devlin hurried toward the village because Tieg said the others were held captive there. As they reached the top of the cliff overlooking the village, Michael saw the mercenaries approach it. He motioned to the others to drop down and watch.

Derek Hammill took in the strange, archaic surroundings. He had learned that the bizarre men of this place were formidable foes. Also, something had gone wrong with the accuracy of their weapons that had his men spooked. "Some of them might be hiding here," he said to his men. "Check the buildings."

"No need." A voice came from back at the gate.

Hammill and his men spun around to see Kohler, Olgerbee and Durham watching them.

"You will find the buildings quite empty," Kohler added.

The two leaders each took the measure of the other. "It's time to talk," Derek Hammill shouted.

"Speak your piece," Kohler invited.

"The woman, Charlotte Reed, is the best bet to get us, all of us, out of here. She also has, or can get, the book I want. We may need those friends of hers to force her to cooperate once we find her again." He eyed Kohler. "I know you fellows also want to leave this place. Let's discuss it. Maybe join forces."

Kohler shook his head indicating he had no interest in talking.

"Wait, listen to them! Let's work with them to find the woman and her friends. We need them!" Olgerbee's voice rang out. "You know we can't do this on our own. We've tried everything over the years. Everything we could think of and then some! Time and again we've walked eastward until the soles of our shoes wore away, and instead of finding any city, we've only seen more empty land. The Atlantic itself was devoid of shipping. Then, when we turned back, in two days we were at the pillars! The same happened when we went west or south, even north." He fought his growing fury. "Always, always, we returned to the pillars. The gateway. We couldn't escape them!"

"We've tried other means as well, ungodly, demonic means, using the book," Will Durham said. "But nothing worked."

"Let Charlotte Reed live, and whoever else she needs to help her," Olgerbee cried. "Let her continue studying the book. It could mean freedom for all of us!"

"He's right," Hammill said. "We want the same thing. We don't have to fight."

"You say that pointing your weapons at us?" Kohler asked. "And look, we are unarmed." He opened his arms wide.

Hammill and his two men lowered their weapons. At that moment, Kohler shouted, *"Now!"* as he, Olgerbee, and Durham dove for cover.

Distant arrows flew at the mercenaries from behind them. Three of the villagers had snuck in the back gate while Kohler kept the mercenaries' attention. But this time the mercenaries were ready for the speed and cunning of the villagers. At Kohler's shout, they hurled themselves out of the walkway, using the buildings for shelter and firing back in both directions.

The villagers released their arrows with incredible speed, but arrows were nothing against rifles.

Michael nodded at the others who had watched the battle with him. All of them felt confident they had seen the last of the village men. Also, they knew the others weren't captives in the village, but were out in the wilderness somewhere.

They could only think of one place where they might be going.

EIGHTY-FOUR

"THE PILLARS," QUADE SAID AS HE LOOKED AT THE SIGHT IN THE distance. "We've made it."

Lionel and Rachel nearly cried with relief, emotionally and physically exhausted. They feared going closer to them, however. They feared leaving the heavily forested area that provided them some protection from the mercenaries, who most likely waited nearby for them.

"Do you see the lights?" Quade asked Lionel, as cold and sanguine as ever.

"Yes, but I don't know what they're telling me!" Lionel cried.

"We need to get closer," Quade said.

"But we'll be exposed! Please, let's just wait here for the others. They've got to come here; this is the only logical place for them." Lionel dropped to one knee, head bowed and chest heaving.

Rachel took Lionel's arm and tried to pull him to his feet. "Let me help you," she said. He resisted.

Quade nodded at her, surprised by her courage.

"Please, Professor Rempart," she pleaded, "won't you try?"

Lionel acquiesced and slowly stood. He and Rachel held each other as they walked toward the mound. Both blinked back tears as they listened for the sound of a rifle shot or the whistle of an arrow. They knew each step could be their last.

Michael ran from the brush towards them. "Stop! Don't go out there."

"Michael!" Lionel cried, as his brother took over his support.

"The mercs will soon be at the pillars," Michael told both Lionel and Rachel. "We'll have to be ready to face them."

He led them back to the sheltered area where Jake, Devlin and Brandi waited.

"Devlin! You're alive!" Rachel cried. To her surprise he opened his arms wide. She ran into them and he lifted her off the ground, hugging her just as tight as she did him.

"Me, too!" Brandi said and joined the hug.

"Wait!" Jake limped toward them. "Where's Charlotte?"

"We don't know," Rachel said. "The villagers caught us, but she managed to get away. We haven't seen her since."

He stopped short at the news, his face ashen.

Michael spotted a glint of light, sun bouncing off of metal, in the distance. "Down, everyone!" He shot toward the light.

Jake flung himself backwards and felt a bullet pass by, missing him by inches. He saw one of the mercenaries duck behind a boulder. "I'll be damned," he muttered. "The mercs are already here!"

Michael, Jake, and Devlin fired the HK-91s, thankful for the powerful weapons they'd found, weapons that provided their only chance of survival. Still, the mercs were not only well-armed, but well-trained. Michael and the others were forced to move back, away from the pillars, deeper and deeper into the forest.

"Toss one of those rifles over here, Sheriff."

Jake spun around with a prayer of thanks at the familiar voice. Charlotte hid behind an outcrop. He saw the relieved smile on her face as she looked at him.

He crawled to her, gave her one of the rifles, and a 30-round magazine. She was bruised, with dirt and scrapes on her hands, face, and clothes, and even her hair was full of leaves and brush, but he thought she had never looked more beautiful.

"You're wounded!" she cried.

"I'll be fine." He started to show her how to release the safeties when she shook her head, and said simply, "Homeland Security training."

She joined the fight.

They were forced to run, and at one point found themselves slipping and sliding down into a low-lying dry creek bed. They hid among the trees and shrubs near the creek as the mercs approached. At one point, the mercs were momentarily exposed.

Only three were left—a surprising and heartening discovery.

Michael circled around as the others held off the mercenaries with steady bursts of gunfire. He quickly became aware of the direction of the person giving orders, the one they needed to take out. With their leader gone the others might be less inclined to fight.

He made his way behind Hammill. He positioned the gun to shoot just as gunfire from two other directions pinned him down. The mercs were protecting their leader. He spun and fired, even though he knew that would leave Hammill free to shoot him. A head shot stopped the one with a black mustache and goatee circling thick, purple lips.

The Hammer smiled as he found Michael in his cross-hairs.

Out of nowhere a bullet struck Hammill squarely in the heart, knocking him backwards. He looked down with shock and horror as his life's blood spread over his chest. He lifted his eyes to the shooter and saw his totem, his lucky charm ... the one he believed would free him from this place. In a sense she had. His last words were her name. "Charlotte Reed."

Charlotte dropped behind a boulder. Her heart pounded and her stomach threatened to empty. The man had killed her friends, had tried to kill her. Her revenge should have been sweet, except that she'd seen too much killing, too much death. Even for revenge, it was more than she could bear.

"No!" Fish cried out in anguish seeing his leader fall. He spun and fired nonstop in Charlotte's direction, his bullets bouncing harmlessly off the boulder protecting her before shots from Michael, Jake, and Devlin's rifles silenced him forever.

As suddenly as it began, the shooting stopped.

"If we're lucky, that's the end of it," Michael said. "If we're able to destroy what's keeping this world going, we'll be free of it."

"That's a kind of big if," Devlin murmured.

"But we can concentrate now," Charlotte said. "Finally our enemies, all of them, are gone."

EIGHTY-FIVE

MICHAEL'S GAZE DRIFTED OVER THE SURVIVORS, HIS HEART HEAVY. They all needed to rest a moment, to somehow find the strength to regroup and overcome the emotional maelstrom of being stunned, sickened and horrified by all that had happened. The villagers had seemed ready to help them fight a common enemy, but then revealed themselves as monsters. This day had been a vision of the power of evil.

The only good news was that Jake had managed to smear some of the poultice Charlotte carried on his gunshot wound and was feeling a bit better for it.

At least no one had been lost when the mercs attacked. Still, Michael couldn't imagine what the students must be feeling and thinking with four members of their group gone. Too much death lurked here. Too much horror.

"I'm ready to keep going," Jake soon told them. The poultice had already dulled some of the pain.

"Why bother? It's hopeless," Devlin said. "I've traveled; I've tried to find help; nothing worked. No one is out there. We're stuck here just like those village men ... until they all died."

"It's not hopeless. I've been told there is a way," Michael said, "and that I'd recognize it. It's got to be near."

Charlotte's gaze narrowed. "Who would say such a thing?"

Michael looked ready to give a flippant answer, but then his shoulders sagged. He gazed at her, then at Jake, wondering how much they remembered of his tale of Mongolia. "Lady Hsieh. And I wasn't hallucinating. She's real ... except that she's been dead for two thousand years."

"Oh, boy," Jake muttered. "Now it's Chinese ghosts. The more the merrier."

"Ghosts?" Quade asked.

"An immortal being, created by her own alchemy," Michael said. "She lived for over two thousand years stuck between heaven and earth in the world her alchemy had created. When I opened her coffin, I somehow freed her to break the alchemical spell she was under. I don't pretend to understand it. All I can say is she thanked me for that, for freeing her to go to the land of souls." He paused a long moment, letting all sink in, and then he added. "She warned me that this place is evil. But she said I'd know how to leave—and that I must."

"Do you think that's possible?" Charlotte asked.

He gave a half-smile. "If you'd have asked me two months ago, I'd have said everything we've experienced was completely impossible. Now, to me, it is the only explanation."

Jake added, "If it gets us out of here, I'll buy the story, too."

"It's got to be the pillars," Charlotte murmured. "Those damn pillars that attract danger like a magnet each time we go near them."

"I see it!" Lionel cried. "I see the array! It's much, much clearer than ever before. I'm not sure what happened. I'll be damned, it's actually beautiful!"

How could Lionel be surprised by its beauty? Michael wondered. It had always been so. "Yes, I see it, too."

"I thought you did," Lionel said. Then, all but dismissing Michael, he turned to Charlotte. "Give me the book. I need it."

"You haven't understood a word in it up to this time," she said. "Why should you now? It's more than reading. It takes an intuitive feel. If anyone here has it, it's Michael." She held out the backpack. "You take it, Michael. Open the gateway for us."

Michael's instincts told him to fight the temptation. He sensed that if he opened the gateway, he would cross a bridge from which no return existed, at least none for him.

Quade's gaze jumped from one brother to the other.

"I agree with Charlotte," Jake said. His voice already sounded stronger as the poultice worked its magic.

Michael shook his head. "I've never studied anything like that book, and

Lionel said he could do it." He faced his brother. "We've never been close because of the way we were raised. But we can change that."

Lionel stared longingly at the backpack. "You're right. We can change."

Reluctantly, Charlotte took out the book and gave it to Lionel.

He climbed to the top of the mound, opened the book to the section that showed an array, and stepped on the lights on the ground as he walked between the pillars. Nothing happened. He placed the book on the lights and walked through again. Still nothing.

Dismayed, Michael watched with growing impatience.

"I told you he can't do it!" Charlotte angrily removed the red pendants she wore and grudgingly thrust them at Michael. "Take these."

His gaze locked on the stones in his hand. "They're beautiful." He reached into his pocket. "The color is the same as this small one from Lady Hsieh's tomb." When he opened his hand to show her the small red stone, all of them began to glow. Bright beams of red light shot from each one skyward, meeting and intertwining. Rolling thunder boomed, and bolts of lightning arched above the pillars.

"My God," Charlotte whispered. "We've never had thunder and lightning on this side; only in the real world. You've bridged something. Made a connection. This just might work."

Jake stood and moved closer to her. "You're right. Michael, go ahead."

Lionel clutched the book to his chest. "What's going on? What are you doing?"

"Wear them, Michael." Charlotte's voice filled with wonder and awe as she lifted the cords holding the pendants over his head.

With the philosopher's stones hanging from his neck, his own small stone still in his hand, a surging power coursed through his body. It felt new, yet familiar, as if he had waited his whole life for this moment, as if he'd found his purpose.

Without knowing why, he climbed up the mound and stood beside Lionel. The pillars began to sway as if they might tumble.

"What's happening?" Lionel cried.

Before he managed to answer, Kohler and the other villagers walked out of the forest.

Michael's flesh turned cold as ice.

The village men no longer wore camouflage clothing, but a much older style, homespun, from the time of Lewis and Clark and the secret expedition. They carried primitive weapons, hatchets, bows and arrows.

The gunshot wounds they had suffered were visible—some gaping open, others puckered, a few had scabbed over. And yet, no blood flowed.

"It can't be," Lionel whispered as he gawked at them.

"How can they be here?" Brandi's high-pitched hysteria carried over the valley. Devlin slipped his arm around Rachel who stood petrified, her hands over her mouth. "They're all shot up! We saw them dead!"

Michael's pulse thudded. Seeing the villagers that way confirmed the suspicion that had grown in him, but one too terrible to contemplate, one he had pushed aside as lunacy. He didn't want to believe it, even now.

"What the hell?" Jake strode toward them, his rifle pointed at Kohler.

Kohler raised his chin high as he spoke. "My true name is Ezra Crouch, captain and leader of our ill-fated expedition. And the young man that you know as Will Durham is in truth Francis Masterson, the scribe who penned the words that taught you so much about us. We have waited over two hundred years for someone with the ability to open the gateway, and now we have found him." He glanced up at the pillars at the two brothers. "Or them."

"Impossible!" Jake shouted. "You expect me to believe you're some kind of ... what? A zombie? A dead man who won't die? You're crazy!"

"He's not," Michael said. "It's the only explanation that makes sense."

"Where are the others, then? The men who came here thirteen years ago?" Jake demanded.

"Dead," Kohler said, devoid of any emotion. He and the others moved closer as he spoke. "They were useful for a time. We learned quite a bit from them with their modern armaments and current knowledge. But then, as all newcomers do, they became exceedingly troublesome and irritating, and we were forced to kill them. We used their identities since they were easier to explain away than our own. They tried to fight us, but they had no chance. No one can kill us. On occasion, our anger boils over and we kill each other. Or those annoying beasts kill us, and we them. But we come back, always. To live and kill another day." He smiled. "Today, for instance."

"So you do know alchemy," Charlotte said.

"If only that were the case," Kohler admitted, "our lives would be far easier. Try as we might, we have been unable to learn it. All we know is that it gives us immortality, for immortal we are. Soon, we will be in the decaying world, your world. There, we will reveal ourselves in power. All men will revere us and want to be like us. They will worship us. We will be more than gods to them, for gods are unseen and live in the heavens, while we will walk among them forever." His gaze lifted to Michael and Lionel. "Now, if you want no harm to befall your friends, you will open the gateway."

Michael realized that if he opened the pillars and the villagers went through it, there was no telling what evil they might do. He envisioned them biding their time, learning the ways of the modern world, and then slowly amassing wealth and power. After all, they had all eternity to achieve their goals. With vast libraries of knowledge and people willing to do almost anything if paid enough money, they could attempt to master the alchemy that had transformed them into immortal monsters.

Once that happened, if they promised immortality to the public, they would own the world. How much would a man give up to live forever? His freedom? His wealth? His soul? Some would see the folly and object, but who knew how many would die before someone stopped the village men forever, if that were even possible?

"I will not help you," he said.

"You have no choice!" Kohler shouted. "I saw what you could do. You must continue. Do you not want to become immortal? You people can be our first conversions. You will go back to your own time, your friends and family, and you will live forever. If not, you will all be killed."

How many people had they already murdered, starting with Abbé Gerard? Michael wondered. They had taken Vince's life without a second thought. Surely, other poor souls had stepped between those pillars in the two-hundred-plus years they had stood, and they, too, must have been killed. These villagers, these explorers from the Secret Expedition, might be immortal, but they weren't men any longer. They had become monsters. He could not reason with monsters.

"Don't listen to him," said Will Durham, who was the journal author, Francis Masterson. "I know him. Once he's through the opening, he'll kill all of you and take *The Book* and the stones." He glanced at Rachel once, sadly, and then faced Kohler. "I will not countenance any more death, Captain!"

"Back away, Francis!" Kohler ordered.

In that moment of distraction, Michael aimed his rifle and fired. Kohler fell, hit in the chest. Michael dropped flat on the ground and continued to shoot at the villagers.

When Kohler dropped, Quade hurried Brandi and Rachel away while Jake, Charlotte and Devlin took cover and fired their weapons. The villagers might be immortal, but they still felt pain, still felt a bullet tear through their flesh and shatter bone. And that should stop them, at least for a little while.

But Kohler didn't stop. He rose again to his feet even as shots to the head and legs rocked his body. He tried to move forward, but the firepower's strength forced him and the others to retreat into the forest, their flesh torn even worse than before.

Michael and the others knew it was only a matter of time before they regrouped and returned. Lady Hsieh had told him he knew the way to free himself and others, not that he would find it, but that he *knew* it, inherently, within himself.

She was right. It suddenly all made sense.

The ability he and the others in his family possessed consisted of no more than that of a conduit between one world and another, no more than a connection through which energy, knowledge, and being could pass.

He didn't want this, but he had no choice.

He put down his rifle and stepped between the pillars. He placed one foot on one peak of light that only he and Lionel could see, and the other foot on another ray of light. Then he raised his arms, palms pressed together, fingers pointing toward the sky so that his body formed a triangle, the key alchemical symbol. Energy from the array ran through him and absorbed his life force to enrich its own before it massed into a burst of energy that streamed from his fingertips high into the heavens.

He felt the array drain his life from him as it absorbed his energy and yet it shared its own with him.

At that moment, the villagers stepped out of their hiding places in the forest to witness the glorious yet frightening event taking place in front of their eyes. Jake, Charlotte, Quade, and the students did the same.

A great ball of light formed above Michael and shined down on them all. A kaleidoscope of colors and images. Michael then spread his arms wide. The earth rumbled. A tree near the villagers suddenly burst into flame, then another farther away. The air crackled with charged sparks of light as those who watched fell to their knees in fright and awe.

Slowly, he lifted his hands. As he did, the pillars rose. His power became far stronger than he imagined, but he knew that once the gateway opened, anyone, anything, could pass from this amoral world to his own.

The chimeras snorted and stomped as they gathered on the western edge of the forest to watch the strange proceedings before them with a human-like intelligence glowing in their eyes. They appeared to understand what they saw perhaps better than the humans.

"Hurry," Michael said to Jake. "Get the students and Charlotte through, and then I'll close the gateway." Quade wasn't with them, but Michael could do nothing about that.

At the same time, Kohler and the villagers began to run toward the mound.

The two groups raced toward the pillars. The villagers were winning.

"Hurry, Jake!" Michael called, but even as he did, he saw that the villagers would reach the gateway before the students. He couldn't let that happen.

The villagers reached the bottom of the mound and began to climb.

Michael began to slowly lower his arms, afraid of what might happen if he moved too quickly and the pillars crashed against the earth and shattered.

"No!" Lionel cried, picking up Michael's high-powered rifle. "Keep the pillars right where they are. We're leaving here! All of us!" He aimed at his brother.

"Lionel, no!" Charlotte screamed.

"We can't let them through," Michael said, both frightened and appalled by the madness that overtook his brother. "They'll destroy everything." He again began to lower his arms.

"Stop! I swear!" Lionel cried. His hand, his entire body, shook as his finger found the trigger and began to squeeze it. Will Durham released an arrow from his crossbow. It struck Lionel in the heart. Lionel's shot went wide, hitting Michael's shoulder, tearing it open and shattering bone and muscle.

As Michael fell, the pillars slammed back to the ground. The earth shook and roared.

"He's not dead!" Kohler shouted to the villagers. "Get up there! Lift him up! We must use him to keep the gateway open!"

The villagers climbed the mound to follow Kohler's orders. The chimeras moved closer as well.

"Lionel," Michael whispered, and dragged himself to his brother. Lionel was already dead. Sorrow shot through Michael for all that might have been between them, for all their lost years, for all that could never be. He bowed his head, overcome, as horror built upon horror in this evil place.

"Enough!" Quade shouted. His long whitish-blond hair looked like an aura around his head, while black eyes took in everything. One hand clutched *The Book of Abraham the Jew* against his chest, while he raised the other hand and again commanded, "Enough!"

A profound authority emanated from him. The villagers stopped moving, unable to do anything but obey Quade's command. Jake, Charlotte and the students stopped as well, forming a tight knot.

"I did not want this." Quade spoke in little more than a whisper that mysteriously carried from the top of the mound to every ear. "I struggled to find some way to avoid it. A misfortune of our fallen arrogant nature is that even a man—such as I—who has lived for centuries still wants to stay alive, curious about what the future will bring to this strange little planet twirling around a giant universe. But I cannot let more people die because of me."

Kohler stood, his body so riddled with bullet holes he had been nearly shredded. "Abbé Gerard? But you cannot be him! We saw you die! We tossed your corpse into the river."

"Die but not dead," the Abbé said with a small, secretive smile. "You've done it yourself, time and again. Why should I, the greatest alchemist the world has ever known, be unable to do the same? Those many years ago, when I revived, I simply kept going. I had the power all along to escape from this place. So I opened the gateway. Several chimeras slipped out with me. To my surprise, in the real world their animal natures, which I did not make immortal, caused them to slowly deteriorate. The bones of the dead created quite a stir among scientists. A couple of them live to this day."

"They live, but they also kill," Michael said as he somehow managed to raise himself to a sitting position, one hand clutching his shoulder, trying to stem the flow of blood.

The Abbe shrugged. "In any case, I never wanted to leave this place. I created it! I loved it! And I did not miss the company of men. They had hounded me from my beloved Paris, from Spain, Egypt, and even from China. In this New World I could live alone in peace, with only the Tukudeka. And then men from the secret expedition came and destroyed my peace. Now, here, all of you shall remain. I want us to return to the village now, my village, where I shall take my rightful place as your leader."

Everything Michael heard, the sheer monstrousness of the story, sickened him. "Tell me, how can a man who doesn't age live in the real world?"

The Abbé's thin red lips tightened with disgust. "I made my way to the Pacific, and from there sailed to Asia, eventually crossing the mountains to Tibet. Tibetans do not question the unquestionable. I stayed with them until the Communist Chinese took over the country. They killed many good men, many holy men." His black eyes raged. "How can you call my world evil compared to the unimaginable horror of *your* world in the twentieth and twenty-first centuries? I left the destruction that once was the beauty of Tibet and returned to America where, for the right price, identities and insider knowledge easily can be purchased. A man who can make gold always has the right price. When I learned all that happened here, I realized my creation caused it, a creation made when I was a very different man from the one you see before you."

"How different?" Michael asked. "You still make yourself a tin god."

"I returned here with hope of freeing the young people and then going on with my life. But once back, I saw that was impossible. I did not want this horror. My deeds have eaten at my soul." He turned from Michael to speak to the students who stood awe-struck at the power that seemed to emanate from both Michael and the Abbé. "Forgive me, but I cannot allow you or those who tried to rescue you to return. Remember the curse that Abraham the Jew placed on his book—*Maranatha against every person that should cast his eyes upon it and is not sacrificer or scribe.* You have seen too much; you know too much; you will desire too much and never again find peace in the real world. You are all cursed! But out of kindness, I shall give you the elixir of immortality. Without it, the men of the secret expedition will surely kill you."

Michael tried to stand, but the excruciating pain almost made him black out. He willed himself to fight past it, but failed.

The scent of flowers...Lady Hsieh. He sensed her beside him. Her words came to him, not as a whisper, but from inside. "You must act, Michael. Destroy this world to save your own. Look to the philosopher's stones, at what they do. When you understand that, you will see that the strength is within you."

She came once more to save him. He gazed at the red stones. *What had she meant?* The alchemist used them to speed up change in minerals and to bring the elements to perfection. The perfect mineral was gold which never decayed; the perfect man was immortal because he never aged. To create the change, the stones compressed time, used untold energy ...

Energy. That was it! Earth, air, fire, and water—the matter of alchemy. The alchemist sped their change ... and that change provided the energy to create all this.

He knew what to do, just as Lady Hsieh had foretold. He removed the philosopher's stones from around his neck and placed them and the stone from Lady Hsieh's tomb on the ground. When he did, lights shown around them forming the symbol of immortality. The stones lay in the black circle, the center of centers.

He remembered once hearing a story about that circle, how a Chinese warrior, a great man, enjoyed invincibility except in one spot—the black circle, the center of centers. It alone made the warrior vulnerable to a terrible, perhaps fatal, wound to body or spirit or both. He thought of Achilles and his vulnerable heel, and the King of the Grail Knights, Amfortas, and his never-healing wound.

"You will let the students go," Michael demanded. "If not, I will destroy this world."

The Abbé faced him, shocked at his new tone. His expression turned fierce, his gaze cold. "This world was a fine place, everything I could possibly want until Captain Crouch who now calls himself 'Kohler,' and his companions wanted to take what was mine. At first, they were good, learned men. I liked them and fed them the elixir of immortality. But then, they wanted to learn alchemy for themselves. They coveted the wealth it could create, the immortality and power it could grant. They became corrupt!"

"*This place* corrupted them, as it did you." Michael's will grew stronger with each breath. "But these young people are innocent. They don't deserve such a fate. You must let them leave and return home."

"I am not evil!" the Abbé thundered. "What I do is for the greater good."

"There's nothing good about what you suggest."

As the Abbé and Michael faced off in a war of wills, their audience stood muted and still, while the earth began to rumble and groan.

"You can't blame me for the evil these men did!" The Abbé clenched his hand into a fist. "I cast an alchemical spell over the pillars causing anyone who found them to forget about them after leaving the area. It's not my fault I could do nothing to prevent a person, once here, from walking between them and entering this world." The Abbe stood straight, regal, chin high as he added, "To destroy the world is to destroy me. You are a part of it, part of my family. In its destruction, you, too, will perish!"

"Then, so it must be!" Michael yanked the arrow from his brother's body and plunged it into the black circle, the center of centers, the only vulnerable spot in this alchemical world.

"No!" the Abbé shouted.

Michael collapsed, too weak and ravaged with pain to hold himself up a moment longer.

The earth trembled. The hieroglyphs at the tops of the pillars developed fissures that grew and deepened. Chunks broke off and fell to the earth.

Michael saw Lady Hsieh then. He watched her image grow faint. "No, not you," he cried. "I can't lose you, too."

"I'm glad ..." she murmured as she faded from his eyes.

Charlotte climbed the mound and tried to pull Michael away, but as much as she struggled, he fought to stay there, as if he saw something beyond her vision. She took Ben Olgerbee's poultice from her pocket and smeared the last of it thickly on his gaping shoulder wound. Immediately, the flow of blood lessened. Michael could not die, she told herself, not now, not in this battle for all their futures.

Jake joined her. They lifted Michael to his feet and carried him off the mound, just ahead of the toppling pillars. "She's gone." His strange words made no sense to them.

The pillars swayed ever deeper until finally they crashed to earth. Dirt and ash spewed into the air.

Jake, Charlotte and Michael fell amidst the tide, choking on the dust.

Michael envisioned the time in Kenya, at his first dig, when the earth collapsed on him and he felt death a certainty. But the paralyzing emptiness that came over him in Kenya didn't happen this time. Life was a gift and held far more wonders and beauty than he had ever believed. He rose to his hands and knees, unwilling to give up.

The sea of ash blinded Charlotte and left her unable to breathe. Strong arms grabbed her. Jake held her close as he led her away from the thick, roiling powder-filled air. Devlin, who had been some distance away with Brandi and Rachel, ran back into the dust and helped Michael escape.

At that moment, a cold, violent wind rose out of nowhere, swept the cloud of soot into a tornado that swirled around the village men alone, and pinned them to one spot.

The villagers' forms faded and then flickered and returned as they struggled against their fate. Kohler stared at Michael with malice while the world that kept him alive collapsed. His body shuddered as he struggled but failed to break the paralysis that came over him.

The others, Francis Masterson who had called himself Will Durham, Noah Handy, who had been Francis' easy-going friend and now called himself Gus Webber; the brothers Orril and Asa Munroe, who pretended to be Sam Black and Arnie Tieg; and the wise elder Reuben Hale, who was known to them as Ben Olgerbee, were also unable to move. All had once been good men, but had been overcome by the evil of this unholy place.

The chimeras watched the trapped men of the Secret Expedition. Hate-filled, they ran towards the men, their eyes glowing with the desire to tear them to pieces. They no sooner reached them when magna from within the earth, hot from fire, rose up and captured both men and beasts in its fiery grasp. The cyclonic wind that circled them grew stronger, forcing them inward even as they struggled with each other. And finally, at their feet, black, brackish water rose up from within the earth. The water boiled.

The villagers and creatures stood in the midst of the elements—earth, fire, air and water. They screamed, and tried to run, but molten rock held them in place as it oozed upward to cover them.

Michael's gaze met Francis Masterson's. As Will Durham, the man had killed Lionel, but did it to save not only Michael, but the world from an unknown horror. And yet, not even Masterson could escape his fate.

Masterson glanced over at Rachel, standing with Devlin's arm around her, then he looked back at Michael as his gaze softened into an uneasy peace and resignation. He nodded, then shut his eyes.

Michael watched with horror as the earth covering them hardened into rock, their final screams echoing throughout the valley.

Michael turned towards Abbé Gerard who remained atop the mound watching the destruction of the world he had created over two centuries earlier. Michael acknowledged, if only to himself, they couldn't have survived without the Abbé's—Quade's—guidance, strange though it had been.

"Abbé Gerard," Michael shouted, "you don't need to die. We'll find a way!"

"It is not possible. I have had far more than my share of life." Tears lined Abbé's face as he looked at the earth, the sky, one last time. "I have seen unimaginable changes in this world, far more than any alchemist ever dreamed of. And they were developed by man, not by magic. I am sad to leave, but some things are not possible to undo." Then, with a strange little smile on his lips, he added, "Man can subvert nature, but never improve it. Remember that, Michael. Always remember that."

The ground quaked more violently and rocks and trees tumbled around them.

The ancient, parched pages of *The Book of Abraham the Jew* caught fire. Before their eyes, the being who was once Abbé Gerard and Simon Quade began to age, his body dried and shriveled. A great whirling tornado of fire rose up, lifting the book and the Abbé high over the earth. At that moment, as if it were some great whale coming out of the ocean, the mound itself began to rise from the earth, to swell, like a terrible malignancy.

As the book burst apart in a fiery blast, the Abbé's body rocked and exploded into a turbulent vortex. The mound split open creating a wide, deep chasm. The men of the Secret Expedition, the chimeras, the pillars, and the charred remains of the Abbé and the book fell deep into the earth.

Finally, as the last echo of the blast drifted away, the vortex collapsed upon itself.

When it settled again, the land lay flat, and all evidence of the terrors they had witnessed were gone.

With balance restored, the earth became perfectly still.

❄

Rachel, Devlin, and Brandi, with Jake and Charlotte supporting Michael, walked silently away from the area where the mound and pillars once stood.

After a short while, Jake stopped and unclipped the satellite phone from his belt and turned it on. Welcoming and welcomed lights flashed. He punched in a number and waited, then tried again. For a while, they heard nothing, but then a faint, crackling sounded, and a voice answered.

"Telichpah Flat Station. Hello? Is anybody there? This is Deputy Mallick. Can you hear me?"

"Mallick," Jake said with a chuckle. "I've never heard a voice so beautiful!"

"Sheriff! Holy crap! Where the hell are you? We thought you were dead!"

"We've got three of the kids...Rachel, Brandi, and Devlin. Charlotte Reed and Michael Rempart also made it. All the others are dead. We could sure use a helicopter and paramedics, Deputy. I'll give you the coordinates."

"Thank God three of the kids were saved! We had given up all hope for them, and for you, too! This is a happy day, Sheriff!"

"Yes, Deputy," Jake said wearily, gazing back at the survivors. "It certainly is."

When Jake hung up cheers and tears erupted in thanks for their impending rescue and return to civilization, as well as sadness for those they lost.

"How will anyone ever believe what happened?" Rachel voiced the question on all their minds.

"They won't," Jake's words were harsh, solemn. "They'll investigate. Point suspicion."

"We've got to tell them something," Charlotte said. "How can we explain? Plus, you and Michael have been shot!"

"We can blame gunshots on stumbling across drug runners or pot growers trying to hide from the law," Jake said. "But as for the students ... whatever we say, we'll all have to agree on it. Anyone who tries to explain what really happened out here will end up in a rubber room."

"A flash flood," Michael barely managed the words. "Before we found Rachel, Brandi, and Devlin, the others were lost, swept down to the Salmon River. That will explain why there are no bodies."

Michael shut his eyes from exhaustion and pain as Jake looked at the others. One by one, they nodded. "That's our story, then," Jake told them, "and it makes sense. There's a reason it's called the river of no return."

EIGHTY-SIX

THE NEXT MORNING THE GOVERNOR DISPATCHED A PRIVATE PLANE TO Salmon City to pick up the students, media, and anyone else who wanted a quick trip back to Boise after the grueling ordeal.

Jake went to the airfield to see them off. Rachel's and Devlin's parents met them there, having ridden up as part of the governor's group. Brandi's parents flew in on their own plane to take her home with them. All the thanks Jake received from parents made him uncomfortable. He looked for Charlotte and Michael, but found neither.

As quickly as he could, he said his goodbyes, got hugs from the students, and hurried to Salmon's emergency medical facility. All the survivors had been brought there to be checked over when they arrived late the night before. The doctors insisted Michael stay, while the state provided the others motel rooms with baths, clean clothes, and lots of food. Jake spent the entire night being debriefed, and pretty much cut off from everyone else. He worried that Michael may have taken a turn for the worse.

Instead, he learned no one knew where Michael went. His doctors expected him to transfer to a hospital in Boise, but a mysterious young Chinese fellow showed up and whisked him out of the medical center before dawn. By the time a furious Homeland Security agent arrived, they were both long gone.

Charlotte hadn't been seen at the hospital either. She might have left with Michael, but Jake found it hard to imagine her leaving without at least saying goodbye. He went to the motel only to learn she hadn't used her room the night before.

It made no sense. He could only think of one other place she might be, if still in the area. He drove like a crazy man out to the Forest Service cabin Simon Quade had used.

She closed the trunk of her rental car as he skidded to a stop on the driveway. She was alone.

She looked happy to see him, but at the same time troubled. He limped toward her, the bullet wound mending but still painful. "You aren't taking the plane back?"

"No. Fortunately, Michael's friend, Li Jianjun, found me as I left the clinic last night. He advised me to stay out of sight of any law enforcement types until a situation involving some murders in Israel was settled. He'll see that the FBI receives evidence that implicates Calvin Phaylor. I don't mind hiding out for a month or two. I was tempted to stay here, but I'm sure the Forest Service will come back to it eventually. You won't turn me in, will you, Sheriff?"

He stood close, one hand on the top of the car to help support himself. "Not to worry. I've said all I have to say on this subject to the authorities, the press, and everyone else."

"I know what you mean." She gave him a lopsided smile. "Ironic, isn't it? I've found the story of a lifetime for both US historians and anyone interested in alchemy, and I can't tell it. No one would believe it, and it isn't the sort of thing I want the parents of all those students to have to live with, or Melisse's little daughter."

He nodded. "True."

"Years from now, when you're old and gray and living in these mountains and no longer care if you're called a crazy old sheriff, you'll certainly have a story to tell."

"If I stay," he said, and glanced out over the mountains. "It's beautiful here, but the winters are long and lonely. At least that's what I'll remind myself when people start throwing blame around for so many deaths. Especially since I won't be able to tell them what really happened, I might not even have a job when it's all said and done. Maybe I'll leave before they ask me to."

"So many deaths," Charlotte said. "So many lives taken, and the lives of those who loved them forever shattered."

Jake nodded. "The public will never know."

"It's for the best," she said, and walked to the driver's door, car keys in hand. Before she opened it, she faced him. "I'm sorry it turned out this way for you."

He shrugged. "I came up here to retire from the world, from people. And look at what I walked into."

"You'll do well wherever you go," she remarked, her face as serious as ever. "Where will you go, Jake?"

"I don't know. A part of me hates the idea of leaving. No matter what, this is home." His gaze swept the area, then returned to her. "What about you, Charlotte? Back to Customs?"

"To look for art and antiquities forgeries after I've found the ultimate antiquity treasure? It's going to be very hard to do my job after that. So, I don't know either." Her troubled blue eyes met his, and she stepped closer to him. "I guess I could return to Jerusalem to finish my Ph.D., but academic life no longer holds any appeal, I'm afraid. It would be finishing what I started, which makes sense, but at the same time, I can't help but feel that would be going backward, not forward."

Washington D. C. or Jerusalem. He could never compete with all that and knew better than to try. "I have never known a woman so serious or so focused on what's logical, scientific and rational. What would you most *like* to do?"

"What would I most like?" She thought a moment. "To what purpose?"

He shook his head and grinned at her. "For the purpose of, I don't know, who you are? What you're all about? Maybe even your very own brand of happiness?" He turned serious and placed his hands on her arms as he quietly added. "You deserve it, you know."

That took her aback. "Well, in that case," she said, regarding him closely, brows furrowed as she contemplated his question, "I think that to be somewhere with a big soaking tub, a soft bed, good books, and lots of peace and quiet would be rather pleasant." Her expression eased, and with some hope in her voice, she added, "It might even be a place to begin to build some new memories. Good ones."

He saw the shine in her eyes, heard a lilt in her voice, but didn't want to believe it. He dropped his hands. "That's all you want?" he asked, wary now.

"Isn't it enough?" Her voice caught.

His mouth went dry. "There's a house in Salmon that has that. My place. You can use it if you'd like. I mean...I've got a guest room. I'm not suggesting...not that I wouldn't want...I mean..." He stopped then.

The two studied each other but said nothing as they held their respective breaths.

She spoke first. "The long winter is just about here," she said, still serious. "And two bodies are warmer than one. That could save a lot of money on the heating bill, especially if we're both unemployed."

A grin played on his lips. "Charlotte Reed, did you just make a joke?"

A slow smile spread over her face, one that broadened as she threw caution aside and put her arms around his neck and pulled him close. "I think I could get the hang of this 'fun' business."

"So do I, Charlotte, so do I." As their lips met and her arms tightened, he crushed her to him. He had no idea if what they had found would last, but knew they would take it day by day, build on what they shared, and value those areas where they differed. Finally each could put aside the ugliness of the past and move toward the future. He hoped with all his heart they would face it together.

EPILOGUE

Goa, India

Michael Rempart walked alone through the narrow streets of the former Portuguese settlement of Old Goa to an imposing black granite and basalt cathedral. His left arm was weak and limp while his shoulder and back still ached from the bullet that might have killed him.

For one month, his friend and assistant, Li Jianjun, stayed by his side, diligently watching over him as his body mended. Once he healed, Jianjun returned to Vancouver.

Michael spent much of his time soul-searching since he left Idaho, and contemplating all he learned about life, death, what lies beyond the grave, and about himself. He feared that a normal life, a life rich with love, marriage, and children would never be his, but for the first time he could think of the woman he had loved but lost without bitterness, and with peace for what they once had known. And as he thought of the ethereal being from another age who had brought him such joy, he knew he would carry the memory of her forever in his heart.

Lady Hsieh—Lin—had been right about many things, but never more than when she said that what he sought was in this world, but not of it. He had learned that, in the endless process of transformation, nothing was destroyed. Death was not destruction, but merely dissolution. In dissolving all things, the cosmos also renewed them. There was fulfillment in life; throughout the whole recurrence of eternity nothing existed that had not lived. He read that Hermes Trismegistus had once said, *'For there never was any dead thing in the cosmos, nor is there, nor will there be.'* He believed it.

He entered the cathedral with its beautifully gilded altars, frescoes and inlays, and turned to a small chapel that housed the relics of St. Francis Xavier, the peripatetic missionary who spent his life in India, the Malay peninsula, Japan, and died while on the way to China.

Michael stood before the silver casket of the saint whose body, many believed, remained perfectly preserved even in death.

Head bowed, Michael's heart filled not only with peace, but also with a sense of purpose. He was alone, but not lonely. He accepted that the convivial life others led was not for him, and never would be. He didn't know where life would lead him, but he had every confidence in Lady Hsieh's words, that he still had much to do. She had never failed him.

His thoughts then turned to Francis Masterson, the gentle but tormented young writer whose journals had guided Michael and the others to understand what they faced and ultimately to safety. He had been a good-hearted man who boldly went to uncharted lands, much like the saint whose name he bore, and now, he finally rested in eternal peace. All of them did, including Lady Hsieh, and even Abbé Gerard.

The unquiet graves were no more; and the secret of alchemy lost forever.

As it should be.

As it must.

AUTHOR'S NOTES

Readers interested in learning more about alchemy can find vast amounts of material, including entire libraries, on the subject. If I had to name one scholarly work that I believe would be most helpful, understandable and interesting, it would be a relatively small book called *The Forge and the Crucible: The Origins and Structure of Alchemy* by philosopher and religious historian Mircea Eliade.

Many writings exist that present the explanation Nicolas Flamel (also spelled Nicholas Flammel) gave of finding and eventually deciphering *The Book of Abraham the Jew*. The material found in this book was taken from the English translation of the French work as printed in London in 1624 for Thomas Walsley, called *Hieroglyphical Figures (Which he caused to be Painted upon an Arch in St. Innocents Church Yard in Paris): Concerning both the Theory and Practice of the Philosophers Stone*. Whether *The Book of Abraham the Jew* ever truly existed, as well as which of several alchemists named "Abraham" might have written it, continues to be hotly debated to this day.

Edward Kelley (also spelled Kelly) is also an historical figure. He is highly controversial, and many of his biographies are filled with unsubstantiated stories. One of the most thoroughly researched works is Michael Wilding's, "A Biography of Edward Kelly, the English Alchemist and Associate of Dr. John Dee," found in *Mystical Metal of Gold, Essays on Alchemy and Renaissance Culture,* edited by Stanton J. Linden. Details of Kelley's life in Bohemia, the ruin of his patron Vilém Rozmberk, and his death can be found there. The real Edward Kelley did not marry Rozmberk's daughter or father her child.

The history of Fort Lemhi, the first Mormon settlement in Idaho, including Brigham Young's visit there and the massacre of the missionaries happened very much as presented, and details can be found in many Idaho history books. The small group that left the main settlement to found a splinter mission called New Gideon, however, is not factual.

The Tukudeka, a small Shoshoni-Bannock tribal group, roamed the area from Idaho's Sawtooth Mountains near what are now Sun Valley, and the Middle Fork and South Fork of the Salmon River. They settled down only during winter. Their name means "sheep eater." Very little is known of them and generally accepted is the belief that the Tukudeka band is now extinct or has been absorbed into other groups. The Sheepeater Indian War of 1879, along the Middle Fork of the Salmon River, is considered to have been the last Indian war in the Pacific Northwest. *The Middle Fork & The Sheepeater War* by Johnny Carrey and Cort Conley is a beautiful presentation of the area and its history.

Last of all, as far as we know, there was no Secret Expedition.

PLUS ...

Don't miss hearing about the next archeologist Michael Rempart adventure and all of Joanne's new books by signing up for her mailing list at www.joannepence.com.

For your enjoyment, here's chapter one of ANCIENT SHADOWS, the next book in the "Ancient Secrets" series:

Michael Rempart pulled the collar of his jacket tight against his neck and side-stepped black, grit-filled rain puddles. The rain had stopped, but the air was damp and cold. He hurried along the narrow city streets unable to shake the feeling of being watched, of being followed.

A high forehead over intense brown eyes and jutting, angular cheekbones gave him a severe demeanor, while jet-black hair without a single strand of gray despite his forty-one years swirled and slapped against his face in the blustering wind. Murky yellow lights from street lamps shimmered on the wet cobblestone. Florence was colorful and charming in sunlight, but in rain it became dank and shadow-filled. Michael first arrived here in the spring to recuperate after badly injuring his left arm and shoulder in a bizarre incident in Idaho. Florence suited his mood then, colorful, green, and lush with flowers, light showers and gentle mists. The summer was brutal with heat and wall-to-wall tourists. He nearly left, but the locals encouraged him to stay, saying the gaggling crowds would soon be gone.

Autumn wrapped itself around his heart, with its waning warm days, cool night breezes, and opulent harvests—fresh fruit, vegetables, cheese and wine, the abundance of Tuscany in all its glory. But far too soon the bone-slicing winds of the approaching winter would hit. He wasn't sure how much longer he would stay in Florence. But if not here, where? He was an American, but no one waited for him back in the U.S. No one particularly cared what he did, or where he went. Nor did he.

He was a solitary figure, friendly but a mystery to his neighbors who were quick to notice that he seemed to have no close friends or companions, male or female, and spent most of his time pouring over books. That night he had gone, alone as usual, to a lecture at the Uffizi Museum given by an archeologist who had recently unearthed a sealed Etruscan tomb not far from Florence. Although Michael's Italian wasn't very good, he found the slides interesting. He, too, was an archeologist—or had been. Currently, nothing captured his interest sufficiently for him to pursue a new dig. He wondered if anything ever would. He had become almost a hermit, burying himself in studies of the Middle Ages and Renaissance. Instead of the tanned, well-toned, outdoor-loving traveler he had once been, he hardly recognized the pale, gaunt figure that looked back at him when he shaved.

The hour was late, and this part of the city still and quiet. A dark, covered walkway off a side street led to the dimly lit courtyard of the nineteenth century building where he rented an apartment. He walked up three steps to his front door, unlocked it, and switched on the light. As he turned to shut the door he was startled to see an elderly stranger standing in the courtyard just a few feet away. He was small of stature, with olive skin, long salt and pepper hair and a scraggly gray beard that reached his chest. Dressed completely in black, his unbuttoned overcoat revealed a large silver crucifix on a heavy chain over his heart.

"C'è qualche problema?" Is there some problem? Michael asked.

"We must speak." The stranger's deep, raspy voice sounded harsh and determined. He spoke English with an accent Michael couldn't readily identify. As the man stepped closer, the light from inside the apartment showed a cadaverous face with a waxy, yellowish cast, and thin, painfully tight skin. His brows, a thick mixture of wiry white and gray hairs, shadowed dark, red-rimmed eyes that never left Michael's. "My name is Yosip Berosus. I am a Chaldean priest. Time is running out for me."

A dark chill rippled through Michael at the priest's odd statement. He was familiar with the Chaldeans, one of the ancient Eastern rites of the Catholic Church, found mainly in Iraq, northwestern Iran, and southeastern Turkey. Their leader was the Patriarch of the diocese of Baghdad.

The priest sounded desperate, but not dangerous. Michael nodded and stepped back, opening the door wider by way of invitation.

As the priest entered the dimly lit apartment, he rested an emaciated, pale hand against the burnt ochre wall and took several deep breaths to steady himself.

Michael moved closer to help him. The old man reeked. Not the usual stink of sweat and filth, but a sour, musky odor, one of rot. An odor that reminded Michael of death. He gripped the priest's arm, so fragile it felt like no more than bone, and led him to a chair at the wooden dining table. Shelves overflowing with books and research papers lined the wall behind the table. A desk, sofa, coffee table, and television on a stand made up the remaining furniture. The tiny bedroom was upstairs.

Michael crossed to the alcove that served as a kitchen, its appliances old but sufficient for his solitary purpose, and poured one glass of Chianti and another of water and set them before the priest. He drank the water first, then reached for the wine. "I've heard about you," Berosus said. "Everything. I know you have been to Mongolia, and what you discovered there."

Michael had wondered why the old man sought him out, but hearing those words, the door to any sympathy he might have felt for the priest slammed shut. A year earlier he had opened the two-thousand year old tomb of a Chinese governor and his wife who had died in Western Mongolia. The wife had been a practitioner of alchemy, and finding her led to a change in Michael's life from which he still hadn't recovered, and most likely never would. He didn't like it that this stranger referred to those unnerving events. "Anything I may have discovered in Mongolia is now lost to the world."

"So be it." The priest's gaze was hard and flat. "You remain the only person I dare give this to." With a shaking hand he reached into his coat pocket. The edges of the sleeves were frayed, the elbows worn thin, and one of the buttons on the cuff hung by a thread. In his hand he held a wadded up cloth, yellow with age.

Placing the cloth on the table, he unfolded it. Michael gaped at the object revealed. Berosus gestured for Michael to pick it up and inspect it.

The bronze vessel was small, with a lid, and stood on three legs. Michael had spent a great deal of time in the Orient with archeological projects, and had more than a passing familiarity with China's past. The bronze appeared genuinely old and cast with a monster design that the Chinese call t'ao t'ieh, a mask with large round eyes, c-shaped horns and an s-shaped mouth. The design had been prevalent in the late Shang dynasty but its meaning was no longer known.

Only tests could determine the exact age of the piece. The workmanship was primitive, but it seemed far too well preserved to be from the Shang, a dynasty so ancient that for centuries Westerners believed it was mythological. Archeological finds proved it did exist, however, from about 1600 B.C. to 1050 B.C.

Michael tried to lift off the lid, but it seemed to be stuck. Gnarled, brown fingers snatched the vessel away.

"You must not open it." Berosus scowled. "Inside is a pearl, a red pearl. Were you to look upon it, you might think it beautiful and harmless, but it is not. It is evil. It will look back at you and know you. From that time, you will be under attack. It has the power to do irreparable harm to you, to destroy your life."

Michael fought the urge to laugh at the irony of the words, considering what a mess he'd made of it. "I don't need a red pearl for that." He would have thought a priest was above such superstitious claptrap. That many significant archeological findings contained "something evil," yet none were ever said to contain "something good" was nothing but an irritating publicity stunt in hopes that the resulting attention would translate into more funding. Not one of the warnings stood up to serious scrutiny. The red pearl wouldn't either.

Berosus frowned. "The pearl was guarded by Nestorian Christians when Marco Polo stole it from them and brought it to Venice. It has been a curse to the Western world ever since. I, alone, have saved the world from its wickedness. Now it is your turn."

"Did you say Marco Polo?" Michael all but spit out the name. *This old priest thinks he saved the world? If so, he's done a piss-poor job of it.*

He wished this visit was a sick joke, but he knew no such jokesters. His one-time assistant, Li Jianjun, Michael's last remaining link to his past, worried about his increasing melancholia and withdrawal from people. He could almost see Jianjun coming up with something like this. Almost, but not quite. This priest was no actor, and Jianjun was currently home with his wife in Vancouver, Canada. "You don't really expect me to believe any of this, do you? What do you want? Money? Do you expect to sell this to me? Where did you get it? If it's truly as old as it appears, it should be in a museum, dated and catalogued."

Berosus' face tightened with anger. The light over the dining table and the one in the kitchen area flickered. The storm, Michael thought, must have gotten much worse. "I am trying to warn you!" Berosus shouted. "I don't want your money. I have no use for it. And you cannot give this to anyone, especially not to some fool at a museum." He breathed deeply, trying to calm himself. "I've spent my life, every waking hour, controlling it, fighting it. But now, my time is short. I came to you because I believed you would not only understand, but if anyone could do what must be done, it is you. Others want the pearl for its power, but they must not get it. You must keep it from them. The red pearl is the only means to control certain demons loosed upon us."

"Demons?"

"Yes! The pearl must not be destroyed or the demons will be set free. The way to stop them is to return the pearl to the Nestorian monastery on the Silk Road, the monastery from which Marco Polo stole it. Only there will the demons be stopped. I tried to get it there, but I failed. You must not."

Michael shook his head. Demons, what rubbish. The old priest was not only sick, but delusional. Perhaps insane. "I've spent a lot of time in China, Father, and studying its history, so I know a bit about the Nestorians—that they went to China after their split with Rome, but were eventually thrown out of the country. It's said they no longer exist anywhere." As he spoke, he sensed the turmoil in the old man, his fear and anguish, and Michael was softened by them. Even if his story was no more than a feverish delusion, the priest's desperation and sorrow were real. Michael's voice turned gentle as he added almost pleadingly, "Even if I wanted to take up the task, Father, it's impossible. I'm sorry."

"The most learned among us are often the least willing to listen. I know what I speak of." Instead of responding to Michael's sympathy, Berosus sounded bitter, his gaze more desperate, fiercer. "You must do as I say. I pray my faith in you was not unfounded."

The priest's black eyes bored into Michael, and seemed to look into his very soul. It bothered him; he had buried too much there to be easy with its revelation to the padre.

Berosus began to tremble. He sipped some wine and when he spoke his words came slowly, his voice thinner and more quavering with each syllable. "For years I attempted to return the pearl to the place where it would do no further harm. I left my order and tried to travel deep into Central Asia, but I was always turned away. I took to hiding, trying to sneak through the area to search for the monastery that most people believe no longer exists. I lived in shadows, a figment of the darkness the pearl cast on the earth. Ultimately, I failed." Increasingly agitated, he added, "An evil lurks about the pearl. Remember, it can read your thoughts. You must hide any thoughts from it. Don't forget. Don't ..."

Berosus shut his eyes, needing to catch his breath after saying so much.

"I am too tired to fight it any longer, and I cannot give this burden to one of my fellow priests, not when there are too few priests and the people desperately need each one of them. And sadly, I cannot think of a single priest who would believe my tale. I fear what will happen upon my death, the evil that will walk the earth. As I weaken, it grows stronger each day, each hour. I believe you feel it as well."

A hacking cough interrupted him.

The air became heavy. Michael's skin prickled. He had walled himself off from others, from emotion, from passion, ever since he learned what he was capable of doing. And now, this old priest threatened the peace he had found here. "What if I refuse? What if I say you're crazy and I want nothing to do with you or with this false Shang dynasty container?"

"You are not as foolish or skeptical a man as such words would have me believe," Berosus said. "I sense your ability. Your power is stronger than my own. I was right to come to you if only you can be made to see, to believe, what your heart tells you is true. You have seen things most men would never believe. But I believe them. You must take up my task, I beg you. Return the pearl."

"But if there is no monastery," Michael insisted, stopping when the old priest's color turned even more ashen.

Berosus stood up, his eyes wide as he faced the window. "There! Begone! Leave me in peace!"

"Calm down, Father." Michael stepped to the priest's side and placed a hand on his back to steady him.

Berosus groaned, raising his fist towards the sky, bending over, his arms tight around his stomach.

"What's wrong?" Michael asked. "Is there someone I can call? A doctor?"

"No, no. I don't need anyone," Berosus said. His hands gripped the tabletop for support. "Not anymore. But I warn you—"

"Sit, please." Michael took the priest's arm. "You aren't well."

"They are stronger now. They must not find me here."

"Who must not find you?"

Berosus clutched Michael's sleeve. "Think! Why did you come to Florence? You knew no one here, yet you remained. Alone. Restless. Waiting. For what?"

Berosus let go and walked shakily to the door. Michael opened it, and as he watched the priest cautiously descend the front steps, a black disquiet crawled from the pit of his stomach up to his brain. The priest's words echoed the questions he'd asked himself. Why had he stayed in Florence? Something held him here, something he had never been able to articulate.

The old man's gait steadied as he crossed the courtyard. Michael abruptly shut the door, relieved to see the man's back. But in the living area he saw the bronze vessel sitting on the dining table, its monster-design S-shaped mouth mocking him. He grabbed it and ran out to return it to the priest.

The priest was no longer in the courtyard. Michael hurried to the street where the rain now fell in heavy sheets, but didn't see him there either. Berosus must have fallen, perhaps was lying in a doorway. Michael rushed up one side and down the other.

Berosus had vanished.

The words the priest had said to him reverberated as he went back indoors, drenched and chilled. Was this the reason he had been drawn to Florence? He grabbed a towel to dry his hair and wipe his face. He glanced at the clock. It was midnight.

He should go to bed and forget the strange visitor, but he couldn't The Chinese bronze called to him.

The priest had warned him against opening it. As an archeologist, he had often been warned not to open tombs, chests, sarcophagi. The popularity of "the curse of King Tut's tomb" only added to common perceptions of the dangers of tampering with ancient objects, despite the fact that all the men who opened King Tut's tomb had died of natural or easily explained causes.

He picked up the bronze, took hold of the lid, and tried twisting it, but it refused to open.

Michael held it up close to the light. It was tiny for a bronze, no larger than a ripe apricot. The three legs, he saw, had been cast separately. He fiddled with them and found that he could twist them. But still, nothing happened.

Then, quite by accident, he simultaneously twisted two of the legs, and with that, the lid began to rotate. It split into five leaves that separated much like a shutter opens over a camera lens. The opening grew larger as he continued to turn. He had never seen such a mechanism in any early Chinese craft. A tiny pillow of black silk lay directly under the opening. He lifted it by its black tassel. Beneath it, nestled in more black silk was what looked and smelled like soil, like earth. He lightly brushed some aside with the tip of his finger, and buried within it, he found a small red stone.

He placed the stone in the palm of his hand and held it under the desk lamp. It was the shape of a perfectly round pearl, but that was where the similarity ended.

He knew what it was.

He had seen a stone similar to this once before, a red philosopher's stone, the source of alchemy, the prime agent needed to perform an alchemical transformation. He had seen it in Idaho ... before his life went to hell.

Now he understood why the old priest had sought him out. But how did the priest know?

The blood of alchemists flowed in Michael's veins going back to Edward Kelley, a 16th century Irishman who claimed to be able to transmute cheap metals into gold. He was popular in Elizabeth I's court, but was later imprisoned by the Emperor of Bohemia when he failed to enrich the empire's wealth. Kelley died trying to escape, but his bastard son seemed to have inherited his abilities, as did a grandson. Those abilities could be traced through historical records, from one generation to another, down to Michael himself.

If alchemists did nothing but turn lead into gold, Michael could easily live with that. But alchemy in its purest state was about power, including power over life and death.

Michael had seen men do terrible things because of it, and he didn't want it back in his life.

But it seemed he had no choice.

As he held the pearl, it began to glow. The lights died in the apartment. All turned black around him except for a faint radiance from the small orb in his hand. Despite the darkness he saw a mist, a black mist, swirling around him. His breathing quickened, and his head began to spin.

The priest's words that when you looked at the pearl it looked back at you filled his mind before he fell, unconscious, to the floor.

(Continue with *Ancient Shadows* wherever e-books and print books are sold.)

ABOUT THE AUTHOR

Joanne Pence was born and raised in northern California. She has been an award-winning, *USA Today* best-selling author of mysteries for many years, but she has also written historical fiction, contemporary romance, romantic suspense, a fantasy, and supernatural suspense. All of her books are now available as ebooks, and most are also in print. Joanne hopes you'll enjoy her books, which present a variety of times, places, and reading experiences, from mysterious to thrilling, emotional to lightly humorous, as well as powerful tales of times long past.

Visit her at www.joannepence.com and be sure to sign up for Joanne's mailing list to hear about new books.

The Rebecca Mayfield Mysteries

Rebecca is a by-the-book detective, who walks the straight and narrow in her work, and in her life. Richie, on the other hand, is not at all by-the-book. But opposites can and do attract, and there are few mystery two-somes quite as opposite as Rebecca and Richie.

ONE O'CLOCK HUSTLE – North American Book Award winner in Mystery

TWO O'CLOCK HEIST

THREE O'CLOCK SÉANCE

FOUR O'CLOCK SIZZLE

FIVE O'CLOCK TWIST

SIX O'CLOCK SILENCE

Plus a Christmas Novella: The Thirteenth Santa

The Angie & Friends Food & Spirits Mysteries

Angie Amalfi and Homicide Inspector Paavo Smith are soon to be married in this latest mystery series. Crime and calories plus a new "twist" in

Angie's life in the form of a ghostly family inhabiting the house she and Paavo buy, create a mystery series with a "spirited" sense of fun and adventure.

COOKING SPIRITS
ADD A PINCH OF MURDER
COOK'S BIG DAY
MURDER BY DEVIL'S FOOD

Plus a Christmas mystery-fantasy: COOK'S CURIOUS CHRISTMAS

And a cookbook: COOK'S DESSERT COOKBOOK

The early "Angie Amalfi mystery series" began when Angie first met San Francisco Homicide Inspector Paavo Smith. Here are those mysteries in the order written:

SOMETHING'S COOKING
TOO MANY COOKS
COOKING UP TROUBLE
COOKING MOST DEADLY
COOK'S NIGHT OUT
COOKS OVERBOARD
A COOK IN TIME
TO CATCH A COOK
BELL, COOK, AND CANDLE
IF COOKS COULD KILL
TWO COOKS A-KILLING
COURTING DISASTER
RED HOT MURDER
THE DA VINCI COOK

Supernatural Suspense

Ancient Echoes

Top Idaho Fiction Book Award Winner

Over two hundred years ago, a covert expedition shadowing Lewis and Clark disappeared in the wilderness of Central Idaho. Now, seven anthropology students and their professor vanish in the same area. The key to finding them lies in an ancient secret, one that men throughout history have sought to unveil.

Michael Rempart is a brilliant archeologist with a colorful and controversial career, but he is plagued by a sense of the supernatural and a spiritual intuitiveness. Joining Michael are a CIA consultant on paranormal phenomena, a washed-up local sheriff, and a former scholar of Egyptology. All must overcome their personal demons as they attempt to save the students and learn the expedition's terrible secret....

Ancient Shadows

One by one, a horror film director, a judge, and a newspaper publisher meet brutal deaths. A link exists between them, and the deaths have only begun ....

Archeologist Michael Rempart finds himself pitted against ancient demons and modern conspirators when a dying priest gives him a powerful artifact—a pearl said to have granted Genghis Khan the power, eight centuries ago, to lead his Mongol warriors across the steppes to the gates of Vienna.

The artifact has set off centuries of war and destruction as it conjures demons to play upon men's strongest ambitions and cruelest desires. Michael realizes the so-called pearl is a philosopher's stone, the prime agent of alchemy. As much as he would like to ignore the artifact, when he sees horrific deaths and experiences, first-hand, diabolical possession and affliction, he has no choice but to act, to follow a path along the Old Silk Road to a land that time forgot, and to somehow find a place that may no longer exist in the world as he knows it.

Historical, Contemporary & Fantasy Romance

Dance with a Gunfighter

Gabriella Devere wants vengeance. She grows up quickly when she witnesses the murder of her family by a gang of outlaws, and vows to make them pay for their crime. When the law won't help her, she takes matters into her own hands.

Jess McLowry left his war-torn Southern home to head West, where he hired out his gun. When he learns what happened to Gabriella's family, and what she plans, he knows a young woman like her will have no chance against the outlaws, and vows to save her the way he couldn't save his own family.

But the price of vengeance is high and Gabriella's willingness to sacrifice everything ultimately leads to the book's deadly and startling conclusion.

Willa Cather Literary Award finalist for Best Historical Novel.

The Dragon's Lady

Turn-of-the-century San Francisco comes to life in this romance of star-crossed lovers whose love is forbidden by both society and the laws of the time.

Ruth Greer, wealthy daughter of a shipping magnate, finds a young boy who has run away from his home in Chinatown—an area of gambling parlors, opium dens, and sing-song girls, as well as families trying to eke out a living. It is also home to the infamous and deadly "hatchet men" of Chinese lore.

There, Ruth meets Li Han-lin, a handsome, enigmatic leader of one such tong, and discovers he is neither as frightening cruel, or wanton as reputation would have her believe. As Ruth's fascination with the lawless area grows, she finds herself pulled deeper into its intrigue and dangers, particularly those surrounding Han-lin. But the two are from completely different worlds, and when both worlds are shattered by the Great Earthquake and Fire of 1906 that destroyed most of San Francisco, they face their ultimate test.

Seems Like Old Times

When Lee Reynolds, nationally known television news anchor, returns to the small town where she was born to sell her now-vacant childhood home, little does she expect to find that her first love has moved back to town. Nor does she expect that her feelings for him are still so strong.

Tony Santos had been a major league baseball player, but now finds his days of glory gone. He's gone back home to raise his young son as a single dad.

Both Tony and Lee have changed a lot. Yet, being with him, she finds that in her heart, it seems like old times...

The Ghost of Squire House

For decades, the home built by reclusive artist, Paul Squire, has stood empty on a windswept cliff overlooking the ocean. Those who attempted to live in the home soon fled in terror. Jennifer Barrett knows nothing of the history of the house she inherited. All she knows is she's glad for the chance to make a new life for herself.

It's Paul Squire's duty to rid his home of intruders, but something about this latest newcomer's vulnerable status ... and resemblance of someone from his past ... dulls his resolve. Jennifer would like to find a real flesh-and-blood man to liven her days and nights—someone to share her life with—but living in the artist's house, studying his paintings, she is surprised at how close she feels to him.

A compelling, prickly ghost with a tortured, guilt-ridden past, and a lonely heroine determined to start fresh, find themselves in a battle of wills and emotion in this ghostly fantasy of love, time, and chance.

Dangerous Journey

C.J. Perkins is trying to find her brother who went missing while on a Peace Corps assignment in Asia. All she knows is that the disappearance has something to do with a "White Dragon." Darius Kane, adventurer and bounty hunter, seems to be her only hope, and she practically shanghais him into helping her.

With a touch of the romantic adventure film Romancing the Stone, C.J. and Darius follow a trail that takes them through the narrow streets of Hong Kong, the backrooms of San Francisco's Chinatown, and the wild jungles of Borneo as they pursue both her brother and the White Dragon. The closer C.J. gets to them, the more danger she finds herself in—and it's not just danger of losing her life, but also of losing her heart.

Made in the USA
Las Vegas, NV
19 January 2021

16204029R00218